DOLL FACE

Sadie Grubor writing as
V Fiorello

ISBN-13: 978-1548840006
ISBN-10: 1548840009

DEDICATION

This one is for shattering comfort zones, exploring new parts of yourself, and for celebrating every part that makes you YOU.

Sometimes you have to embrace the darker parts too.
(But don't go to jail.)

Love, Sadie G.

SPECIAL THANKS

To Mr. G for not thinking I was demented or crazy for writing this story. I love you.

To the BETA BABES (Marie, Ruth, Kara, Leanne, Tracy, Pam, Bronwyn, Katie, Stephanie, & Michelle), You guys are so amazing. Thank you for all the conversation, discussion, and hours of reading, critiquing & the ego boosts. ☺

Monica. <3 You complete… my sentences, because apparently, I forgot how to write one this time around. Thank you for all your hard work and putting up with my insecurities! Without you, I very well may have never published this story.

To the G Spot (Groupie Zone), Thank you for keeping me entertained and answering my weird questions.

Special thanks to Carrie Waltenbaugh!! You are amazing! Thank you for all your support of this new venture.

TABLE OF CONTENTS

BLURB

Most kids don't grow up wanting a deadbeat dad. Those kids don't understand how much worse it can truly be—how it feels to grow up wishing your father was neglectful and not a living nightmare.

I did. I do. And my safest place is to hide among the monsters. So, that's what I do. I blend into a sea of criminals, the depraved, the evil lurking in the underground of Chicago.

That's how I ended up here, applying too much makeup and too little clothing, dressing up just enough to entice, yet subdued enough not to draw too much attention. Getting noticed not only puts you in the position of private dance rooms, but it makes them curious. They want to see you—all of you—and possess you. Even if it's all a part of the game, their night of fantasy, it's too risky.

For two years, I've stayed safe.

For two years, I've kept the balance.

For two years, I've been someone else, living another person's life.

I've taken on the occasional businessman, random bachelor, and even the rare, everyday good guy, but never a regular client or patron. Sure, the money, gifts, and hell, even the attention and pampering, are more tempting than the drugs readily available, but the fear of being discovered again...it tampers the temptations and desires for more.

Then, he walked through the dark red lacquered doors of my hiding place. His eyes searching, probing, knowing. He sees through my fabrications. Buried beneath the corded muscle and smooth tan skin, lies a darkness I know too well. He has his own secrets.

It's terrifying, seductive. The temptation swirls on the tip of my tongue, teasing my taste buds, making me want to confess all my sins to a man who could punish me and free me in the most wonderfully worst ways.

chapter one

Mei

The face looking back at me is familiar, but not my own. The eyes shouldn't be green, the blonde hair is unnatural, and the layers of foundation, blush, shadows, and charcoal liner are just a mask—a façade topped off with glitter and red lips. All of it, everything about me is as false as the lashes glued to frame the eyes of a stranger.

No, that's wrong. A stranger is someone you don't know. I knew her once—long before darkness unleashed from within the sins born to me. It crawled its way through my veins with whispers of seduction. Promised freedom and a life beyond the shadows closing in around me. If only I'd been strong enough to fight against it. If only I'd realized the very sin providing my escape would also imprison me. If only the face staring back were a stranger and not a reminder of what I'd done. If only.

"Meissa," Tricia shouts, planting herself in the chair to my left.

Blinking, I emerge from my dark thoughts and focus on her reflection.

"Have you heard anything I've said?" she asks, leaning toward the mirrored wall behind the makeup table.

"Sorry," I say, flat, unable to shake the murky memories plaguing me.

"What the hell is up with you tonight?" Her eyes meet mine in the mirror before she goes back to primping for the private dance requests she no doubt got after her incredible performance on stage.

"Nothing." I give a shake of my head. "Just tired, I guess."

Forcing a smile, I look away, my gaze falling on the text alert I read a few moments ago.

10th Anniversary of Dollhouse Killer's Discovery. After years of no leads, authorities speculate Gilbert Dandry, aka The Dollhouse Killer, has died in hiding. Click here to continue...

Gripping the edge of the table, I swallow the sudden flood of saliva in my mouth. Bile rises, lingering at the base of my throat.

"I still don't understand why you don't work the audience more. With your figure and the moves I've seen during rehearsal, you could easily have a couple regulars." Tricia sighs.

"I've told you before—"

"Yeah, yeah, you aren't looking for a sugar daddy or regulars," she mocks with a roll of her eyes. "Look, I don't know what you're running from, but—"

"Who says I'm running from anything?" I snap, hating when people get too close to the truth.

"Girl, please, it doesn't take a fucking genius to see you're running from something..." she pauses, turning to meet my eyes, "or someone."

"You don't know shit," I state, looking away.

"I know you are running, or hiding, or both—just like I know Kelly's here because she's got four kids to feed and no fathers in sight, Natasha isn't even fucking close to being in this country legally, and Candy is fucking Joey. You think any of us grew up hoping to work in this place?" She purses her lips.

"Candy's fucking Joey?" I ask on a whisper, glancing toward the curvy redhead in question. "She's so young and—"

"And has her fucking reasons, like extra money for the college courses she's always going on about," Tricia cuts me off, motioning to the young student caught up in this depraved life. "Just like you have your reasons." She lifts one shoulder in a half shrug.

Tensing, I bite back the urge to rage at her. To tell her to shut the fuck up and leave it alone. Instead, I turn back to the mirror and touch up the mask I wear every night.

"The problem with you is you're either crazy or fucking stupid," Tricia says, deciding to continue.

Placing both hands on the table, I clench my fists, close my eyes, and take a deep breath. A darkness, one that lives within in the depths of me, begins to boil.

My eyes dart to the pair of scissors resting at the corner of the table, and I lean my head to the side. It would be so easy to grab them and make a horror show out of Tricia. It would be a spectacular sight, one I could even sell tickets to... Shaking my head, I blow out a breath and push down my anger, fear, and twisted thoughts.

"It's really none of your—"

"I mean, if you're gonna hide in a place like this only to bury yourself in the sideshow, I'm guessing you've got legal problems."

If only that were the worst of my worries.

Misery, pain, and death follow my every step. And if Tricia doesn't shut the fuck up, she's going to end up another casualty in my selfish choice to live instead of just ending it all—ending me, and not just this false me, but taking the real me to the grave.

But I won't. I've survived this long. I may hide behind the mask in a crowd of Chicago nightlife debauchery, but, selfish or not, I will not surrender.

"You need to play this smarter, honey, not harder," Tricia prattles on, uncaring or unnoticing of the way my back stiffens and jaw tightens. "I mean, you realize this place is owned by Giovanni Accardo, right?"

"I don't fucking care about Giovanni Accardo," I say through clenched teeth.

"Girl," she drawls, "you should. He's like a major player in the Chicago Syndicate. And I mean he's *in* the family."

Giving a humorless laugh, I cross my arms over my chest and slouch back in my chair. I know who owns this club and exactly which *family* he belongs. I also know I do my best to stay out of their way when the expensive suits arrive. Instead of putting on a show for them, I let the other girls flirt and catch their eyes.

Sure, the money flowing from those silk-lined pockets would

rejuvenate my dwindling cash flow, but the danger radiating from them is enough for me to stick to my routine.

Take the stage, dip, twist, and wrap around the pole just enough to make the drunks, cheaters, and first-timers practically dump their wallets on stage. And, on occasion, when necessary, I emerge from the depths of backstage and work the floor. I've perfected my client radar, able to spot the married men, traveling business types, and the couple here to spice up their marriage. Those ready to venture, but not get attached—they are my preferred targets.

"So, what? He's just going to erase any legal woes one of us *might* have because we strip in his club? I'm pretty sure it doesn't work that way," I respond with sarcasm.

"Okay, so we're leaning toward the stupid side of this scenario," she insults.

Twisting my head in her direction, I allow my eyes to drop to her neck, focusing on the pulse. One puncture to that delicate spot would shut her up.

"Major players come in here regularly, which means you just need the attention of one." She lifts a perfectly manicured finger, all of them dark red with sparkling black tips. "All it takes is one of those guys to put you on a favorites list and poof! Your troubles to go away."

I snort. She acts like trouble doesn't follow these guys or danger doesn't radiate around them like a mud-thickened aura.

"You don't believe me?" There's a level of anger to her question. "Bitch, do you know how many of those guys come here just for certain girls? Fuck, it only took Vicky three goddamn private dances to get Felix Ricci on her regular rotation, then only a couple months before she was upgraded to mistress."

"Who's Vicky?" I ask, unfamiliar with the name.

"She's the girl who's spot you filled, 'cause she's now living in an above-the-law and untouchable penthouse downtown," Tricia answers, a slight jerk to her head.

"Who is Felix Ric—?"

"You really don't know shit, do you? Maybe it's time to look up once and awhile to see what the fuck is going on around you, huh?"

It's not really a question she wants an answer to, because after delivering the snotty remarks, she pushes away from the table and sashays out of the dressing room.

My eyes flit back to my cellphone. Tapping the screen, I glance over a second text alert.

Missing girl case goes cold after 7 years. Kayla Mearson Presumed Dead.

Deleting the alerts, I close my eyes. Unfortunately, the memory of the first time he came for me plays behind my eyelids.

"Come to Daddy, doll." His hand stretches out, dripping red. "I'm going to take you home."

Slowly raising my arm, I fixate on the familiar man before me.

"That's it. Come to me," he urges, taking one step forward.

A scream pierces the air, breaking the trance and pulling my gaze to the contorted face of the beautiful girl I share a room with.

Mr. and Mrs. Branson made Kayla and I sisters, friends.

Following her horrified stare across the room, the man speaks to me once more.

"Come here, doll," he pleads, sounding closer. "Your family misses you. Your dolls miss you."

My eyes land on Mr. and Mrs. Branson. They lay on the floor in weird shapes.

"What's wrong with—?"

"DOLL, COME TO ME!" His yell snaps my eyes back to him.

This crazed man sounds nothing like my father. This can't be him.

This time, both his arms reach for me, blood soaked and holding a knife.

Kayla screams once more, gripping my arm. My body jerks from the tug of her hands, but I'm frozen in place. Nothing makes sense. Not the man before me or the fear climbing up my throat.

My gaze moves back to Mr. and Mrs. Branson. They were so kind to me. Mr. Branson was going to show us how to catch fish tomorrow. Why are they laying like that? Who—?

"Come on!" Kayla yells, pulling harder on my arm as his stained hands fist the front my flannel nightgown.

How could he do this? They aren't dolls, and the mess isn't acceptable. I bite my bottom lip, remembering all the times he scolded my messy room, or when my hand slipped and—

"Let go of her," Scott yells, charging from the darkness of the dining room and knocking him to the floor.

"Scott!" Kayla cries out to our foster brother.

Studying the fear etching her face, I touch the tears streaking her cheeks.

Why would she fear Daddy? He's—

"Run," Scott yells. "Go get hel—"

A gurgling sound fills the room, and I turn to the source as Kayla wails once more.

Daddy sits over Scott.

He'd been the one who showed me how to ride a bike when I first arrived.

Daddy brings the sharp metal down over and over. Scott's chest, his neck, his face...so many times his face.

"You. Can't. Have. Her!" he shouts, each word accentuated with a stab. "She. Belongs. With. Her. Family!"

Knots twist in my stomach and dread weighs down my limbs. Bringing my hand up, I touch the dampness on my chest, then pull it back, staring at blood. My eyes wide, I look back to my father.

Burying the knife into Scott's chest one last time, Daddy twists his blood-covered body and reaches out for me to take his hand.

A sharp pain in my arm makes me glance down. Kayla's fingernails bite into my skin.

"He's dead," she sobs.

Shaking my head, I look back to Scott. His face is unrecognizable and his body ruined. A pool spreads beneath him, slowly darkening the carpet.

Daddy rises to his feet, dropping another knife to the floor. The thud of it makes me jump and sharp realization slices through me. The Bransons and Scott weren't dolls. They were real.

Memories of all the doctors, the questions, the looks each person gave me when I told them about our dolls, flash in my mind, and it all makes sense. It was all wrong. Daddy was wrong. I was wrong. The dolls were wrong.

Shame I didn't completely understand and a fear I'd never felt before surged through my veins. Before I can think twice, I grab Kayla's hand and run from the man who just took away the people who cared for me, showed me so many things, who took all the dolls out of the *house without scolding me for what I did with them. Wrong things.*

Running blindly, Kayla and I end up deep in the woods behind the house.

"We aren't allowed to be this far into the woods," I remind Kayla. "Mrs. Branson will be angry."

"Mrs. Branson's dead," Kayla cries, shoving me. "They're all dead, because of you."

"Doll!" We jump at his bellow, our eyes darting around. This new fear makes my stomach flip and twist.

"We should hide." I point to a hollow tree, my brow furrowing. Kayla is bigger than me, older. I'm not sure we'll both fit.

"He wants you." She shoves me again. "He can have you."

She disappears farther into the woods, leaving me behind. The darkness closes in. The damp wooden smell grows thicker with each breath. My fear turns into something all encompassing. I'm frozen in place.

"Come to Daddy! Don't be afraid. I've come to bring you home," he yells, closer, more urgent, terrifying. "Damn it! Come to me now!"

It's enough to push my body into motion.

Scurrying to the hollow tree, I climb inside and bury myself in dirt and leaves. Covering my ears, I block out his curses and demands. Eventually, when he falls silent, the sounds of the woods and calls of a search party find me.

"Don't let Tricia push your buttons." Candy slides into the recently vacated seat, her light brown eyes soft with understanding and pity.

"It's fine," I choke out, pushing down the nausea caused by the memory.

Fucking hell, in the two years I've worked here, I've never had one, let alone two, fellow dancers decide it was time for a stripper heart to heart.

"She does have a point, though," she continues.

Snapping my eyes to her, I furrow my brow. So much for understanding.

"Look, I know people around here talk. I'm well aware my arrangement with Joey is public knowledge." She lifts one shoulder. "I

13

have an end game, and in this life, the cards I was dealt were shit. So, I'm now stacking the deck in my favor."

"So, you sleep with him for money?" I ask, maybe a bit too much snark in my voice.

"Look, call it what you want, but my arrangement with him has already paid for my first year of college. The rest, I'm banking, 'cause I know it won't last forever with a man like him," she confesses. "But Tricia's right, you gotta be smarter and play the game better."

"And what happens when the game cashes you out?"

This time, she lifts both shoulders.

"At least I tried to make my life my own. I didn't fucking sit around waiting for shit to happen or not happen to me," she states, smirking. "Look, I just wanted to make sure she didn't upset you, but I also know what it's like to be stuck in a place you desperately want outta. If I've learned anything in my short time here, it's that there are far more dark kings than white knights. It's up to you to save yourself, and sometimes, that's by any means necessary."

A sharp twinge of another memory, a necessary means, whispers in the back of my mind, wanting me to remember things I try not to.

After touching up her lipstick, she leaves me to myself.

Finding the strangers eyes in the mirror once more, I take in her face.

Can I really put my trust in a criminal? Is my only saving grace in those who lie, cheat, steal, and kill?

Hell, are you really any better than them?

Closing my eyes, I inhale deeply. Opening my eyes on a slow exhale, I silently answer my own question.

No. You're worse. You're a monster born from the darkest evil and shaped by sin.

But what if my past is dead? It's a possibility, though I can't be sure. It's not like I can go looking into it or risk exposing myself. The moment I do, the instant I give anything away, he'll be here covered in red, or they'll be here in blue with their badges and handcuffs.

Unable to put Tricia's comments out of my head and tempted by the idea of choosing my sins rather than them choosing me, I decide to observe the club guests and Joey's special VIPs a bit closer.

In the following weeks, hidden in the dark corners of the club, behind curtains and through two-way mirrors, I watch these men, professional criminals, in some of their baser moments. The sex is usually rough. Like when one guy grabbed a girl by the throat, pinned her to a table, and fucked her hard enough to move the table a good couple feet. And then there are the drugs. Plentiful and readily available for any purpose they desire. Afterward, the girls are carried out of the private rooms, either heavily drugged or exhausted from use.

The darker part of me, the one I try to lock deep down, relishes in the voyeuristic moments. And when my hand is between my legs, it's these dirty, depraved instances I recall with clarity to ease the throb.

Having spent so many nights observing the behaviors that take place behind the velvet curtain within VIP rooms, my curiosity about the mistresses has grown exceptionally. And tonight I finally get the chance to see what occurs with these kept women. Vicky, the very one Tricia worships, has returned to the club covered head to toe in designer clothing on the arm of an important man. His expensive suit is tailored perfectly to meet his height and broad shoulders. Dark blond hair is brushed smooth against his head, highlighting the defined bone structure of his face. A strong square jaw, high cheekbones, and defined brow.

A cigar held firmly between his full lips, he speaks to the large entourage of men surrounding him. Some have their own Vicky counterpart, other's partaking in the women readily available at the club. The moment this group arrived, it was evident they were different. There's a dangerous power vibrating around them the groups from previous weeks didn't have. The dangerous aura they create is why I avoided them in the past, putting my head down and remaining unnoticed.

From shadowed corners and previous hiding spots, I watch the interactions. There's a certain hierarchy, a pecking order in the group. The men seated are definitely the ones in charge, though Vicky's suit is unquestionably the nucleus. Joey looks like a lap dog, running at the center man's command and doing his bidding.

I don't watch the group too long, fearing they'll discover my inspection. Having learned enough of what can happen to those seen as a threat from previous observations, which I'm sure my spying would be considered, I slip away from the hidden corner, and rub the back of my neck, the feeling of being watched overwhelming. Refusing to glance over my shoulder, I walk toward the dressing room.

"No more," Natasha's soft plea in heavily accented English rings out, and I slow at a private room, leaning toward the door.

"Be a good girl," a man grunts, followed by Natasha's whimpers.

A dull ache forms between my fishnet-covered thighs, and I shake my head, disgusted with myself. Though, it doesn't stop me from moving closer. The door inches open, and I clench my eyes shut, fighting back my darkness as her seductive whispers swirl in my head, telling me to watch, to listen.

"Please," Natasha cries.

"You're going to take it like the whore you are," another voice growls, and my eyes snap open, taking in the man pounding into her ass, his fist wrapped in her hair. He reaches around, placing his other hand over her mouth.

"Fuck, easy, Don," a man commands, and my eyes dart to the sound, finding the other voice naked from the waist down lying beneath Natasha.

Pumping up into her, he collars her neck with his hand and his fingers flex.

The skin on my neck tingles with craving.

"Don't be a pussy," Don barks, thrusting into her harder, pulling me out of my sick desire.

Her muffled scream pours from between Don's fingers as the other guy releases her neck to grab her hips and slams up into her harder, groaning before lying still beneath her. Releasing her, he delivers a heavy slap to the side of her thigh.

I clench my thighs, my clit pulsing, battling between disgust and a sick fucking desire to be her—to be punished.

On a grunt, Don releases her mouth and hair, then slides from her body, stumbling back a couple steps. Natasha climbs off the man beneath her, and he croons, grabbing her by the arm. "Tash, come here."

She turns, a large smile on her face.

"I clean you," she states, running her fingers down his wrinkled dress shirt.

The broken English is clearly an act, exaggerating her Russian accent to play a part.

At his dangling legs, she leans forward. Face to now soft cock, she licks and sucks.

"Such a good girl." His fingers move through her hair.

"Christ, she does that every time?" Don asks.

"Natasha enjoys the clean-up," he states, pulling her off his dick by her hair. "Take care of our friend, babe."

At his command, she crawls on her hands and knees to Don, licking her lips. Removing the condom, she performs the same "clean-up."

Pushing away from the door, I step back until my back presses against the wall and clench my eyes shut, trying to calm the wicked desire running through my body.

The rattle of the doorknob snaps me into movement, the sound of a slap, and then the two men laughing follows me as I make my way back down the hall.

When I reach the curtain leading out to the main floor, I realize I've walked in the wrong direction.

It opens in a swoosh of thick velvet and I come face to face with Joey, feeling the presence of the group behind him.

His eyes widen in surprise.

"Turn around, Mei," he orders.

Still trying to come down from the lust-induced high, I only blink at his command.

"Move," he barks, and I fumble back, trying to make myself as unnoticeable as possible.

"Who's this?" a deep voice inquires, and my eyes dart to the group leader.

The bad guy nucleus.

Vicky's suit.

And his attention is solely focused on me.

"Felix, she doesn't—" Joey starts to explain my lack of private dance participation, among other things.

"I don't believe we've seen her. Have we, Joey?" Felix steps closer, taking my chin in his soft hand, and my stomach knots as I seek out Vicky, or any of the designer-clad arm candy from earlier.

"She's not on the VIP menu," Joey explains, sounding defeated.

VIP Menu? Is that what the other girls are?

"Exceptions shall be made," Felix states, releasing my chin. "Won't they, Gio?"

"Of course," an unseen man chuckles.

Felix offers me his arm, and I just stare, unblinking.

"Mei," Joey prompts, and my eyes move to him, though I'm frozen. "Take the fucking arm."

"Joey," Felix scolds, "is that how you talk to my precious girls?"

"Meissa," Joey growls, spurring me into action.

Sliding my satin-glove-covered hand over his arm, I reign in the desire still burning my inner thighs and my panic at this turn of events, and channel it all into the deceitful armor I wear.

Chapter two

Saint

I watched her skulk in the shadows of this dilapidated shithole where my cousin insisted we conduct his business tonight. Felix was unimpressed with this place from the moment Gio convinced him to visit two and a half years ago, and if it weren't for his obsession with Vicky, he would've never returned. Now, we're back in this cesspool of junkies, drunks, and whores to deal with Gio.

Not that he's aware of this fact. He only thinks Felix wants to visit the very place Gio's deceptions started.

So, when I locate the little spy, my own observations begin.

Her curious eyes roam over each person in Felix and Gio's party, her relaxed stance portraying how inconspicuous she thinks she's being. When her gaze lingers on Felix in great length, my suspicions escalate. Pushing away from my own dark corner, I begin my journey across the dirty red carpet.

Her body stiffens, and I pause, watching her eyes dart around the room before she takes off. Swirling lights illuminate her long blonde hair, fair skin, and barely covered ass as she steps farther and farther away from me. It's enough to identify her as a performer, but not one I remember seeing on stage since our arrival tonight.

Now, she's latched onto the very man she'd spent so much time examining.

Stepping inside the VIP room, Felix guides her to a high-back leather chair, then sits, looking up at her and patting his leg.

The shy, shock-filled girl from the hallway gone, she steps between his legs, sliding her curvy little body against his before planting her heart-shaped ass on his leg. Felix, always the man whore, grins wide, eating up her act.

And it's definitely an act. Her previous body language was anything but the seductress before me now. Panic and fear flashed in those pretty green eyes before she put her mask into place. Scanning over her, I look for anything that could be a wire or recording device. She doesn't have the smell of Fed about her, but you never know who they've recruited or blackmailed into doing their dirty work.

"You've been holding out, Joey," Felix scolds, running his hand along her fishnet-covered thigh.

"Sorry, sir, you know the girls have to agree to the VIP menu," Joey says, trying once more to let Felix know this girl hasn't consented to the things Felix surely wants.

Sliding his hand between her legs, Felix takes her chin in his other hand.

"Mei? That's your name?"

She nods.

"Such a shame, Mei." His thumb runs over her chin. "The things I could give you."

"Would you like me to bring in the girls?" Joey asks, drawing Felix's attention away from the girl.

"Not yet." He releases her chin and thigh. "There's something I want from pretty little Mei here."

It's a slight movement, but her spine straightens, and he slaps the side of her ass, gesturing for her to stand.

"Dance for me, Mei," Felix requests, motioning to the pole at the center of the room.

Her lips part, but close when Joey steps forward and whispers into her ear.

Determination sets her face and she gives him a nod before strutting to the pole located on a raised section at the center of the room.

The rest of the group settles into the chairs and couches lining the room, their eyes fixated on the little blonde, waiting for a show.

Stepping over to my cousin, I lean into his ear.

"You need to be careful, Felix. This one is hiding something," I inform him.

He meets my eyes as I straighten back to my full height and raises one brow.

"It's just a dance, Dante. Relax and enjoy the show," he says, waving off my warning, his eyes focused on his current distraction.

The blonde grips the golden pole, walking the circumference of the small stage, and I sigh, walking away and leaning against the wall behind Felix. He may not be concerned, but every instinct has me on high alert. There's something different about this girl. Something not right.

As uninterested as I am in whores, the moment soft music fills the room, I find my gaze drawn to her. Instead of the typical stripper anthems, the words *"You don't own me,"* float in the air, and the moment the classic song turns into a heavier, newer beat, I'm caught.

The sway of her hips, curve of her leg, and her hands moving over her body has every man in the room riveted. The moves are graceful, her face serene, and her eyes...fuck, her eyes blaze. But not with an act of innocence. No, there's a darkness deep within them—a contrast to her fair complexion. Her satin-covered fingertips dig into her skin, clawing their way up to remove the scraps of material she wears. She's sin wrapped in porcelain flesh.

My urges scratch their way up from the black pit deep inside me—the place where every sin, every terrible act I've done, resides. It's drawn to *her.* Every muscle tenses as she finishes the song with the arch of her back and slow slide to the floor. One hand on the pole, head tossed back, the ends of her hair brushing the spikes of her heels, and the soft, rounded flesh of her breast on display, my fingers twitch against my thigh. The need to dirty her, mark her, to break her surges through my veins in a rush of need.

The music lowers to make conversation possible again, and in a practiced move, she lifts and spins her body from the floor. Joey appears, handing her the dark red satin top and skirt she discarded moments ago before taking her arm and leading her toward the door.

"She stays," Felix says in a way no one would question or

argue.

Joey stops, turning to Mei so only she can see his face. Speaking too low for me to hear, he releases her arm before continuing to the door.

"Come here," he orders.

Her eyes stay on Joey's back for a moment, before turning them on Felix.

In the briefest of seconds, panic flashes across her face before the seductress is back in place. Holding the scraps of satin against her chest, she struts toward us.

Felix stands before she reaches him.

"Allow me," he says, motioning for her clothes.

Hesitating just a moment, she places them in his outstretched hand.

Clenching my fist, I find it filled with leather and glance down. At some point, I'd pushed away from the wall and grabbed the back of Felix's chair.

Furrowing my brow, I release the chair on a shake of my head, and watch as he wraps the top around her body, securing the ties at the front before tossing the skirt away.

"Come." He takes her hand, pulling her back to his seat and placing her on the arm of the chair opposite where I stand.

Reclaiming the chair, he settles in, and calls out, "Joey, please bring them in."

Moments later, the room falls silent as Vicky is led into the room with the other whores and mistresses.

In my peripheral, I notice Mei tense.

The women gravitate toward their male counterpart. All except Vicky.

She stands across the room, a small smile on her red lips.

"Are you trying to make me jealous again?" she asks, her question teasing.

When Felix doesn't respond, Vicky struts around the room, running her fingers over shoulders, backs of chairs, and even stepping up to the pole.

"You forget I know your preferences," she continues, starting to move against the pole.

"My preferences?" Felix finally acknowledges her remarks.

Grinding against the pole, she nods, licking her bottom lip.

"She's too young." She gives him her back and glances over her shoulder. "And far too skinny."

Clasping the zipper at the back of her dress, she lowers it, allowing the material to fall away from her left shoulder.

"You prefer a woman's body," she continues, letting the dress fall completely.

In only a black thong and stilettos, Vicky returns to her dance, her ample breasts and full, round ass swaying and rolling. My fingers don't twitch to touch her, nor do my dark urges swirl to possess me.

Pushing out of the chair, he pulls his gun from inside his jacket and holds it to her eye level.

Fear flashes across her face before her eyes widen and a smirk forms. Opening her mouth and closing her eyes, she takes the barrel into her mouth and sucks.

"Mirage Hotel."

Vicky's eyes snap open and fade to black as her head jerks back, blood spraying the wall behind her as he pulls the trigger.

Feminine screams drown out the shouts of surprise from half the men. The other half, Felix's half, are aware of tonight's purpose. We have a traitor, and they are dealt with swiftly.

Not missing a beat, Felix turns the gun on Gio. The visible swallow and rounded eyes give away Felix's plans for the evening. A curvy blonde scrambles off his lap, backing away to the nearest wall.

My eyes flicker to Mei, and lock on. She stares at Vicky's body, but there is no hysteria or shock. In fact, there is absolutely no fucking expression on her face, and not a peep left her lips.

Felix's voice pulls both our attention to him.

"Did you think a whore would be my undoing?" he shouts, moving closer to Gio.

"Felix, I don't know what she—"

A second shot from his gun drives a bullet into Gio's left knee. His shrieks of pain pierce the air as my eyes shift to Mei once more. The corner of her lips twitch, but I'm unsure whether she wants to cringe or smile.

"The only words I want to hear from your mouth will be ones begging for your life," Felix shouts, spit spraying Gio's face, adding to the tears coating his cheeks. Straightening, Felix looks around the room.

"Anyone else want to challenge me?" He meets each man's eyes, pointing the gun at them to emphasize his question.

When they land on me, he motions to the moaning Gio. "Saint," he says, addressing me by my feared nickname, "he's yours."

The creature inside me, the culmination of every dark urge lingering in my deepest parts, roars to life, my eyes zeroing in on my prey. Injured and easily captured is my usual preference, but I won't walk away. I can't. I've been groomed and shaped into this demon that haunts the dreams of criminals and psychopaths—their own living, breathing nightmare.

Stalking over, I unsheathe my knife with my left hand, grab him by the back of his jacket, and drag him out of the room. Most look away, but the heavy weight of one set burns into me, causing me to glance over my shoulder. The curiosity and desire lighting her face is almost enough to make me forget the traitor begging Felix to listen to him, but the creature will not be denied his prey, regardless of how drawn I am to feed off the darkness in her.

Mei

I wait for the scream, the shock, to come, but it doesn't. Instead, I close my eyes and travel back to the Victorian style house. To the room beyond his study, beyond the doll room, beyond the place where I was designed and corrupted. I remember the books, the drawings and pictures—a place I would continue to sneak into whenever I could...until that day.

"Please, let me out," she cries from the toy box.

"You want to play?" I ask, thrilled to have a doll who can talk.

She falls silent for a long time—so long, disappointment washes through me.

"Yes," she finally answers, my excitement growing once more. "But I can't play in here."

Rushing to the toy box, I push on the lid.

"Do you see a key? You need a key," she starts to cry.

Squatting down, I glance through the small opening between the slats. Her face is wrong. She's too dark. Her eyes widen at the sight of me.

"Oh my God," she gasps, tears pouring from her eyes. "You're just a baby."

"I'm not a baby," I argue, crossing my arms over my chest.

"You're right. I'm sorry." She wipes at her cheeks, brushing away tears.

"Why are you crying?"

"I want us to play and I can't get out," she explains.

My eyes move to the large silver lock.

Glancing around the room, I find a wall of little hooks and keys.

"I'll get you out," I shout, eager to play with a new doll.

Jumping up, I run to the keys and hop until I get some to fall. Carrying them over, I start trying different keys, until one fits and opens the lock.

"I did it!" I shove the lid open.

The doll rises, grabbing the sides of the box to steady herself.

"Let's play," I shout, clapping.

Climbing out of the box, the doll rubs her face and runs for the door.

"Hey," I shout, following after her. "You said you would play."

In the large play room, she stops, turning in a circle. Tears still stream over her cheeks.

"What...what is this?" she asks, her voice nothing more than a whisper.

"Our dolls," I explain, smiling proudly.

"Oh my God," she gasps, then thrusts her hands under my arms to lift me.

"I like that you can play back with me," I tell her, wrapping my arms around her neck. "The others don't talk or move."

"What?" The doll pulls back, studying my face.

"Some can blink, though," I brag.

Her hold on me tightens and breathing becomes difficult. Then, she spins and runs from the room.

"The dolls have to stay in the play room," I protest.

Still in her arms, I squirm and shove to get free.

Inside my father's study, my efforts become too much for her and she places me on my feet.

Lifting my head, I watch her scan the room.

Unsure what she's looking for, I take her hand and try to pull her back into the play room.

"We aren't allowed to—"

"Let's play outside," she suggests.

Shaking my head, I explain again, "We aren't allowed."

"Can't we make an exception, since I can..." she closes her eyes, taking a deep breath, "talk and play back?"

Her eyes open, staring down at me, and I bite my lip, knowing it's wrong, but the excitement is too much. Grasping her arm, I pull her behind me and show her the outside.

I'd had no idea what that day would bring, what I would learn about my family...myself. That I would learn how wrong it was, how wrong I was...about everything.

Felix's angry words drag me away from the memory, but also call to the evil lurking inside. It feeds off the scent of blood and fear pouring from Gio.

Opening my eyes, I can't help but focus on Vicky. Her once perfectly lined red lips are smeared and gaping. Her jaw is slack and skewed, her head tilted slightly to the right. The shining golden hair fanned out around her head grows darker, redder.

Vicky's blood is darker than the dolls, and he would never mess up her face. There are other ways—cleaner, prettier ways.

The second gunshot sends a rush of ecstasy coursing through my veins, but it's Felix's next words that change everything.

"Saint, he's yours."

The room falls silent as the large man standing to the right of the chair straightens to his full height.

Glancing at the men on the other side of the room, there is a mixture of knowing and fear on their faces. The air grows thicker, a dense collection of horror and anticipation. My skin tingles, prickling with the dark excitement tonight's events have unleashed.

Without any further hesitation, this man, Saint, slips a long knife from his jacket. Moving with purpose and certainty, he fists Gio's collar, dragging him out of the chair and to the floor.

"Felix, please," he begs, causing Saint to tighten his collar until it chokes off his airway.

Malevolence vibrates in his wake, causing others to sit straighter, to look and lean away from him as he passes, but not me. No, I can't tear my eyes from this dark figure. When he turns and our eyes meet, I recognize the uninhibited excitement. Every sin, every lie, every depraved thought dances beneath my skin, begging for me to follow the creature calling from behind his eyes. When he turns away, disappearing through the doorway, the muscles in my thighs tense, wanting to follow.

"Now," Felix waves toward Vicky, "dispose of that," he orders, his eyes fixating on me.

Gun still in his hand and blood spattered across the lapels of his expensive suit, chin, and white dress shirt near his neck, he approaches. *Covered in red.*

Slipping from the arm of the chair, I stand, putting the chair between us.

At my movement, he stops.

"No one is going to hurt you," he says.

Dropping my eyes from his face to the gun in his hand, I grip the back of the leather chair.

"I wouldn't hurt you," he reassures.

I glance to Vicky's lifeless, twisted body, then back to his face. He furrows his brow.

"Come here," he calls to me.

Planting my feet, I tense, preparing to use the chair as a shield if necessary.

With a sigh, he lifts the gun out to his side and shakes it.

A large man in a dark suit steps forward, taking the weapon.

"There," he offers me his empty hands, palms up, "better?"

Before he forces me to respond, the large man clears his throat.

"What is it, Nico?" Felix asks in annoyance, his eyes staying on me.

Nico pulls a white handkerchief from his pocket and holds it to him.

Felix's eyes move and focus on the white fabric, but before he can reach out, Tricia, who had been on Gio's lap, appears at his side.

Taking the cloth, she brings it close to his chin, but doesn't touch him. He briefly studies her face before nodding. At his silent permission, she cleans away the blood.

"Everyone out," he commands.

Advancing on Tricia, she drops her hand away and steps back, preparing to follow his orders, but he moves, blocking her.

"You stay," he states, grabbing her bicep. I move with the rest of the crowd toward the exit, but pause at the door, glancing back.

Relaxing his grip, Felix slides his fingers down her arm until he reaches her hand. Taking the white cloth, he moves to stand in front of her once more.

"Open," he commands, his voice deep, restrained.

Tricia parts her lips, but barely in enough time before he shoves the blood-stained handkerchief into her mouth and twists her torso, pushing her over the side of a chair so hard, the legs screech against the tiled floor. Her face contorts as she cries out, though the cloth muffles the sound.

In flurry of movement, he moves in behind her, undoing his pants. Tearing the micro skirt away, her body jerks. Tricia's head comes up on a stifled yelp, and the fear in her eyes turns to regret the moment her thong is yanked out of his way.

Nico appears, blocking the scene and using the size of his body to force me into the hallway. He closes the door behind us, but not before I hear Tricia once more.

Her cry is soft, pitiful, and no matter how much of a bitch she's been, I can't help but take a step forward, wanting to help her. But Nico stands guard at the closed door, not letting me pass. His meaty hand grips my shoulder, causing our eyes to lock in a silent battle of will.

"Mei," Natasha says, wrapping her arm in mine, "come," she whispers, pulling me away from the room.

"Tricia...?"

"Made her choice," Natasha states, leading us to the dressing room. "She knew exactly what she was getting into with Felix."

I want to ask why, but I know why. Felix's attention is exactly what Tricia thought she wanted, and I can't help but wonder if she still feels that way.

I don't. It was stupid to even consider these men an out, an escape. In reality, it's simply choosing which cage you want. The dark seedy, rusty cage I currently find myself in, or the gilded cage of a mafia mistress.

Vicky's broken body flashes in my mind. Giving myself a mental shake, I focus on getting back to the dressing room, collecting my shit, and getting the fuck out of here.

As soon as we enter the room, Natalia grabs my bag and starts helping me pack. I furrow my brows, following her actions. Glancing up, she catches my questioning look and shakes her head.

"I overheard Joey," she says, setting my bag on a chair and meeting my eyes. "Saint wants you."

Mouth now dry, I swallow twice.

"Out of all the men, you don't want Saint," she explains, her eyes pleading for me to understand.

I want to shout at her, tell her I don't want any of them, that she's just as much the fool for getting involved with these men, but I don't. Mistaking my silence, she grabs my hands, squeezing them.

"Every man in that room fears him for a reason, Mei," she says, her accent always making my name sound rougher. "Even Felix would cower if faced with Saint."

"Why?" My curiosity wins out. Though I saw his darkness, I know why they are afraid.

"He's sick," she spits out. "I've seen some of the things he's done. He's their butcher—the hired killer no one wants to cross. The last time he requested a girl..." she pauses, "we never saw or heard from her again."

I swallow once more—only, this time, I'm swallowing my shame. The excitement I felt in that room, surrounded by menace and death. The way my body reacted to a man so dangerously dark and deadly. Dropping my face, I shove the last of my things into my bag, not wanting her to see what lives inside me.

"You don't have time to change," she says, throwing a long coat at me.

Wrapping it over my shoulders, I secure the buttons, throw my bag over my shoulder, and run from the room.

At the exit, I come face to face with Joey.

His eyes, hard and set, search my face before softening.

"Go, Mei, and don't come back for a few days," he says on a sigh, shoving the door open, aiding my escape. "You got lucky tonight, but just in case, you need to stay away from here. If you were smart, you wouldn't come back at all."

I hesitate a moment too long, and he shouts, "Damn it, Mei, go!"

Instead of my usual bus stop, I power walk three blocks before hailing a cab back to my apartment—where I lock myself inside, leave all my lights off, and try to shower away the desire and shame.

Climbing into bed, I mentally calculate my savings and contemplate running. I have enough to do it. To find a new dirty city and hidden away strip club, but these aren't the kind of men to give up. No matter where I go, they'd eventually find me and deal with their loose end—and I'm not done in this place yet.

Burying my face into my worn pillow, I scream.

He won't give up.

They won't let me disappear.

Always the hunted, the prey.

Rolling back over, I allow a few tears to fall, vowing they will be my last as I stare at the stained ceiling in the darkness.

No more. If they want me, they can come find me. I won't give up, not without a fight. I won't make it easy.

Shoving the covers away from my body, I climb out of bed and move to the mirror on my wall. There's just enough light from the street lamps to make out the pale face in the mirror.

It's time to accept the fact that the girl I was is gone. It's time for the blonde hair, green-eyed women staring back to become me, and for me to get comfortable behind this mask.

Pressing my palms against the wall on either side of the mirror, I lean closer and focus on my reflection. "You will no longer be the prey. You are Meissa Winters, stripper, whore, survivor."

chapter three

Saint

"What do you mean she's gone?" I try to keep my voice level, calm, though I'm feeling anything but when Joey returns without the blonde.

"By the time I got to the dressing room, she was gone," he repeats.

"Where does she live?" I ask through clenched teeth, slipping my arms back into my white dress shirt.

"How the fuck should—?" he begins, before remembering whom he's speaking to.

Pausing on the third button up, I glance to him and raise one brow, and his tone changes quickly.

"I mean, I don't know."

"Christ," I growl, snagging my tie and black suit jacket from the wall hook as I charge from the room.

"What am I supposed to do about—?" He motions to the carnage behind me.

Gio proved to be an excellent outlet for my needs. Now, I just need to get my hands on the tiny little blonde to ease this new curiosity and suspicion.

"Call the cleaner," I shout, not letting him finish.

Loud thumping permeates through the VIP room door where Nico stands guard. "He's busy," he informs on a strangled rasp.

Knowing Nico would put his life on the line before disobeying Felix, I pause and let my eyes wander to the thick, jagged scar running across his neck. A wound inflicted during an attempt on Felix's life and forever altering Nico's vocal chords is a testament to his loyalty.

The thumps begin to increase in volume and frequency as a woman's voice calls out. "I want it," she shouts. "Yes, do—" she cuts off on a strangled gurgle as Felix groans.

"Sounds like the fun is over." I nod to the door.

Moving aside, he knocks three times, pauses, then two hard thumps. It's the code to tell Felix who's at the door—my code.

"Come in," Felix responds, and Nico opens the door, waving me in.

I have to give him credit. He's loyal as fuck and follows procedure regardless of what I could do to him.

The smells of sex and cigars filter through the space. Felix lounges in the leather chair, pants pulled up but his fly and dress shirt still undone.

"Finished so soon?" he asks, placing his cigar between his lips.

"I could say the same for you," I taunt.

He grins, glancing down at the crumpled woman on the floor.

My eyes follow the same path, waiting to see if she shows any signs of life, his tie dangling from her neck and red marks decorating her back.

"Christ, Felix, is she even fucking breathing?"

"Of course," he abolishes the very idea, like he hasn't done it before.

Leaning forward, he grabs her chin, pulling her up to her knees. She clasps his forearm with thin, shaking fingers, her chest rising and falling in quick succession, bruises already starting to form on her thighs.

"She's a good girl," he praises, placing a kiss to her forehead before releasing her face.

The woman rests her cheek against his knee.

"Joey's calling in the cleaner," I tell him. "I've got some business to attend to."

"Does this business have anything to do with the sexy little blonde I had in my lap earlier?" He drags from his cigar before continuing. "You're losing your touch, Saint."

I scowl, causing him to chuckle.

"You think I didn't notice the way you watched her?" he presses, and I remain silent. "It only made me want her more." On his confession, I tense.

"Then where is she?" I ask, spiteful.

Felix may be a boss, but his easily sidetracked dick puts blinders on him.

"She couldn't handle things," he releases a white cloud of smoke, "and this one," keeping his eyes on me, he runs his hand over her head, "stepped up to play."

"Too bad you weren't watching the other blonde as well as me," I insult. "Maybe you would've caught the same odd behaviors I did."

Felix laughs, until he sees my face. His smile falls. Shoving the woman from his leg, he stands. With only a foot between us, he narrows his eyes on mine.

"Where is she?" he asks, finally catching on.

"Gone," I bark. "I asked Joey to bring her to me while I dealt with Gio, but..."

"But what?" he demands, buttoning his dress pants before starting on his shirt.

"Apparently, she bolted," I explain, crossing my arms over my chest. "If this girl is a Fed or working for someone, then we've already wasted too much time and she's long gone by now." At the thought of her being gone, for good, my fists clench.

"Nico," Felix shouts at the closed door.

The minute it cracks open, he barks out, "Bring me Joey."

"He doesn't know where she is," I advise. "I already asked."

"I know," the quiet rasp of the forgotten woman at our feet draws both our attention. Grabbing her throat, she visibly swallows, then tries again, "I know what building she lives in."

Felix's head snaps back to me. "Find her, Saint. Deal with it."

I clench my jaw, grinding my teeth, to keep from punching the arrogant asshole in his face. I don't take orders from him, but Nico is watching. So, out of respect for my cousin's position, I give a tight nod before collecting the used woman from the floor and leaving the room.

It doesn't take Tricia long to give up all the information she has on Mei. Not just her apartment building, but also her own uncertainties.

The last person I'm going to listen to is a jealous whore willing to endure Felix's attention when she's clearly not into the lifestyle. Still, the information Tricia provides about Mei's purposely toned-down acts, being so closed off from the rest of them, and that she's sure Mei's running from someone piques my interest more than any of the reservations.

Finding Felix still in the VIP room with Vicky's body isn't entirely surprising, but the scent of death is starting to take over. I quickly relay the location information Tricia provided, but keep the rest to myself.

"Bring me Christian and Jimmy," Felix orders Nico, who stands just inside the door.

"I'll deal with her," I state, letting my curiosity trample down the suspicions. His eyes move from Nico to me, glancing between us. The muscle in my right cheek twitches, relishing in his uncertainty. He's loyal to Felix, but they're all afraid of me, The Saint—the dark creature residing where my soul should be. A place long ago obliterated, only to be infused with blood, tears, dirt, screams, and darkness.

"Seems a bit out of the ordinary for you," he comments, studying my blank face.

At an early age, I learned to keep my emotions buried deep. My mentor wouldn't accept anything less, so by the tender age of seven, I could watch a man lose limbs, teeth, and tongue without blinking. If I had, my punishment would've been worse than the tortures I'd witnessed and cleaned up after.

Giving a casual raise of my shoulders, I admit, "I'm curious."

Felix grins.

"The Saint is curious?" It's a taunt, not a question. "Perhaps you've developed new..." he pauses, waving his hand in front of him, "practices in the little game you like to play."

Anger rages a war beneath my skin, knowing exactly what he's insinuating. I lean forward in my seat, elbows to my knees. Our eyes meet and a moment of fear flashes in his eyes before he blinks it away.

"I have no need to force myself on a woman," I state, calmly.

His top lip curls, just a bit.

"You forget, Dante, I'm well aware of your *preferences*," he scoffs.

Snorting, I settle back into my chair.

"Felix, you only know what I allow you to. You should remember that," I say, my words carrying threat and promise.

He opens his mouth, but I continue. "The small glimpse you stole into my private affairs is part of a larger picture you couldn't fathom. It's not for..." I pause, mimicking his hand waving motion from moments before, "men such as yourself."

Eyebrows drawn over narrowed eyes, his lips thin. He's pissed and ready to challenge my authority. Raising one brow, I welcome the confrontation. Felix is getting a bit too full of himself. He forgets who I am. Forgets that, in the life we were born, we may be blood, but I outrank him.

"You arrogant—" he begins, reaching inside his jacket. Before he can get his fingertips beneath the lapel, his chair is on its side and I stand behind him. My knife to his throat and hand fisting his hair, I focus on the always loyal Nico, who's gun is trained on my head.

"Don't be a fool," I warn. "I'm not going to hurt my dear cousin."

Letting Felix feel the steel of my blade against his throat, I release the dark blond strands on his head and step away.

"Put the gun down, you idiot," Felix barks at Nico.

Grinning, I slide my blade back into place. Nico lowers his gun, hard eyes focused on me.

It's been this way with Felix since the day I did what he could not.

The request was simple, yet gruesome. Felix froze up the moment he met the eyes of his father. I didn't. Not even with my own mother and father.

While we both wear the title of "boss," I, unlike him, answer only to the head of the family—Angelo Ruggiano, our uncle. So, on occasion, Felix likes to test the boundaries of our relationship, like

35

tonight.

After helping him from the floor, Felix sends Nico on his errand and straightens his clothing. When Christian and Jimmy arrive, he orders them to follow my every instruction.

I give them the location of the building they will be watching. With my final direction to observe, not engage, and to report all information back to me, we go our separate ways. In the hallway toward the exit, Felix and I pass a dirty janitor. Felix doesn't pay him any attention, but my eyes briefly meet his with a knowing look. The cleaner, meant to be unnoticed, has arrived for Gio and Vicky. Before exiting, I wonder if they will dissolve in the same barrel, mixing together forever like a morbid fairytale ending.

On my way to my Chicago penthouse, I receive confirmation of Meissa's whereabouts, closing curtains spotted in a third-floor window before the lights went out.

At the information, the demons possessing me stir. Tightening my grip on the steering wheel, the urge to reroute to her tenses every muscle in my body.

Her response to Vicky's death and the curious excitement in her eyes as I dragged Gio to his end calls to the darkest side of me. Their connection, something he craves to explore, in pain, blood, and tears—all the things even monsters are afraid of.

Reaching inside my jacket, I run my fingers over the cold steel of the blade tucked away in the special pocket I have custom added to all my suits. The urge settles, calming enough to keep me from tracking down what I currently desire.

Arriving home, I make my way through the unlit rooms and climb the stairs to the master bedroom. Once I've stripped out of my stained clothes, I stuff them into a black bag to be disposed of tomorrow.

Naked, my knife in hand, I make my way to the bathroom. Placing the knife next to the sink, I climb into the shower to wash away the events of the night. There's only one thing I can't seem to cleanse from my system. And when I climb into bed, it's with thoughts of the tiny blonde and all the secrets she carries. Skeletons I want to unearth and put on display, just to see how she reacts.

Waking so sudden, and unsure of what caused it, I scan my dark bedroom.

Empty.

Taking my gun from the side table, I slide naked from my oversized bed.

With the heel of my palm, I slap the control unit on the wall. The mechanical hum of the blinds opening fills the room. Gripping the gun with both hands, I bring it up and scan the room again.

Empty.

Dropping my arms, I furrow my brow.

The fuck woke me up?

Tossing the Glock onto the bed, I sigh and rub the back of my neck.

With a deep breath, I shake off the weird anxiousness coursing through my body and begin my day.

I'm halfway through my workout when my phone beeps.

Flexing my taped hands, I still the punching bag and glance down at the cell phone resting on the bench.

She's on the move.

The text from Christian sends an unfamiliar tingle up my spine.

Typing my response, the uneasiness from earlier returns.

Follow. Do not engage.

There are a million other things I need to take care of today, meetings that cannot be missed, but a tiny woman with fake blonde hair and a glittery painted mask has become my number one objective.

Unable to concentrate on the rest of my routine, I leave the workout room to prepare for the day ahead of me. I don my own mask—a custom-made, dark blue thousand-dollar suit hiding the malicious, blood-thirsty creature lurking beneath my skin.

Forgoing my driver, I need to do this on my own. This task, this woman, is more personal, but I don't spend time trying to figure out why. I opt for the less conspicuous silver SUV. Unbuttoning my jacket, I slide into the black leather seat, start the car, and back out of the reserved space. Before exiting the underground garage, I send a text requesting Christian and Jimmy's location. It doesn't take long for them to respond and me to drive in that direction.

Alerting them when I'm close, they pull out of their parking space along the side of the street, allowing me to pull in. Moments later, Jimmy steps up to the driver side window, and I lower it halfway, allowing him to recap her day so far.

"She left her building at eight thirty-two this morning, walked three blocks to a small diner, and stayed there until nine forty-eight. Now," Jimmy nods across the street, "she's in there."

Moving my gaze from him to the run-down fitness center, I scan the large, dirty windows. In the left window, four out of five treadmills are being used. None of them are her. In the right window, one man bench presses while another spots him. Still no sign of her.

"She's been in there for almost an hour," he finishes.

Without taking my eyes from the building, I nod.

"I assume you both have things to do. Go take care of them and find me in a couple hours," I instruct, rolling the window back up without waiting for a response.

I study the business front—the peeling white logo, the cracked glass in the corner of the right window, and old signs taped on the inside of the double door entrance that announce a new spin class, new business hours, and a heavy weight champion boxing instructor.

There's no way this place makes enough money to stay open on its own. Reaching for my phone, I'm about to do some research on the business, to inquire whether it's one of our fronts, when Mei emerges.

Face flush and messy hair knotted at the top of her head, not one swipe of the makeup-created mask she wore last night. Her skin is like porcelain, creamy white, aside from the natural flush of her cheeks. The lashes framing her eyes aren't nearly as dark or thick as before, but do wonders at highlighting their largeness. All of it could be out of place, odd, but there's a natural, almost youthful appeal. Something very doll-like.

Her face turns toward me, and for the slightest moment, I feel exposed, discovered, then she scans the rest of the street before stepping out from beneath the faded awning. I observe her from my spot for as long as possible, but when she rounds a corner, I have no choice but to pull out into traffic.

I turn the same corner and watch as she disappears into another shop—a used bookstore. Driving around the block, even while knowing I risk losing her, I hit the car's Bluetooth to make a call.

"Saint?" Sketch answers, sounding distracted.

"I need information," I respond. "I'll send you the subjects."

"And I'm..." he releases a soft grunt, then continues, "sending you new developments in regards to your other requests." A slap comes through the phone.

"Which one?" I inquire.

"Both," he says on a pant. "And one is going to put you in a gutting mood," he reveals. "Just don't slice and dice the messenger, okay?"

"When will I have it?" I ask, ignoring his gibe.

"Later today. Check out your porn," he instructs, referring to the secure laptop he provided. The one that dons a large XXX sticker on it.

"How deep do I go with these new...principals?" he asks, knowing not to reveal too much over the phone. A muffled groan in the background follows his question.

"I want to know the business's history, if it's one of ours, and the owner. I want everything."

"Got it," he confirms.

"Are you sure, because you seem focused on other things," I growl into the phone.

"Have I ever disappointed?" he counters.

Fortunately for him, Sketch is right. No matter the shit going on around him, he's never failed me.

"It's in your best interest not to let this be the first time you do," I inform before ending the call.

Pulling into an empty space down the street, I send him her name and the name of the fitness center. As if sensing the mention of her name, she emerges from the store, an old backpack over her shoulder, and once again searches the street before heading the opposite direction of where I parked.

All afternoon, she barely interacts with others, keeping her head down and moving with purpose from the bookstore, a salon, and a convenience store, a revolving enter and exit. And when she's done, she climbs onto public transportation and takes a seat farthest from the passengers already on board.

My head swirls with questions and assumptions. If she's a Fed, then she's buried herself so deep into the game, she's now a permanent member. But maybe she's just this good at diversion. Or perhaps she's very aware of being monitored, watched, and this is her attempt to throw us off her scent.

My phone buzzes with an alert from Christian, confirming he and Jimmy are waiting at her building.

I have other matters to take care of, but the yearning to follow her causes the demons to rouse, feeling like barbs burrowing into my gut. He will only be denied for so long before demanding his prey. And once she's in our grasp, I almost regret what I'll allow him to do to her.

When her bus turns right, back in the direction of her home, I turn left, toward the warehouse. Angelo's request cannot be ignored. Special treatment for a business partner is needed—The Saint treatment. The promise of things to come is the only reason my dark half allows his new prey out of our sight.

Mei

Three days. It doesn't sound like much, but when you're not used to having this much free time, it is. Not to mention the hit my minimal savings is taking without the steady tip money from the club. My apartment isn't much, but it's secure. In my neighborhood, that's crucial and expensive.

Taking a deep breath, I close my eyes, and on an exhale, I punch the weight bag.

"You know better, Mei," Junior scolds, holding the bag in place.

My eyes flit open, focusing on the worn, cracked material.

"Never close your eyes on your target," he continues.

One of the few positives to having so much time on my hands has been getting overdue errands taken care of—selling and purchasing text books, hair and body touch-ups at the salon, and the extra training I've gotten in at the gym.

"Focus on where you want to strike, memorize their face, study their movements," he goes on.

After a year of self-defense and kickbox training, I'm very familiar with the ground rules and lectures that follow when I break them. His lectures are much better than what happens with my mixed martial arts instructor, Jake. If I mess up there, it ends with bruises and sore spots courtesy of leg sweeps and surprise jabs.

"Okay, girl, cool down," he instructs.

Dropping my gloved hands, I roll my head on my shoulders.

"Good job," is the last thing he says before walking away.

A man of very few words and barely interested in me aside from our sessions. *The perfect man*, I think, removing the gloves. *If only he weren't old enough to be my grandfather*, I finish my thought before chugging down half a bottle of water.

When I arrive home, I take care of one last errand. Stopping at the apartment next to mine, I lift my hand to knock. The door jerks open, but in place of the thin, seventy-something-year-old woman with dark black hair and paper-thin skin, a woman with light brown curls stands.

Tension fills every muscle, my flight instinct kicking in.

"Can I help you?" she asks, furrowing her brow.

"Is Ms. Waltman here?"

"I'm afraid my grandmother has fallen ill," she states, blatantly examining me from head to toe.

"I'm sorry to hear that." I cross my arms over my middle. "I just wanted to see if she was finished with the stuff she was mending for me."

My relationship with Ms. Waltman started over a year ago, when she fixed some tears and reinforced the lining of one of the bustiers I wear at the club. She claims to have found it outside my door, but I suspect she took it out of my laundry before returning the item along with the offer to mend any others—for a price, of course. It turns out she was a seamstress back in the day and most definitely one hell of a hustler. Instead of sending her away, I respected her game. We all have a game, and she does amazing work. We just vary the level we play at based on our needs and desires.

"What things?" she asks, leaning out the door and glancing down the hallway.

I take a step back.

Her curls fall over her shoulders, framing her oval face. She doesn't look anything like her grandmother.

Ms. Waltman is tall and seriously thin with pointy features. She often made me think of the evil witches I'd read about in books. This woman is average height, not thin, but not fat either. More like abundantly curved. And her skin...well, it's peaches and cream, not the pale white of the old woman.

Noticing my retreat, she says, "Sorry." Then forcing a smile, she explains, "I'm expecting someone. Now, what was she mending?"

"There should be a couple bras and—"

"I wondered why Gran would have those things." Her face tightens briefly before the friendly mask slips back into place. Her smile forces, she lifts one finger. "Just a second."

When she moves back inside the apartment, an awareness creeps over my skin and the hairs on the back of my neck rise. Glancing to the left, then the right, I find the hallway empty, but it doesn't change the feeling of being watched. My instinct to run surges and I'm about to bolt for my apartment when she arrives to the open door.

"Here you go," she announces, holding out a handful of items.

Taking them quickly, I forge my own smile.

"Thank you," I state, giving a nod.

Turning, I start for the safety my apartment offers.

"My name's Caroline, by the way," she calls out to my back.

Glancing back, I give a wave, but I stumble when I see a shadowed figure down the hallway, a hundred knives exploding in my stomach.

Quickening my pace, I get inside my apartment, drop my lingerie, and secure the knob lock, both deadbolts, and the chain.

Leaning against the door, I slide down to the floor, close my eyes, and breathe deep. *No, it can't be. He was much taller. It can't be him.*

"There's no way he found you. It was just the person your new neighbor was waiting for," I reassure myself. "Get a fucking grip," I growl, slapping my hands against the scuffed, hardwood floor.

Angry at my overreaction, my weakness, I open my eyes and start to collect the clothing from the floor. I scan the area around me for a dark purple satin bralette.

"I know I gave it to her last week," I mumble, looking through the items again.

Assuming Caroline missed one, I carry the rest to my dresser and put them away. My stomach rumbles, reminding me I haven't eaten since this morning. Mentally ticking off the things I have in my small kitchen, I decide on grilled cheese and canned fruit cocktail.

The sandwich and fruit on a plate in one hand and a glass of pop in the other, I sit on the floor in front of my worn couch. It, the cracked pleather chair, and small dresser came with the studio apartment. The twin box spring and mattress are my only real contributions. Unless you count the makeshift coffee table I made of plywood and two milk crates I swiped from behind a grocery store.

Setting my food and drink on said table, I glance around the open space. I don't have much as far as possessions go. Aside from the need to be frugal, I prefer to be a minimalist. It's less to leave behind or attempt to take with you. Given the very real possibility I'll need to take off at a moment's notice, it's for the best.

There's a small microwave and toaster I bought during a collective secondhand sidewalk sale a year ago, enough Dollar Store silverware, dishes, cups, pans, and cooking utensils to get me through two days before I absolutely need to wash things, my bathroom sports a clear shower curtain and enough towels to last a week, and my bed is covered in a simple green plaid comforter with green sheets.

There are no decorative items on my walls—no pictures or artwork. My curtains are a combination of green and red, both found in a discount bin because the matching panels were missing.

I return my focus to my grilled cheese, take a large bite, and reach for the new-to-me text books I picked up today and my GED Study Guide. Having been on the streets since barely fifteen, and given my upbringing, I had the equivalent of an eighth-grade education. But now, I'm so close to understanding everything in this study guide, I can feel the diploma I'll never have.

They don't give degrees to dead girls.

I stare at the print within the book, but don't see it. Over the years, I've died many times out of necessity–survival. My eyes grow blurry, remembering the first time.

"We've got twenty-two dollars." I raise my head from the small bag we keep our money in.

Our adoptive street mom, our leader, who calls herself Winter, walks ahead of me. She says the money is necessary, urgent even. We need five hundred dollars before tomorrow, but I'm still not sure what the rush is.

"Did you guys hit the streets we talked about this morning?" she asks over her shoulder.

"Yeah," two of the older boys say in unison.

Sighing, she stops, and the five of us circle her like puppies wanting to suckle, but instead of milk, we want instruction, orders, or even tips on the best cars to break into, pockets to pick.

"Okay," she points to the two older boys, "you two, go to Main Street. It's a risk, so be careful of who's pockets you get into."

With a nod, they dash off down the street.

"You two," she points to a younger boy and girl, "I want you to put on the cute kid act."

Their deceptively sweet faces split into wide grins, revealing their true devilish natures.

"You're with me, baby doll," she calls me by the nickname bestowed soon after she found me freezing and covered in blood. I hate it, which is partly why I think she keeps using it.

Putting her arm around my shoulders, she silently guides me down the block.

"Today, we're going to utilize your most valuable asset," she tells me, turning a corner.

"I don't have anything," I remind her.

"You're innocent," Winter states.

"I'm not—"

"You're a virgin," she explains. "Right?"

Swallowing hard, I give a nod. "Yeah, but..."

Stopping us, she moves in front of me. Placing both hands on my shoulders, she stares into my eyes.

"You're sixteen now, and I can't be the only one working for us, our family," she says, softly and persuasive. "Don't you want to help your family after we took you in, gave you protection, and a place to stay?"

Knowing she's right, I give a nod. I owe her and the rest of them so much. They could've left me in that alley, scared, starving, and freezing. And she could've easily taken me to the police, given the blood covering me, but she didn't. She welcomed me into their underage street family.

After months of learning the ropes, the tricks of the street, and the hierarchy of the group, Winter's taken to me like a pet. Where she went, I was to follow. This is how I know exactly what she has planned for my "asset." I've stood in the shadows many times while she disappears into cars and alleys with strange men. I've sat on fire escapes overhearing all the things they would do, and on occasion, the fire escape was right above where the action would take place in the alleyway.

Cupping my face, she lifts it to hers.

"Good." Releasing my face, she turns, looking down a familiar street. "Let's see if Peter's home," she says, reaching back for my hand.

I take it, allowing her to tug me down the street.

Peter, a drug dealer and sometimes pimp, doesn't have a stable of girls like the others we deal with. Instead, he makes arrangements between willing women and seeking men.

"He's definitely the least of a prick," she finishes.

A part of me warms at those words, her caring enough not to shove me at some random stranger.

Until she continues. "We can get more money from him, especially if he's high."

My only solace is the fact that it will probably take at least a day for Peter to make the arrangements—and that is short lived when we reach his place.

"How old is she?" he asks, circling, examining me.

"Does it matter?" another man asks.

I've never seen him before, and I would certainly remember a man dressed as well as him. No one on this street wears a suit this expensive.

Unzipping the oversized black hoodie I'm wearing, Peter tugs, pulling it off of my body and dropping it to the floor. Standing in a pair of oversized jeans and t-shirt, my stomach turns. Peter steps close to my back, and I try not to flinch when his hand grips my shoulder and slides along my spine.

"You have to know someone who–" Winter begins.

"Go shower," the other man instructs, motioning toward the bathroom.

Peter shoves me in the same direction.

Stumbling, I ask, "What? Why?"

"Because I need you clean." The look in the stranger's eyes knots my stomach.

"Max, I didn't know you were such a sick fuck," Peter insults on a laugh.

"Hold on," Winter's words halt my steps. "She's not doing anything until we talk money."

The suited man, Max, stands to his full, intimidating height. "Tread carefully, little girl," he warns.

"Talk money to me, Max," she bites out.

Max steps closer, fists clenched.

Stepping close, her chest presses against him. Pushing up on her toes, she narrows her eyes and pokes his pectoral. If there's one thing I know for certain, her temper flares when challenged. It gets the best of her almost every time. I close my eyes, hoping she's mad enough to call it off.

But Peter knows her too, so he tries to diffuse the building tension, offering, "Three hundred dollars."

At his words, I open my eyes.

"Five hundred," she counters, eyes now on Peter. "She's completely untouched. Not even a kiss."

My mouth goes dry and heat flushes my chest. I want to yell. I want to run away. But I'm suddenly frozen mute.

"One thousand," Max interjects, "and no more. Now, get her cleaned up." He pulls out a roll of cash, shoving it at her chest.

"I'll have clean clothes brought with my car." His words send a chill across my skin.

"Car?" she asks, brushing her long blonde hair from her forehead. "She's not going anywhere."

"The deal is made. She comes with me," Max sneers.

"No," I squeak out, shaking my head, and all eyes move to me.

"Go shower," she states, fisting the money.

"Don't worry, pet, I'll have you back here by morning." Max's words do nothing to reassure me.

When I don't move fast enough, Winter helps me into the bathroom and shower.

"If they offer you anything to eat or drink, don't take it," she warns. "Ask for bottled water, and make sure it's unopened."

Rubbing the thin, rough towel over my head, I nod and fight back tears.

With the knock of the door comes a bag of clothes and instructions to hurry up.

It starts with an apprehensive touch, giving me false hope that he might not be able to go through with it. Until I realize it's just for show. From slow to quick, eager movements, the blouse and skirt I'd been given are torn away, ruined. My body is then put into position on top of the comforter—on display for all. A haze settles over my eyes, blocking out what's happening.

My defiler's hands and mouth move over my flesh, both teasing and brutal.

Blood roars through my veins, creating a deafening thrum between my ears that begins to rival an unfamiliar throb between my legs. The first thrust tears through me like a knife, setting off a rage I've never known before.

The deep chuckles and taunts from the men observing, witnessing my death, slip over my bare body, each word soaking into my skin, creating a spark deep inside me.

Fingernails bared, I claw the defiler's face and fight against him.

Stilling the thrusts, his hand comes up, and I brace for the hit, but he grabs both wrists with one large hand and pins them to the bed. The moment he resumes the assault between my legs, my body responds. Lifting my face to his, I find his dark eyes swimming with ferocity.

Clenching my jaw, I narrow my eyes and meet his stare, unblinking, until an explosion swirls across my nerve endings. The room and my anger fall away as my eyes snap shut and my back bows. A scream escapes my mouth, plummeting into an oblivion of tingles and warmth. The fall is too much, too fast. I'm dying.

A roar of applause and laughter breaks through the oblivion, bringing me back to my surroundings. My eyes snap open when wet fingers are shoved into my mouth. A mixture of salt, copper, and something unfamiliar slip over my tongue.

"That's the taste of me owning you, little whore," the man on top of me states before pushing off my body and the bed, his fingers now in his own mouth.

Men congratulate, praise the performance, and eyes shift to me. Leering, taking in my naked body, they lick their lips.

"Careful, Max, the boy may want to keep her," a salt-and-peppered-haired man taunts.

"My son has better taste than that, I would think."

At another man's heavily accented words, the room falls silent. Bodies part, clearing the way for the tall, large-shouldered man with black hair. Unlike the others, he doesn't share a second of his attention on me. Instead, he strides toward the killer of my innocence. Clapping his bare shoulder, he grins before bringing him in for an embrace. Then, over his son's shoulder, he takes in my naked body with his dark eyes. Stopping between my legs, he licks his lips. Even when he releases him to the rest of the group, his focus remains on me. The look on his face is familiar, predatory.

Sitting up in the center of the bed, pain pulls my eyes down my body.

Legs still parted, red tinges my skin and the bedding. I quickly close them, bringing my knees to my chest. Everything throbs, and nausea coils in my stomach realizing I enjoyed what happened, what he did. Suddenly, the taste in my mouth sours on my tongue. Wrapping my arms around my knees, I bury my face as the shame settles over me.

The first time I died...I liked it.

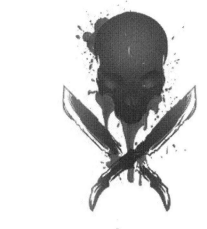

chapter four

Saint

The photos Sketch sent don't surprise me, nor do the documents attached with dates, times, and locations. With the number of our men who have met death's door as of late, I was already sure they were connected. Our syndicate has an assassin on their hands, even if the others don't want to admit it. Part of me suspects our very own boss—our Godfather, if you will—Angelo.

When I click on the first sound file—one of three Sketch was able to get his hands on—there's no keeping the creature calm. Angelo is guilty, all right. And not of just what I've assumed. His guilt runs much deeper than I could have ever fathomed.

That voice. The fucking traitor providing information to Max, Angelo's righthand man. Dates, details, and disclosing what he's overheard.

I don't have to click anything for the second or third audio file to begin. This time, it's Angelo and what he says unleashes the monster I am.

Fisting my hands, I punch the desk on either side of the laptop before clearing pens, papers, and a lamp with a swipe of my arm. I push away from the desk, draw my blade, and stab the now empty corner. A guttural shout escapes me at the same time I bend forward and press my palms to the dark wood.

My office door slams open.

I don't look up at their entrance, but they've been in my service long enough for me to know who it is. Russ, Vince, and Tony—my diligent, dedicated, and loyal soldiers.

I snort at the thought of loyalty now.

"Boss?" Russ is the bravest.

Inhaling deep, I push off the desk and yank my Jagdkommando knife out of the desk.

I lift the blade in front of me, keeping my eyes on it, and slowly make my way to the three men.

"Did you know the Jagdkommando," I nod toward the steel in my hand, "is one of the deadliest knives ever created?" I tighten my grip on the handle. "It's got a comfortable grip, but it's the tri-dagger fixed blade and the way it swirls around like a sharp serpent that makes it deadly."

Glancing up, I find the three men, each holding a gun at their hip, looking back and forth between the blade and me. Their eyes follow the weapon as I drop my arm to my side.

"Is," Russ starts, swallows, and then perseveres, "everything okay?"

"No," I admit, my voice low, deep.

Each of them straighten and move closer together. I'm not sure if it's a safety in numbers or unified front move, but it brings my target closer to me, to the creature. It's too late for the traitor now.

Taking a step forward, I'm not sure if I should be proud or offended they don't back away.

"A team of surgeons would need to be readily available to fix the damage it could do," I continue.

Three sets of eyes drop to my right side before raising back to meet mine.

Lifting the knife, I point it at Russ. His eyes widen and he swallows hard, but he doesn't move.

"What's he done?" Tony asks, hands raised as he steps forward.

Eyes focused on Russ's, I respond, "Nothing."

Flipping the knife in my palm, I grip it with the sharp edge aimed at Tony and strike. The metal pierces his face, and with a twist my wrist, his long scream fills the room.

Grip still on the handle, I hold him in place and finally move to face him.

"You're the fucking traitor," I ground out.

Having landed the knife in the lower socket, his eyeball bulges out, ready to pop. With another twist, the flesh splits across his cheek bone. I let him drop to his knees, and when his lips part on another scream, blood fills his mouth.

I lift one foot, place it on his chest, and pull the knife free.

He falls back on the floor, bringing his hands to the mutilated flesh.

"What else have you told him?" I shout, moving to stand over his writhing body.

"I didn't—"

The roar inside my head is deafening.

Crouching over him, I take his protruding eye in my fingers and rip it out.

"Fuck," he screams.

I toss the eye on the floor and close my eyes. His scream satisfies one of the cravings, but we have many more to go and a lot of hours left in the night.

Dark urges getting an unexpected fix the night before, I slept surprisingly well for someone who still holds the secrets of a deadly and protected man.

When I enter my office, part of me is disappointed the cleaners have already erased all my fun, but the other part needs to get down to business. Taking a seat at my desk, I pull out my cell and place a call to Felix. If anyone will feel the same way I do about this new information, it will be him. At least, I hope he does, or I'm about to give him enough ammo to get me *dealt with*.

Getting his voicemail, I only invite him to join me at the strip club Friday night. As much as I want to start dealing with Angelo now,

Tony's unfortunate accident will draw attention, and I don't need further suspicion falling on me.

Besides, I have another interest—a tiny bleach blonde who taunts my fucking thoughts.

Felix enters the VIP room with Nico and two other men at his back.

"This is a private conversation," I inform, lifting my tumbler glass and draining the amber liquid.

He raises one brow, expressing his surprise, before raising his hand and motioning for his men to leave us.

Crossing the room, he settles into a leather seat adjacent to mine.

"I'll admit, I was a bit suspicious when *you* requested to meet here."

"Given our recent events here, I figured it wouldn't look too conspicuous. I also had the room secured before your arrival."

Resting back in the chair, he places one ankle on his knee.

"Well, now you have me intrigued," he states, a small smile playing at the corner of his mouth.

"You remember the death of Evgeni Volkov's wife and infant son?" I pause, allowing him to confirm.

"The death of the Bratva Queen, their prince, and the blood bath Evgeni began is sort of a hard story to forget," he states.

Nodding, I agree, "Yes."

"Did you bring me here to discuss romanticized blood wars?" he asks, wearing a teasing smile.

"No," I clip out, growing annoyed at his sarcasm. "We're here because Angelo is the one behind the deaths."

The grin melts from his face.

"Why would he—?"

"Greed, power, because he could," I interject.

"What would murdering a woman and infant accomplish? Other than to upset the truce we have with the Bratva?"

"You're not stupid, Felix. You've seen what Angelo really is."

Felix snaps his mouth shut. Eyes narrowing, he studies my face.

"I'm not trying to set you up," I assure him. "There's something else too," I admit.

His brow furrows and the muscles in his jaw flex. "What?"

"I'm not convinced Evgeni's son died in the explosion."

He opens his mouth, but I lift a hand to silence his protest.

"It's not confirmed," I divulge, "but I suspect Angelo has him. Or had him. He could've disposed of him later, I suppose."

When I reach into my jacket, he stiffens, only relaxing when I pull out an envelope.

Lifting it up, I meet his stare and toss it in his lap.

Opening the envelope, he pulls out three documents and looks them over. The first provides dates, locations, and times—one particular entry highlighted. The second, a copy of a time-stamped photo placing Angelo right where the first document states, and, finally, the third, a transcription of the audio file I listened to.

"How do I know this isn't some—"

Tossing a black recorder device in his lap cuts him off.

He picks it up, puts in the earbuds, and presses play.

Every emotion flickering across his face is like an out of body experience. I can almost see the moment he hears Angelo reference the loss of AJ. *"Sacrifices must occur in order to make it to the winner's circle."*

"That fucker killed his own son!" Felix shouts, yanking the earbuds out.

"He's the reason AJ is dead yes," I correct.

"It's the same fucking thing," Felix argues. "If he hadn't started a fucking blood war with Evgeni, we wouldn't have been ambushed that day and AJ—his own damn son, Saint—would still be with us."

Faulting him for his anger would be hypocritical. The day we lost our cousin was hard on both of us.

Lifting the device, Felix smashes it on the floor.

"He treats it like just another fucking casualty in his greater picture," Felix rants, pushing out of the chair and pacing.

His reaction is bittersweet. I know he'll be on board with my plan to deal with Angelo, but he's also struggling with the loss of AJ once again. Only, this time, it's with the added callousness of our uncle.

"He'll pay," I vow, pushing out of my chair.

Felix twists his head in my direction. "And how do you plan to accomplish that? Not even The Saint will come of out of something like that alive."

Tugging on the cuff of my sleeve, I begin, "The difference between you and me, Felix," I pause, giving him my back and making my way to the door, "is I never plan on survival." Grasping the door handle, I pull it open and exit.

When I reach the end of the long hallway, I draw back the velvet curtain leading to the central area and freeze.

Under a golden spotlight, my current obsession caresses a metal pole with one leg, cigarette smoke swirling around her body as if she's commanding it to do so.

Mei

"What the fuck are you doing here?"

Ignoring Joey's question, I lean in close to the mirror and swipe black kohl along my lash line, pretending he's talking to one of the other dancers.

"Mei," he barks, gripping the old chair and shaking. "I told you—"

Meeting his hard eyes in the mirror, I drop the liner.

"You said a few days, Joe," I remind him. "It's almost been a week."

Five days, to be exact. While the extra gym time has done wonders for my technique, I can't even stand the thought of staying locked up in my small apartment any longer. Between feeling watched every time I step out of my building, my new neighbor's midnight bedroom performances, and my dwindling spending money, getting back to work is my only choice. Regardless of the men who scared me away from the club, who had me locking myself away in fear, I can no longer cower. I made a vow, a promise to myself, and it's time to take control.

"Barely a week, Mei," he says on an exasperated sigh.

"I need the money," I confess.

Surprise widens his eyes, unfamiliar with my volunteering

anything personal.

Swallowing down the anxiousness and apprehension, I continue. "And I'll need one of the main stages tonight."

His features morph, giving me a skeptical glance.

"You want the floor tonight?" he asks, the underlying tone making his silent inquiry clear.

If he gives me a main stage, then I agree to work the floor and private dance rooms.

The darkness stirs deep inside, twisting my stomach with its feverish anticipation of delving into the wickedness sure to follow.

Keeping my mask in place, I nod.

Joey's eyes narrow for just a moment before he licks his lips. "Fine, but I have my own conditions."

Steeling my spine, I sit up and wait.

"You can have stage three..." he starts, and I fight the urge to cringe. Stage three is where the regulars hang out: the sloppy drunks, gropers, and men who come in here too often for my liking. Joey isn't stupid. He's picked up on my preference for the casual visitor or passer through.

"Or you get on stage one and put the full show on," he finishes, dropping into the seat next to me. The bustle of the dressing room quiets and I feel their eyes on us.

"Fine," I bite out.

"I'll let Chase know," he says through a grin.

I start to turn back to the mirror, but he keeps talking. "Oh, and Mei, start with the sweet and innocent act." It's not a request.

Standing, he reaches over my head. Grabbing an outfit from the wall rack, he drops it in the now vacant seat. Knowing exactly what he chose, I don't look at it until I know he's gone from the room.

Given what I ran away from years ago, the irony of this particular outfit is not lost on me. Facing the mirror, I take a deep breath to calm the terrible desires tingling beneath my skin. Getting myself under control, I grab the outfit and set it on the table in front of me. The flesh-tone bralette and G-string are fine. It's the sheer, white babydoll mini dress that makes my head swim with unwanted feelings and memories.

"Where is your hair?" he asks, urgency in his tone and a box under his arm.

"It's too hot," I whine.

"But a ragdoll has red yarn hair," he insists, scanning the room.

Biting my lip, I twist my hands in my aproned lap. I know I'm supposed to wear the red hair with this dress. I'm expected to match Annie, my favorite doll to bring to my tea parties with the shadow in the mirror.

"Doll," he warns, stepping so close, his shiny black shoes almost touch my tights-covered leg.

Sighing, I reach behind me under the bed, pull out the wig, and place it on my head.

"That's better," he praises, slipping his hands beneath my arms. Bringing me to my feet, he guides me toward the tall wall mirror.

"Why do you have your table against the mirror?" he asks, pushing it and my most favorite of the toy dolls out of his way.

"To have tea with my friends," I explain.

"Your dolls?" he inquires, glancing back to the table, Annie, Penny, Teddy, Sarah, and Betty now knocked over in their chairs.

I nod.

He picks up Sarah, my dark-skinned china doll, and runs his finger over the curve of her face before touching a dark curl.

"Do you want one like this," he holds Sarah out to me, "from daddy?"

I nod once more, excited at the thought of a new friend in Daddy's doll room.

"You love them more than these toys, don't you?" he asks, placing Sarah onto the small table set for imaginary tea. "They're more fun, aren't they?"

His eyes light with excitement.

"Oh, yes," I agree. "It's much more fun with them. When I touch them, they are warm, and they blink, and...and..." Guilt sets in. "But I love these too," I declare, making sure these dolls know I love them too, " and my shadow friend," I admit, searching the mirror for her to show up.

But, like every time Daddy is here, she doesn't.

He stills, hands taking my shoulders in a firm grip, eyes roaming over my face.

"Shadow friend?" he presses.

Before I can respond, he smiles. "Like Peter Pan?"

I nod, grinning at the mention of my favorite bedtime story.

Conversation about my shadow friend over, he situates me before the mirror.

"See how perfect you are?" he says, moving against my back.

The heat of his body adds to the warmth of the hair. Before I can step away, he clenches my shoulders, pulling me closer. More and more, his touch feels different. His stares linger, searching. Fingers tip my chin up to meet his gaze.

"I have something for you," he informs, grinning wide.

"What is it?" Excitement laces my question, though I know what it will be before opening the ribbon decorated package. Removing the box from under his arm, he places it on my tea party table.

It's another stuffed doll which would be followed by a matching outfit. The dress would be in my size, and I would model it for the only friend who could move like me—my shadow in the mirror. If I twirled, she twirled. When I touched the glass, she touched it too. And sometimes, she would do something for me to repeat.

Lingering too long on the past, I rush to get my curled pigtails in place. Fighting back the memories of the shadow in the mirror, what I decided later was just the creation of a child's imagination, I hurry out to the stage. My trip down nightmare lane means I don't have the time to look over the crowd. Tonight, I won't be able to assess them for my preferred customers.

With a quick introduction and the sickening sounds of jewelry box music, I approach the pole and grip. The deeper beat kicks in, an innocent voice sings the lyrics about having no strings to hold me down, and I sway gently, giving my innocent act.

After two years, I'm still not sure whether Joey is a twisted or brilliant asshole. Twisted because it's a goddamn children's movie song, or brilliant because the crowd always eats it up. There's never a sound out of the crowd or an eye anywhere but on me. He swears it's because of my *youthful* appearance, but I'm pretty sure any of the girls would get the same reaction.

Hell, even I feel a reaction—an unwanted one. The dark desires begin their own dance inside me, reaching, stretching, trying to break out of the box I lock them away in.

At the crescendo, I take a breath, calming the urges just in time for the next song to start up.

Music with a heavy beat plays through the club and I start the roll of my body, swing of my hips, and make eye contact with a couple men scattered around the stage.

Switching from sweet girl to crazy nympho, I lip the words and move across the stage. Unhooking the mini dress, it floats to the floor, leaving me in nude-colored lingerie covered in gemstones.

When I remove the bralette, I barely notice the money thrown at my feet. The dark urges battle for freedom. Dropping to the side of the stage, I try to distract myself with the singles being slid against my skin and beneath my G-string. For the moment, it works, until a man grabs my thigh and squeezes.

Gripping his wrist, I pull his hand away and shake my head with a scolding purse of my lips. Crawling away from Mister Handsy, I reach the other side of the stage. On my knees, I close my eyes and grind down toward the stage. Running my hands up my body, I slip my fingers into my hair and reopen my eyes to the one they call Saint.

The ferocity in his eyes should scare me, but it does the opposite. The malevolence in them titillates, excites. Our eyes locked, I rise to my feet and back up against the pole. Twisting my hips, rolling my body, I'm caught in his depths, and the darkness I lock away seeps through the confines of its cage, crawling, stretching through my limbs. Every dirty, terrible urge I fight surfaces, raising each hair on my body. My nerve endings crackle with anticipation, excitement, and fear. Sucking my lip into my mouth, I bite. The metallic taste slipping over my tongue sends a throb between my legs.

Caressing my hands over my hips, I follow the crease where my torso meets my leg. I'm one fingertip away from slipping beneath the G-String to ease my ache, when a man shouts out, breaking the trance.

"Come here, baby!"

Turning, I grip the pole and spin, fighting to lock everything back down inside me. As soon as the song ends, I collect the money and rush from the stage. Pushing through the backstage curtain, my bicep is seized in a rough grip.

"Hey—" I start, but my protest is cut off with a palm pressed to my mouth as I'm dragged down the hallway and shoved into a private room. I stumble forward before finding my balance. Clutching the minimal clothing to my chest, I turn to face my attacker, and freeze.

"If you want a dance, you need to make the arrangements with Chase," I say with a bravado I don't feel at all.

One side of Felix's mouth quirks, though I can't tell whether it's in amusement or disgust. He settles onto a couch along the wall, resting his left ankle on his right knee.

"We need to get a few things cleared up, doll," he says, scratching his scruffy jaw, and I stiffen at the endearment.

"Relax, I just need to be sure we understand what happened last week." Dropping his leg, he plants both feet on the floor and leans his elbows to his knees. His eyes stay focused on me, though they peruse my body, lingering on the barest spots.

"I don't know what you're talking about." I'm amazed at the boldness in my voice, especially with the way my palms are sweating.

A grin splits his stern face.

"Good girl," he praises, standing from the couch.

With smooth, confident strides, he backs me against the far wall.

"You look so sweet." His eyes roam my face.

In a flash of movement, Felix grabs my wrists and yanks my arms out to my sides, my clothes falling to the floor. His light brown eyes drop to my chest and he licks his lips.

Leaning forward, he presses his face into my neck, and whispers, "So sweet."

His tongue runs over my skin, causing an unwanted shiver, and the urges begin to stir once more. Running his nose along my jaw, he inhales. Then, his lips are on mine, pressing, pushing.

When I don't immediately return the kiss, his grip on my wrists tightens painfully, and I force myself to comply to his unspoken command.

Felix releases my wrists, cupping the sides of my face and deepening the kiss. Pressings his body into mine, he gives one hard thrust as his hands slide down over my neck and collarbone, until he can palm my breast.

"Boss?" a deep voice calls through the door, followed by three hard knocks.

Ignoring them, Felix swipes his thumb over my left nipple, but the knock comes again.

"Christ, Nico," he growls, pushing away from me. "What is it?"

he shouts at the door.

The door cracks open and the large man from the other night leans in. "There's a pressing matter," he rasps.

His eyes shift to me, and to his credit, he doesn't look at my bare breasts before focusing back on Felix.

"Angelo," is all his says, and Felix tenses for the briefest moment before turning back to me.

"Another time, doll," he says with a grin, and the endearment makes my stomach roil. Then, he's gone, out the door with Nico.

I collect the discarded clothing and leave the VIP room. It may be time to move on, after all—a new place, new strangers, and less attention from men like him. A pair of bright hazel eyes flash in my mind, sending tingles down my spine and stirring the darkness inside me.

Back in the dressing room, I don the black strapless bra and matching garter and panties. Rummaging through my bag, I select a pair of black, silk, elbow-length gloves. Innocent may have been the game on the stage, but naughty is the way to go when catching the eye of those seeking private time. And I can get away with no gloves on stage, but the roughness of my fingers makes the use of them essential—just as necessary as the lengths I go to make my fingerprints unrecognizable.

"Mei." Joey's call stops me right outside the dressing room. His brow is furrowed and lips drawn tight. "Room five," he clips, looking more pissed than usual. He can't still be angry about me being back, especially since he got what he wanted on stage.

"I haven't—"

"You have a request," he cuts me off, not meeting my eyes. Worry starts to gnaw at my gut.

"What's going—?"

"No questions. Just go," he interrupts once more. "Now," he orders.

At the rough command, I make my way down the dim hallway

to the room farthest from everything. Outside the door, I pause, running my silk-covered hands up my arms. He didn't give me the client's name or any details. *Damn it*, I mentally curse, *he's sending me in here blind.*

Opening the door, I step into the dimly lit room. Thinking they aren't here yet, I reach for the light switch panel.

"Leave it," the deep baritone voice slices through me. I don't have to see him to know it's him—the one they call Saint. Excitement prickles my skin, anticipation kicks my heart into overdrive, and fear...the fear steels my spine and constricts my lungs. I want to run, but I'm not sure whether it's away from or toward the voice.

"I'll catch you," he informs, and a new wave of terror slices through me. "Close the door."

As if my body has fallen under his control, I shove the door shut behind me.

Arms wrap around me from behind, one at my waist, the other across my chest. His rough hand clamps down on my shoulder, while the other squeezes the fleshy part of my hip. He's so much larger than me, stronger too, and his arms act as unwavering bands, confining me against his chest.

At his rough touch, my body flares to life. Parting my lips, I inhale and lean back into him. Below the surface of my skin, a slow burn begins, seeking release from the confines of my flesh.

Felix had drawn a reaction, a coaxed one, but this man calls to me, luring every deep dark desire from within.

The heat of his mouth caresses my ear, encompassing me in a cocoon of want.

"Who are you?" The words stroke my lobe, and I close my eyes, trying to battle the response my body has to him.

At my silence, Saint releases my shoulder, his large hand sliding over my chest and collaring my neck.

"Who the fuck are you?" He accentuates the question with a flex of his fingers.

The briefest bite of pain shoots through me, and I gasp, reaching up to grab his arms with both hands. Fear swirls with a deadly combination of need. The darkness seeps through the cracks in my armor, and I arch against him.

He stiffens, releasing the hold on my throat, and the

movement is enough to push the desires back down.

Shoving at his arms, I twist out of his grip and face him. Even in the dim lighting, his hazel eyes gleam. It's both scary and enticing. His eyes roam over me, taking in every part slowly and deliberately, allowing me a moment to study the dangerous man in front of me.

His dark brown hair is cut close to his scalp around the sides, but left a bit longer on top. High cheekbones, strong jaw, and an angular nose give him a severe but handsome face. A broad chest and muscular shoulders fill out the undoubtedly expensive gray suit, and I'm sure the white, button-down shirt protests the flex of his biceps. He's over a head taller than my five-foot-seven stature. He's attractive—extremely attractive—but it's the fierce dark aura surrounding him that sends normal, sane people running.

I'm clearly not normal, or sane, because it's this I respond to the most. Even now, I want to offer myself up as a sacrifice to the danger and sin I sense in him.

Snapping his eyes back to mine, I'm caught once again in his allure. Like a practiced predator, his gaze distracted me from the hand reaching out to surround my throat.

At the warning squeeze, I grab his wrist and tug. Fear rushes through me, washing away all the other unwanted feelings.

Leaning down, he brings his face less than an inch from mine, and growls, "I won't ask you again."

I'm trapped and vulnerable—something I've fought so hard not to be. And this man comes right in and destroys all the careful protections I set in place. Pushing down the fear, I let anger and desperation surge. Channeling all of it, I release his wrist, fist my hands together, and give an upward thrust. My double fist meets his arm. He's solid muscle, but my action caught him off guard.

Using all my weight, I force myself into his chest, and he stumbles back. It's not much, but I take the opportunity to grab for the door handle.

A band of hard muscle wrenches me back by the waist. Opening my mouth, I prepare to scream, but a large, calloused hand seals my lips shut.

Lifting me off my feet, he turns and carries me farther into the room. Digging at his hand with my fingertips, I try to free my mouth, but the damn gloves won't allow me to find purchase on his skin.

"You can scream all you want," he rasps into the side of my head, "but no one will come for you."

He releases my mouth, and I scream and I kick back into his leg with the heel of my stiletto.

"Fuck," he groans, dropping me down, and I turn, kicking off my heels, preparing to make my stand. I've fought for too long to survive. There's no way I'm letting them take me out without a fight. Fists up, I brace myself for the battle of my life.

Chapter Five

Saint

Fuck if she isn't a ferocious little thing.

When Sketch called, instead of using the laptop to send over the information he found on Mei, I grew even more suspicious. But then he revealed his findings. Not much surprises Sketch, but the mystery surrounding this woman has riled his curiosities. His interest in her uncharacteristically annoys me.

"You're a dead girl," I state.

Lifting her chin, I watch her rise to a challenge, and it's fucking glorious.

"You can try, but I won't make it easy," she informs.

Straightening to my full height, I remove my sport coat and toss it onto a chair. Her eyes follow the action, as well as when I remove my cufflinks and roll up the sleeves of my shirt.

"No, sweetheart, you are a dead girl," I explain.

The slight flinch at the words wouldn't be noticeable to an average person, but I'm not normal. I catch the furrow of her brow, tightening of her lips, and slight jerk of her body before she puts a blank face in place.

Grinning, I step closer. Her fists tighten, and she squares her shoulders, ready to fight me. Reaching out, she slaps away my hand, but I lash out, undeterred, grabbing both her fists in mine. Surprising me, she spins, bringing her extended leg out and around. Slapping her leg away, I shove her face first into the wall.

"So, I'll ask one more time. Who are you?" I press, way too curious for the answer. I crave the response, the truth from her red lips.

An elbow lands into my side, knocking the wind from me, but not enough for me to release her. "If that's how you want to play it," I growl, using my forearm to hold her tighter.

With my free hand, I reach into the waist of my pants. The cold steel in my hand, I lean in close to her body. Her scent fills my nose, a mixture of earthy vanilla, musk, and fear.

The creature stirs, eager to be set free. Releasing the blade next to her creamy skin, my cock twitches, wanting in on the action.

Her mouth parts on a gasp and she inhales sharply as I press the cold metal to her face. Careful not to break the skin, I run the tip over her cheek and down the side of her neck.

She leans her body into the blade and tilts her head to allow better access, shocking me again. An unfamiliar feeling surges inside, the dark merging with the desire to fuck her. My cock hardens painfully, forcing my hips to thrust against her round ass for relief.

Closing my eyes, I hold the blade flat against her shoulder and press. Her moan fills my ears, drowning the need to know who she is and what game she's playing.

Burying my face into the back of her neck, I inhale deep. Her heady vanilla scent isn't like cupcakes and sunshine. No, it's a thick, dark vanilla, like it was found in the depths of a decaying forest.

Forehead pressed to the back of her head, I twist my neck and open my eyes. With the flick of one finger, the blade pierces her skin, and her body melts against me as she pushes her ass back, giving my cock the friction is seeks.

One crimson drop forms, dangling as precariously as my control. It's so unlike me. And I'm sure she still fears me, but she likes it—she's getting off on the fear, my steel.

The drop of blood slides down the side of the blade, and my control snaps. Bringing my mouth to the puncture of her shoulder, I lick, and she gasps as my tongue trails over her shoulder, up her neck, and to her ear.

"What are you?" I ask on a strangled breath before pulling back. My eyes dart to the trail of red along her skin, and I spin her around, forcing her back to the wall. Knife to her throat, I grip her face in my other hand, lift it to mine, and study her.

Fear and lust sparkle in her eyes, but I want more. I want the familiar darkness hidden deep within. I dive deeper, hunting, searching, waiting. Glittering like an oasis for demons—for my demons—the black soul rises, her eyes turning darker, more pronounced. The creature inside me grows, sliding beneath my flesh until it's presence seeps from my pores.

Control gone, I remove the knife from her throat, and cut the button of my pants and the front of my shirt, running it along my skin. Her eyes follow the blade, widening in both horror and curiosity as I break through my skin. When she parts her lips, I press the bloodied steel to her mouth, silencing her.

Nostrils flaring, her green eyes snap from my chest to my face. The right side of her mouth twitches upward as her fingers touch my stomach, making my muscles jump. Her right hand slides up, flattening over my sternum and pushing against me. Unmoved by her shove, I frown down at her, and her tongue peeks out between her lips, touching the blade while her hand curves around my wrist.

Pushing once more, I allow her to remove the knife from her mouth and guide me back until she sits me in the chair holding my jacket. She steps closer, and I part my legs for her to stand between my knees.

The blood-stained silk of her glove glides up and around my neck. Tilting my head back, I look up at this seductress. Her eyes closed, she swipes her tongue over her stained lips, and my cock throbs against the confines of my clothing. My demons burn within every cell of my body, ready to combust with the urge to devour her, but it's not the typical need to maim and destroy. His hunger is for ownership, possession. He's found the solace of another broken soul. Not one that will stifle his need, but revel in our dark oblivion.

Wrapping my left arm around her right thigh, I pull her closer. Gripping my switchblade in my other hand, I run it up the inside of her leg and watch her head fall back as a moan leaves her mouth. The hand at my neck disappears as she brings it to her chest and runs it up over her body. The blood-stained trail against her creamy skin unlocks the need to devour her.

Slipping the blade beneath the edge of her black panties, I slice through the flimsy material, exposing the smooth, bare skin of her pussy. Burying my face between her thighs, I inhale. She's so aroused, her cunt so wet and ready for everything she doesn't know I'll want. Done denying myself, I slide my tongue past her softest part.

"Shit," she moans, hands coming to my shoulders, and I delve deeper, my tongue flicking and twisting over the most sensitive part of her. I push my hand against her ass, squeezing, drawing her closer, and she whimpers at the contact. A low hum releases as I remove my mouth and slide the flat side of my knife over her, revealing the wettest and pinkest part of her. The heavy thrum of the blood rushing through my veins consumes me. On a growl, I shove my tongue against her once more, licking and sucking the sensitive flesh. She thrusts against my mouth, wanting more, seeking to extinguish the same ache my cock feels.

Sliding my hand over her ass, I bring my thumb down until I feel the wet opening. Leaving my fingers splayed on her ass, my middle finger slipping deep between the globes, I press the tip against her tight hole.

She jerks forward, but relaxes when I don't penetrate.

Middle finger pressing against her asshole, thumb plunged inside her cunt, and my mouth sucking at her clit, she rocks faster, harder against me.

Her hands claw at my head, trying to find purchase in the short strands, and she screams, "Oh fuck!"

Dropping my knife, I palm the back of her left thigh and do every deviant thing I want—starting with devouring her until she comes against my mouth.

As she starts to come down from her orgasm, I release her legs. Back on both feet again, she sways unsteadily.

Taking her by the hips, I fist the black satin dangling from her hip. Her body jostles from the force it takes to rip the panties off.

I palm behind her knees and pull her between my legs until my nose brushes her stomach. The smell of her cum mixed with my saliva fills my nose.

The door to the room opens, and Mei tries to pull away, but I hold tight.

"Room's taken," I growl without looking at the door.

"I never took you for a sloppy seconds kind of man, Dante," Felix's voice cuts through me.

Straightening my spine, the thought of him touching Mei blurs my vision. Jealousy isn't something I feel often, but like any other emotion someone as fucked up as me experiences, God help the person responsible.

Mei's whimper clears my vision. Her hands grip at my wrists, trying to remove my hands—hands I'd been digging deep enough into her skin to leave bruises.

Releasing her legs, I grab both her wrists and yank her down to me.

"Did you fuck him?" I ask through clenched teeth.

"She's not worth it. Let her go, Dante," Felix orders.

Snapping my head toward him, I narrow my eyes. He leans against the wall, Nico at his back. The arrogance he displays eats away at the anger and irrational jealousy I already feel. I'm not sure what his game is, but he's purposely forcing my hand.

"I didn't fuck him," her words are just above a whisper, but enough to lessen the rage boiling inside me, though it doesn't lessen my need to put Felix in his place.

"Undo my belt," I order without taking my eyes from Felix. I don't miss the way his body tenses or the hesitation from Mei when I release her wrists. Turning my attention back to her, I raise a brow.

"Unless you'd rather go to Felix," I challenge. "The choice is yours, sweetheart."

Burying the rage, nausea, and bite of unfamiliar jealousy at just the mention of her choosing Felix, I settle back into the leather chair. My limbs want to lash out and hold her against me, but I rest them on the arms of the chair, giving the perfect example of relaxed calm.

"Are you sure you want to do this?" Felix asks, his question surely accompanied with a smirk.

"Make your choice, *Mei*," I stress the name I know doesn't belong to her.

"Yes, Mei," his saying her name makes darkness claw inside me, "choose carefully. I can see he already introduced you to just the tip of his predilections."

My fingers twitch, wanting to wrap around the handle of my

blade and take it to his throat.

Mei's eyes glance down her body, taking in the pink and red streaks across her chest. When she lifts her head, she focuses on Felix, and I clench my jaw.

Eyes still on him, she sinks to the floor, the scrape of metal against the tile breaking the silence before she stands back to her full height. Not breaking eye contact, she slips the knife between her breasts and slices the material of her bra. The cups fall away, baring herself to both of us.

Dropping her arms, she lets the material join her ruined panties at her feet. Then, in a flash of movement, the knife is pointed at my face.

Felix chuckles, thinking he's victorious in this standoff, until Mei brings her gaze to mine.

The sinister look in her eyes and twisted half grin on her face takes my breath away. Grabbing the blade of the knife in her left hand, she releases the handle, extending it for me to take.

I wrap my fingers around the base, but instead of letting go, she fists the sharp edges and yanks her hand along them. Blood immediately soaks the silk of her palm, spreading through the fabric along her fingers.

"The fuck," Nico exclaims.

"Christ," Felix growls, knowing he's lost. "She's as fucked up as he is."

Stepping closer, her knees touch the edge of the cushion between my legs. She leans down and presses her bloody palm against my chest. My mouth parts on a relieved sigh, and I begin to relax, but she's not finished.

Straddling my lap, she slips her palm down my body and into my pants.

It's wet and slick against my aching flesh. Each stroke makes me grow harder, rousing the demons back to the surface. All my depraved urges gather in preparation to possess the woman before us.

Grabbing her hips, I lift her over me, and she releases my cock from its confines, positioning me at her entrance.

"What are you?" I ask again.

Regardless of the answers I seek, the ones I *will* get, it doesn't change the fact that she just publicly handed herself over to me. She's mine, no matter who, or what, she ends up being.

"A curse," she gasps, taking me into her body.

"Fucking hell," Nico rasps from the doorway.

"Fuck you, Dante!" Felix exclaims. "You can have the whore," he says, followed by heavy footsteps and a slamming door.

Taking the wrist of her injured hand, I press it to her chest and draw it across her skin. The dark crimson stain taunts the creature, making him want more.

Wrapping my arms around her, I guide her up and down my length faster, harder, the force causing her to bury her face in my neck and scream. Fisting the hair at the back of her head, I pull her face to mine and watch the orgasm form an O on her lips as her skin flushes and eyes lose focus.

It's fucking glorious watching her come undone on my cock. So much so, my release pulses at the base of my dick to the point of pain before exploding through me and into her.

Long moments later, breathing back to normal, I pull her off me and place her back on her feet. Naked, streaked in our blood, and cum dripping down her thigh, the feelings of ownership and possession creep back in and take hold.

Standing from the chair, I tuck my dick back into my pants and reach for my jacket. I grab my cell phone, tap the screen, and put it to my ear.

My eyes find Mei and watch the discomfort set in. Her palm has definitely started throbbing by now, and as hard as we fucked, she's probably sore between her legs too.

"Yes, sir?" Jimmy answers.

"Your boss reassign you yet?" I inquire.

Felix likes to throw his power around when he loses, so I'm sure he's informed his lackeys they no longer do my bidding.

"We've been given a new job," he responds, dutiful and politically correct.

"Very well, but if you share any information about her, I'll be paying you a special visit," I warn.

Mei's wide eyes come to mine as a visible shiver slides over her body.

"Do you understand?" I press at his silence.

"Y-Yes," he stutters.

"Pass the information on to your partner as well," I state before ending the call.

Shaking out my jacket, I step closer to Mei and wrap it around her naked body. She relaxes enough to offer a minimal smile of thanks.

"Collect your things," I order, watching her tense.

Brushing a loose strand of blonde hair behind her ear, I slide my hand to the back of her neck and bring her chest to mine.

"We still have a lot to discuss, dead girl," I remind her, smirking at the determination lining her face.

"Go get your things," I instruct, motioning to the door. "I'll collect you shortly, so don't take forever."

"Collect me?" she asks, brow furrowed.

"Yes," is the only response I give.

She doesn't need to know there is no getting away from me now. Above the answers she'll give me, the craving for and connection to her has only increased after tonight.

"Where are—?"

"It doesn't matter," I cut off her question. "Get your things, Mei, or whatever your name is."

Tension and unease pour off her so thick, the room starts to feel stifling.

"Fine," she concedes, squaring her shoulders and walking to the door.

"Be quick, dead girl." The nickname makes her footing falter, and I turn away. Bringing my phone to my ear, I call my own men—the ones waiting outside in the car we arrived in tonight.

"Yo, Boss," Russ answers.

"Bring the car to the rear exit. I have a guest with me," I inform him. Glancing at the now open door, a feeling of unease settles over me.

"On it," he responds, hanging up.

Straightening my shirt, I exit the VIP room.

My first stop is the private restroom, where I wash away the visible blood and find a new shirt hanging in the closet. It's a half size too small, but will do until I get Mei back to my apartment.

When I reach the dressing room, the chatter goes silent. My reputation seems to have reached the whores of this establishment.

Good. They should be scared. Fear keeps people in line. Glancing at the faces, I don't find Mei.

"Where is she?" I ask, anger burning in my gut.

"W-Who?" a very young redhead stutters.

"Mei," I bite out.

"I haven't—" she starts, but doesn't finish. I follow the young redhead's gaze, finding Tricia.

"She left," she confesses.

"Tricia," the redhead hisses.

"She ran out of here ten minutes ago," Tricia continues.

"I see," I say, turning and exiting the room. My anger lowers to a simmer, the darkest part of me eager to play hunter.

Chapter Six

Mei

I clean up, change into baggy jeans and an oversized hooded sweatshirt, and escape the club before he can *collect* me. Fear, not paranoia, makes me glance over my shoulder.

Saint, or Dante, or whoever the fuck he is wants answers and my actions back in the VIP room, baring my dark side to him, started something I'm not sure I'll survive. I handed a dangerous man a glimpse behind the glitter and lace. A front seat view to the sick and perverse parts I work so hard to keep locked away.

Fuck!

My mask slipped and now he's determined to tear it away.

Climbing the stairs to my apartment, I fight back tears of frustration as I mentally run through my plan. It will take him at least a day to find out where I live. The club doesn't have my correct address and I've never invited anyone to my place. That gives me a morning to pawn, pack, and get the hell out of this town. It's much sooner than I'd planned, but after tonight, there's no other option. This time, I'll get far, far away from here. Much farther than Chicago. Tomorrow, I'll see just how many states I can get between me and—

Lost in my thoughts, I crash into a solid, warm body.

"I'm sorry," a male voice says, sending ripples of concern over my skin, raising the hairs.

"Sorry," I mumble, stepping around him.

"I thought I was the only one who took the stairs," he says, a hint of humor in his voice.

Nodding, I keep my head down and continue up the final flight.

The feeling of being watched is too much, and I glance over my shoulder. My step falters when I find the unknown man staring after me. I'm not familiar with him, and he's not dressed like one of Felix or Saint's men, but my night has me on the edge of panic.

Perhaps it's my fright, but the look on his face, his build, and features feel all too familiar, setting my raw nerves on fire. Warning bells sound in my head, and in times like this, I've learned to listen to them. Doubling my efforts, I rush to my apartment, locking and bolting the door.

I drop my bag and glance around, taking stock of my belongings. With a fortifying breath, I empty my bag and set it on my bed along with a large backpack.

Rummaging through my clothing, I put all the frilly and slutty items I took from the club and shove them into the bottom of the duffle before moving on to my minimal wardrobe. I've kept my possessions light for this exact reason—the ability to cut and run at a moment's notice.

Stripping, I climb into the shower and lean into the spray. Placing my injured palm on the wall, I use my other hand to scrub at my chest, over my belly, and between my legs. There's no stopping the tears while the hot water rinses away the blood, sweat, and cum. If only it could wash away the night of allowing myself to even consider the temptation Tricia laid out before me.

"What were you thinking?" I ask, pressing my forehead to the dingy tile wall.

The moment he spoke, my control was gone. The instant he touched me, my inhibitions disappeared. When the switchblade pressed against my skin, want grew into need. My darkest desires rose up in reverence, spilling over as easily as the blood from our split skin.

Wrapping my arms around my body, I sink down to the floor, the spray beating against the top of my head.

That knife.

A shiver rolls through my body, making me hug myself tighter.

The cold metal across my skin. The terrible darkness in his eyes watching me enjoy what he was doing. Knowing every sick thing he did turned me on in a way I'd never let myself imagine. That his every command felt like a spell binding me to him in the worst way.

"You're sick," I chastise. "Sick, sick, sick," I chant, accentuating each word by hitting my head against the wall.

When the water runs cold, I drag myself out and remove my contacts.

Looking into the mirror over the sink, I find the familiar blue eyes of my true self staring back. I can bleach my hair and cover my skin in makeup, but there isn't a lens big enough to mask what you are deep down. My eyes fall out of focus and play tricks, my hair darkening to its true color, accentuating the natural bright blue I was born with.

The thought of revealing everything to Saint, the dark seducer, starts a burning throb between my thighs. An unreasonable certainty that he wouldn't run in fear or be disgusted by my darkness takes root deep inside me. He'd bathe in it, coax it to the surface, and wrap it around my neck like a leash.

I rub a hand over my face, groaning. Gripping the sides of the sink, I drop my head. Shame swirls low in my stomach because my body craves to let him.

"What the fuck has he done to me?" I ask the empty bathroom, taking deep breaths to get myself under control.

Dressing in jeans, a t-shirt, and sweatshirt, I finish packing everything and gather the items to pawn in the morning. Running shoes on my feet, I sleep, fully ready to bolt if needed.

Waking to loud pounding on my door, I scramble until my back presses against the wall. Looking around the apartment, I try to even my breathing.

Bags still packed and sitting next to the bed, I glance to the door. The bolt is still in place and all the windows are closed with curtains pulled tight.

Swallowing down my nerves, I wait for the noise to return, but it never comes.

After five long minutes, I wonder if I dreamt it.

Standing from the bed, I lick my dry lips and take tentative steps to the door. When I reach it, I look through the peephole. Finding the hallway empty, I sag into the door and rest my forehead against the wood.

"I'm losing my mind," I mumble on my way to the bathroom.

After relieving myself and brushing my teeth, I braid my hair down my back and pull the hood of my sweatshirt over my head. Strapping on my backpack, I place my duffle bag next to the door.

Ready to take care of my first order of business—liquidate for cash and obtain a bus ticket—I grab my pawn-worthy items and exit the apartment.

"Shit," I yell as my foot catches on something and I stumble into the door opposite mine. "What the fuck?" I growl, turning and looking at the floor.

A brown package lays on its side. I immediately glance up and down the hall, finding it empty. Stepping closer, I crouch down to the box and find a pink tag dangling from the twine tied around the brown paper shoe box.

Fingering the pastel square, I flip it over. Elegant script spells out one word.

Doll.

My stomach twists and lungs stop working. Pounding in my head matches the beat of my panicked heart. A hand clamps onto my shoulder.

"Don't touch me," I scream.

"Are you—"

I lash out, using my forearm to beat my attacker in the leg. A loud male grunt sends me scrambling back to the door.

"Hey, calm down," he tries to soothe.

Sliding up the wall, the world tilts, and I claw at my hood, trying to get more oxygen into my lungs.

"What's going on?" a female voice asks.

"I found her on the floor hovered over a box," he defends. "I was just making sure she was okay."

"What is it?" At her second question, I look and find Ms.

Waltman's granddaughter, Caroline.

Slowly, my breathing starts to regulate along with my heart.

Kneeling down, she lifts the lid from the box.

"Don't," I exclaim, putting a hand out in warning, but it's too late.

"It's just a rag doll," she states, irritation clear in her words. "An old dirty one at that," she adds.

She lifts the doll by its red yarn hair, holding it up.

My eyes focus on it as I press farther into the door at my back. I don't know how, but I sure as hell know who sent me this piece of my past. Annie, my favorite doll, dangles from my neighbor's fingers.

"Just put it back," I order, closing my eyes.

"Oh-kay," she drawls.

"Put the lid back on," I snap, quick to follow with, "Please?"

There's a rustle of paper before she confirms, "It's put away."

Relaxing my shoulders and opening my eyes, I find two sets on me—one belonging to Caroline, a familiar annoyance present, and the other a shade of blue, reminding me of the ones I hide behind my contacts.

They also belong to the man from the stairwell last night. Today, he wears a gray beanie cap, pulling it low and only allowing black hair to peek out around his ears. He's tall, lean, and the resemblance is there. A shiver of apprehension prickles my skin at his presence.

I close my eyes, and in a familiar practice, mentally remind myself there are millions of dark-haired, blue-eyed men in the world, and this man too young to be him.

"Are you okay?" he asks.

Reopening my eyes, I nod. "Yeah, thanks."

"Are you afraid of dolls?" he presses.

Just like last night, I don't miss the intense way he watches me.

"It's nothing." I shake my head and grip the straps of my backpack.

"It didn't look like nothing," Caroline states. "Did it, John?"

"Okay, yes, I'm afraid of dolls." It's partially true, and right now, I'd agree to just about anything to get away from here. "It's just someone's sick idea of a joke."

Bending at the waist, Caroline picks up the box, holding it out to me.

"Here," she says, almost gleeful.

"You can have it or get rid of it," I tell her.

"You're just going to throw it away?" the man I now know as John clips out. His lips press into a thin line and a muscle in his jaw ticks.

I furrow my brow, not understanding why he's so angry.

"John," Caroline hisses.

"I mean," he gives a small shake of his head, "don't you want to report it to the cops or something?"

I shake my head again, the thought of the police getting involved sending a new fear through me.

If he can find you, it won't be long before the authorities find you too.

"No," I blurt. "Like I said, just a bad joke."

With trembling hands, I take the box from Caroline's hands, unlock my door, and I toss it inside before locking it back up.

When I turn, they both stand watching me, John's hands in his pockets and Caroline's arm wrapped around his. The unwanted memory of their late-night sex sounds flashes in my mind and heat crawls over my chest.

"Thank you for checking on me, but I really need to get going," I tell them, hoping they'll turn and leave. They don't.

"You sure you don't want to call the cops?" John mentions once more, only this time, it's with more curiosity, while Caroline studies my face a bit too intently.

Everything about these two confuses me. I don't know what they want from me, why they react in odd ways, but I don't have any more time to waste. Nor will I have to deal with them after tonight if everything goes as planned.

"Very well," he finally concedes. "If you need anything, you know where we are." He motions to their door with a lift of his chin.

"Thank you, but I'm sure I'll be fine." *As soon as I can get the fuck away from this place.*

I get even less at the pawn shop than I'd planned, leaving me with minimal funds after purchasing the bus ticket to Vegas. But surely the hotels are cheap and the stripping gigs plentiful in the City of Sin. The next obstacle in my plan: my bus doesn't leave until tomorrow morning. I could've hidden out in my apartment until night, then crashed at the bus station, but after the special delivery today, there's no fucking way in hell I'll wait for him to come for me. There is also the possibility of Saint showing up.

With my bags strapped over my body, I exit my apartment for the last time and mentally go through my plan. I'll move from place to place around town, starting with the used bookstore, until it's late enough to hide away at the bus station.

"Going on a trip?" John's question surprises me, and I jump.

"Sorry, didn't mean to frighten you." He smiles, leaning against the open door to Ms. Waltman's apartment.

"Um, yeah, I'm gonna go stay with a friend for a while." I force a smile to accompany my lie. "We've been thinking about moving in together, so this is sort of a trial run."

The pleasant smile drops from his face.

"Boyfriend?" His voice sounds tight, restrained.

"Yeah," I lie again, watching his face flush.

"I see," he clips, pushing to his full height.

"Well, I should get—"

The sound of the elevator draws both our attention, but it's the men stepping off that silence my farewell.

Saint's eyes locate me with practiced accuracy. My flight instinct makes every muscle twitch in anticipation. He lifts one dark brow, like he's challenging me to try to run.

Glancing to the stairwell door, I mentally calculate whether I can make it before he reaches me. Or perhaps back to my apartment and down the fire escape.

"Mei," his deep voice calls to every dark fiber of my being. "I'll catch you."

The sick side of me revels in the promise, wanting to be caught. Swallowing hard, I fist my hands around the straps of my bags.

"Hurry, inside," John orders.

Grabbing my forearm, he pulls me toward his apartment door, and my duffle slips from my arm, landing with a thud at my feet.

"I advise you to take your hands off her." Saint's voice is closer, accompanied by the sound of a gun click.

John's hands tighten on me, causing me to flinch.

"This is the last warning you'll get," his deep baritone threatens.

John's eyes come to mine as a familiar arm wraps around my waist.

"Let go," I whisper in defeat. Saint has me now. And his touch tears down any defense I have—calling to my depravity with the promise of stripping away my secrets and lies, cracking me open, freeing the darkest of my sins.

One of the men accompanying Saint presses the barrel of the gun to John's temple. The moment he releases my arm, I'm dragged toward the elevator and away from my escape.

"Grab the bag," he calls over his shoulder.

In the elevator, he turns to me, pressing my back to the fading brown wall.

Jaw flexed, his eyes bore into mine, and he asks, "Do you love him?"

Lost in the ferocity of his gaze, I can only shake my head. Cupping the side of my head with his large hand, he runs a calloused thumb over my cheek.

"Does he love you?"

"What?" I blink, breaking the trance between us. "No. He's just a neighbor who lives with his girlfriend," I rush to explain.

I don't feel any loyalty to John and Caroline, but I also don't want to be the reason these men make any special visits.

"Boss?" one man asks, holding the doors from closing us in.

Twisting his body to face the two men, I take a moment to look at them.

One wears a suit like Saint's, but doesn't fill it out the way he does. He's at least a head shorter with paler skin. The other, the one who spoke, is tall, lean, and wears a light gray suit. He's the same height as Saint, but leaner.

Turning back to me, Saint runs his hands over my body. Upon finding my keys, he removes them from my back pocket and tosses them over his shoulder. The taller man catches them and waits.

"Collect her things," he orders.

"On it." The man moves. "We'll meet you at the penthouse," he says before allowing the door to slide shut.

I tense, but finally find my voice.

"Where are you taking me?"

Caging me in with his arms, he lets his eyes roam over my face.

"Tell me who you are," he counters.

Straightening my spine, I let anger and fear strengthen my resolve. "I'm Meissa—"

"Don't lie to me," he cuts me off, pushing away and standing to his full height. "Meissa Winters is dead. Found by utility workers fixing a sewage issue."

I flinch at the memory of Mei's attack, but lock it all away before I get to the worse part.

"You don't look like a dead girl to me," he states, crossing his arms over his chest.

"What does it matter?" I ask on a humorless laugh. "I'm on my way out of this town, so just give me my bag and—"

He snorts. "You think it's that easy, do you?" A grin parts his lips. "You've seen too much, dead girl."

"I haven't seen anything."

"You've also revealed too much," he adds, ignoring me.

"I haven't—"

Dropping his arms, he takes my face in his hands, pulling me to him. Leaning down, he crushes his mouth to mine before biting my lip. At the nip, I jerk, but when his tongue invades my mouth, and the tang of copper mixes in the kiss. Fisting his jacket, I bite back.

Chuckling, he breaks the kiss, and slips his hands down to collar my neck. He extends his thumbs, running them along the sides of my windpipe and propping my chin up. Grinning again, he releases me, causing me to sway back from his loss.

He swipes his tongue along his bottom lip, collecting the blood before sucking it into his mouth. Instinctively, I run my tongue over my injured lip. Nostrils flaring, his eyes follow the action.

"I assure you, I'll find out who you are, but I'll give you one more chance to tell me, dead girl." His eyes come to mine.

"I am no one," I respond as the elevator chimes our arrival to the first floor.

"Have it your way," he states, taking me by the bicep and tugging me along at his side.

An older man dressed in a plain black suit opens the rear door of a silver SUV.

"Sir." He bows his head.

Saint shoves me into the backseat, and the scent of new car and leather fills my senses. If my fingers weren't encased in my thin gloves, I'm sure the seats would be the softest I've ever felt. Saint climbs in behind me, pulling me out of my assessment of the vehicle.

The door closes, sealing me in. "Let's hope what I find out doesn't get you into trouble."

Wrapping my arms around myself, I glance out the window. "That's the catch, Saint," I admit, turning my face back to his. "What people find out gets them into trouble—not me."

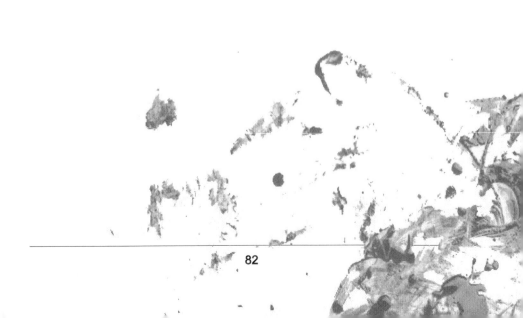

Chapter Seven

Saint

Her words send a jolt of truth through me. She's an enigma, and the intrigue she inspires is dangerous to the male population.

The way her neighbor looked at her, grabbed her...it took everything I had to lock down the urge to pull the trigger. Fuck, this woman has me twisted in a way I've never known.

I've even contemplated murdering Sketch, the very one helping me uncover her secrets. The puzzle she creates for a man like him, one used to find every last detail about a person, sparks the thrill of the challenge. And it has me wanting to cut his fucking throat, the overly curious bastard.

I don't do jealousy. There was never a reason for this emotion in my life. The fact that this little female who doesn't exist brings it out of me is disrupting everything. Sketch is one thing, but having it happen in front of Felix pisses me off. There are plans I need to put into place—dangerous and careful plans.

"You could just let me go," she whispers to the tinted window. "I was leaving town and have no interest in—"

"You weren't going anywhere," I inform her. "The moment you stepped into the bus station my men would have brought you to me."

She sighs and her shoulders sag.

"It's for your own good, dead girl," I reveal.

Her head snaps to me, eyes searching my face.

"You made a choice last night." Her mouth opens, but I continue before she can make a sound. "Felix wasn't there for just one night of fun." I can't stop the curl of my lip. "However, you denied him."

"I...I..." she stutters, giving her head a shake. "He was called away. I didn't deny him anything."

Grinning, I rub my thumb along my chin.

"When you sank down onto my cock in front of him, giving yourself to me," she stiffens at my words, "you made your choice."

"So?" She drops her arms, turning her body to face me. "I leave town and the problem is solved."

I snort. "You'd think that, but Felix is a proud man. You bruised his ego."

What I don't tell her is, even without a name, without her history, she's claimed. The moment she tore away the mask and revealed the dark and dirty beneath that lovely costume, she became mine. When she drew the blade over her palm, coating me in her blood and taking me inside her body, she became mine.

"That's ridiculous," she snarls, gripping the edge of the seat. I stare at her gloved hands. It's not cold enough yet for gloves. Thinking about it, she's had them on every time I see her. It's barely fall in Chicago and the weather is warm for the most part.

"You want me to drop you off at the bus station right now?" I dangle her freedom like a fucking carrot she'll never get. "Tell me who the fuck you are and I'll tell Frank to head to the bus station."

It's a goddamn lie. I've caught my prey and, like the animal I am, playing with them is the most fun. However, Felix will press the issue of her identity. If I can't figure her out, and soon, his vengeful ass will take it to Angelo. The last fucking thing I need is Angelo getting involved. He'll order the hit and my loyalty will be tested. Again.

Straightening her spine, she clenches her mouth shut.

"Very well then." I lift one shoulder. "I'll get my answers."

Taking the cell from inside my suit jacket, I locate Sketch and press the call button.

"Why does it matter?" she asks, her question barely audible.

"Yeah," Sketch answers on a grunt.

There's a female moan in the background.

Rolling my eyes, I inhale through my nose, and on the exhale, say, "Your services are needed."

The damn exhibitionist is all about being watched and/or heard.

"When?" he grounds out.

"Now," I say, feeling Mei's eyes on me.

"Fuck," he groans. "I'm sort of in the middle of something."

"You've got twenty minutes to meet the dead girl and me" I order.

"You have her?" he asks as a female voice protests and curses.

"Careful. Your eagerness isn't appreciated," I growl, ending the call before he can respond.

Her round eyes stay fixed on me. Fear lines her face, mixing with a hint of curiosity, surely wanting to know who and what Sketch is.

"Because I'm sure you aren't a fed," I finally respond to her question. "But I have to wonder what or who you are hiding from. The last thing we need are the police looking for you."

"Then let me go and you have nothing to worry about," she rushes out on a breath.

"So, the police are looking for you?" I press.

Her lips press into a tight line, locking shut.

"I'm afraid that's not a possibility," I rumble, the suggestion of letting her go causing the dark creature to claw at me.

Her body sags back into the seat. "Then just kill me and get it over with."

The car comes to a stop in front of the building I call home.

"Frank, give us a moment." At my request, he exits the car and stands next to the closed driver side door.

Mei scoots closer to her door, wide eyes moving from the exiting driver to me. Her bottom lip begins to tremble, and it makes my dick twitch. She's unsure and afraid, but the sudden lift of her chin and tightening of her hands into fists means she's also ready to fight. The fear coming off her sends a rush of excitement through me. The thrill of the battle she's silently promising has my cock as hard as the steel blades I carry.

Reaching out in a flash of movement, I grip her thigh and tear her legs apart. The move surprises her long enough for me to put my body between her knees.

Hands claw at the door handle, and I shackle them in my grasp. Lifting her arms over her head, I transfer both her small wrists into one hand and squeeze. Her body jerks and bucks, fighting my invasion.

Using the weight of my body, not all two hundred and thirty pounds, but enough to still her, I take her chin in my free hand and turn her head.

"Please," she whimpers, a silent plea for her life. One tear falls from the outside corner of her clenched eye, mesmerizing me and causing my dick to throb.

Placing my forehead just above her temple, my tongue darts out, catching the tear. The moment is so perfect—too fucking beautiful—the creature surges beneath my flesh, wanting a piece of her as well.

With a small shift of my head, my mouth hovers over her ear.

"I plan to kill you..." her body stiffens, "in so many ways—ways you'll beg for me to kill you, over and over again."

Mei

The words should scare me. His behavior should terrify me.

I know he thinks it does. That the fear rolling through me, the fight I put up and tears I let escape are a result of his actions and promises. He has no idea he's only part of it. My past and unreasonable attraction to him intensify every mixed up emotion.

His fingers tighten once more, a silent indication to look at him.

"Let's go," he orders, releasing my face.

Wrists still locked in his large hand, he pushes off me. The heat of his body disappears, chilling me. When the door behind him opens, the night air sends a shiver up my spine. And without releasing me, he backs himself out of the car, pulling me out with him.

"Will there be anything else, sir?" the driver, Frank, asks from our right.

"No," Saint clips out.

Moving my eyes beyond his broad chest, I focus on the wide glass doors to the tall building before us. Lifting my head, I glance up and take in the sky-high structure.

A tug on my arms brings me back to my captor. Stumbling behind him, he strides into the building. Walking passed the four metal elevators, he turns a corner into a narrow private hallway.

Craning my neck, I try to find our destination, but he's too wide for me to see around. Frustrated and nervous, I begin to chew on the bottom of my lip. He stops at a wooden panel and holds a card up to a small black circle. I jump at the sound the panel makes when it slides open to reveal a single elevator.

Even knowing it's pointless, I plant my feet in defiance. Saint enters the lift, pulling on my arms. His head snaps around at my resistance, his eyes narrowed. Bringing my hands to his chest, he steps toward me, and I back up with each of his steps. Raising one brow, the right side of his mouth lifts.

While I try to determine whether it's a smile or sneer, he swings my arms out to the side, releases my wrists, and wraps his thick arm around my waist.

My back to his chest, he walks us backward until we are inside the elevator.

"It's in your best interest to stop fighting me," he says, a hint of strain in his voice.

"Go to hell," I growl, feeling bold.

He's going to kill me, anyway. Probably torture me first, given his threat, so why should I make it easy on him?

To accentuate my words, I reach for the closing elevator door. I'm only able to get my fingertips curled around the metal's edge before he jerks me back and slams his card against another black circle. If I ever regretted the gloves I wear, it's this moment.

The tightening of his arm takes my breath away. I claw at it, even though it's pointless, and freeze when the scruff of his cheek brushes my ear.

"Your defiance isn't getting your desired effect," he rumbles, running his nose over the shell of my ear.

"Obviously," I choke out, confused by the threats and dark seduction.

The penthouse is what you would think it to be—dark wood flooring, shiny, light surfaces, and windows. The moment I'm forced into the foyer, we're greeted by two men in dark suits. Only their heads turn our direction, giving Saint an expectant look.

"Is everything set up?" he asks, nudging me forward.

I struggle to get out of his hold, and his arms tighten until I still. Then, he releases me.

In two strides, I stand next to a dark wooden staircase and look through an archway. Curious, I step through, stopping to take in the room.

The ceiling is so high, it holds a large glass chandelier. Every wall is covered in windows framed with large stone looking arches. They instantly remind me of a church I saw on TV once. Beyond the windows are railings to a wraparound balcony.

My body twitches to step out one of the floor length windows, though I'm not sure whether I would simply look at the view or jump and finally free myself.

The pieces of furniture are muted and look like a piece of untouched art rather than comfortable seating. The shock of bright blue in the massive rug seems too cheerful for a man like Saint.

"If she runs," his words recapture my attention, "shoot her," he finishes, walking down a small hallway in the opposite direction.

I don't miss the matching grins the men give each other.

"Come on, dead girl," Saint calls over his shoulder.

Turning, I walk until I'm next to the penthouse elevator, my eyes lingering on the silver door. This is my chance. Probably my only opportunity to attempt an escape.

"I'll catch you."

Snapping my head around, I find Saint watching me, arms over his chest and one brow raised.

Squaring my shoulders, I take tentative steps in his direction. Before I reach him, he turns and walks away, continuing down the hallway.

"Get comfortable," Saint instructs, motioning to a large sofa covered in dark gray material filling the far side of the room. This furniture is definitely for comfort, unlike the other room, and could probably seat twenty people.

Standing behind the couch, I wrap my arms around myself. "I'm good," I say, turning my head to look out the massive wall of windows.

Without taking my eyes from the view outside, I feel the vicinity of his body as he moves around the room. The swoosh of material is finally the thing to draw my attention back to him.

He discards his tie onto a chair at the breakfast bar before approaching.

Dropping my arms, I take a step back.

"It's time to tell me who you are, dead girl," he states.

Taking my arm in his large hand, he pulls me around the oversized piece of furniture. I dig my heels into the floor, resisting, but one solid tug and I'm forced to follow. Moving from the hard wood to a super thick rug, he brings me to the other side of the couch and turns to face me, his muscular body outlined by the cityscape behind him. Eyes locked on mine, he slides his hand up my arm to my shoulder and pushes down, giving me the silent instruction to sit. The more he stares at me, the harder it is to fight him, so I give in.

Sitting slowly onto the couch, I don't dare look away. My ass sinks into the cushion and I grip the edges. The moment my head is level to his belt, his lip gives a familiar twitch.

Pulling his hand away, but keeping his eyes on mine, he slides his suit jacket from his shoulders, and I fight the urge to reach out and touch him. It's fucked up and so wrong to want him this way, but desire moves like lava beneath my skin. The burn crawls over me, settling in the most sensitive places.

His cufflinks gleam in my peripheral as he removes them and slips them into his pocket. The muscles in his forearms flex and bunch while he starts releasing the buttons of his shirt, displaying dark inked designs on his olive skin and a white tank beneath.

Pulling the dress shirt from the waist of his pants, he tosses it to the cushion on my left. The personal strip tease continues until he's standing in just pants and the white tank.

I push farther into the couch when he drops into a crouch in front of me. Bringing his hands to my knees, he grips.

"You aren't Meissa Winters," he says in a way that dares me to challenge. I lock my jaw, keeping my lips pressed together and words mute. "You're really going to continue this game?" he asks, offering me my last chance.

But I can't. No matter what I do, say, it won't end well for me.

I tell him, and his curiosity ends. Probably right along with my life. They could turn me over to the police or worse—*him*. I would choose death before returning to *him*. I may have been young and naïve all those years ago, but I'd learned so much in my time away from that man, that house. Even when part of me, the sick, twisted part, yearns to go home.

A shiver shakes my body at the thought of what would've most likely happened to me in that house. Alive or dead, I would've been another piece in his collection. In fact, I would've been the prized doll. His finest work. Part of me still is.

"Fine," he barks, shoving at my legs, pulling me out of such morbid thoughts.

Standing to his full height, he casts a shadow over my body, sending fear through my veins. I pull my feet up, curl them beneath me, and settle into the back of the couch.

"Sir?" One of the suits draws Saint's attention from me.

"Yes, Tony," he responds.

"He's on his way up now," Tony states, standing with his back to the wall.

I tense. *Who is on his way?*

"I'll have my answers soon enough, dead girl," Saint says with a smirk.

Minutes pass before a tall, lean man enters the room. His dark shaggy curls look wet.

"Saint." The man nods in greeting.

"Sketch," he returns.

"You don't look dead to me," Sketch says, smiling wide. "Fuck me, look at that face. You look like a little doll." His gaze moves to Saint. "No wonder you want to play with her."

His eyes are so dark, they look black, and his smile feels off and manic. The way he stares at me sends off warning signals.

"Did you bring everything you need?" Saint asks, an annoyance I don't understand in his question.

Sketch pats a sleek black bag at his side. Approaching the sofa, his fingers run up the strap slung across his chest and pull it over his head as he sits next to me, his gaze never leaving mine. There's curiosity, intrigue, and something else behind those dark irises. It calls to my evil desires, making them fight against the internal place where I lock them away.

He slides a thin silver laptop, a flat black mat, and a couple other items I'm not familiar with from an army green messenger back onto the coffee table. The speed that he sets up his equipment is almost as fast as the hand he uses to grab my forearm.

Gasping, I yank at his hold. Sketch may be lean and long, but it's evidently pure muscle beneath the black, long-sleeve shirt and jeans.

"This is quite the fashion statement," he teases, pinching the material of my glove.

I make a fist—my last-ditch effort to ensure the glove stays on. I should've known it was pointless. With his thumb and finger, he applies pressure to the skin between mine, and I yelp, my fist unclenching. In the next moment, the glove is slid from my hand and dropped to the floor.

Before I can close my hand again, Saint has it captured in his.

"What the fuck did you do?" he asks on a growl.

"Jesus," Sketch breathes out. "They're mutilated," he says looking over my fingertips, then to my face.

"Can you still run them?" Saint asks.

I pull at my arm, my heart racing and lungs constricting. They can't run my prints. I'm in the system. All foster kids are. I'll be found.

Lashing out with my free arm, I jab Saint in the ribs, the need to get out of here becoming overwhelming. The surprise of my action makes him drop my arm and cough, and I use that distraction, pushing up with my legs and jumping the back of the couch.

"Not so fast," Sketch yells, grabbing my ankle mid-air, and I fall awkwardly along the back of the sofa, my lungs seizing as the air is knocked out of me. I can't even scream.

Large hands clamp on my arms, and the familiar feel of his callouses against my skin is unmistakable. While Sketch's wrongness may call to the darkness inside me, Saint's touch unleashes it. Battling the urge to surrender to him, I twist my hips and kick back. Blocking my leg, he kneels on the couch. Gripping his hands into my hips, he pulls my back to his chest, wraps his arms around my body, and seats us so we face the man who will unleash my personal hell.

"She's feisty," Sketch says on a laugh. "And limber as fuck."

Trailing one finger over my knee, he runs it up my thigh.

"Your talents kept you alive before," Saint growls over my head, "but if you continue to touch her, I'll finish what I started years ago."

Sketch's eyes widen for the briefest moment. Removing his fingers, he gives a small tilt to his head as a grin slides over his face, reminding me of a cartoon villain I saw once.

"That's not like you," he says, his tone teasing.

Saint says nothing, but his body tightens around mine.

"Perhaps when you're through with your toy..." Sketch shrugs.

"She's mine," Saint rumbles low, deep, animalistic.

His hand slides over my chest, collaring my neck. Fear would be the rational response, but the flex of his fingers at my neck excites me.

Sketch stares at us for a moment, gives a nod, and turns back to his equipment. He reaches for my bare hand, but I slip them under my thighs. Gripping my forearm, he easily brings my hand to his face.

"How the fuck did you accomplish this?" There's awe in his words as he runs his fingers over the damage I regularly inflict on myself. I curl my fingers into my palm, breaking his focus. Half grinning, he squeezes and twists my wrist, eliciting a sharp cry as my hand falls open. Without wasting another second, Sketch presses it to a flat pad, placing his hand over mine and holding it in place.

I attempt to squirm away, but Saint stills me by tightening his arms.

"Got it," Sketch confirms, releasing me. "Though, I'm not sure what we'll get off those fucked prints." He nods to my hands in my lap.

Balling them into tight fists, my anger rises and survival instinct flares to life. I jab out, catching his arm, then kick out with my free leg, finding his rib.

"Fuck," he shouts, grabbing his side.

"You won't get a damn thing from them," I say on a humorless laugh.

Sketch's eyes come to me, flashing with rage. Grabbing my face in his hand, he leans in close enough for me to feel his breath. "Be careful which monsters you provoke, dead girl," he warns, and a whimper slips past my lips at the bite of his fingers on my jaw. His fingers flinch before falling away as Saint holds his wrist until I hear a snap. Sketch groans, pain contorting his face.

"Next time," Saint drops the arm, "I'll rip it from your fucking body," he threatens, pushing from the couch with me still in his arms. Sketch follows our movement, scowling.

"How long for results?"

"We may need to do dental records," Sketch says, rubbing his wrist.

Unable to hold back, my lip twitches. They'd have no luck with that either. Sketch doesn't miss my self-satisfied look.

"Even if you had them changed, doll Face, there will be records," he states arrogantly.

Maybe it's the nickname. Maybe it's the fact that these men, men who think they can unveil the shroud I've carefully placed over myself, aren't going to get what they want unless I give it to them. Whatever the reason, the power is heady and shifts something inside me.

"*You* would think that," I taunt, and his eyes narrow.

Saint pulls me to face him, his eyes roaming my face.

After long minutes of silence, he asks, "What does that mean?"

Pulling from his grip, I take a step back and snort.

"You think dentists don't visit strip clubs? That there aren't plenty of dirty old men with dental degrees willing to provide services to someone willing to fulfill their depraved fantasies?" I can't keep the disgust out of my words.

Remembering the full weekend of the little girl performance I put on for a man old enough to be my grandfather makes my skin crawl. The way he made me call him daddy and treated his "little girl" stuck with me for months, bringing terrible nightmares and memories with it. But, in the end, it got my teeth reconstructed.

Saint's eyes narrow, his lips forming a thin line.

"Christ," Sketch voices his disbelief. "Who the fuck are you?"

At his question, I meet his eyes. "No one. I'm absolutely no one."

The words are so true, more honest than I ever realized. For a moment, a long lost part of me — the real me — screams to be set free.

Saint's broad chest blocks my view of Sketch and I raise my eyes to him.

"What else can be done?" he asks without taking his eyes from me.

"Fuck, man," Sketch sighs. "Maybe face recognition," he offers, then adds, "unless she's fucked favors from a plastic surgeon too."

"Fuck you," I growl, leaning around Saint to deliver the words to the asshole behind him. I shouldn't feel insulted, but I do.

"I'll gladly add myself to your bedpost notches," he sneers.

"Enough," Saint growls, crossing his arms over his chest.

"Just let me leave town," I try once again. "I don't give a fuck about—"

"No," Saint interrupts.

"Why can't you—"

My question is cut off by the arrival of two men. It's the same men from my apartment building. They have my bags as well two cardboard boxes.

"Take them to her room," Saint instructs.

Snapping my head back to him, I furrow my brow.

"Follow me," he orders, turning and walking.

When I don't fall into step behind him, he turns back to me and commands, "Now."

"Run along, doll Face," Sketch taunts, moving two fingers in a mock running motion.

"Mei," Saint's use of the name pulls my scowl off Sketch. "Follow me," he orders once more.

The way he growls the command pushes me into motion. He watches every step I take until I'm a foot from the archway, then he turns, leading the way into an adjoining room.

Before disappearing into the space, but keeping my eyes on Saint's wide back, I lift my right arm out behind me and flip Sketch my middle finger.

Sketch's bark of laughter causes Saint to look back over his shoulder, and I drop my arm, scurrying behind him to catch up. He studies my face. Not finding the answer he seeks, he leads me to a staircase.

Cold realization wraps around my neck, making it difficult to breathe. If I go up these stairs, I'm signing my death certificate. Instead of taking the first step, I inch back, contemplating the likelihood of making it to the elevator before being caught or shot. Deciding to take the risk, I spin around and land into a chest.

"Not so fast, doll face," Sketch's hands shackle my biceps, guiding me backward. The back of my heels meet the base of the staircase and he releases me. The room tilts as I start to fall back. Reaching out, I claw at the material covering his chest, but can't grip. Before I fall, a large muscular hand hooks me at the waist. Saint hauls me up until only my toes touch the floor.

Sketch offers another cartoon villain smile as I'm dragged up the stairs by the man I'm sure will be my executioner.

chap ter eiCht

Saint

While I pride myself on self-control, where Mei is concerned, I can only take so much.

Just thinking about how possessive I feel over someone I barely know makes my blood boil. Meissa Winters is dead and this creature struggling against me every step of the way is a complete fucking blank space. Not knowing is a risk I can't allow in my life. Lack of control, of information, will end a man like me. I'm too close to my ultimate goal for this doll-faced girl to disrupt my carefully constructed plans.

My cell phone vibrates against my leg as I reach the second floor of my penthouse. A floor full of extra rooms, including the one I set up for the dead girl in my arms.

Walking down the hallway, through an extra room, and then into another, I drop her onto the wrought iron bed. She lands in the thick light blue blanket with an *oomph*.

"Your things are there," I motion to two bags and three boxes piled beside the walk-in closet.

Her eyes move to everything my men collected from her apartment.

"That's not mine," she rushes out, and the panic in her voice draws me to the items.

"What?" I ask over my shoulder.

"The small brown box." She visibly fights to stay calm.

My cell vibrates again, but her reaction has me intrigued. Lifting the box, I flip the lid off and furrow my brow.

"Get rid of it," she demands.

Reaching inside, I fist the faded, dingy, tattered rag doll. The red yarn hair is frayed and one button eye is loose. Glancing from the worn doll to the box, I see a small white card.

Frowning at the inscription, I turn to Mei, finding her on the bed. Back pressed to the swirling bars at the head, her eyes focus on the items in my hands.

"Who gave this to you?" I ask, approaching her as she presses harder against the bars.

"Why would someone send you an old doll?" I press, needing to understand the situation and her fear.

"Just get rid of it," she begs on a strangled cry.

"Tell me who sent it first, then—" My demand is cut off by a knock on the door. Without waiting for a response, Vincent leans inside. Narrowing my eyes at his intrusion, I watch him swallow hard.

"Sorry, boss, but..." his eyes shift to Mei, then back to me, "you're being requested."

The vibration of my cell punctuates his statement. Removing it from my pocket, I glance at the screen. Every muscle in my jaw tenses, grinding my teeth together.

Keeping my eyes on Mei, I instruct Vincent, "Put Russ on her door. She doesn't leave this room."

Her mouth presses into a thin line and anger lights her eyes. It's glorious, beautiful. I want her to rage against my orders. To fight me the way she does just before our darkness consumes us, mingling in a primitive joining.

The cell vibrating once more pulls me from my haze.

"We aren't finished here." I toss the doll on the bed and watch Mei recoil as it lands next to her.

Leaving her with the doll, I exit the room with one last instruction to Vincent, "Have food brought up."

97

"I don't like to be kept waiting, Dante," Angelo scolds from behind the ornate mahogany desk in his townhouse.

"I had something to attend to," I explain in a bored tone.

The man before me, the head of our syndicate, demands respect and loyalty, but lately, I find it far too difficult to give a fuck.

"Yes...well, we have a situation." He places his elbows to the desk, linking his fingers, aside from the two forming a triangle against his mouth.

His silence puts me on edge. I'll never show it, but it doesn't mean my nerves aren't firing warning shots of adrenalin through my body. There is too much at stake right now, and Felix has surely run to our uncle. I know him well enough to feel confident in assuming the bastard is crying disrespect, drawing Mei and me into the spotlight—his attempt to gain the favor Uncle Angelo bestows on me regularly.

I'm not sure why he singled me out to receive his attention when I was just a child, instructing my mentor, his brother and my father, to teach me things no child should know, let alone see. The first time I saw a man killed, I was a six-year-old boy seated at Angelo's side.

Flexing my fingers into the leather arm rests of the guest chair, I prepare to go to war. Typically, Felix's embarrassment and forcing him to run to Angelo are enough to entertain, making him look like a child. But even with my plans, I won't be so easily persuaded to concede where Mei is concerned.

She's mine.

"There have been a series of recent...incidents," Angelo finally breaks the silence.

"The accidents," I confirm, relaxing my fingers at the unexpected direction of topic. Surprise flares in his eyes for short moment.

"What do you know?" His question is cautious, but there's also a hint of pride.

"That three of your major players have been met with unfortunate...*accidents*," I stress the final word.

"And what do you make of them, Dante?" he presses, trying to vet me out.

"That you may need a new cleaner," is all I offer.

His jaw tenses and eyes narrow.

The deaths of three bosses over the past month and a half caught my attention because I was an eye witness to the first. Of course, at the time, I'd assumed Angelo was taking care of a loose end by having the man stabbed, then covered it up in a gas leak explosion.

When Sketch brought the second and third deaths to me, I paid closer attention. They both followed a similar pattern, except these two had a design carved into their flesh—a symbol Sketch identified as Japanese Kanji, one spelling out "geisha", and the other, "daughter."

"Perhaps you're right," he concedes, dropping his hands and settling back into his large chair. "Or perhaps you've gone a bit rogue, taking matters into your own hands."

The words are said lightly, but the accusation is still there.

"What would I have to gain?"

Angelo grins. "When have you needed more than the thrill of spilling blood?" He pauses, sneering, "After all, you are The Saint."

Heat crawls up my chest, and the creature stirs again, wanting to be released. Lifting the right corner of my mouth, I snort.

"Easy prey aren't exactly my style," I remind him, and a full laugh escapes his mouth.

"You're right, son." His jovial tone tells me the accusation was never serious. Still, at the label, I tense. My father wasn't a good man, nor loyal. In the end, his harsh lessons and training, along with his disloyalty, had catapulted me into my place in the family. It had made my rise as easy as pulling the trigger three times—three bullets and a cold-blooded killer delivering three targets instead of the two assigned.

Clenching my teeth, I fight down the all too familiar feelings of anger and revulsion for the man before me. My own flesh and blood, my boss, my creator, my keeper.

"Does your *source* have information you care to share?" I don't miss the abhorrence in his voice when he references his wife's nephew.

Angelo's never trusted Sketch, given his skillset and ability to fall off the radar. And Sketch sealed his place with Angelo years ago when he stole from him, which brought me to his doorstep late one night.

"Nothing more than you already know, I'm sure," I admit, and he nods.

"I'm putting this on your plate," he says, eyes watching for my reaction.

"What about Felix?" I ask.

"What about your cousin?" he returns.

I raise one brow in response. Angelo damn well knows about the power games Felix likes to put into play, and they often involve attempts to knock me from favor.

"I love your cousin, Dante. He's family."

I nod, knowing blood means everything.

"But I've grown tired of his hunger for power."

Internally, I snort. This greedy motherfucker has no room to talk.

"I'll take this, but..." I purposely bate.

"But?" Angelo presses.

"I need Felix out of my affairs," I state.

"Would these have anything to do with the little whore?"

I'm not surprised he knows about Mei. If there is anything I know about Uncle Angelo, it's that he trusts no one. I've been followed by his spies since I was a young boy, but it wasn't until recent years I realized he mostly follows me out of fear.

"It doesn't matter what my affairs are," I counter.

"Keep your plaything," he grants. "I doubt she'll last any longer than the others," he finishes with a sickening grin. "Besides, Giuliana will only put up with it for so long. Won't she?"

I don't miss the taunting tone, the gleam in his eye or the way he licks his lips. The sick fucker in front of me hid his demon well enough, only a select few knew of the sick urges Angelo carries with him.

Many fear the darkness I unleash and death I leave in my wake, but they should fear the secret evil in Angelo. And they don't even know it.

"Is she still visiting with her sister?" he inquires. "Or has she returned to the house?"

Gripping the brown leather of the chair, I work to loosen my clenched jaw.

"She's home," I say, much calmer than I feel. "Her parents are visiting," I tack on, making sure he realizes she's not alone. I don't know what she ever did to garner his attention, and I'd thought his interest would wane as she grew older, but it hasn't.

He rubs his chin, lost in thought it seems. The silence brings forth the memory of the day my fate was sealed.

"Promise me, Dante," he coughs around the blood clogging his throat.

"Hang on, AJ," I order, gripping under his armpits.

Fisting the material of his blood-stained shirt, I drag him through the mayhem of gunfire and small explosions. Finding an overturned table, I jerk his body behind the makeshift shield, and he groans at the jostling.

Glancing around the room, my gaze locks on Victor. The look on my face must tell him everything, because his eyes widen and he risks rushing through the crossfire to reach us.

"Promise me," he repeats on a groan barely audible over the gunfire.

AJ's fingers dig into my arm, pulling my attention back to his prone body.

"Protect her, Dante. Protect her from him," he says, his plea a gargle.

"There's no need for promises. You will protect her yourself," I state, flinching when Victor rips open AJ's shirt.

Multiple bullet holes puncture his chest and stomach, but it's the one at his neck Victor focuses on.

"Put pressure on his neck," Victor orders, and I comply, pressing my hands against his body.

AJ coughs again, gags, and spits blood to the floor.

My demon awakens, wanting their blood, wanting vengeance.

"Pro—"

"I promise," I shout, quieting him. "Giuliana will be safe."

"Fuck," Victor sighs, stopping chest compressions to check AJ's pulse at his wrist.

"What the fuck are you doing?" I yell, grabbing his hand and placing it back on AJ's chest.

"Dante," Victor says, shaking his head, "he's gone."

Dropping my chin to my chest, I take two deep inhales through my nose and release the wound at his neck. Once he heard she would be safe, he let go.

Closing my eyes, I sit back onto my calves. Anger boils in my gut and rage rises in my chest. Tossing my head back, I unleash my fury in a loud roar, then pull both my guns from their holsters and rise from behind the table.

"Dante!" Victor shouts, but I start to fire, ignoring the sharp burn ripping through my shoulder and left thigh. The demons take control, shooting, killing, and reveling in the bloodbath we create.

"Bring me the person responsible," Angelo's orders bring me back to the present.

"I'll put people on it," I say, giving a slight nod.

"Good," he returns the gesture. "Max will see you out," he dismisses, eyes conveying our conversation is over.

Pushing out of the chair, I button my jacket and turn to leave.

"I'll expect to see you tomorrow night," he says to my back.

Fuck. I'd forgotten about the party. All levels of the organization would be in attendance. Felix's younger brother was being brought into the fold and tomorrow night would be a "men only" event. Well, the women would be plentiful, but no wives were invited.

"I expect everyone to be there for the announcement," he orders, his voice rougher.

"Of course," I concede over my shoulder before leaving his office.

Fighting the urge to draw my knife and do humanity a favor, I close the door behind me.

In the car, I focus on what I can currently control: Mei, the little dead girl in my apartment. We have much to discuss. Her past, why she mangles her fingertips, and who the fuck she's hiding from.

The right side of my mouth hooks up at the thought of the fight she'll present. The challenge is only surpassed by one thing: her submission. A woman so dark, hungry, and tormented, I'm impressed by her ability to suppress the urges. I'm also fucking ravenous to get another glimpse of the monster hidden inside her.

Mei

Since my phone is nowhere to be found and there isn't a damn clock anywhere in my current prison, I have no idea how long Saint's been gone, nor how long I've been trapped here. Though it was long enough for me to eat half a sandwich and drink two of the three bottles of water brought for me.

Catching my reflection in a wall length mirror, I see just how out of place I am in yet another lavish room. The light colors, brightness of the lightning, and clean surfaces feel suffocating. It's as if the light is trying to snuff out my dark.

Turning from the mirror, I reenter the main portion of the bedroom. My feet sink into the thick carpet, tempting me to walk barefoot. But I don't. I need to be prepared for any chance to escape.

The worn doll on the bed catches my attention. Just like me, it doesn't belong here. It's frayed red hair, torn blue checked dress, and dingy apron clash against the pristine look of the bed. We have more in common than our past.

My knees touch the side of the mattress before I realize my past has drawn me to it like a moth to a flame. Swallowing the panic and fear, I shake my head.

"It's a fucking doll," I tell myself. "It's not a bomb."

Climbing into the middle of the bed, I take the doll in my hand and scoot back to the swirled wrought iron at the head.

"You may have found me there, but you can't get me here," I whisper, face to face with my old friend.

The doll's head flops forward just as the bedroom door opens, causing me to inhale sharply. Sketch appears in the doorway and I relax, placing the doll in my lap.

What the hell does he want?

At my apparent relaxing, he tilts his head just a bit and eyes me.

"Little dead girl, if you think Saint is the only monster you should be afraid of, you are terribly wrong." He grins, entering the bedroom.

Quietly snorting, I glance back down to the doll. I know it's dumb. I can sense the danger on this man, but I can't seem to care. If they are going to kill me, I'd rather they did it and got it over with. I've been played with my entire life—figuratively and literally.

"You think I'm kidding? He isn't the only one who can end you," he presses.

Looking from under my lashes, I watch him grip the edge of the footboard.

From fist to shoulder to face, I trace him with my eyes. He is long, lean, strong, and definitely dangerous. This man carries demons. I can feel them calling from the depths of this dark brown gaze.

"I'm not the one who's terribly wrong," I mumble, sounding calmer than I feel.

Grin returning, he raises one brow, and asks, "Oh really?"

"Really," I deadpan.

"I've seen the way you tense and pull away, wanting to run from him," he laughs humorlessly. "Saint isn't someone to not be afraid of. Fuck, he scares me. So I'd think you were fucking insane if you didn't worry about what he'll do to you once he's done with you."

Unable to keep the evil sneer off my face, my skin prickles with the heat of my anger. The pleasure I get at the way his stupid grin falls from his cocky face feeds my dark urges, emboldening me.

Setting the doll to my left, I raise onto my knees and lift my chin.

Sketch releases the footboard, straightening to his full height.

"Your first mistake," I say through clenched teeth, "is assuming I'm sane. For someone who prides themselves on figuring people out, you sure do suck at it with me," I taunt, knee walking to the end of the mattress.

Sliding my fingers over the edge of the footboard, I fist the metal. "I bet it kills you to be..." leaning over and propping my body on the wrought iron, I close the distance between us, "failing."

The muscles in his jaw tick as his hands shoot out, gripping my biceps. The touch does nothing to shut me up, though. In fact, his reaction only spurs me on.

"Your second mistake is thinking I haven't died before," I sneer, lifting both brows.

"Is there a third?" Sketch's question wafts over my face, a mixture of whiskey and cigarettes.

Grinning, I embrace the evil within me and stare straight into his dark eyes. "Is that I'm afraid of Saint."

His eyes bore into mine for long moments before they widen and his hands relax. "You really aren't," he breathes out, disbelief and curiosity slackening his jaw.

I smirk, pulling myself from his grip. Settling back onto the bed, my eyes never leaving his, I get comfortable in my previous spot and place my hand on the discarded doll.

"No, Sketch, I'm not *afraid* of Saint," I confirm.

"But I've watched how you act with him," he argues.

"It's in my nature to want to run," I partially lie.

"It's more than that," he says, shaking his head.

"Yes, it is." At the sound of Saint's voice, I tense. Hairs raise on my arms and anticipation zings across my nerve endings.

His presence fills the room, seducing and torturing me.

I fist the doll at my side.

"Tell him, dead girl," Saint pushes.

To curb the exhilaration I feel when he's around, I lock my mouth shut and try to slow my breathing.

"Tell him who you are when the light is gone and the innocent girl act is stripped away," he challenges.

"Go to hell," I growl, not angry at the truth he speaks, but that he knows it at all.

The evil lurking within recognizes and wants him. Even now, the urges swirl beneath my skin in a choreographed dance designed just for him.

He grins, walking around the bed, and my eyes follow every languid movement of his large body. Stopping at the right of the bed, he leans down, fists burrowing into the mattress.

"I've been in hell for years, dead girl," he informs. "Now, I'm bringing you with me."

The minimal light in the room gives the illusion that his eyes are darkening, disappearing into pits of blackness. It sucks me in, making me want to delve into those depths and saturate myself in every dark fantasy.

I'm inches from his face before realizing I've leaned forward. He's planted both his knees onto the bed, and I blink, trying to break the spell. Before I can pull away, he palms the back of head and takes my chin in the other.

With smooth execution, he straddles my lap and his nostrils flare just before he crushes his mouth to mine.

My body ignites, ready to hand myself over to do what he will with me. Fisting his jacket, I feel the knife just below the expensive material and reality creeps back into my lust addled brain.

Sliding my hands over his chest and beneath his lapels, I curl my fingers around the handle and yank the blade out in a swoosh. It slices through his jacket and nicks the back of his arm.

He barely makes a sound. Fuck, he doesn't even take his mouth from mine.

"Saint," Sketch shouts a warning, but he's already tense and prepared for my fight.

Our mouths still fused together, I battle to dominate the kiss. Locking his tongue between my teeth, I extend my arm. Before I can bring the blade back down, he grips my wrist and squeezes. It's painful, but not unbearable.

Lifting his head from mine, both our chests rise and fall in rapid succession.

The gleam in his eyes sends a shiver of euphoria straight between my legs. A murky, thick cloud of lust cyclones out of control. Spinning, spinning, spinning, until I'm dizzy and disoriented by him.

Hand still on my wrist, he guides the knife to my neck, holding it against my skin. Lust turns to want, and want grows into need, burning me from the inside out. If he doesn't touch me soon, I'm sure I'll combust.

Dropping my head back, I offer myself to him, allowing him undeterred access—to kill me the way he wants.

The flat of the blade presses to my neck.

"Saint," Sketch cautions from beyond our dirty, depraved, sick foreplay bubble.

"Get out," he growls, low and feral.

I squeeze my thighs together for relief, but get none.

"Saint—" Sketch tries again.

"Get out," he roars.

A heavy sigh and the sound of a door slamming are the last I hear of Sketch. The right side of my mouth hooks up, knowing he was sent away like a punished child.

Saint guides our joined hands, running the blade down and beneath the neckline of my shirt. Twisting the handle, he tries to cut through the cotton, but the fabric won't give.

Impatient, he yanks the weapon from my hand and shoves me onto my back, fists my t-shirt, and slices it open. The soft material falls to my sides as the tip of his blade returns to the hollow of my neck.

"I'm going to kill you." His whisper is rough and throaty.

"I know," I gasp, arching my back enough to bare my throat to him.

I'm not sure why I do it. Maybe I'm tired of running, hiding, or maybe, just maybe, my darkness can't think of a better way to die. The shiver that runs through me at the thought of his monster taking control of my fate tightens my nipples.

"Beg me to do it," he orders on a groan, dragging the tip down, over my chest, stopping in the valley of my breasts.

He slices through my bra, revealing the way my nipples reach out for him.

Sliding the dull side of the blade over my left breast, the cold metal sends a flurry of tingles to my belly, and I close my eyes.

The knife disappears, only to return in a quick slap against the already pebbled tip.

Opening my eyes on a gasp, I find him studying my face. I lick my dry lips, and he slaps my breast again.

The sharp sting of the metal hurts, but it also sends a pulse of pleasure from my belly to my clit. The sensation is so intense on the third strike, I can't help my squirm and fist the blanket beneath us.

"Who are you?" he asks, slapping my other breast with the metal blade.

"No one," I answer, breathily.

One dark brow raises over a hazel eye. "You're going to tell me who you are, dead girl." His words are a promise.

He strikes my nipple once more.

"Oh God," I moan, clenching my thighs tighter.

He leans down, bringing his face less than an inch from mine.

"There's no God here, dead girl, only demons," he clarifies in a hot breath.

"Beg me to do it. Beg me to kill you," he says against my lips, possessing them, forcing them to form the words with him.

Closing my eyes, I admit, "I've already died once, just get it over with."

Everything stills, his body, the air, and my heart.

He pushes away from me, putting space between our bodies. His eyes search my face and I look away, but he takes my chin, turning it back to his. He studies me for an uncomfortably long moment.

Feeling far more exposed than when I'm stripping on stage, I cover my chest with my hands and try to look away. His eyes drop to my hands on my breasts, releasing me from his gaze, but not the hold on my chin.

Looking back at my face, he brushes his thumb over my lips and furrows his brow.

"We will be going out tomorrow," he states, letting go of my face and pushing off my body.

Swallowing down a mixture of relief and disappointment, I pull my shirt closed and sit up.

At the side of the bed, he removes his jacket and tosses it over the end of the bed. My eyes focus on the guns holstered at his sides.

Sliding them off, he hooks one strap on the end of the bed. My fingers itch to grab the weapons and escape.

Turning to face me, he begins unbuttoning his shirt.

"Not curious about where we will be going?" he asks.

"I'm sure I won't like the answer," I respond, inching to the opposite side of the bed. Though, the more I think about it, the more I realize the reasons I'm running from him. I need distance from this man who ensnares me in his presence and consumes with a touch. If I submit and confess all my sins to him, I choose this gilded cage.

His shirt falls away, and he undoes his belt. The jingle of the metal buckle pulls me out of my thoughts. Ignoring the revelation, I focus my efforts on reaching the opposite edge of the bed.

"There's nowhere for you to go," he says, belt dropping to the floor with a thud.

Attention solely on me, he pulls his t-shirt from the waist of his pants. My jaw tightens and I glare.

"You're magnificent," he growls, kneeling onto the bed.

Twisting, I try to crawl away, but Saint shackles my ankle with his large hand. Pulling me across the bed, I struggle until he pins me beneath him once more. Seizing my neck in one of his calloused hands, the fight leaves my body and I melt into the caress of his thumb along my jaw.

"Your death starts tonight," he says, his voice gruff, low, promising.

I fist the comforter, trying so hard not to touch him, but my resistance crumbles beneath every possessive stroke. Each piece of my mental armor is swallowed in wave of primal, raw need.

Most people say the dark is cold and alone. Those people don't know a fucking thing. Craving, lust, and belonging wash through me, searing every inch of my skin.

It is so far from the alone and empty I've been living. My soul feeds on the intimacy, triggering my surrender to the monster.

"Please," I beg, verbalizing my submission.

"Fuck," he says on a breath, flexing his hand. "It won't hurt..." he speaks against my mouth, "too much."

Holding me the way he wants, he claims my mouth just the way I need him to. The kiss is every bit a possession of my body. The edges of his darkness dance across my skin, wrapping around my limbs, drawing out the depravity I lock away.

Chapter nine

Mei

Jerking awake, I fight off the lingering aftermath of the nightmare. I take a deep breath, trying to shake off the phantom feeling of being chased. It's been a while since I dreamt about *him* and being within his reach.

My surroundings slowly creep into awareness. It must be early morning. The room is dimly lit from the windows, but the night still clutches to the black shadows at the corner. My arms ache as I push myself up the bed. Leaning against the headboard, the memory of Saint's hands on my body accompany the soreness. My thigh muscles twitch in anticipation, wanting the feel of his hip bones digging into them. A tingling begins in my exposed nipples, from how raw they feel and in memory of his attention.

Closing my eyes, I drop my head back against the metal.

I'm so weak. I did exactly what he wanted. Idiot!

"We're going to talk about this doll," his voice startles me, "but first, you're going to tell me who you are and what the fuck has you crying out in your sleep."

Pulling the sheet up my naked body, I hold it to my chest and glance to my right.

Saint sits in a light gray, high-back chair. The darkness swallows his upper body, leaving his bare feet, legs, and forearms exposed. The knife in his right hand gleams in the low light of early day and the rag doll dangles from his left fist.

"Tell me who you are," he demands, leaning forward. His face surfaces from the inky shadow, eyes focused on me.

Licking my bottom lip, I wince. His kiss had been punishing and demanding, sealing my unknown fate with this man.

"I'm just..." I hesitate, every practiced rule urging me to lie until I can get out of here.

He pushes out of the chair, his naked body emerging from the darkness like a fallen angel. The scars I'd felt on his chest are now visually confirmed. The ones at his shoulder, just above his left hip, and high on his thigh look like bullet wounds. The long line crossing his right pectoral is jagged and raised higher than the others, most likely a knife or other sharp object. Anticipation swirls in my stomach, wondering if I'll get to see the ones I felt on his back.

The doll is tossed into my lap, breaking me out of my perusal of battle wounds.

"I'm just a runaway," I admit, and it's not a lie. I've been running away for years.

Stopping at the edge of the bed, he taps his knife against his leg.

"How did you become a dead girl?"

Folding his arms over his chest, I watch the way he tucks the blade so it doesn't cut him. It's practiced, like he does it all the time.

My mind flashes back to that night and my terrible sin.

Every time I'm left alone with Winter to work the neighborhood, I'm scared—terrified I'll be forced to repeat what happened to me months before. To say the night I lost my innocence ended with the single encounter would be a lie. There was another more brutal encounter.

"Watch where you're fucking going," Winter scolds, pulling me away from a taped and poorly fenced-off open manhole. "And stop thinking about it," she demands with a roll of her eyes.

"I'm not," I lie.

"Bullshit, you have that look on your face again." She sighs, taking me by the shoulders to face her. "The trick is to forget about it, block it out. It gets easier," she reassures.

I didn't tell her everything about that night. Embarrassment and shame wouldn't allow me to confess all the sordid and evil things that happened to me, what I enjoyed, and what was forced upon me. But Winter had seen the bruises, blood, and emotional damage when she found me curled against a dumpster on the street near Peter's apartment.

"Hey," the sound of a male voice makes me shudder.

Winter turns toward him, and responds, hesitant. "Yeah?"

She's feeling him out, making sure it's not a cop setting her up. *Her lessons in selling yourself started the very next day after I returned to the abandoned apartment building we called home.*

"How much?" he asks, looking up and down her body.

"I'm not selling anything," she lies.

She dragged us out into the cold night for this very reason. We needed the money and she was prepared to get it by any means.

When I asked about the large sum of money we, or I, just earned, she slapped me for my act of defiance. Though, I later found the needles she'd been hiding inside her boot, answering that question. Apparently, you can't always forget some things. Sometimes you need chemically enhanced escapes.

The man moves into her personal space. When he catches sight of me, he grins.

"How much for both of you?" He rubs his chin. "I have a friend with me."

Winter looks over her shoulder at me. I shake my head and take a step back. Rolling her eyes, again, she turns back to respond to him.

Before she can get more than a "She" out of her mouth, two men emerge from the shadows and grab her.

Frozen in terror, I watch them drag her into an alley.

"Run," she screams, snapping me into action, but the guy who approached latches his hand to my arm.

Leaning down, I bite his hand until I taste blood. He shouts in pain, releasing me, and I run. I run and run and run.

Squeezing between two dumpsters in an alley, I hide in the filth and darkness. My heart pounds in my ears, making it impossible to hear if someone chased after me. Tears streaming over my cheeks, I hold my head in my hand and rock.

When I finally find the courage to peek out from my hiding

spot, my body is stiff and protesting the movement. Unsure how long I've been there, I glance around the corner of the brick building, finding no one.

Turning, I prepare to head home, hoping Winter will be there waiting and ready to yell at me for disappearing. But something won't let me.

Sticking to the shadows, I retrace my steps until I reach the place I last saw Winter. The moment I hear laughter, I take cover in a boarded-up doorway and crouch low.

"Fuck, man, next time I'll find the girl," a deep voice says, and the click of a lighter cuts through the air.

"Shut up, asshole, she's the best piece you've had," another responds with a laugh.

"I can tell you her ass was tight as fuck," a third man praises, earning humored agreement from the others.

"Greg," a new voice shouts.

"Can't keep it up, Jare," he taunts in response.

"She ain't fucking breathing," the panic in his voice makes my stomach knot.

"What the fuck are you going on about?" Footsteps follow the question.

"Fuck," he shouts. "She ain't breathing!"

"What the fuck do we do?"

Their voices blend together as one, panic, yelling, and then heavy footfalls. I don't even flinch when they run by me, too lost in the words they spoke.

Slipping out from the doorway, uncaring if they turn and see me, I enter the alley where she was taken.

Winter's naked body is sprawled out on a large piece of cardboard. Bruises cover her hips, thighs, and chest. There's blood smeared on her mouth, chin, and cheek. Her head lays at an awkward angle.

Kneeling, I reach out and poke her shoulder.

"Winter?" I whisper.

No answer.

"Winter," I say louder.

No answer.

With both hands, I shove her body, and scream, "Winter!"

Tears escape my eyes, soaking my face and dripping from my chin. Leaning forward, I press my head to her arm and sob.

After what feels like an entire night, I collect her discarded and torn clothes. Her pants, still caught on one ankle, are covered in grease, grime, and dirt. Gripping the waist of them, my hand encounters something in her pocket and I pull out a canvas wallet.

The tear of the Velcro sounds like a scream in the quiet alley, making me look around to see if anyone else heard it. Inside, I find a couple hundred dollars and her ID.

Meissa L. Winters.

I don't know where the idea comes from, but it comes just the same. Biting my lip, I glance between the wallet and Winter's lifeless body.

One word floats in my mind.

Freedom.

"Silence isn't going to work this time," Saint's voice causes me to start. Swallowing the tears lodged in my throat, I tell him something no one else knows.

Eyes unfocused, I confess my greatest sin, "I killed her."

My admission feels like a piece of my armor; my mask has been torn away. It's freeing and terrifying at the same time. The dark urges start to crawl through me, until I bury them beneath the guilt.

"You killed her?"

I should've known better than to expect shock or disgust from a man like him, but the nonchalance in his question still surprises me.

Nodding, I lick my bottom lip and explain how I found her.

"Then you didn't kill her, those assholes did," he grounds out.

Shaking my head, I argue, "No, you don't know the rest."

Before he can interrupt, I explain, "I collected all her things and tossed them into the manhole, except the wallet and her jacket." I turn my eyes to his. "Then I went back for Winter."

Bringing both hands in front of me, I glance down at them.

"With my bare hands, I dragged her body by the arms to the street," I choke on the last word and take a deep breath. "I'd already had it all planned out in my head. I didn't know how or where, but I would become her. I'd be old enough to work, get an apartment..." I let the words die off before my next admission. "And then, she moaned."

This time, I can't keep the tears at bay. A sob wracks my chest.

"She wasn't dead. Small tremors began shaking her body, but instead of taking her to get help or bringing help to her..." I move my water-filled eyes back to his face, wanting, needing, to look him in the eye, "I shoved her head first into the manhole."

A humorless laugh escapes between the sobs. "Sometimes I can still hear the cracking of her skull against the metal rungs and the crunch of her body to the wet cement below the street."

The room grows so silent as my crying subsides, and I wipe the tears from my face.

"Then, you became her." It's not a question, but I nod anyway.

His eyes search my face and I notice the room has brightened by the rising sun.

"What time is it?" I ask.

"Early," is his response. "How old are you?"

Another humorless laugh escapes me and I shrug.

"Now it matters?" Answering his question with one of my own earns me a deep scowl, but he lets it go–for now, anyway.

"You go to that salon to keep up the appearance." Again, not a question, and I stiffen, realization drying up my emotional outburst.

"You followed me?"

"Is the gym to maintain your body for work?" This time, he's inquiring.

"How long did you follow me?" I press, moving to my knees.

Did he draw attention to me? Is he the reason that doll reentered my life?

"Explain the gym," he demands, trying to piece together whatever information he has about me.

"Explain following me," I growl.

Dropping his arms from his chest, he tosses his knife into the chair behind him.

"You aren't exactly in a position to ask me anything," he says through clenched teeth. "Tell me who the fuck you are."

Defiance surges into every muscle, and I launch from the bed, run for the bathroom. Before I reach the door, his arm wraps around my waist.

"Let go," I shout, anger rushing through my veins.

"There's nowhere else for you to go," he says in my ear.

One arm at my waist and the other over my chest, he restrains me, and I struggle against him.

"Tell me who you hide from," the plea in his voice stills me. "Tell me everything and I can set you free of them." His face buries into the back of head.

"You think you can free me?" The anger in my question tenses his embrace.

Before I can deliver the verbal assault lingering on the tip of my tongue, I'm turned and pinned to the wall by his body. His hand caresses my face, tracing my jaw.

"You aren't free," he says, his rumbled words accented by the grip of my chin.

Our eyes clash and the mix of emotion in his puts every hair on end. Grasping his wrist with one hand and pressing my other to his chest, I try to look away, but he doesn't allow it.

"You will never be free," he pauses, bringing his face closer to mine, "of me."

The words, his promise, should terrify me, but they don't, and I'm not sure why. Maybe it's the way he's chipping away at my façade. Maybe it's that he's glimpsed the dark urges, the evil, inside me, and still desires more. No, he commands more.

His grip eases enough for him to slide the pad of his thumb over my lips, and I wince when he reaches the sensitive spot. Dipping his head, and licks the swollen area, and my body reacts the opposite way it should. The pain dissolves into a flurry of desperation. The need for him to conquer and consume me stirs the urges back to life.

"Tell me," he demands against my mouth.

Needy and frustrated, I blurt, "I'm a dead girl."

Saint

Standing at the end of the bed, pants pulled on but not fastened, I take in every mark. A good and decent man wouldn't see the swollen lips, purple marks from my mouth, and reddened skin— the evidence of my touch on her body—and feel like I do.

Sure, most would be lying if they denied the primitive desire to own someone completely. The difference between them and me is I'm doing it, but there's so much more to it than even I expected.

I didn't anticipate the protector to emerge with the possessor, or the submission accompanying my dominance. I want to own her, yet free her. Need her to submit to me, yet challenge everything. And fuck if I don't crave her devotion as much as I want to give mine. This little dead girl passed out on the bed has twisted everything.

Having committed every word she spoke to memory, I play it on repeat in my head. I know there's more, so much more. Rubbing a hand over my face, I turn from the bed, collect my things, and leave the room.

Instead of going up to the master bedroom, I find myself on the first floor of the penthouse making a drink at the bar.

I feel his presence before he speaks.

"Christ," he exclaims.

The sting I felt on my back since I climbed off the bed confirms the scratches she left on me. Turning around and seeing the look on Sketch's face tells me she clawed me up good. A surge of satisfaction straightens my spine.

"Are you fucking smiling?" he asks, his question full of disbelief.

Until he asked, I hadn't realized the corners of my mouth had curled.

"I guess I am," I state, erasing any amusement from my face.

"Did you at least get a name?" he presses, leaning against the doorway.

"No."

He shakes his head.

"But she did explain how she became Meissa Winters," I share before draining the remaining vodka from my glass.

Sketch perks up, straightening to his full height.

"How?"

"You'll know what I want you to," I growl, and the surprise on his face matches the way I feel. Telling him would help his search for answers—a search I put him on—but I don't want to share anything about my little dead girl. Not when her death has just begun. I've already torn away a piece of the life she's been living, and while I want answers, I'm also enjoying the slow death of Meissa Winters.

Instead of sharing further, I switch the subject.

"She'll accompany me tonight," I say, setting my glass on the bar.

"To the club?"

"Yes," I confirm.

Bringing her to the party tonight would be a statement, making it known she belongs to me. And given this celebration is for Felix's younger brother, and my cousin, it could definitely escalate hostilities between us.

"What about Felix?" Sketch apparently carries similar concerns.

"Angelo's made a deal," I explain, and his brow rise high on his forehead. "He wants more information about the accidents."

Reaching into the pocket of the jacket draped over my arm, I take out a flash drive and toss it to him without giving any more details. Sketch is very much aware of the men being taken out, the carvings into their flesh, and all the *other* details I'd left out during my talk with Angelo. Like his assumption that it's a man or one person may be completely wrong.

He may be family, my boss, and the leader of this organization, but he's led me around for far too long. Used me in ways a man shouldn't ask of a boy. And I had been just a boy the day he used my loyalty to deceive and manipulate in the worst way.

I could respect the deceit and manipulations. In fact, I did for the longest time, until I discovered just a few of his traitorous acts. The biggest being my parents were not the disloyal conspirators he'd made me believe. No, he used me to clean up a mess he created and to hide the devious acts coming back to haunt him.

"You know you can't trust him," Sketch interrupts my dark thoughts.

"Felix?" I ask.

"Angelo," he clarifies. "Even I don't know how deep his shit goes."

I know it pisses him off not being able to get all the details and dirt on Angelo, in the same way his dead ends with Mei's past are pushing him to the breaking point. Especially with her shoving the fact in his face. I'm sure if I hadn't interrupted them late yesterday evening, I would've found her tied to a chair with a gun to her head. Fuck, he may have even gotten chemically creative and used drugs to make her talk.

"You sure about this? I can keep an eye on the little doll," he offers, nodding to the stairs.

"She's with me," I state, pushing away from the bar and moving to the stairs.

"Be careful, Saint." His warning stops me. "You don't know a fucking thing about this girl. I wouldn't get too invested."

Keeping my back to him, I take the first, then second step. "It doesn't matter who she is," I confess. "She belongs to me now."

"Fucking hell," he swears on a loud exhale.

chapter ten

Mei

Saint didn't return, not later in the morning or this afternoon. He's had food sent up twice, though, as well as more of my things.

It's both a blessing and torture. I need distance and time to rebuild the walls he's tearing away, but the smell left behind on the bed and my skin drives me to distraction.

Taking my things into the bathroom, I lock the door, then remove my contacts before stepping into the glass shower. The warm water cascades over my skin, easing my muscle aches. My raw nipples take a bit longer to adapt, and I refrain from directly washing them.

Standing beneath the spray, I give myself a moment to regroup.

"What color are you hiding?"

The surprise of his question pulls a scream from me. Spinning, I press against the tile wall and clutch a hand to my chest.

Damn it! I'd been so lost in my own head, I didn't hear him enter. I keep making stupid mistakes with this man.

His dark figure approaches the foggy glass, filling the door with his shadowing outline. He yanks open the door, and his eyes meet mine.

"Blue," he rumbles, glancing down at the white contact case in his palm.

Realizing my other mistake, I close my eyes. *Stupid, stupid, stupid.*

Hands slip around my arms, pulling me away from the tile and out of the shower. Lifting me at the waist, my wet, bare ass is planted on the double sink vanity.

"Open them," his words warm against my chilled skin.

"Give them back to me," I counter.

He clasps my chin.

"Open," he orders.

Blinking, I do as he instructs. Hazel eyes bore into mine, searching, probing, as if he can see my soul.

"Blue is better," he states, releasing my chin.

Stepping back, he purposely pockets the contact case.

"Do you have extras?" he inquires, and I begin to shake my head, but glance at my bag.

He raises a brow.

"Yes," I answer through clenched teeth.

Grinning, he reaches into my bag and takes out my last extra set, pocketing those too.

"What color is your hair?"

"Blonde," I respond, knowing he's asking for the real color, but not wanting to give it to him.

The right side of his mouth turns up and he closes in on me. Fisting my hair, he brings his mouth to the curve of my neck.

"What is your real hair color?" he asks, flicking his tongue against my skin.

The chill instantly leaves my body.

"Pink," I whisper.

His fist tightens and hips press between my naked thighs until he is flush against me. The feel of him hard and ready beneath the cotton of his pants makes my thighs tense and clit throb.

"If I were a patient man," his hand moves from above my ass and slips to my inner thigh, his thumb brushing over my bare pussy, "I'd wait to see what grows out, but I'm not."

The pad of the torturous digit presses to the top of my slit, just grazing my clit. My hips jerk forward, and I gasp.

Easing the pressure, he lightly glides along my lips. The touch is agonizingly slow and easy. My pussy tingles, throbs, and the walls contract in anticipation. If he slips inside, I'm sure he would find me slick and ready.

"Tell me the color, dead girl, and I'll give your cunt what it desires," he promises.

He presses once more against my clit and tightens his grasp in my hair. Releasing my hold on the edge of the vanity, I fist his white t-shirt and fight the urge to reveal everything to this dangerous man.

Running his tongue up the side of my neck, he uses a knuckle to push into me. It's enough to drive me further insane, but not enough to fill where I need his touch most.

"Is this what you want?" He finally slips one finger inside me and stills.

"Yes," I moan, squirming to get friction.

"Uh-uh, dead girl," he scolds, curling and locking his finger inside me so I can't get any relief.

Growling in frustration, I shove at his chest. It does nothing but earn me a wiggle of the tip against the most glorious spot inside before he stills once more. It's not enough. I need more, so much more.

"You know what to do," he reminds, emphasizing with another lick where my shoulder and neck meet.

"Brown," I surrender. "Dark brown!"

He growls in satisfaction, withdrawing his finger and releasing my body.

"No," I protest, ready to crumble to the floor, until he returns, slamming his cock inside and collaring my neck.

"Oh, yes," I yell, bringing my hands to his thick arm and holding on.

With a large hand spanning my lower back, he pistons in and out, circles, and repeats, fucking me hard and thorough. His cock slides and grinds deep within me, drawing my climax just to the precipice. The flex of his fingers around my throat pulls a moan from my mouth just before he shifts his hold, hooking his thumb between my parted lips.

I suck on it and gently bite.

He thrusts so hard, I'm sure the inside of my thighs will bruise. My orgasm bursts behind my clit and burns through my body, consuming every care, every worry, and every shame.

I step out of the bathroom in a pair of sweatpants and a t-shirt, my socks in my hand.

Saint sits, pants undone, in the same chair from earlier this morning. This time, he's not focused on me, too busy speaking in clipped tones into his cell phone.

Padding quietly to the end of the bed, I sit and pull my socks on.

"I don't care how you handle it, just do it," he barks.

Reaching for my shoes, I slip my toes inside.

"Where do you think you're going?"

At his question, I jerk the running shoe all the way on, lace it up, then start on the left. A shadow falls over me as I create the last knot.

"I prefer to have my shoes on," I admit without giving any more detail.

He doesn't need to know I like to be ready for anything, including running. Nor does he need to know that sleeping naked, as I did, is not my norm. I prefer to be fully dressed with my shoes on or next to the bed.

Looking up, I find him staring down in his observant way.

"A stylist will be here with a team of people within the hour," he informs, watching me for a reaction.

"Stylist?" I question.

"Yes, I told you, we will be going out this evening, and this," he motions to my current ensemble, "won't work."

"Okay," I answer, hesitant. There's obviously more he has to say.

"I've asked for a hairstylist as well," he states.

The air leaves my lungs and I swallow down the dread lumping in my throat. "I can't," I blurt, dropping my eyes from his face.

"You won't be wearing the contacts, *Mei*." I don't miss the way he stresses my name. Closing my eyes, I try to keep the panic at bay. I can't go out without the mask, the façade. He's exposing too much.

Fingers grip my chin, pulling my face back to his.

"Your death is imminent," he informs. "They will bring options for you to choose from, but there will only be shades of dark brown."

"I won't," I defy.

"You will," he releases my chin. "How soon you forget," his fingers comb into my hair, "my skills of persuasion."

I want to slap the half grin from his face. Opening my mouth, he continues before I get a word out.

"Perhaps this time, it will be persuasion by tongue," he grips my damp hair, pulling my head back, "before I secure your arms behind your back and fuck your ass."

My lower body clenches and nipples tingle at the thought. Jerking my head, I'm pissed he's so easily discovered the dirty and depraved girl locked away inside.

With a knowing smile, he releases my head and steps back.

"I'll kill you yet," he promises before turning and leaving the room.

Twisting and dropping face first into the bed, I scream, then inhale, his scent wrapping around me like a vice I never want to escape.

Sketch arrives an hour later, showing three blonde women and one redhead into the room. Two carry thick garment bags, another rolls a large trunk, and the last has two black bags over her shoulders.

Pushing off the bed, I stand and face my current firing squad. Distracted by the women moving about the room, I don't see Sketch approach.

"Let's see how well hidden you stay with your costume torn away, doll," he taunts, and I want to slap the cocky grin off his face.

"When you still can't figure me out," I begin, watching his face fall, "please mention me in your suicide note," I finish with a sugar sweet smile.

"You don't know wh—"

"Step back," Saint booms, pulling our rounded eyes to him.

"Sketch, have you finished your task?"

A muscle jumps in Sketch's jaw.

"Someone's gonna get grounded," I taunt in a whisper.

"I hate you," he growls low.

"Aw, but I love you," I say in my normal tone.

His eyes bug before he slides them to Saint.

Saint raises one brow before one side of his mouth curls. Sketch visibly relaxes and leaves the room. I frown, unsure of what just happened in their silent exchange.

"Have you come to dress your doll?" I ask, tilting my head.

Smirking, he enters my personal space, but I refuse to back down. I've given this man too much power—too much everything.

"Once I kill you, dead girl, Doll may be a perfect name. I will have you however I want you," he rumbles.

Stupidly, excitement thrums through my body at his words instead of the fear and terror they should invoke. Especially being called doll. It's obvious I need to get out of here and away from him, but how?

A throat clears from across the room and I take three steps back from Saint.

"Sir, we will need to begin if we are to be ready by eight o'clock," the redhead addresses him.

"Just a moment and she is all yours," he promises, then turns back to me. "We will be going to a club with my associates this evening."

Remembering the women who arrived on the arms of his associates at the club, a flash of Vicki enters my mind and I worry Felix will be there. Swallowing, I wrap my arms around me.

"No one will touch you," he reassures. "You are with me and that makes you untouchable. Unless I say otherwise," he adds.

Before I can voice a concern or protest, he's walking for the door, and I resign myself to play along with dress up while using it to my advantage. The first opportunity to run I get, I'll take, and in a crowded club with dark corners, I'm sure the chance will be there.

"You have until eight o'clock," he says, exiting.

The moment the door clicks shut, the women surround me.

"Hello, dear, my name is Megan. I'm your stylist," the redhead smiles before motioning to the rest of the women. "These are my assistants, Julie, Helen, and Amy."

Fighting back the dread of the upcoming evening, I put on a smile and greet them, "You can call me Mei."

"Come along." Megan takes my hand, pulling me toward the bathroom.

They drape me in a protective black cape before trimming, dyeing, and styling my hair. Next comes Julie with her manicure set, then Amy with her makeup tackle box.

At least I'd have that mask in place.

"Based on your shape and body size," Helen starts upon my reentry to the bedroom, "these five dresses are the best to choose from." She motions to the garments hung along the closet's double doors.

"With your eyes, I suggest this one." She unhooks a blue dress, carrying it over and laying it on the bed next to an array of undergarments.

Taking a deep breath, I tug off my clothes and slip into the black satin and lace thong. I finger the spaghetti strap of a black lace slip and hold it up.

"What exactly does this accomplish?" I ask, knowing it serves none—unless you count wrapping for a man to remove.

"That's just for fun," Megan giggles. "We'll leave that in the bathroom for later." She winks.

Remembering these women have no idea of my situation and this is just one step closer to escape from this room, I bite back my annoyance. Amy holds out the dress, and I step inside. The blue velvet material is like a thousand kittens climbed up my body. Megan quickly zips up the back and turns me toward the full-length mirror on the back of an open closet door.

The knee-length dress would be modest if it weren't for the way it hugs to every curve and the deep V neckline knotting at my stomach. Now I understand the lack of bra.

"You look like a different person," Helen sighs, kneeling and helping me into the gold strappy heels.

I move closer to the mirror, allowing myself to take in the full effect of the changes. My blue eyes exposed. The blonde hair replaced by dark chocolate locks. Gold jewelry. Sultry, yet demure makeup. My burgundy-tinted lips part. Placing a hand to my stomach, I try to stop the riot.

"No," Megan says, stepping next to me. "She looks like she was meant to."

My eyes dart to hers in the mirror, and she smiles.

"I don't see it often, but there are moments, like this one, where a person transforms into themselves." Clasping her hands, she gives her head a small shake and turns to her team. "Now, we must clean up." She claps, and they move into action.

Refocusing on my reflection, I stare at the women looking back.

"He did it," I whisper. "He killed me."

Meissa Winters is gone. A single tear escapes my perfectly lined eye.

Saint

"Let it go," I warn Sketch for the third time.

"How are you so sure this is a good idea?" he presses.

Lifting my glass, I drain the last of my vodka and raise a brow at him.

"I think you're fucking crazy," he announces on a heavy sigh. "You don't know a fucking thing about this girl. Felix isn't known for stepping down so easily, regardless of what Angelo says, and..."

His words fall away, the focus of his eyes now over my shoulder.

Turning on the couch, I find Mei standing in the archway.

"What do you think?" Megan asks, ushering her team through.

"Who the fuck are you?" Sketch asks, part wonder, part growl.

"Careful," I advise, but can't fault him.

My dead girl is stripped down and exposed. Blue eyes and creamy skin framed by long dark hair. The only hint left of Mei is the small tattoo on her ribcage. The rest...fuck me, if the real version of this woman isn't the most glorious thing I've seen.

The combination of anger in her eyes and that damn dress conjures my cock and the demon. Both wanting inside her—one to please, the other to possess.

Pushing up from the couch, I watch Mei straighten her spine at my approach. Reaching inside my jacket, I retrieve an envelope and hold it out to Megan.

"Thank you for your services," I state, cupping Mei's face in my right palm.

"If you aren't happy with —"

"Let's go," Sketch says, leading the woman away. "I assure you, he is thrilled with the results."

"Welcome to your death," I whisper, and she tenses, pulling her face away from my touch. Frowning, I drop my hand.

"I wish you would just kill me..." she begins. Before I can shush her, she finishes on a quiet whisper, "Before it's too late."

Gripping her chin, I force her face back to mine.

"What do you mean by that?"

She tries to shake her head, but my hold prevents it.

"Tell me," I demand, moving closer. The smell of her perfume swirls around me. It's the same dark vanilla scent, the kind only mythological creatures could smell of.

"It doesn't matter," she says. "You've done what you set out to do. You've killed me—killed Meissa—but you really have no idea what you're sentencing me to."

Her eyes take on a dead look, and I fucking hate it.

"Explain," I command.

"Never," she spits back.

Before I can stop myself, I ask, "Why?"

She blinks twice, just as staggered by the question as I am.

"Because I don't trust you," she says on a whisper. "No one can be trusted."

I want to shake her and demand answers, but how can I when I live by the same code? Trust no one. Releasing her and taking a step back, I offer my arm.

Surprise fills her face when I don't press further. She visibly inhales and exhales once before placing her small hand around the bend of my elbow.

At the door, I present her with a gold clutch purse and drape a black coat around her shoulders.

"Keep the clutch with you at all times," I instruct, ushering her onto the elevator.

Inside the lift, she furrows her brows in question.

"If we get separated at any time, there is trigger button that will signal me," I explain. "However, you will be by my side, with me," I wrap my arm around her waist, "and it will send the necessary message that you are not to be touched."

"Except by you," she snaps.

"Of course," I respond, giving her a squeeze.

"Will Felix be there?" she asks.

"Yes, but he won't be a problem."

She snorts at my response.

"I've taken measures," I assure her, letting some of my anger saturate the words.

At the car, Frank opens the door and I motion for her to enter.

She's silent for a beat. Then, as we pull away from the curb, she asks, "What am I supposed to do, say, not say? Should I speak at all?"

Placing my hand on her knee, I let my fingers dance along her soft skin.

"Be honest," I finally respond.

"Honest?" she scoffs.

"Yes."

"I'll just tell them how you're keeping me against my will and you are okay with that?" she pushes.

Turning my eyes on her, I find the challenge I crave so much. Without her contacts, it burns so much brighter. Her eyes drop to watch me adjust myself, but my response brings them back to mine.

"Careful what you say, dead girl," I warn. "Complain too much, and someone may feel the need to *save* you," I stress. "And trust me, they won't be the white knight you seek."

"I don't need a white knight or someone to save me," she grounds out, crossing her arms over her chest and slouching back into the seat.

The behavior brings back something she said during her confession. *"I'd be old enough to work, get an apartment..."*

"How old are you?"

At my question, I watch her squirm.

"Why does it matter now?" she responds, the same as before.

"Tell me you aren't fucking underage," I demand, tired of her avoidance.

Her head slowly swivels to me, our eyes lock, and she smirks.

"Technically you'd be fucking someone underage," she taunts.

Snaking my arm out, I palm the back of her head and pull her face close to mine. Her small hands come to my chest, bracing and shoving at the same time.

"This isn't a fucking joke," I remind her, my voice gruff.

"I'm not underage," she mutters hastily, the fear rounding her eyes making both my demon and dick stir.

"That's not what I'm looking for," I firmly prompt.

"Nineteen," she says, her voice thick and unsteady.

Nineteen.

"Fucking hell," I exclaim and release her head, not missing the harshness in my words or the way she presses into the car door.

Rubbing my hand over my face, the scent of her perfume fills my nostrils, teasing the demon. He doesn't give two shits that, in this day of teenage parents, I'm old enough to be her father. No, all he wants is to open her up and seduce her into his black pit, bathing her in the blood and fear he collects.

Eyes still closed, trying to get my urges under control, I ask, "The club?"

"I was seventeen, but with Mei's ID, I was almost twenty," she responds, her voice sounding detached. I turn my head, finding her staring out the window. It's too dark to see anything at the speed we're traveling.

We should be reaching the club soon, so I remind her, "Keep the clutch with you at all times."

She gives a slow nod and lifts her chin.

"We're here," I announce as the car pulls onto the curb.

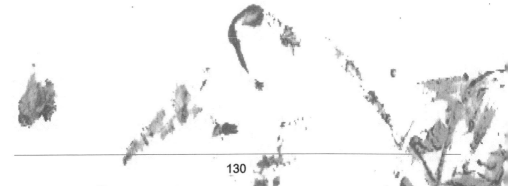

Chapter eleven

Mei

The club is definitely classier than the one where I work—or worked. The valet service, clear glass entrance, and shiny gold and black décor would be enough to make it a hundred times better, but it's the opulence that sets it far above.

Conversations stop and the crowd parts as Saint leads us to a large bar running the length of the wall opposite the band.

"Tired of your toy already?" Felix's familiar voice teases from behind, and I stiffen.

"Not at all," Saint replies, not turning or looking back.

He only stops once when an older gentleman speaks, but it's only a moment in passing. At the bar, he releases me to order two drinks from the waiting bartender.

Staring at Saint's back, I tighten my hands around the clutch he's so concerned I carry. Before I can dwell on all the reasons I shouldn't even be here with him, fingers lock around my bicep and turn me around. "This is definitely an upgrade from—" Felix studies my face as his words die off. His brow furrows just before his eyes narrow.

"Remove your hand," Saint orders, loud enough to draw attention.

Eyes filled with recognition, he asks, "It's her, isn't it?"

Sliding his arm around my waist, he pulls me away from Felix into his side.

"I believe you know Mei," Saint says with a hint of patronization. "She *used* to work at your club."

Felix's jaw tightens as his eyes move from me to Saint.

"She cleans up well," he concedes. "On the outside." He drinks from the tumbler in his hand and grins. "But a whore is always a whore on the inside," he says, mocking.

Saint's body stiffens and he tightens his hold on my waist. It starts to hurt, but I keep it to myself. This is clearly some standoff I don't understand the rules to.

"You do seem to have an expertise with whores, Felix," Saint counters, the edge in his voice slicing through the tension. "Thankfully, mine knows the right *choice* to make."

The glare on Felix's face could not be mistaken for anything but murderous—a look I'm sure has to do with the night I sealed my fate with Saint.

The room suddenly falls into quiet murmurs, like everyone's eyes are on their current exchange.

Felix forces a smile, followed by a loud laugh, and claps Saint on the shoulder.

"Come now, cousin. I'm only teasing," he says, a bit too loud.

I don't miss the smirk lingering at the corner of Saint's mouth. He's won, but the look in Felix's eyes, the one he can't mask with a fake smile and laugh, holds a promise of retribution.

The conversations around us pick back up and others approach Saint.

Thankfully, no one does more than look over my body, mostly my bared cleavage. Leaning against the bar, I keep to myself, drinking whatever the bartender keeps bringing me.

Over the rim of my wine glass, I let my eyes scan the room. At first, I take in the multiple exit signs showing the path to my freedom, then my eyes fall on a familiar face.

Natasha sits on a man's knee. When he tosses his head back in laughter, I see it's one of the men I watched fuck her. Remembrance tingles my inner thighs as him ordering her to clean the other man flashes in my mind.

Instead of the black lace lingerie, thigh highs, and cat ears she's known for at the club, she wears a strapless black dress. Sitting on his lap, the hem is precariously close to sliding over her hips. The smile I see on her profile makes me wonder if it's an act or genuine. When she glances toward the bar—at me—I fight the crazy urge to wave.

It's an odd thing. I've never been a person to call myself out in a crowded room, so I'm not sure where the desire to do something so out of character comes from. Not that it matters. Natasha doesn't see *me*, the Mei she knows. She glances over a girl she has no recognition of.

I'm about to move on, check out the rest of the crowd, when her head suddenly snaps around to the man. His hand slides up her back into the nape of her hair, where he fists, pulling her face to his.

The other men in the group laugh, drink, and watch the two intently.

His free hand grips her knee, yanking her legs apart, and Natasha's spine stiffens.

A flex of his arm pulls her head back. The smile on her face doesn't surprise me, not after seeing her previous interaction with him. In fact, the moment her mouth parts on a gasp, my eyes drop knowingly. Hand beneath the short skirt of her dress, it moves rhythmically. Her ass squirms and he stops the movement, yanking her head toward him.

With a restrained nod, she agrees to something, and the show commences. I watch his mouth move, though I can't hear or make out the words, and Natasha exposes her breasts.

Men around them laser in on the performance, adjusting themselves, loosening their ties, and licking their lips. A man seated two chairs away with a beautiful brunette shoves the woman toward Natasha. She looks to the man with his hand between her legs, and with a nod, she cups Natasha's breasts before kneeling between her parted legs. Gripping the man's wrist, she removes his hand, sucks his fingers, smiles, and delves between Natasha's legs.

A rumble of laughter carries over the crowd, including from Natasha's man.

This time, I can make out what he says. "Look at my good girl," he praises before turning her head to kiss him.

Aware I'm squeezing my glass too tightly, I spin and set it down on the bar. It clatters with a thud, gaining attention I don't want.

Is that what's expected of me tonight? Will he show off his new doll—the way he can dress me up and make me moan for a crowd? The club is one thing, but this...this is humiliating.

Shame swirls in my belly at knowing how wet I would feel if I reached between my legs at this moment, how aroused I would be by the display I'm condemning.

"What's the matter?" Saint's question breaks through my worry and shame, and I shake my head.

"I have to ask," a man I don't know, but who has been speaking with Saint at length, says, "what does Giuliana think of your new development?"

"She doesn't," Saint growls, and the group falls silent.

Giuliana? Is she his usual companion for these?

I don't have time to dwell on the thought or how it makes my stomach turn. Saint's chest presses to my back, his arms caging me against the bar.

"I asked you a question," he says, his words unyielding.

"Where's the restroom?" I ask, though I'd already figured it out during my perusal.

"I'll escort you," he states. Twisting my head, I scowl over my shoulder.

"You think I'm going to let you roam free in here?" he snorts. "I thought you were smarter than that."

"Dante." A light feminine voice interrupts our disagreement.

Releasing the bar, Saints stands to his full height and turns. Glancing around him, I find a tiny wisp of a girl. Her dark hair lays in a loose plait over her bare shoulder. The silver dress is like a second skin, leaving little to the imagination, but she doesn't match the rest of the women in this room. I'm not a large chested woman, yet I'm double her size. She's thin with minimal curves, reminding me of a young girl playing dress up in her mother's clothes. I would think I was right if it weren't for the knowing in her eyes. She may be young, but she's seen a lot.

"Nina," Saint greets.

"Angelo has requested you," she explains, her chin held high.

Her bravado is false. It's clear she's afraid of him—The Saint— like everyone else. Like I should be.

His hand raises expectantly, and I reach out to place my hand into his grasp when Nina adds, "No women." She swallows, and finishes, "Felix is already with him."

Saint's eyes shift to me, and he scowls.

"She'll be with me," Nina assures, moving to my side and wrapping her thin arm around mine.

Gripping my chin, he leans into my face. "There's nowhere you can run from me, dead girl," he reminds. "Keep the clutch with you and use the button if you need me."

Warmth spreads through my belly at the concern lying beneath the menace in his words. His lips press to my mouth before he disappears into the crowd.

Multiple sets of eyes hone in, glancing me over from head to toe.

"Where's the restroom?" I ask, turning to Nina.

"This way," she motions, leading me by the arm.

We pass the group I watched earlier, and Natasha, ass high in the air, catches my attention as she buries her head in a lap. It's not the man who's lap she was sitting on. He's fucking her ass while she puts her mouth to good use on the brunette, apparently returning the favor.

Locked in a bathroom stall, I lean my head against the cool wood of the door and breathe deep. My hand stays on the lock, afraid someone will interrupt my attempt to collect myself.

Nina hasn't spoken a word, not on the way here nor when we entered.

The chime of a cell phone fills the room before her voice breaks the silence.

"I've gotta take care of something for Angelo." The nervousness in her voice betrays how important she tries to sound.

"I'll be fine," I assure, hoping she leaves.

"Don't leave the restroom, okay?" Her heels click on the tile floor. "I'll be back in a few minutes, but don't leave."

I know why she's afraid. Angelo has made a request, but she doesn't want to suffer Saint's wrath either.

"Got it," I say, fighting back my elation.

The door closes, and I take three deep breaths before opening the stall, dropping the clutch on the floor, and moving to the bathroom exit.

"Sorry, Nina," I whisper an apology she'll never hear.

Opening the door, I step into the brightly lit hallway. I should know by now the worst things happen in the light, because there's nowhere to hide.

At the mouth of the restroom hallway, I tentatively glance around the space before me. I can stick to the walls, but that brings me into contact with groups like Natasha's, and walking through the crowd puts me at risk of being spotted.

A yelp from my left draws my eyes. It's not Natasha, but one of the waitresses. She looks about my age—my real age—and at the moment her arms are secured against her back by a man standing behind her. Another server, a young man, has his head shoved between her legs, forced there by another *guest*.

"What's the matter little boy, not man enough to please her?" He pushes the boy's face in deeper, but this time, I don't feel aroused. The tears streaming her face are a mixture of pain, humiliation, and terror.

"Maybe you're better with cock." The man yanks his head back. "Is that it?"

Similar tears stream the boy's face.

"Let's see," the man states, pulling the boy's face into his own lap.

I hadn't even seen his pants undone. My mouth opens, ready to yell, but then there's a gun to his head.

"I feel one tooth and you're fucking gone," he threatens, sitting back in a leather armchair.

The girl shrieks, but I look away, unable to stomach anymore.

"You're quite the lovely thing," a husky male voice says, accompanied by the backs of his fingers on my cheek.

I recognize him immediately. He's older, grayer, but it's definitely him. I could never forget his brand of evil. Freezing in place, I wait for his recognition to kick in, but it doesn't come.

"You shouldn't be alone," he purrs, stepping into my personal space and making me retreat into the hallway. "I can help with that."

I try to tell him I'm not alone, but the words get caught in my throat. Instead, I remember the night years ago when a man took my innocence, his father shredded my soul, and this man—charged with returning me—took what he called his *fee for service*. There had been no one to hear me scream in the backseat of that car, nowhere to run, and certainly no darkness to hide. In broad daylight, on the side of a street, no one stopped him. Not even the two people who happened upon us. They averted their eyes and walked faster. My screams meant nothing.

Finally finding my voice, I protest, "I'm not alone."

He sneers, reaching out and gripping the fabric knotted at the bottom of my plunging neckline.

Grabbing his wrist, I yank. "I said, I'm not alone," I shout, pulling at his hand and wishing I still had the clutch.

Tugging me forward against him, he buries his face in my neck and starts to suck.

Remembering my training, I bring my leg up and put my knee to his balls. Yelling, he releases me to grab his crotch. Stepping back, I hit the wall and inch to the side.

My attempt to get around him is thwarted when he grabs my arm. Throwing me back against the wall, he limps forward.

"You little fucking cunt," he growls. "Still think you're too goddamn good for me."

Snapping my eyes to meet his, he grins.

"Yeah, now you remember," he sneers.

The back of his hand lands against my cheek, snapping my head to the right. Bright bursts of light flash behind my clenched eyelids and my ears ring. My body slams into the corner of the hallway, something digging into my bicep. I force my eyes open, not daring to take my eyes from him.

"I bet your ass is plenty loose now, whore, but I'll make it work," he threatens.

Lunging forward, he slams my face into the wall, pinning me while lifting the skirt of my dress. I stomp my heel, trying to find his foot, and his thick arm presses into the back of my neck, subduing me with pain.

Dry, calloused fingers push inside my underwear and pinch my skin, trying to get between my ass cheeks.

"Are you insane?!" a voice bellows, and I suck in much needed breath as the asshole's body is torn away from mine. Tugging my dress back down, I focus on my savior, my eyes widening.

Felix.

"This isn't any of your business," the man barks, moving toward me. "We're old friends, aren't we, little girl?"

A shiver runs up my spine and tears sting the backs of my eyes.

"The fuck it isn't," Felix shouts, grabbing him and throwing him against a wall. "She belongs to Saint!"

"Bullshit," he retorts. "Saint doesn't have women."

Felix lifts his brow, giving him a look that clearly reads, *are you questioning me, asshole?*

My attacker stills, his eyes moving to Felix, who gives him a slow nod. "Yeah, you stupid fuck. You're a dead man."

"I didn't know," he blurts, grabbing Felix's arm. "You gotta tell him I—"

"There's no fucking helping you," Felix scoffs. "Who do you think you just fucked with?"

His eyes move to me.

"I'm sorry, I didn't—"

"I hope he eats your heart," I sneer, my dark side reveling in the fear and promise of this bastard's death. Not just a death, but a torturous and painfully slow redemption.

At my words, Felix fixes wide eyes on me.

Panic fills my attackers face.

I smile, hoping it conveys every ounce of the vengeance and evil coursing through my veins. My eyes follow my attacker as he shoves by Felix out of the hallway.

"You can't run from him," I whisper, looking to Felix.

He visibly swallows, and I don't miss the way he flinches at my face.

"Go clean yourself up," he sighs. "I'll send for—"

"What the fuck is going on?"

My eyes flit to Saint. He fills the entrance of the hallway, four other men at his back and Nina at his side. His eyes narrow on my face.

"I'll kill you," he growls, advancing on Felix.

"It wasn't him," I blurt, putting myself in his path.

He examines my face, gripping my chin and turning my head. Knowing he'll see the marks on my neck as well, I grimace.

"Who did this?"

I try to look up at him, but his grip is unrelenting.

"Arman," Felix says, signing the man's death sentence.

"And what are you doing with her?" Saint presses, still holding my face.

"He stopped him," I grunt, trying to free my face from his hand.

The hallway falls silent, until I whimper. Letting go of my chin, he wraps the arm around my waist, pulls me to his side, and turns us.

"Find him," he orders.

The men nod before disappearing into the crowd.

"He won't get away," Saint promises without sparing one glance at me.

"No one ever does," I whisper, and his arm curls around me, bringing my front to his chest.

"Stay close. We're leaving," he orders, walking me into the crowd, and just like before, they part, letting him through.

At the car, I look up from Saint's chest to see Frank waiting with the door open. As soon as his eyes take me in, a small flinch catches my notice. Saint palms my head, burying my face once more until he can place me in the car and climb in behind me. Pulling me close to his side, he throws an arm over my shoulders.

The silence grows long and uncomfortable. There are no words, only the sound of his heavy breathing and the car moving through the streets. Multiple times throughout the drive, I consider putting space between us or saying something to break the tension, but each time, I chicken out.

Rage vibrates off him, almost suffocating me. By the time we finally arrive to his building, my left cheek pulses beneath the tight skin.

The door opens, Frank steps back, and Saint pulls me out of the car behind him.

The trip through the lobby, up the private elevator, and into his penthouse is much the same as our exit from the club and the ride in the car. That is, until Sketch looks up from a laptop set up on the long dining table.

"What the fuck?" he exclaims, pushing up from the table. "What happened?"

His eyes move from my face to Saint, and whatever he finds there shuts him up. Saint tugs me up the stairs. As soon as we hit the second floor, I move toward my posh prison room, only to be jerked back. I look up at him, but his face remains stoic as he guides me up another set of stairs. The unfamiliarity of this floor pushes every warning button in my head. Fear rushes through my body, tensing every aching muscle.

We come to a set of dark wooden doors, and he guides me inside first.

I pause as we enter, and jump when his large hand comes to my shoulder, my sense on overdrive. *Is this where he'll finally kill me completely?*

He walks me farther into the small entrance hallway, and guides me through a door on our left.

Inside is a bathroom like the one I've been using, but much bigger. The vanity, mirrors, shower, and tub all feel bigger. Not to mention the gas fireplace in the wall above said tub.

"Undress." His command startles me, and I spin, finding him in the doorway watching me. Fear, anticipation, self-consciousness, and annoyance form a ball of discord in my stomach.

"Wh-What?" I ask, though I heard him just fine.

He arches his left brow, and I untie the knot at the bottom of the deep neckline and slip the blue velvet off my shoulders. The material catches at my hips, and I shove it down.

Standing in just my panties and high heels, I watch as his eyes roam over my body. I hook my thumbs into the lace at my hips and drag the thin fabric down my thighs until they fall to my high-heeled feet.

"Stop," he commands as I lift one foot. He comes so close, the heat of his body engulfs me. My nipples tighten, reaching out for his touch.

Then, he kneels at my feet.

Straightening my spine, I wrap my arms around myself.

Reaching up, he takes a hold of each wrist and pulls my arms down to my sides.

"Did he touch you?" he asks gruffly, the heat of his words falling against my stomach.

"You can see my face," I respond, focusing on the pale wall over his head.

His hands slide up my arms, flatten at my shoulders, then glide down to palm my breasts.

"Did. He. Touch. You?" he repeats, unable to hold back the anger.

Releasing my breasts, he moves to my sides, following the outline of my body with his fingertips. At my hips, he clutches, pressing his forehead to my stomach.

"No," I whisper.

The need to touch him is almost unbearable, but I don't understand why. I fist my hands at my sides to get the emotion under control, and look down at him.

Lifting his head from my body, his hands continue their slow descent.

Saint is all dominance, push and pull, and overpowering. This light touch is confusing and makes me nervous.

At my ankles, he unbuckles each strap of the heels before freeing my feet from my panties and shoes. Slipping his hands back up my legs, he stops at my thighs, gripping. For a long moment, he doesn't move, then he rises to his full height.

Towering over me, he lifts my face. Our eyes meet for a moment, then he lets go, steps back, and walks around me.

Blinking, I can't help but wonder what the hell that was about.

Turning at the sound of water, I find he started the fire and the bath.

"Wash him off you," he commands, eyes on the rapidly filling tub.

Anger tears down my fears and apprehension.

Now I'm unclean?" I ask, incredulous. Marching up to his side, not caring that I'm stripped bare before him, I get up in his personal space.

"I'm a whore, Saint," I remind him. "I've sold myself so—"

The snap of his head in my direction and the fury in his eyes silences me.

"They were your choice," he growls. "Did you offer yourself to Arman?"

Nausea washes over me at the thought of the man who abused a teenage girl and tried to repeat the act tonight.

"Exactly," he grumbles. "Now, get in the fucking bath and wash his goddamn touch from your skin!" He stabs his hands into his short hair before running them over his face.

"I can't stand the thought of his hands on you," he confesses.

His voice, though quiet, holds an ominous quality that makes me comply with his demands.

The moment I'm chest deep in the warm water, my muscles relax and a feeling of relief encompasses me. I sigh, resting back against the tub.

When I slip down, submerging myself completely, the sting on my face reminds me how fucked up it's is going to look.

Saint

My teeth clench as I lock my jaw. In the small entry hallway of my bedroom, I place my palms on the wall and breathe through my nose. After this evening, trying to keep the demon from emerging is just as difficult as the thought of her being out of my sight.

Bringing her to my bedroom wasn't in the plan, but not being there to protect her has done nothing but fuck with my head. It's so overwhelming, even the dark creature feels it. He usually consumes feelings, not experiences them, and now...he wants blood.

Closing my eyes, I inhale one last time, exhale on a whoosh, and push off the wall, exiting my room. On the second floor, I stop at the large abstract painting in the long hallway and touch the bottom of the frame, unlocking the special wall closet with my fingerprint.

Gripping one of my favorite blades, an amputation knife from the 1700's, I continue to the first floor where I find Sketch in the same place as before.

The moment I enter the open area, his eyes move from the screen of his laptop to me, then down to the blade I'm tapping against my leg.

"Find Arman," I demand. "I want him alive."

Understanding flashing in his eyes, he responds with a single nod and focuses back on his screen.

Approaching the long wall of windows, I look out at the night covered city of Chicago, but I don't see a fucking thing. The roar of my blood drowns out the world and the many ways Arman will suffer for touching her play on repeat in my mind. He'll also serve as a lesson to anyone else who thinks they can mess with what belongs to me.

I don't hear my cell, but I feel it vibrate against my chest. Removing the suit jacket, I retrieve the phone before tossing the fabric on the back of a couch and press it to my ear.

"Yes?"

"You can't kill him," Angelo says, no greeting, just orders.

"He's a dead man," I inform, still staring unseeing out the window.

"Arman's uncle would not be happy if—"

"Then he shouldn't have touched what belongs to me," I say, the words raw and harsh in my throat.

He sighs heavily.

"Dante, this will create a problem, and right now, we don't need any further problems," he tries once more. "She's a whore, not a wife."

"Angelo," I say, much calmer than I feel on the inside, "tell his uncle to back down or I'll have to remind him of the favor I did for him with a reenactment on his wife," I threaten, probably revealing too much.

Angelo isn't aware of everything I do, and if he knew the favors owed me or direct relationships I've been building, he would have probably tried to kill me years ago.

"What favor?"

"Just pass that along," I state, hanging up and tossing the phone to the couch.

"He's not going to let that go," Sketch says from behind me, but my rage doesn't allow me to care about my overshare. Turning, I focus my gaze on him.

"You have multiple fucking things to take care of, Sketch," I remind with a sneer. "How about you get me what I've asked for before I acquaint you with the sharp edge of this blade," I say, holding up the knife.

He stands, unmoving, and I can't fight the smile tugging at the corners of my mouth. He knows damn well I'll do it; I've done it before. I also know he fears me, but still, he stands, undeterred. I respect that, hence why he's the closest thing I have to a friend.

The sound of my cell phone ends our standoff. He grabs it off the couch and glances at the screen.

"Answer it," I say, turning back to the window.

"Hello?" Sketch greets. "Yeah, I'll pass it along."

"Can't find him, can they?" I snarl.

"I'll have him by tomorrow," Sketch assures.

"I'm not sure I can wait that long," I admit.

"Is she all right?"

At his question, I turn to face him again. "She's not your concern," I say, the warning in my tone clear.

Hands up in defense, he's quick to retort. "Just want to know if we need the doc to make a visit. That's all."

"No," I clip out, heading for the bar. Snatching up the vodka, I drink straight from the bottle, letting the alcohol burn my throat and suppress the demon until I can unleash on my target.

"Let them know they have twenty-four hours to find the asshole," I growl, slamming the bottle onto the bar. Feeling a presence, I spin, finding Mei standing on the stairs. Her cheek is red and swollen, having reached the corner of her eye, causing it to partially shut.

Regardless of the damage done, her dark wet hair lays in long, wet strands, framing her face, giving her skin a translucent quality and brightening her blue eyes.

Moving my appraising eyes back to the mark she currently wears, I grind my teeth and grip the handle of the amputation knife. Arman will know my creature intimately as it devours his life one cut at a time. And if she would tell me her real name, I'd carve it on his heart before ripping it out with my bare hands.

By the flash of fear in her eyes, I'm sure my look is murderous. But instead of running, she squares her shoulders, and says, "I need ice."

Her appearance is enticing, but, fuck me, if her defiance and challenges aren't motherfucking glorious. My balls tighten, sending a pulse to the tip of my cock.

I watch as she descends the stairs. Her eyes drop to the knife in my hand and she pauses. It doesn't last long, just a couple seconds.

When she makes to pass by me, I reach out and grab her arm. Her head whips in my direction, surprise flushing her face.

Dropping the knife to the floor, I grip the back of her neck and pull her against my chest. With a fist in her hair, I tilt her face to mine and scan the swollen mark as well as the sucker bite on her neck. Tilting her head, I latch my mouth over the mark and suck.

She tenses, knotting her fingers in my white dress shirt. My cock aches, urging me to push her against the wall and fuck her until I've absorbed her into my skin.

Removing my mouth, I examine my bite mark, making sure it erases his. Pleased to find it does, I release her. Her hand comes up, covering the spot.

"Ice is in the freezer," I tell her, turning back to my vodka.

Closing my eyes, I grip the edge of the bar, fighting against the demon's demand to consume her.

chapter twelve

Saint

It doesn't take twenty-four hours. It only takes three for my men to tell me where Arman is hiding. Well...to tell who is hiding him.

"I told you," Sketch snaps, slamming his laptop shut. "You can't trust that asshole!"

Bent at the waist, my palms pressing to the dark wooden dinner table, I stare at the stained grain, satisfaction curling the corners of my mouth.

"He probably had him when he fucking called," Sketch continues, crossing his arms over his chest.

Smile still on my face, I raise my head and watch Sketch's brow draw down, wrinkling the skin above the bridge of his nose.

"What the fuck are you smiling about?"

Straightening, I lift one shoulder, and say, "I know where he is."

"Yeah, fucking Angelo has him hidden away. How the hell do you expect to—?"

My smile grows larger, silencing him mid-sentence.

"The fuck are you up to?"

"Angelo isn't the only one who can play this game," I remind him. "I may not get my hands on him tonight, but..." I stretch my arms out to my sides, drop my head back, and exhale a long breath, letting the creature move beneath my skin. "I'll have my vengeance," I growl, reigning it in before it's too late.

"Vincent?" I call out to the apartment.

"Yes, sir." He appears instantly, and I turn toward his rough, baritone voice.

"We'll be needing the country estate," I inform.

His eyes grow round. Having been with me since he was young, he knows what my parents' abandoned home means. Over the last few years, it's become both my sanctuary and my creature's playground— the alter for redemption and forgiveness I'll never get or deserve.

"You know what needs to be done. And you have one week."

"Yes, sir." He nods before leaving the room.

"The Country Estate," Sketch says, quiet and factual.

"Yes," I confirm, though it wasn't a question.

Sketch has only been brought to the estate once, when he ended up on the other side of my dark creature. It's a place he never wants to be again, and, luckily for him, he's become an asset, so going back hasn't happened.

Now, knowing where and who has Arman, the thrill of returning to the estate and promise of blood have awakened the beast. Keeping him subdued is growing more difficult with his obsessions so close. The certainty of being released, of blood, and the woman upstairs in my room...he's so close to surfacing.

"Saint?" Sketch's question is full of nervous tension.

Closing my eyes, all I see is the lift of her chin. The way her damp hair stuck to her face. The taste of her skin.

"I'll be upstairs," I say through clenched teeth. "You should probably sleep," I toss over my shoulder. "We have a lot to do in the coming days."

"Is everything else on hold then?" His question is accented by the screech of his chair.

"Of course not," I respond, rounding the corner for the stairs.

Stopping on the second floor of the apartment to return my knife to the hidden wall safe, a soft thump comes from the room Mei's been staying. I secure the painting back into place and follow the noise.

Quietly, I enter, finding the room dark out a sliver of light coming from the bathroom. Keeping to the dark corner, I watch her emerge. She's fully dressed, even wearing fucking shoes.

Walking to one of her bags, she crouches down and rummages around.

"Fuck," she growls, slamming her palms on the leather duffle.

"Where do you think you're going?"

Having not noticed me, she jumps up and spins.

"You scared the shit out of me," she grounds out.

"What are you doing?" I ask, stepping out of the corner.

"Getting dressed," she responds immediately, but there's something about the way she says the words. It's too innocent.

Rewording my question, I ask, "Do you think you're going somewhere?"

In the light streaming from the bathroom, I watch her shake her head.

"The shoes," I point out, not missing the way she straightens or the tension in her posture.

"Mei, you don't honestly believe you can walk out of here, do you?" I cross my arms over my chest.

"I'm not—"

"There are codes you don't have and my men are all over this building," I explain, dropping my arms and walking toward her. "They are downstairs, at the front doors, in cars outside the building...I could go on. The only way you get out of this apartment is with my permission or on my arm."

I reach for her chin, but she turns away from my grasp.

"I'm not stupid," she spits out, taking two steps back.

"Really? Then perhaps you'd like to explain where the clutch I gave you went," I prompt.

The flash of surprise on her face and part of her lips gives away so much.

"I'm not stupid either," I tell her, keeping my voice low.

Her mouth snaps shut.

Out of curiosity, I ask, "How far did you think you would get?"

She steps back twice more as I move to sit in the high back armchair.

"I think I forgot it in the bathroom," she finally responds.

"Yes, I'm sure you *forgot* it," I play along with her lie, but only for a moment. "My men were at the door, Mei," I confess. "There isn't a way to escape the choice you made."

"What choice?" she snorts. "I didn't have a choice. Your pissing contest with your cousin wasn't my doing," she argues.

"I didn't strip away your mask that night," I retort, pushing out of the chair.

I advance. She retreats.

"You stripped away the good girl act all on your own," I remind her. "*You* gave me a taste of the real woman behind the façade. That was of your own doing."

Having backed her against the wall, I cage her in with my arms.

"That was all you, my pretty, dirty, little dead girl," I say, bringing my face so close each of her heavy breaths warms my mouth. "I've glimpsed your darkness," I whisper, feeling her body tense, "and it's fucking beautiful."

Unable to fight the need to feel her, taste her, I take her mouth with mine. The moment my tongue touches the seam of her lips, she sucks me inside. Bringing one hand down from the wall, I grab the back of her neck, drawing her closer. And just like every time my mouth is on her, I forget my need for oxygen until my lungs protest.

On a large gasp for air, she turns her head, putting her marked face in my line of sight. Even in the dim light, her darkening swollen skin is obvious. The anger and bloodlust returns.

"He's a dead man," I say on a low growl, feeling her stiffen.

Panting, she asks, "Who are you?"

The question confuses me at first, but she continues.

"When Felix told him I was yours, he...everything changed," she says in whisper. "Everyone in that club feared you, but I know you aren't the leader or whatever you call it."

A quick laugh bubbles up from my chest.

"No, I'm not in charge, but I..." I hesitate, unsure how to explain without scaring her more.

My rank in the family was earned with respect, but also in apprehension of my dark nature. My creature, what earned me the nickname, The Saint, is well known and feared. Mei carries a darkness, but if she knew, saw, my basest nature at work...there's no coming back from that. Even a few of the men in our organization who thought themselves badasses cower in the face of my true self.

"I'm high within the ranks," I finish, deciding she doesn't need to know all my demons—yet.

"The ranks?" Her eyes search for mine.

"It's not important," I state, releasing my hold on her neck and taking a step back. "Take off the shoes," I order, and she hesitates. Watching her battle within herself, wanting to fight me, but knowing she needs to pick her battles, makes my dick throb. Finally, she toes off her running shoes.

"I didn't put them on to escape," she confesses, kicking them to the side. "I prefer to have them on or next to my bed when I sleep."

"Why?" I ask, taking her hand.

Pulling her out of the room, I motion for her to climb the stairs.

"What are we doing?" she asks, looking at the stairs like they're a death sentence.

"Tell me about the shoes," I press.

"Tell me why we're going upstairs," she retorts, glaring at me.

Recapturing her hand, I tug her up the stairs to my bedroom and guide her down the small hallway past the bathroom she used earlier.

"Strip," I order, unbuttoning my shirt and slipping it off.

"Wh-What?" she stutters, watching as I unbuckle my pants and let them fall to the floor.

"Strip," I repeat.

Pulling off my socks and white t-shirt, I approach her.

"I left the ice downstairs," she says, her eyes roaming down my almost naked body.

Reaching around her, I press a button on the wall.

"Yes, sir?" comes through the intercom.

Holding the button down, I say, "Send up an ice pack," and release the button.

Locking my eyes on hers, I grip the bottom of her shirt, pull it over her head, and toss it to the floor before hooking my fingers into the front of her jeans. Our eyes stay on each other's as I undo the closure, lower the zipper, and push them over her hips.

Pressing my barefoot on the denim between her feet, I say, "Step out."

She blinks a couple times, then complies.

I lower my gaze, taking in the woman before me. She stands next to my bed in a tight gray tank top and white panties, and her youth has never been so very evident. I should be ashamed for the horrible ways I want to dirty those little white panties.

The knock on the door brings my eyes to her face and the fresh mark. My wicked desires are replaced with a fierce protectiveness. I straighten my spine, trying to resign myself to this feeling. I'm used to possessiveness and protecting what's mine, but this need to keep her safe, untouched, while at the same wanting to own every part of her, goes deeper than I want to admit.

"Get in bed," I say, aware of the annoyance in my voice. "I'll get the ice."

I turn, not waiting to see if she obeys. Part of me, the sick part that wants to possess her, hopes she doesn't.

Mei

As he walks away, I watch the flex of each muscle, making his dark tattoo look like it's moving. What first looks like feathers, turns out to be wings made of sharp pointed blades.

When he rounds the corner, I plop my ass on the edge of the bed and fist the comforter on each side of my body. Closing my eyes, the night comes back into mind, but in a fast-forward version. The pain in my face and exhaustion of the events crash over me.

I'm in so much trouble, and I don't know how to get out of it. And the most fucked up part of it all: do I really want to escape?

Lifting one hand, I tentatively touch my cheek, and wince.

"Take these." He thrusts his palm out, offering me two large white pills.

"What are they?" I ask on a whisper.

"For the pain," he responds.

Dropping my hand to my lap, I stare at the pills.

"I'm not trying to drug you," he assures.

"That's what they all say," I tease, but my words fall flat.

Crouching down, his eyes find mine. Our gazes lock. Gripping my wrist, he turns my hand and places the medicine in it.

"Take them," he orders, presenting a small glass of water.

I toss the pills in my mouth, release the grip my left hand has on the blanket, take the glass, and chase the medicine down.

Taking the glass from my hand, he stands and places it on the bedside table.

I let my head drop, fist my hands in my lap, and close my eyes.

"Can I go to my room now?" I know the answer, but I have to try.

He's so dangerous and overwhelming. Everything he does strips away another layer of my carefully built illusion, and he does it with practiced ease. He doesn't make promises. No, he makes declarations of protection and safety, but what would he really do? If he knew the fucked-up evil, the rest of my dark tale, would he feel the same?

Long, strong fingers clamp on my trembling chin, lifting my face to his. I open my eyes.

Maybe I should just confess it all. He's already killed me. Why not return the favor and kill his intrigue? There's a very real chance he'll set me free then. Whether it's six feet deep or back on the streets, I'm not sure.

I'm prepared for the no, braced for the no, so my body involuntarily jerks when he responds with, "That's not your room."

His gaze is penetrating, conveying the finality of his words.

He's so right. It's not my room. "My cage?"

The right side of his mouth twitches with amusement.

"Tell me your name."

I roll my eyes, continuing to evade his favorite question. "Dead girl."

The grin slowly grows on his face, while his thumb glides along my bottom lip. A fuzzy sensation tingles across my skin, though I'm not sure whether it's his touch or the pills.

"Sleep," he says, another command.

Warmth crawls across my shoulders and up my neck. Everything from my eyelids to my limbs grows heavy.

I try to ask, "What did you give me?" But it comes out garbled.

I wake with a groan. My face throbs and my head and body ache.

Rolling over, I find myself the sole occupant of Saint's bed, but the soft padding of feet on the thick carpet tell me I'm not alone.

"You're finally awake." His deep, rich voice draws my eyes across the room.

Saint stands at an open closet, slipping into an expensive suit jacket. I push myself up to sit, and wince. My head is really paying the price without the adrenalin coursing through my system.

"Take the pills on the stand," he orders, turning to a floor length mirror to adjust his collar and tie.

"Like I'll fall for that again," I say, but allow my eyes to slide a glance at the pills and water waiting.

"Did you wake or feel any pain last night?" he asks, already knowing I didn't. "These aren't the same."

Moving away from the mirror, he approaches the end of the thick, dark wood footboard. Last night, I'd been too distracted to take in the king-sized sleigh bed or overall largeness of the master bedroom.

His bedroom.

"I have business to take care of this morning, but I'll be back early," he says, coming around the bed.

At my side, he picks up the pills and water and holds them out to me. Shifting my eyes between the pills and his face, then back, I take his offering. Like the night before, once I'm done, he takes the glass. But this time, he leans down, fists to the mattress, and levels a look at me.

"You have free reign of the apartment..." he hesitates, allowing the words to sink in, "but don't attempt to leave. I assure you, it's pointless to try."

Pushing up to his full height, he reaches inside his jacket and tosses a cell phone between my knees.

"If you need me." He nods toward the device and begins to

turn.

I stare at the phone, afraid to touch it.

"It won't bite you," he teases over his shoulder.

"Should I call Joey to let him know I won't be back to work until my indefinite time as your captive has ended?" I ask sarcastically.

At the mouth of the small hallway, he faces me. The smile he wears makes me nervous.

"He's already been made aware you aren't returning," he states before disappearing around the corner.

I'm not surprised by his admission, but I can't help but feel annoyed.

"Motherfucker," I groan, falling back into the pillows.

Rolling onto my side, I close my eyes and wait for the pills to kick in.

Chapter thirteen

Saint

Stepping out of the elevator, I'm greeted by Vince and Russ.

Glancing around the room, it's empty. The television is on, but the sound is turned down. Not a fan of television, I search for the remote to turn it off.

Rounding the couch, I find the remote and Mei. Seeing her wrapped in one of my dress shirts and curled up on the sofa causes a sharp pang in my chest.

Moving close, I trail my fingers from her ankle to where my socks stop just below her knee. Her thighs, on display, beg to be touched. So, I do, palming her knee and running it up her smooth skin. With my other hand, I brush the dark strands of hair from her face.

Everything inside me tightens at the sight of her face. The redness and swelling are significant. Experience tells me the ugly purple and blue color will form soon. My anger seethes at the sight, knowing another man put his mark on her.

"Ow," she cries, her voice filled with sleep.

Her hand comes to the one I have on her thigh.

Realizing I've tightened my grip, I jerk my hand away.

Wary eyes meet mine.

"I apologize." The word feels foreign, like I'm pronouncing it wrong.

Propping up onto her forearms, she crawls backward until she's pressed against the couch cushion.

"Dinner will be here soon," I tell her, unable to stop my eyes from raking over her in my clothing.

She fists the unbuttoned part of the shirt, closing her cleavage from view.

"I'll get dressed." She tries to climb onto the back of the couch and over it.

Grabbing her by the arm, I pull her to me instead. Lifting her wrist, I finger a brown stain.

"This shirt costs three hundred dollars," I tell her just to see her reaction.

She doesn't disappoint. Shock flashes in her eyes before she rebelliously lifts her chin and says, "Well, next time I'll walk around in my underwear."

Slipping an arm around her waist, I haul her into my chest.

"If you walk around in your underwear, I'll bend you over every piece of furniture in this apartment and fuck you in front of my men," I warn.

Her lips thin and nostrils flare. She blinks a couple times before challenging me once more.

"Wouldn't be the first time someone watched us. Now would it?" she says, referring to Felix back at the club.

Bringing my face closer to hers, I growl, "But I didn't kill him afterward."

Mei's lips part on a small gasp, telling me she got my meaning.

Like I'd let them watch us fuck and live to tell about it. Her dirty little dark girl is mine alone.

Seated at the head of the table, I glance over the Chinese take-out containers.

My eyes drift to Sketch, finding him staring at Mei.

"Is there a problem?" Mei throws the question like a punch.

"Who the fuck are you?" he grounds out.

Pushing away from the table, he pulls his gun from behind and aims it at her.

Mei's eyes widen, but not in fear. The flare of her nostrils reveals the dangerous high of her darker side coming to life. She's fucking beautiful.

"I'm sick of this shit," he shouts.

Settling back in my chair, I bring the paper takeout box with me. With a bored tone, I instruct, "Put the gun away." Then I fork low mien noodles into my mouth.

"Fuck you," he yells. "You won't deal with this, so I will!"

Curling one side of my mouth, I drop the container onto the table.

"Holster your fucking gun," I demand.

"Fuck—" My knife landing in his hand changes his tune. "Shit!" The gun lands in a container of rice.

"Fucking hell, Saint," Sketch growls. Yanking the blade from his hand, he drops it next to the gun. He swipes a cloth napkin from the table, wraps it round his hand, and ties it off.

As a professional deliverer of pain, I don't miss how little it registers on his face. Interesting. His tolerance wasn't that high years ago.

"You should probably get that looked at," Mei offers, a taunting grin on her face. "It could get infected," she says in a sickening sweet voice.

Sketch reaches for his gun, his intention clear.

"Enough," I shout, tired of the bickering.

Redirecting the conversation, I turn my gaze on Mei.

"Tell me about the doll," I demand, motioning to Sketch with my hand.

His chair scuffs against the hardwood floors as he stands.

Gripping the arms of her chair, her eyes follow his every movement until he disappears from the room.

"Look at me," I command.

She takes a deep breath and turns back to me, her eyes raging like an angry sea.

"What's the significance of the doll, Mei?"

"I just don't like dolls." She shrugs, then stares out the large window across from her, eyes glazing over. Lost in her own mind, her mask slips a bit more.

"Then why would someone be sending them to you? And why old used dolls?"

Placing my forearms on the table, I shove the containers away and lean forward.

Eyes still on the window, she lifts one shoulder, and says, "You tell me."

Sketch drops a shoebox on the table, and Mei practically jumps out of her chair. The stuffed legs of the rag doll flop over one side while the red yarn on its head sticks up from a different corner.

"I don't believe you," I say, keeping my voice low.

Trying to keep up her charade, she reaches out with one pale, shaking hand. Her fingertips graze the worn checkered dress as Sketch drops a second box.

"Fuck!" she screams. "Quit doing that, asshole!"

Manic grin on his face, Sketch presses his palms to the table and leans down. Instead of speaking, he uses one long thin finger to flip open a new box.

This time, she does climb out of her chair. Hand over her mouth, she stares down at the special delivery.

The doll rests in pink tissue paper, creating a stark contrast between it and the dark curls and ceramic skin.

"Sarah." Her whisper brings me out of my chair. Shaking her head, she backs away from the box like it's going to explode.

"Where?" she rasps.

"Tell me," I demand.

"Where?" her voice raises.

Rounding the table, I growl, "Who's sending the dolls?"

The soft body of the glass doll in my hand, I shove it at her.

Retreating two more steps, she asks, "Where was it?"

"It was sent to the club," I share. "Now, fucking tell me who sent them to you and why you—?"

"A dead man," she shouts. "A fucking dead man sent them!"

She spins, her dark hair swirling around her head, and rushes from the room.

As Sketch moves, I reach out with my free hand and grab his arm. My eyes stay on the archway she fled through as his eyes bore into me. I give a small shake of my head, and he stills.

The sound of her feet against the stairs is followed by the slam of a door.

"Did you find anything?" I ask, examining the doll in my hand again.

The light pink silk of the dress is faded in spots and frayed in others. A single half inch crack stretches from its hairline toward the tiny nose. One bright blue eye is scuffed, while the other tells of a better time.

"Person said they were a courier service, but none of the ones in town had a delivery to the club," Sketch answers. "They brought it to the rear delivery door. The camera there sucks and the person had a ball cap on, but I'm still trying to get something from it."

"Male or Female?" I ask, dropping the doll back into the box.

"Male. *I think.*"

"You think?" I growl, annoyed with the lack of fucking answers where she is concerned.

"The security camera is shit," he defends. "And it's all I have to work with for fucks sake."

She almost had me believing it's the dolls she's afraid of, but it's not fear I see flash in her round eyes. It's absolute terror. The feeling so deep, she looks ready to snap, to fall into madness.

"Get me something," I demand.

"How about I get you one of your favorite toys and you go carve the goddamn information out of her like you normally do," he growls, throwing himself into the chair near his laptop.

Snapping my head in his direction, I clench my jaw and wait for him to backpedal, but he doesn't.

"What the fuck, Saint? If you won't put a fucking knife to her throat, then maybe I should place a gun to it. I bet we'd get all the fucking answers then."

Narrowing my eyes on him, I lower my voice. "Maurizio, if you touch her, I'll kill you."

I don't miss the way he cringes at his real name, but it's quickly replaced with emotions ranging from defiance to anger. Out the corner of my eye, I catch the way his hand twitches, surely tempted to pull the gun on me right now.

Sketch doesn't say anything else as I finish my drink, grab the doll, and walk from the room. He doesn't quite get that my little dead girl is twisted and dark on the inside.

Just. Like. Me.

Knowing she didn't go to my room, I enter the second floor bedroom and find her in front of an open window, head drooped and hands pressed to the ledge. She lifts her head, but doesn't turn to look at me.

"Tell me about the dolls," I demand, tossing the item she fears at her feet.

"Tell me about the other girls," she retorts, her words harsher than expected.

When I don't respond, she pushes up from the ledge and faces me.

"Not so eager to talk now, are you?" She crosses her arms over her chest.

"What other—?"

"Don't," she exclaims, "pretend you don't know," her voice drops.

Lifting one brow, I can't help but smirk. Her glare is like a reward for the inner demon. He wants her to fight us, to resist.

"They aren't your concern," I continue to evade, hoping to rouse her dark side out to play.

"At least you aren't denying it," she mumbles.

Dropping her arms, she turns back to the window.

Her lack of challenge, tampering of her emotions, sends red hot rage through my limbs.

Taking four long strides, I press my chest to her back. Her body tenses, but she doesn't pull away. Bringing my arms up, I reach around her and grip the bottom frame of the window.

Mouth to her ear, I request again, "Who sends the dolls?"

"Why should I tell a strange psychopath any—"

I slam the window shut, cutting her off and making her jump. Still, she doesn't pull away from me.

"Anything?" she finishes.

Fisting the hair at the back of her head, I jerk it to the side.

"Because you're less afraid of this strange psychopath than the one sending the dolls," I rasp into her ear before running my nose down the side of her neck.

The scent of dark vanilla assaults my senses. I close my eyes, savoring it, and wrap my arms around her body.

Arms pinned to her sides, she struggles against me, and my

cock hardens further. "If you tell me their name they'll no longer be a problem for you."

"You going to save me, Saint?" she snorts, still struggling.

"No." She stills at my confession.

"You have it all wrong," I say, turning her in my arms.

I flex my fingers into the hinges of her jaw, and her head lifts to mine, eyes wild with anticipation and fear. With my other hand, I withdraw a card from my back pocket and hold it up.

Her eyes move to the notecard and widen.

Soon...

Lashing out, she grips my wrist with both hands, the rough calloused pads of her fingers digging into my flesh. A squeeze of my hand stills her attempts.

"Please," she begs in a whisper, and I bring my face inches from hers.

"He wants what's mine, and that won't be fucking happening," I growl.

"I'm not yours," she argues. "And I don't need you to save me," she retorts.

One side of my mouth curls. "I'm not saving you. I've condemned you."

Her nostrils flare and the muscles in her jaw tense beneath my fingers.

"Get ready for bed," I instruct before crushing my mouth to hers in a quick, hard kiss. Pulling back, I release her face. Chin raised and her eyes not leaving my face, she walks to where her bags used to be.

"Where are my things?" she asks, looking down at the empty spot.

"Upstairs." At my admission, she spins around, unspoken questions in her eyes. "I told you last night this isn't your room."

"I'll sleep in this," she says like it's a threat, standing immobile as I approach her. When I pull my knife out from behind my back, her body gives a slight jerk, but she doesn't move.

Taking the material at her shoulder in my fist, her hands clasp my forearm, and I spin her around, breaking her hold on me and making her curse.

I lift the blade and press the tip into the back of the shirt and slice through it. The action stops her fight. Three cuts of the expensive fabric later, the shirt is practically shredded.

Twirling the knife in my hand, I release her and head for the door.

Before I exit, I instruct once more, "Get ready for bed."

Instead of heading upstairs, I return to the first floor. Sketch's eyes find me the moment I enter the room and he pushes away from his laptop.

"Get anything?" I don't miss the bite of annoyance in his voice.

Using the tip of the knife still in my hand, I tap on the screen of a cell phone currently wired to his laptop.

"It's basically a burner phone," he says on an agitated sigh. "No contract to tie her to anything. Just an account to re-up with more data and minutes." He motions to the screen with a wave of his hand.

Coming to stand behind him, I look down at the screen.

"She's not a professional, but she isn't a fucking amateur either," he warns.

"Explain," I order.

"If the feds were involved, she'd be buried deeper and behind false identities and accounts."

"But..."

"She keeps herself off the grid really well. Like she's been doing this for a fucking lifetime." He rubs a hand over his face.

"So, you still have nothing," I grumble.

"There's one thing that doesn't fit, but..."

"Sketch," I warn, my patience growing thin.

"There's a Google alert she received about a Kayla Mearson. The alert is out of character for someone who tries not to have any attachments," he says, pausing to tap on the keys in front of him.

A picture of a young girl comes up on the screen with the word MISSING printed above her.

"It's clearly not doll Face."

I tense, hating how my insides twist with his familiarity of her.

"Don't get attached, Sketch," I growl, clamping my hand on his shoulder.

"Fuck," Sketch complains, leaning away from my hand. "I get it, Saint. She's yours."

His hand replaces mine once I release him.

"Christ," he snaps, rolling his shoulder. "You realize you're acting like an obsessed asshole, right? Not to mention I don't want any part of the kind of crazy you're harboring in your bed."

Reclaiming my seat at the head of the table, I meet his eyes.

"You know what I am," is my response.

"I'm not sure I do anymore," he clips.

Gripping the handle of my knife, I flip it above my head and catch it by the blade before flicking my wrist. The knife stabs into the wood table an inch from his wrist.

"Christ," he exclaims, jerking his arm from the table.

"Consider yourself reminded."

"Here," he clips, tossing a folder.

The manila file lands on the table and slides across the smooth surface until it's within arm's reach of me.

Placing my palm on the folder, I keep my eyes fixated to it, and ask, "Is it confirmed?"

"It's all there." I don't miss the edgy cadence of his words.

Before I can pull it to me, Sketch's hand lands over mine. Our eyes meet.

"You need to know," he pauses, furrowing his brow and licking his lips.

Narrowing my eyes, I pull the folder and my hand out from under his. This level of nervousness isn't like him.

"What?" I bark out.

"There's more than..." he visibly swallows, "there's just more and it's going to change everything."

Flipping through the pages is like digging up every dead body Angelo buried. The skeletons pile up until I'm submerged. Everything I already know and those I suspected are confirmed. Staring down at the undeniable proof of Angelo's twisted games, I thought I knew his greatest. That he is, in fact, the catalyst in killing his own son in his quest for power.

"This is everything we..." I turn to the final section of the file, and the rhythm of Sketch's pacing becomes the soundtrack to a revelation I never saw coming. "This doesn't—" the final page, the one with genetic proof, is enough to cut off my protest.

Curling the right side of my mouth, disgust, anger, and venom stir my dark side. The demon wants flesh and bone beneath our hands—another soul to add to our collection.

Since I was a boy, his word was law. My father preached and beat it into me on a regular basis. Do not question. Do not hesitate. Do not show fear.

"Dante, please don't—"

Her cries are cut off by the back of his hand and she crumbles to the ground.

The urge to protect her tenses my muscles, but I school my features.

"She's a traitor," he shouts. "And a whore."

The words slice me open. Anger starts to burn in the pit of my stomach. But his word is law and must be obeyed.

"Still making up your own truths I see," she shouts, spitting blood at his feet.

He fists her by the hair and pulls her up on her knees, bowing his head until their faces are only inches apart.

Words are exchanged, too quiet for me to hear, but the defiance melts from her face, replaced with terror.

"No," she gasps, tears pouring over her blood-smeared cheeks.

"Yes, Theresa," he hisses, tossing her to the floor. "She's just another whore."

Grunts of protest draw my attention from the sobbing woman on the floor.

"Dad," Felix shouts from the other side of Angelo before moving toward the bound and gagged form of Uncle Dino.

"Stop him." Angelo's orders are always obeyed.

Reaching out, I grab Felix's arm, and eyes flashing with confusion and anger meet mine.

"Control yourself!" Angelo's demand falls on Felix's deaf ears.

He pulls from my grip, only to be subdued by two other men.

"Let go of me," he shouts, struggling against their hold.

A loud grunt draws my attention once more.

The look in my uncle's eyes is clear. He's silently warning my cousin about his outburst.

Felix quiets, but the men don't release him.

"Welcome, brother," Angelo greets.

He tries to step forward, but his shoe meets my mother's leg.

Every muscle bunches and my chest feels like it's going to explode. Crossing my arms over my chest, I try to hold myself together and in place. Every moment with my mother flashes to mind.

Her singing me to sleep.

Her telling me stories.

The way she overfeeds me when I visit the house.

The sad look in her eyes when I walk out the door.

Fighting back the urge to collect her in my arms and protect her becomes physically painful. A pit forms in my stomach, like a churning of needles and glass.

Spreading my legs farther, I plant my feet. To go to her is weakness. She's a traitor to our family, and disloyalty comes with a high cost. It's one we all know.

With his expensive Italian shoe, he kicks her leg, causing her to whimper.

"Max," Angelo calls over his shoulder, "prepare the whore."

Turning my head at the muffled shout from my uncle, I watch him struggle against the men holding him.

"Don't worry, you too will get what traitors deserve, brother," Angelo says, the final word drawn out in disgust.

"Dante, please," my mother cries softly.

When I don't look at her, sharp tips of my pain pierce my soul.

"Please, look at me," she begs.

"Shut up," Max growls, and I don't have to look to know there's a gun to her head.

"It's not your fault," she rebels against the order.

"Bitch, what did I say?" The crack of bone slices through the room, followed by her cry of pain.

"Stop trying to help her," Angelo says.

For a moment, I'm sure he's talking to me, but then it becomes clear the words are meant for my uncle.

"You've helped her quite enough, haven't you?"

Uncle Dino's eyes narrow in defiance.

"Where's the other traitor?" Angelo asks, make me start.

Another? The question swirls around my head.

It's a muffled response, but Uncle Don's face makes his intended "Fuck you," evident.

Angelo's laugh is humorless and sadistic.

His hand comes up expectantly. A switchblade is placed in his palm, and within seconds, the blade pierces my uncle's thigh.

Felix tenses, taking a step forward, but he doesn't get any farther.

"Dante," my mother rasps, her words broken by gasps for breath, "you are not like them."

Looking down at her kneeling form, Max's hand in her hair keeping her upright, our eyes meet.

In them, I find love, forgiveness, and understanding, and it confuses me. She knows what's coming for her.

Her lips part in a bloody smile.

Surprise unfurrows my brows.

"Get them in place," Angelo orders, and like the well-trained soldier I am, my attention moves to him.

Uncle Dino is pushed to his knees next to my mother, the pain in his carved up thigh making him bow forward onto his hands. My mother is forced to all fours when Max shoves between her shoulder blades.

"Dante, Felix, come," Angelo beckons us to his side.

"I forgive you." My mother's words earn her a booted kick in the side.

"Damn it, Angelo," Uncle Dino curses, placing an arm protectively around her.

In a flash of rage, Angelo stabs Dino in the shoulder, over and over, until he falls away from my mother.

"Don't touch the whore," Angelo warns, a new edge to his voice I'm not familiar with.

Straightening to his full height, he regains his composure before addressing us.

"The time has come for you two to prove your loyalty, devotion, and make your oath of blood," he announces reverently, and everything becomes clear. I know what he wants us to do and the reason for her words of forgiveness.

"You bastard," Dino exclaims, and another grunt of pain follows.

Guns are thrust toward Felix and I, and Angelo motions with his head for us to take them.

Taking the gun, I hold it at my side.

Felix reaches out, his shaking hand hovers over the weapon.

"Take it," Angelo urges. "Prove your loyalty."

I can feel the tension growing as Felix hesitates.

The dark pain blossoms along with my full understanding of this situation.

Felix is more of a brother than a cousin and his suffering is only feeding the pain growing inside me. It's like nails being hammered in my gut.

Tightening my hold on the handle of my gun, I step forward, lift the barrel to my mother's forehead. The action takes Angelo's focus off Felix.

My eyes lock with hers, love and forgiveness still shining from their depths before they close.

"Open them," I demand, making her blink in surprise.

Her head jerks back with the force of the bullet before her lifeless body crumbles to the floor.

"Now, Felix—" Angelo begins.

Before he can finish, I sidestep, aim and pull the trigger a second time.

Uncle Dino collapses into the puddle of blood soaking into the cement.

Tossing the gun on their bodies, I step back to my previous position.

The room is quiet, but inside, I'm sliced open and raw.

"Well, that didn't go exactly as planned," Angelo jokes, getting uncomfortable laughs from the rest of the men.

The same men who stare at the emotionless and deadly fifteen-year-old boy who killed his own mother and beloved uncle without a second thought. The one who walked out of that room like nothing had happened, although it had unleashed the darkest side of him. One that would grow into a stronger, darker, needier, and vengeful creature.

So much had led up to the moment I stood before my mother and shot her executioner style. And while most thought I'd forced her to open her eyes because I was a sick fuck, the truth was, I needed to see the love and forgiveness for what I was about to do. Even believing she and my uncle had both betrayed our family, I still needed that from her.

And now, with the information Sketch just gave to me, I am

back in that room with them.

The woman I called mother had supposedly been trading secrets and information to Leonid Vasechkin. At the time, Leo was head of the Russian Mob and this information is what I believed was the reason Angelo's son, AJ, was killed.

As Angelo's word was law, I didn't dare ask for proof. Now, my suspicions of being used to cover up his actions are confirmed. I just didn't realize the depth of his deceit and part he played in the death of my beloved cousin.

I retrieve my cell from the table.

"You're still going through with this? Knowing what this all means and what it will begin?" Sketch asks.

Scrolling to my cousin's number, I tap the screen and prepare to set my plan in motion.

"Do you know what time it is?" Felix growls.

"Yet, you answer," I tease.

Not amused, he barks, "What the fuck do you want?"

"I need to request an audience with you," I inform.

"And this couldn't be done at a more reasonable hour?" he snaps.

I allow him his anger. Only because what I have to talk with him about will not only flip his world upside down, but also our family. Felix will soon learn the truth of the organization we've dedicated our lives to, that we took a blood oath to serve and sacrifice for a greedy, selfish bastard.

"Tomorrow," I say, ignoring his question. "On sacred ground. Noon."

At the mention of where I want to meet, he goes silent. Understanding this conversation has everything to do with our previous discussion, and could leave one, or all of us, dead.

"Done," he says, ending the call.

Placing my phone back on the table, I lean forward, forearms to the table.

The grain of the dark wood table blurs. My thoughts race with the words I'll share with Felix. Words that could unite us or tear us apart. The latter will possibly sign my death certificate, but Angelo has gone too far. His twisted manipulations have finally caught up to him.

Chapter fourteen

Mei

Jerking awake from another nightmare, a sadistic reminder of my past, a heavy darkness and the weight of a large body settles over me.

Panic pushes my flight instinct into action. I bring my hand up, preparing to use the heel of my hand to smash this person's nose. Before I can make contact, my wrist is caught in a giant hand. Not wasting any time fighting to get free, I wrap my legs around his thighs and buck beneath him, rolling us from the bed.

"Christ," he growls, releasing my wrist.

His arms come around me in a protective cocoon while the thud of his body makes the nightstand rattle and knocks the air from his lungs. Palms planted on his face, I shove hard. For a moment, I'm free of his hold, only for him to grab my forearms.

"Christ," he exclaims. "Calm the fuck down."

The recognition of his voice, his smell, and my surroundings, stop my defensive maneuvers.

Shit! I'd been tempted to disobey and stay in the blue bedroom, but it took only one look at that doll, lying twisted in an unnatural way on the floor, to send me up to his room.

In a swift move, Saint sits up, pressing me to his chest. One hand finds my ass and the other the back of my neck, holding me in place.

"What the fuck was that?" His question rumbles against my chest.

"I didn't..." I pause, remembering the nightmare he dragged me out of. As the adrenaline subsides, my muscles begin to twitch and my emotions rise to the surface.

"Mei?" he asks, giving a squeeze to my neck.

"I didn't know it was you," I answer quickly.

"Who the hell did you think it would be?"

"No one," I say, not wanting to confess a damn thing about the twisted shit my subconscious and memory show me at night.

"Up," he orders, releasing my body. I scramble away and stand at the foot of the bed. Rising from the floor, his eyes rake over me.

"All that's missing are the shoes," he notes my choice of bed clothes.

I cross my arms over my chest, suddenly feeling more exposed than when I strip on stage.

He takes a step toward me. I take a step back. The cold look in his eyes and set of his jaw stops my retreat.

Sitting at the foot of the bed, he snares my waist with a muscular arm and repositions me between his knees. His face lifts, and our eyes lock. There's a brief moment of vulnerability, and it scares the shit out of me. This is Saint, *The Saint*, cold, dark, and deadly. I feel like he's showing me something, intentional or not, I shouldn't be seeing.

I open my mouth. To say what, I don't know, but he blinks and the moment is gone.

At my hips, he fists my sweatpants and underwear, then yanks the material down my legs until it pools around my ankles. His calloused hands run up my thighs and over my bare ass, then dig in, pulling me against him and forcing me to straddle his lap.

Gripping the hem of my tank top, he tears it over my head, then reclaims my ass and neck with his hands. Eyes locked on mine, he asks in a low, rough voice, "Tell me who haunts you?"

"Tell me what happened to the other women," I counter in a hushed tone.

"Why do they interest you so much?"

Swallowing down my nerves, I confess, "I'd like to know my fate."

Sliding his hand from behind my neck to my jaw, his eyes drop to my lips as he brushes his thumb over my mouth.

"You aren't like them," he admits, shoving two fingers into my mouth.

I roll my tongue around the digits and suck as he removes them.

The thrill I feel at his words isn't normal or sane. Regardless, a need so powerful and consuming takes over. Wrapping my arms around his shoulders, I grind down against the hard ridge of his cock. The friction is glorious, pushing me closer and closer to the precipice of release.

"No," I whine, so close yet denied.

The hand on my ass lifts, keeping my pussy from what it wants most.

Slipping my arms under his, I curl them up, trying to force myself down on his clothing-covered cock. I'm so close. I just need—

"I want to feel you come around me," he growls.

Wrapping his arm beneath my leg, he inserts two wet fingers inside me from behind.

"Oh God," I cry out. The relief is exquisite.

Tossing my head back, I fuck the fingers of his right hand.

His mouth latches to my throat, sucking, licking, biting, adding to the sensations sizzling across my skin.

"You're so wet," he rasps against my skin. "My hand is soaked."

The words inch me closer to bliss.

I just need...I need...

His left hand tightens on my ass, spreading me open. Then he slips a third finger through my wetness and into my ass. At the invasion, I tense.

"Take it, Mei," he orders, pumping his fingers into my pussy and ass in a delicious and dirty rhythm. "That's it," he praises when I start meeting each thrust of his hand. "You belong to me, dead girl," he states. "They can't have you."

The gravity of this moment is lost in my overwhelming need to come.

"Say it," he demands, squeezing my ass cheek enough for the pain to ebb my pleasure.

"Fuck," I cry, dropping my head to his shoulder. I was so close, and the ache just grows stronger.

Saint's hand begins a painfully slow assault on both holes, and the moment he knows I'm close, I get a painful squeeze on the ass.

"You belong to me," he repeats, increasing the thrusts.

Opening my mouth, I bite down on his shoulder, the fabric of his shirt dry on my tongue.

"Say it," he demands, slowing once more.

I nod against him, trying to fuck his hand faster.

"That won't do," he reprimands, removing his fingers.

My guttural cry is the only way I can express the pain. Two wet fingers enter my ass, and I gasp. My pussy clenches in anticipation, but it doesn't come. Each contraction seeking fulfillment, relief, sets my clit pulsing like a ticking time bomb.

Crying out in frustration, I press my body against his stomach seeking any type of friction I can get—anything to set off the orgasm lingering and burning me from the inside out.

A third wet finger joins in the probing of my ass, stretching and filling. It's not enough to set off my release, but it's enough to torture me.

Releasing his shirt from my mouth, I turn my head, and beg, "Please."

"Say the words, dead girl," he coaxes, "Tell me who you belong to."

"Okay," I gasp against his neck, sliding my body against his like a cat in heat.

"That won't do, my dirty little girl," he admonishes, using another finger to tease my soaked slit before taking it away.

"Please," I beg on a strangled cry.

My hands find their way over his stomach. Just one touch of my finger and my body will have what it seeks, but he figures me out too soon.

One moment, I'm straddling my captor, begging for him to fill me in every way. The next, I'm on my back, hands pinned above my head, empty without his fingers. His body looms above me as I wiggle my ass like a mindless, sex-starved whore.

His free hand moves between my thighs, but no matter how I squirm or thrust, I cannot reach him.

When his hand comes to my throat, a thumb presses my chin up.

"Who do you belong to?" The edge to his voice gives away how close he is to losing control.

"Fuck me," I demand, hoping the dirty words will push him over the edge. His hands flex, but he doesn't concede.

"Those aren't the words I want to hear and you know it," he growls, and I bite my lip, keeping myself from making the declaration that will seal my fate. But my lips part on a gasp the moment his dick slides inside me.

"Yes," I exclaim, trying to move against him.

Using his lower body to hold me still, I'm only allowed to feel the fullness of him filling me.

"Goddamn it," I cry in frustration, struggling against his hold.

"Tell me what you already know is true." The hot words fan over my nipple, then he licks the hard tip. I feel it all the way to my clit and the walls of my sex tighten.

"Fuck, Mei, say it."

I clench around him again, earning a groan. Pulling back, he gives a demanding thrust, and every part of me immediately focuses on only one thing: the need for him to fuck me, hard, rough, and punishing.

I can feel every inch of him, smell the mixture of lust, need, and sex. The sound of my blood rushing through my body is all I can hear. This man is the key to my demise, and I've never wanted anyone to possess me more than I want him.

"Christ, you're dangerous," he growls, giving one more punishing thrust before withdrawing.

Closing my eyes, I drop my head back to the mattress and fight a sob. The loss of him is the last thing my body can take, and it overrides all rational thoughts or concerns.

"I'm yours," I cry out, raising my hips to him. "I belong to you."

Thinking my admission, my oath, would earn me immediate satisfaction and release, I'm surprised when my wrists are freed and the heat of his body disappears.

Opening my eyes, I look up and find Saint staring down. His

shirt hangs open, allowing me to see the dark ink on his defined chest. Moving my eyes lower, I find his pants barely clinging to his hips and the tip of his hard cock exposed. I can't tear my eyes away from the glistening tip, knowing it's my wetness.

Then, the feeling in the room changes. The dark gleam I saw in his eyes the night of Vicky's death was nothing compared to what's blazing in them now. The air around us grows thick, and I can't catch my breath. His lips curl at the edges in a sinister smile, the intensity sending a chill along my spine. Instinctively, I crawl backward to get away from the creature standing over me.

Before I get too far, his hand clamps around my ankle. I try to use my other foot to free myself from his hold, but he grabs that one too. With a hard tug, I'm yanked across the bed. He releases my ankles and grips my thighs. Shoving them open, he moves between them.

"You belong to me." His words are raw, and not to be argued.

He presses my legs as far as they will go.

"Your body only receives mine."

His cock slides inside me.

"Yes," I agree on a heavy sigh.

"I'm yours," he says, but there's an unexpected question in his words, and I don't know how to respond.

This isn't some romance, of that I'm sure. The only feelings involved here are fear, lust, and something like Stockholm. I've chosen the gilded cage and become his possession, until he tires of his new toy.

In a Saint move, my jaw is seized in his large hand, and he squeezes until my eyes meet his.

"I'm yours," he presses.

"Yes," I whisper, giving him the answer he desires.

Surprising me, it sends a wave of satisfaction through me.

Releasing my chin, he trails his hand down my neck, over my collarbone, between my breasts, and over my stomach. When he reaches the cleft between my legs, he pulls out, dips his fingers inside, and collects my wetness before rubbing them against the entrance of my ass. Swirling, coating, entering, he prepares me.

Now prepped and ready, he enters in a slow, deliberate act of ownership.

Once fully seated inside, his large hands grip the back of my thighs and he rocks in and out. My inner thighs tense and my pussy clenches, seeking anything to fill it.

Finally, two fingers slip deep inside, providing the sought after relief. He finger-fucks me to the point I'm so wet, it drips down to coat his cock between each thrust. The double assault sends my already sensitive body into a frenzy, feeding my need to come.

Unable to take any more of the teasing, I reach down between our legs. His fingers entwine with mine and use both our hands to bring my orgasm crashing over me, consuming me like a hurricane.

"Feel how you come for me," he boasts, thrusting harder into my ass.

My body jerks and spasms in the most delightful way until I melt into the mattress.

Not finished with me, he grunts with force he fucks me. His fingers, covered in my orgasm, slip against my skin, but he doesn't relent. Not until his back stiffens on an animalistic groan.

He collapses over me, catching his weight on his forearms in the bed. His damp forehead presses between my breasts, each pant of his breath warming my skin.

"You're mine," he reminds, nipping the side of my breast.

Too exhausted to argue or even comply, I say nothing. Instead, I close my eyes and try to catch my breath.

Saint slips free of my body, taking the weight of his body with him. I gasp from the sudden loss and the ache, my muscles contracting at the emptiness. I don't have to open my eyes to feel his body cage me in. His knees pressed into the mattress next to my thighs. His fists planted on each side of my head. The warmth of his body reaches my skin before his tongue presses to my breastbone. Sliding up my body, he leaves a wet trail to my ear.

"Tell me who torments you," he whispers.

I snap my eyes open and stare over his shoulder. Shadows darken the ceiling, and the longer I focus on them, the more they grow and close in around me. Just like my past and present, everything swallows me. Exhaustion and anger swirl up from deep inside.

Tired of being out of control, pissed off at his relentless questions, and hating myself for wanting to hand everything over on a blood-covered silver tray, my emotions bubble over.

"Who torments me?" I retort on a laugh, and he lifts his head and grips my face, forcing me to meet his eyes.

"The person who looks back at me in the mirror," I admit through clenched teeth.

Wrapping my fingers around his wrist, I try to remove his hold on me, and just like all the times before, he doesn't release me. Instead, he brings his face an inch from mine.

"I'm growing tired of this game," he growls. "I've killed men for less." His fingers tighten, and the bite of pain brings my other hand into the effort to remove his grip.

Ignoring my attempts, Saint continues. "And they didn't belong to me, Mei."

With a flick of his wrist, he releases my face, causing my head to jerk to the left. It's not enough to hurt, but enough to make his irritation clear.

I close my eyes, fighting back the urge to tell him everything. I want to throw every dirty detail of my deranged and dangerously insane past in his lap just to watch him recoil.

Saint may be a dark, bloodthirsty killer, but not even *The Saint* could shrug off the damaged goods spread out beneath him. Killing Winter was one of my greatest sins, but it's not what stained my soul. No, the blackness was born unto me, nurtured and praised by the sickest kind of evil.

I clench my eyes shut tight, trying to fight the memories from emerging and fail.

"Isn't she lovely?" he coos, running a hand over the glass.

Instead of responding, I approach the large water-filled case. Reaching out, I run my finger over the condensation.

"It's cold," I state, a question in my young voice.

Running his hand over my dark curls, he says, "Mermaids can only survive in colder water, doll."

She looks so much like the mermaid toy I have for the bath. The white shells of her top sparkle and her tail is almost the same shimmering green. Her blue hair flows through the water as she swims, but the movements aren't smooth and graceful like the stories Daddy reads. No, she jerks, shoves at the glass, and pulls at the shell on her face.

"She doesn't swim very well," I note, looking up to him.

"Mermaids are used to the open ocean, my doll." His hand runs over my head. "She just needs to get used to her new home."

Focusing back on the mermaid, I grow curious. "Why does she have a shell in her mouth?"

"We don't have ocean water. The shell is magic, helping her with our water."

"Can she go in the bathtub with me?" I ask excitedly.

"I'm afraid she's much too large to fit in your tub with you," he explains. "But perhaps you can swim together one day."

For days, I spent as much time as possible watching the mystically beautiful creature. She would often press her hands on the glass, and I would place mine in the same spot.

Her movements were often jerky and erratic. Adjusting to her new surroundings, Daddy said. Until one afternoon, she didn't place her hands on the glass, didn't swim, and didn't open her eyes. Bored, I left her to sleep.

The next day, the tank was empty, and I cried. Like a spoiled child having its toy taken away, I cried.

Until Daddy brought me the marionette.

Yes, the urge to offer it all up to him is tempting. It would ensure my freedom. The moment he learns exactly who and what I am, I will be released from his penthouse prison and back to the streets or freed from my life altogether. But now there are two dolls. One where I lived, and the other where I worked, meaning he's found me. And that right there keeps my lips from parting with my confession. I'd rather die than fall back into the nightmare of my past.

So many doctors, so much therapy, and still, the peace I find in those terrors is what feels like home.

Saint pushes away from me and off the bed, instantly chilling my body. Fighting against the threatening shiver, I prop up on my forearms and meet his hard gaze.

"With or without you, I'll find them. And when I do, I will have all your secrets."

Grabbing the blanket beneath me, I wrap it around my body and move to kneel on the bed before him.

"I look forward to the day you have them all," I hiss. "Just so I can watch each one of them unravel everything you *think* you own."

In a flash of movement, he grips the back of my neck, pulling me to him. His right hand comes up, splaying against the side of my face.

"Make no mistake, *doll,* you belong to me."

Raising my chin, I glare into his eyes.

His thumb rubs over my tightened lips as he whispers, "You should know by now, I enjoy your resistance, the fight. It makes taking you so much more gratifying."

"Let go of me," I growl, hating the way his words relight my lust.

Smirking, he flexes his hands, letting me feel the possessive hold he has on me before releasing me and wrapping his arms around my waist. Hoisting me up his body, he brings my face so close, our noses touch.

"You should be thankful for my interest," he grounds out. "It's the only reason you get to keep breathing."

"And when you lose interest?" I ask, not liking the way my stomach knots in worry. I can't be sure whether the anxiety is from the thought of losing my life or losing Saint.

"Tell me what I want to know and we'll find out," he responds, dropping me on the bed.

His hands make quick work of divesting his clothes. Knees in the bed, he plants his fists in the mattress, the weight of his cock hanging between his thighs.

"Why make it so easy for you?" I ask, scooting up the bed until my back presses against the headboard.

Tilting his head, he scans my body before crawling on hands and knees toward me.

Drawing my legs to my chest, I wrap my arms around my knees, close my eyes, and wait for his touch.

I can feel him close, within reaching distance, but instead of grabbing me like I thought, the bed dips next to me.

Peeking out of one eye, I find him stretched out, one muscular arm bent over his face.

Uncoiling, I slide to the edge of the bed and scream when my wrist is caught.

"Don't do anything stupid," he warns.

Pulling at my arm, I snap, "I'm going to the bathroom to clean up your mess."

Lifting his arm from his face, he turns his head.

"My mess?" he asks, the twitch of his lip giving a hint to amusement.

Ignoring the question, I yank at his hold and he jerks me to the side, then pulls me on top of him, running his hands down my back and over my ass until his fingers curl into the flesh at the back of my thighs. Pulling my legs apart, he positions one at each of his hips so I straddle his waist.

I push against his chest to sit up, but a hand between my shoulder blades stops me, holding me in place. When he's sure I won't move, the hand moves into the back of my hair and fists, bringing my face closer to his.

"I like my mess on you," he admits, his hands moving up to my ass and caressing one globe before dipping a finger between my spread cheeks and slipping around the sore hole.

My mind attempts to dredge up the memory of the first man to take me there, but his rough admission pulls me from the dark thoughts.

"I like my mess in you."

Saint presses his hips up from the bed, teasing the sensitive skin between my ass and pussy with the tip of his cock.

"The way your body opens to me." He rolls his hips, and I can't stop my own from seeking out the friction he promises.

"Even now, tired, angry, and afraid, you want me."

The more he speaks, the more strain I hear in his words.

"I'm not afraid of you," I lie.

Twisting my head by my hair, he places his lips close to my ear.

"Good, because remember, doll, I'm yours." The warmth of his breath against my skin causes my nipples to tighten and my clit to throb.

Keeping us chest to chest, he maneuvers us so his back is against the headboard. My pussy slips over his hard length, the tip pressing to my clit.

One hand on my hip and the other back in my hair, he commands, "Take what you want, doll."

"What are you?" I whisper.

It makes no sense the way the fight leaves me and I surrender to his demands.

Lifting his hips, he slips between my wet lips, and I gasp, but don't move, fighting the desire to let him climb inside and own me, though I know it's a losing battle. The heat of his body, smell of his skin, the feel of him beneath mine, and the surrender he's laying out before me...it's all too tempting. It's something I want to possess.

The Saint, the dark killer, is submitting to me.

Nostrils flaring, eyes wild with frustration, he jerks against me.

"Fuck, Mei, take it!" he demands, accentuated by the collaring my throat and putting a foot of space between our chests.

The act should frighten me, but, like all the times before, it sends my libido into overdrive. With one hand, I grip the thick arm holding me and jerk my hips against him.

"That's it," he growls in approval.

It's a praise I never would've thought I wanted, but I do. Oh, I want it so much, my body burns, leaving the wet evidence between my legs and along the ridge of his hard cock.

Using my other hand to position him against my entrance, I drop down, taking him inside me. Every nerve ending explodes and my dark desires blossom into a craving, a need only he can appease. I'm unraveling with no chance of holding it together any longer.

"Take what's yours," he urges, relaxing the hand at my neck and sliding it down my chest.

Moving over him, faster, harder, our eyes lock.

The dark gleam is there, reveling in my depraved descent.

"There it is," he growls.

The sound of skin slapping, heavy breathing, and the smell of sex fill the air around us.

Gripping the back of his neck with one hand and pressing the other to the front of his shoulder, I close the space between us. Rising above him, I press my breast against his mouth.

Without hesitation, he opens, sucking the hard tip between his lips. When his hands come to my hips, I move them to cup my breasts and grind down on his cock. On a groan, he moves to my other nipple, then wraps my arms around his neck and head. Holding his face to my chest, I fuck him fast and hard. My thighs burn to the point of pain, but the ache in my clit and maddening anticipation of orgasmic escape are too powerful. And the force of what's to come emboldens me.

Wanting him to watch me fuck him, I release his head and collar his throat with my hand while my hips never cease their assault on him. He allows me to use my new hold on to push him back against the headboard, but the satisfaction, pride, and hunger in his eyes are enough for me to falter. His hands find my hips, assuring I find my rhythm again, and I lean in, licking his mouth before taking his bottom lip between my teeth.

"Fuck," he moans, painfully gripping my hips and increasing my pace.

Screaming my orgasm, I release his lip. The coppery taste on my tongue, I drop my head back and ride out the most intense orgasm of my life. White spots burst behind my eyelids and a long, guttural moan tears from my throat. The force of it all turns into over stimulation, every touch sending a jolt of pleasurable pain through me.

"We aren't finished," he promises as I slacken against him.

Shoved to my back, Saint kneels above me. Placing one ankle on his shoulder and pressing my other leg open wide, he slips the tip of his dick through my cum saturated lips.

"Fuck, you're soaking." Without hesitation, he drops my leg and buries his face between my thighs.

He eats me with fervor, wanting every last drop, then he's back inside me, ankle on his shoulder and palm pressing me open wide. His thrusts are hard and punishing, exactly what I crave. When his thumb presses to my clit, I moan, lost in the sensation of it all.

"So. Fucking. Good." His thrusts accentuate each word as my head hits the headboard.

"Yes," I moan my agreement, earning me a swirl of his hips. "Fuck yes," I cry.

"You. Belong." His hips once again emphasizing his words, but on the last he shouts, "To me," staying deeply planted inside me.

Slipping an arm beneath me, he rolls us to our sides.

His cock slides out, resting against the inside of my thigh as he entwines our legs. Running his hand up the back of my thigh, he uses his fingers to slip through his cum.

"I like my mess in you," he repeats, and my body jerks as two fingers reenter me and stay there.

Chapter fifteen

Saint

Unsure of how today's meeting with Felix is going to go, I'm distracted.

So, when I'm stopped short on the last step by Sketch, I'm unprepared for his verbal assault.

"You're starting a fucking war," Sketch states, blocking my path.

"I'm well aware of what I'm doing, but if we're being honest, it's Angelo who started the war," I remind him, lifting one brow before pushing past him.

Removing my vibrating cell from inside my suit jacket, I glance to the screen.

"Fuck," he growls from behind me. "You're going to get us all killed."

Ignoring his concern, I swipe the phone, and answer, "Yes?"

"You watching the news?" Felix asks.

"Should I be?"

"Mick and Harry are dead," he states, his words lacking emotion.

"Who?"

"You fucking know who," he growls, frustrated.

Taking a deep breath, I respond on a heavy exhale, "The assassin."

"Assassin? Please tell me you aren't buying into all the fucking rumors," he shouts, disbelief lacing the hypothetical question. "You know who carves into their fucking targets, Saint. They even threatened to carve out Cosimo's eyes." Felix's fiery temper escalates.

"The Cartel is sorted," I remind him. "Cosimo is no longer of interest to them."

"That's bullshit and you know it!" The line goes dead.

"What the fuck was that about?" Sketch asks, standing next to me.

"I need you to add Nick and Harry to your information," is my response.

"She strikes again." It's not a question, but a statement filled with awe at our latest nuisance.

"You're so sure it's a woman?"

"I fantasize that it's woman," he admits with a shrug.

Shaking my head, I continue toward the kitchen. I may find Sketch ridiculous at times, but I would be a liar if I said I wasn't a bit impressed with this killer—or killers. They are ballsy and swift to act.

"If they continue this way, you'll all be dead by the end of the year," Sketch teases.

He's not too far off in his assessment.

"Mr. Ruggiano?"

Shoving my cell back inside my suit jacket, I glance up at my personal associate. Jacob Colmbs came into my service when I was just a kid, my father and mother bringing him on as security.

Knowing damn well Jacob hasn't called me by my given name since I was a child, I taunt, "Still so formal after all these years."

"Would you prefer Mr. Saint?" I don't miss the edge to the way he says my nickname.

"Welcome home," I greet, ignoring his question. "You were missed."

"And *you* have a new pet," he responds, lifting a brow and holding out a mug.

"Mei," I stress her name, making it clear that's what he's to call her, "is still asleep."

For a moment, my mind flashes to the image of Mei twisted in the sheet of my bed. The way the soft cotton wrapped around her waist and cross beneath her body leaving the bare globes of her ass on display. The urge to leave my hand print on her fair skin had been almost undeniable.

Shaking off my lust filled thoughts, I continue. "She has free reign of the penthouse, but isn't to leave."

I don't miss the way his eyes flare with curiosity before I turn to Sketch.

"I want you to focus your efforts on the flash drive, today's development, and I need you to check on Raul's recent activity," I instruct.

"So, you think The Cartel has something to do with it?"

"No." My answer earns me a frown.

"Care to tell me why I'm risking getting caught checking up on him?"

"Thought you don't get caught," Jacob tosses back words he's repeatedly boasted over the years.

Sketch glares. "I prefer to work under full disclosure," he says to Jacob before turning to me, "Something that's not happening much lately." His words accusatory, but I can't find it in me to give a fuck.

"You'll know what I want you to," I inform.

Placing the now half full mug on the island, I glance at my watch.

"I'm late."

"I'll message for the car," Jacob says, falling right back into his routine.

Adjusting my cuffs, I give them a nod and leave the penthouse.

Frankie moves the SUV through the streets of Chicago in silent familiarity while a stiff and tense Vincent quietly sits in the passenger seat. They may not know the reason behind this meeting, but the men I keep in my inner circle are there for reason. They aren't fucking stupid and have a skill set. Perception and intelligence are two, while being loyal as fuck is another. After that, they each possess their skills in different levels.

Frankie's capability to maneuver a car and his split-second reflexes and Vincent's ability to read a room or a person are only matched by his skill to find people. Russ, who follows in a separate vehicle, is a decorated sharp shooter who will be covering us from higher ground in a building across the street.

I know each of their minds are on this meeting, but I can't say the same. Mine drifts back to the woman in my bed—my dangerous obsession.

"Boss?" Vincent pulls me from my deviant thoughts. "Two things." Not waiting for a response, he continues. "We're about twenty minutes out."

"And?"

He turns sideways in the passenger seat, holding up his cell phone.

Requested package delivered to destination.

The feeling of victory is quickly replaced by the rage I've been locking away.

Arman is in place, just hours away, and all I want to do is turn the fucking car around and introduce him to all the reasons people fear The Saint, and why touching what belongs to me is a terrible idea.

Vincent pulls his phone away, casting his eyes down, and I follow his gaze.

My custom talon blade spins around the fingers of my right hand, my body moving on autopilot, seeking out the comfort of a sharp edge and familiar handle.

Smirking, I glance up and catch his eyes with mine.

My men aren't pussy's. They're strong and brave as fuck, but, as I said, they aren't fuckin stupid. It's smart to fear me—especially when Vincent is one of the few to see the aftermath of my own particular skill set.

Leaning back into the leather seat, I raise my right hand and continue to twirl the knife. The vibration of my cell phone does nothing to calm my current mood. Taking my knife in my left hand, I use my right to take out my phone, swipe the screen and answer.

"Yes?"

"Look who's still alive," she responds.

Closing my eyes, I inhale through my nose, trying to keep my temper under control. She only uses this tone when someone is within listening distance. It still grates on my fucking nerves and it's only in honor of AJ's memory that I continue to put up with this game.

"You haven't been home in weeks," she continues with the charade of nagging. "And I need you to come home."

"I'm busy," I say, much calmer than I feel.

With the game about to change and Arman's demise so close, I can already smell the metallic hints in his blood, this is the last distraction I need.

"Yes...well, we have a problem." Her voice lowers enough for me to know she's free of eavesdroppers. "Rosario is planning a *family* dinner before my parents return to New York." I don't miss the annoyance and exhaustion in her voice.

"Christ," I grumble, pressing the heel of the knife handle between my eyes. Being summoned to play my dutiful domestic role isn't what I need at the moment. And it's a role that, if it weren't for AJ's plea, I wouldn't have. Anger burns in my gut. It's all because of Angelo and his greedy, power hungry, God complex.

"My thoughts exactly," she whispers before the charade returns. "You need to be here tonight by seven and don't you dare call and tell me you'll be late. I don't ask for a lot and you know it."

Clenching my jaw until it aches, I loosen it enough to growl out, "Fine," and toss the phone across the car.

At the clearing of a throat, I look up and realize we're parked on the side street next to the Holy Name Cathedral. Frank stands next to my door, knowing not to open it yet.

I take one last moment to collect myself and my thoughts before tapping the tinted window. Frank opens the door and a breeze sweeps inside, helping to cool my temper.

Standing on the curb, I roll my head on my shoulders and quickly scan the street, finding Felix sliding out of a car a few spaces down. His men gather at his side and move at a steady pace with him.

"Dante," he greets, giving me a quick nod before ducking inside the church.

I follow close behind. Frankie stays with the car, while Vincent is the only man at my side.

Inside the church, I'm met with the smell of incense and wood polish, and the soft lighting is almost romantic.

"Good morning, my sons," Father Esposito greets from the doorway of his office.

"Father," we respond in unison before locating the dark

wooden panel at the back of a hallway. Releasing the hidden latch, we descend to the secure and secret part of the basement. It's deep enough to prevent any type of radio transmitted wires, cell phones, and once the door is closed behind us, it becomes sound proof. Reaching the concrete and stone destination, Felix turns to me.

"What the hell is going on?" he demands.

Eyes on Felix, I order, "Leave us."

Vincent doesn't hesitate, but Felix's men don't move until he gives a lift of his chin. Once alone and the door sealed behind us, I straighten my spine and cross my arms over my chest.

Felix raises one brow, a prompt for me to begin.

"Angelo's fucked us since the beginning," I begin.

"I think we already covered this," Felix barks.

"Yes, he's the reason we were ambushed and AJ was killed," I state.

"Again, shit I already know," he says with annoyance.

Taking a seat at the large table in the center of the room, he sighs, running a hand through his hair before asking, "Are you going to tell me anything I don't know?"

"Evgeni's son isn't dead."

"The fuck," Felix exclaims. "Does the sick bastard have him locked away somewhere?"

Part of me is relieved to hear how he refers to Angelo. It gives me hope I've made the right choice bringing him in on this—that our relationship isn't so strained we will be on opposite sides of the coming war.

"No," I quip, gripping the back of the chair next to him.

Pulling it out, I turn the chair to face him and sit.

"He's kept him close, hiding him in plain fucking sight the whole time," I hint a little more at the truth. I don't want to overwhelm Felix too quickly. He's known for his cold fury. Where others are hotheaded and explode in times of severe anger, Felix gets calm—too calm—until he smoothly executes you how he sees fit.

"You?" he guesses with an incredulous laugh. "Of course, you're the fucking missing Bratva son everyone thinks is dead."

"No, Felix." I shake my head, but hold his eyes. As the silence stretches, I watch realization soften his face.

"You're wrong," he denies.

I stay silent.

"It's impossible," he snaps.

"It's not," I finally confirm. "Felix, you were born Kazimir Leonid Volkov, son of Evgeni and Diana Volkov. The fucking Bratva son is you."

Pushing out of the chair, he spins around and paces the side of the room.

"How is that possible?" he asks, and without waiting for a response, adds, "They found the evidence of his wife and infant son's body in the car after the flames were extinguished."

"Angelo arranged the car accident, but it's not what everyone thought. Diana was barely alive when the car was put into motion and the infant was already dead."

Felix stops and looks at me, his eyes burning for answers.

"Angelo used the body of your parents' first child, a newborn son, who conveniently died around the same time the 'accident' occurred," I explain, letting my suspicions on that matter seep into my words.

"My mother would never have allowed him to—"

"You think he asked?" I snap. "How many open caskets have you seen for an infant, Felix? Most people don't want to see a dead adult, let alone a child."

"Evgeni knows?" His eyes search my face.

"I don't believe so," I shake my head.

"So, the day we lost AJ..." he trails off.

"Was Evgeni taking what Angelo took from him, though I think it was done on a gut feeling. I don't believe he had any real proof. If he did, I think he would've found you long ago."

"But why?" Felix asks the same question that bothered me.

Why would Angelo murder Evgeni's family and break a long-standing truce?

"Greed, power, a fucked up tactical move to supersede the Bratva's power and influence," I offer the only educated guesses I've come up with. "I hope I'm not the only one who sees how obsessed he's become with power and ruling like a goddamn tyrant."

It's not a question, but Felix nods in agreement.

"Christ," Felix growls. "How could my mother fucking keep this from me?"

He begins pacing again.

"I don't think she knows who you are," I explain. "I'm pretty sure Angelo just swooped in as the big brother saving the day. She'd just lost her first child, Felix. She wouldn't think past having a baby in her arms again, besides the fact that Angelo has sheltered her since she was a child."

His eyes meet mine, understanding shining in them. No one in the family needs to say exactly how protective Angelo is of his sister. It's evident in every over-the-top protective action where she's concerned.

"But my father," he stops short, snapping his head in my direction. "He figured it out. That's why he..."

Tightening my jaw, I give a firm nod. This will be the true test between Felix and me.

"The fucker called him a traitor just so—"

"He could get rid of a loose end," I say, dropping my eyes to the floor.

I don't lower them in regret or apology. I am a monster, a demon, and death is what I do, but this has always been a point of contention between us.

"I'm not an idiot, Dante." Felix's unexpected words bring my eyes back to his.

"I know you did it so I wouldn't have to," he confesses. "Not at first," he continues, returning to his previous seat. "But eventually, I figured it out. You thought I wouldn't be able to kill my own father."

"No." Now it's my turn to surprise him. "I didn't doubt for one minute you would kill him."

His brow furrows. "Then why?"

"Felix," I lean forward, elbows to my knees, "by the age of fifteen, I had more blood on my hands than anyone in that room."

His eyes widen just a bit.

"I did it so you wouldn't have to *live* with it," I admit, sitting back into my chair. "My soul was already twisted and black."

"A saint owned by a devil?" Felix tries to tease.

"I am the devil. I just go by the name Saint," I retort.

Snorting, he gives a nod.

"What the fuck are we going to do, Dante? It's not like we can confront him, and we sure as fuck can't bring in the rest of the family without risking Angelo's wrath."

"Evgeni," I suggest.

"Fuck," Felix breathes out the word, rubbing his bottom lip with his thumb. "Why the fuck would he believe us?"

I give a shrug. "A father's love? I'm sure he would need proof, but that's where DNA comes in."

"What if I don't want to be his son?" Felix tosses the words like a challenge. "What if *he* doesn't want a son?"

"Then we find another way," I state, letting him know I'll stand behind his decision. Then I continue, "You aren't the only one with reasons."

Tilting his head to the right, he lifts his brows in a silent question.

"My mother and father," I remind him of the other two lives Angelo coerced me into taking on the false charge of traitor.

"Fuck," the word whooshes from his mouth. "He had you..." Felix doesn't finish, choosing another direction instead. "He's a fucking piece of work, isn't he?" Felix asks. "Screwing with people's kids for whatever sick reason he had."

"My mother belonged to Angelo before my father married her."

"Belonged, as in...?" he presses.

"As in she was his mistress," I explain. and continue, "After marrying Rosario, she laid down the law."

"She made him give up his mistress?"

I nod.

"But she's very aware of Nina. I don't understand," he says, disbelief in his words.

"He loved my mother, and Rosario knew she was second to her," I clarify. "It was pure jealousy."

"And your father just swooped right in for his brother's leftovers? That doesn't sound like Uncle Don."

"Angelo forced my mother onto him," I snort, because what comes next ultimately sets the stage for how Angelo would operate for years to come.

"But why would—"

"My mother had caught Evgeni's attention during sit downs she would attend with Angelo. So, once she was released from Angelo's side, a place she apparently didn't get to by choice, he knew

Evgeni could push his advance. To prevent that, he ordered my father to take her on," I continue. "But he didn't count on my parents falling in love."

"Fucking hell, Dante, how many times did you have to run this through your head before it stopped sounding like those damn daytime soap operas Nonna used to watch?" He asks.

"It still sounds like one, but it doesn't change the fact that Angelo has fucked with our lives since before we were born," I remind him.

"So, you think your mother and father were working with mine?"

Giving another shrug, I tell him, "I can only assume they found out about your real bloodline and were working with your father against Angelo. I'm pretty sure your mother was sheltered from all of it."

"Why not just have them taken out quietly? Why the big show of killing them?"

"His power hunger started years ago," I remind. "And what better way to assert and show off his power than to have their own children kill them."

Felix shakes his head.

I continue. "I was and still am his killer, his butcher. He's pulled my strings for far too long, thinking he's got control of his creature, but," I pause, smirking, "he's not immune to the fear I invoke or the vengeance I seek."

"Don't give me your I want to see what your insides look like glare," he growls. "Your point is made."

"I'm taking him down, Felix," I say, revealing my plan.

He focuses on the table, silent and unmoving, for five long minutes.

With a nod, he asks, "Are we sure it's not Angelo taking everyone out?" His eyes come to mine. "I mean, if he's picking off people one by one, it could be him clearing out anyone he feels is a threat to his secrets. That means we could very well be next on his list."

"No." I shake my head. "I considered that, but things are pointing in another direction."

"What direction?"

"You won't like the answer."

Felix squints his eyes in thought before the wrinkles smooth out and he grins. "Not this fucking Geisha Assassin bullshit again," he says, astounded.

"You're so quick to discount it?"

"Okay, say I believe one woman is doing all this, have you found anything on this *Geisha*?"

"Not enough," I admit, "But I do know she has ties to the Yakuza I can't explain yet."

"So, it is a she?"

"More like a collection, I believe," I reveal. "My research makes it difficult to believe the murder of our men is a single person, and the conversations in Japan are of a group called the Jōshitai."

"So, there isn't a Geisha, per say?" He assumes wrong.

"Oh no, there is definite mention of a Yakuza hitwoman who is referred to as The Geisha," I correct.

"She's their leader?"

"Mostly she's mentioned as a revered hitwoman in service to the Yakuza, but, as I stated, I don't have enough information. Though, you are correct about one thing."

"And that would be?"

"We could be next on the hit list." It's true, and he needs to understand Angelo isn't the only place to focus.

"I feel like my life has just been shot to hell," Felix admits, rubbing his hands over his face.

"I need to know where you stand, Felix," I say, every word a warning.

"He really is a twisted asshole," he breathes out.

"I killed my mother just to hide his secrets and perpetuate his desire for power," I say aloud, grabbing Felix's full attention. "He lied to me, used me. The only traitorous thing she did was not love or want him. Then he had me hunt down my father, like a fucking animal. I've been used as his death bringer for the last fucking time."

Standing from my chair, Felix's eyes follow me.

"I know what I am and what I do, but it won't be by his control again," I declare.

Felix nods, a murderous expression forming on his face.

"What's your plan?"

"We need to find allies," I confess.

"I know a few," he divulges.

At my look, he gives a one shoulder shrug. "You aren't the only one who knows it's time to dethrone our tyrant."

Chapter Sixteen

Mei

Two days.

Two nights.

No Saint.

During the morning routine I'd started, I sit on the tiles of the shower floor, letting the tears of realization fall from my eyes.

I surrendered to him, handed myself over on a blood-stained platter. And now that he's gotten what he wants, the thrill of the chase, or the challenge, is no longer there. Any fight I once had has been demolished. Now, I need to resign myself to this gilded cage. The life of a mistress, plaything—an afterthought.

Pressing the heel of my palms into my eyes, a guttural cry escapes me. I rub my hands over my face before lifting it to the stream of water.

Descending the stairs, I overhear Sketch having a one-sided conversation. Curious for any information about Saint, his whereabouts, or anything beyond this apartment, I stop before rounding the corner to the open living, dining, and kitchen area.

"He's fucking with you," Sketch barks. "You can't tell me he wasn't behind getting Giuliana and her family involved," he continues.

Giuliana. It's not the first time I've heard her name. After studying the men who came to the strip club, I'm well aware most of them have wives, mistresses, and other affairs. I'm also not so naïve that I don't believe Giuliana is most likely Saint's wife. He's been with her these past two days.

"When are her parents leaving?" he asks, pausing. "Because we got another special delivery for your little toy upstairs," he informs.

At the mention of a special delivery, I step around the corner. Eyes searching, I locate the brown paper and twine wrapped box sitting on the sleek black dining table. My chest constricts at the familiarity.

Uncaring if they know I'm there or what seeing inside the box will do to my mental state, I take long strides to the table.

"Someone's awake," Jacob announces.

Over the past two days, Jacob has been my solace. Conversations and showing me the exercise room where he works on boxing techniques with me, he's the only real source of company I've had.

Lost in my own thoughts, the weight of both their stares still registers, but doesn't take mine from the brown box.

"Fuck," Sketch exclaims. "You need to fucking get here."

Placing my hands on the package, I curl my fingers into the paper and tear through it.

"Stop," Sketch shouts. "You don't fucking know what's in there!"

He approaches, but I maneuver myself and the box around the table. Ripping the top off, I cover my mouth and step back. The green eyes and blue hair are the first things I recognize.

"The mermaid," I whisper through my fingers.

Jacob's massive presence fills my right side as Sketch reaches inside the box.

"What the hell—" Jacob begins.

"You will swim with mermaids," Sketch reads out loud, cutting Jacob off. Sketch's eyes come to mine, and he finishes, "He didn't keep his word, but I will. I promise."

Bending at the waist, I grip the edge of the table and take deep breaths, attempting to stop the bile from rising into my throat.

"What is this?" Jacob asks, reaching out for the doll.

"Don't touch it," I say in a rush.

"Who the fuck sent this sick shit?" Sketch grabs my arm, pulling me away from the table.

"Sketch," Jacob warns, taking my other arm in his hand. "You should probably call Dante," he instructs, pulling me toward him.

Sketch looks at his forgotten cell, releases my arm, and curses. His phone has multiple missed calls. Tapping the screen, he inhales, blows out the breath and puts the phone to his ear.

"Don't fucking start with me, Saint. I can't help it that your fucking pet lost her shit," he exclaims minutes later.

"Yeah, it's another one," he answers.

He glares at me.

"The message is different this time." His hard eyes stay on me. "It's extra fucking creepy. That's what it is." Dropping his head back, he sighs at the ceiling.

"You can't do shit unless you get your goddamn pet to talk."

I stiffen at his words and pull myself out of Jacob's hold. Moving closer to the table, I steel my resolve, tear away the rest of the packaging, and study the doll.

Her hair is matted in different spots. Where her white shell top used to sparkle, it's dull and scuffed. The green shimmer tale is faded and worn. Reaching out, I run two fingers over her smooth face and close my eyes.

Unbidden, each doll flashes in my mind. Annie, my beloved rag doll. Sarah, my treasured china doll. Now, the mermaid. But it's not the child's toys I remember with such fondness, it's the real dolls. The greatest gifts my father would bestow upon me. Tea parties, brushing their hair, dancing for them, cherishing and loving them. A sick, twisted warmth settles in my chest.

Shoving the morbid feelings down deep, I lick my dry lips, and whisper, "I never got to swim with her."

"What did you say?" Jacob asks, shock saturating his question.

Removing my hand, I wrap my arms around all the pieces of me and hold them together. My eyes fall on the notecard, focusing on one terrifying sentence.

He didn't keep his word, but I will.

Hugging myself tighter, I slowly turn and walk away.

"Mei?" Jacob calls at my back. "Where are you going?"

"Who the hell is sending them?" Sketch demands.

Rounding the corner to the stairs, I hear Jacob say, "Let her go."

Back in Saint's room, I sit against the headboard with a pillow over my bent-up knees. Burying my face into Egyptian cotton, I unleash all my pent-up tears.

Warmth travels along my cheek and down my neck, curling around. Blinking awake, a dark blur lies next to me on the bed. Panic grips my chest, locking all my muscles. Preparing to shove away, the warmth at my neck tightens, fisting the hair at the nape.

"Relax," he says, and my body instantly obeys Saint's order. Each muscle loosens, settling back into the side position I lay.

He tears the pillow I'd been cuddling out from between us and pulls me against his chest. I expect him to demand answers, sex, or anything else, but he just holds me.

"You need to eat," he says against the side of my head. "Jacob tells me you haven't all day."

"What time is it?" I rasp, my throat dry and unused.

"After seven," he answers.

"I've never slept this long," I say absently.

When I push away to climb off the bed, he allows it. On my way to the bathroom, I stop briefly to stare at a tray of food on top of a dresser.

"Jacob," is his explanation.

Not hungry, I continue to handle my business, then stare at myself in the mirror.

"Hello, stranger," I say to the grown-up version of the little girl I used to be. "It's been a very long time." For the briefest of moments, I see a shadow in the mirror, but I blink and it's gone. A trick of my warped mind. A mind slowly but surely slipping into madness.

I take note my bruise is starting to fade to greens and yellow before everything comes rushing back. Saint's absence, most likely with his wife and family, the dolls, the memories...the message on the card.

Washing my face, I rub my hands over it hard enough to make me wince. It does nothing to scrub away the chaos in my mind. Exiting the bathroom, I turn for the bedroom door instead of the bed and leave Saint behind.

"Mei," he shouts, but I walk faster, able to reach the first floor of the penthouse before he catches up.

"Where are you going?" His question draws Sketch's attention. His eyes are on us the moment we enter the room.

Keeping my emotions in check, I tell him, "I want to leave."

My arm is captured and he spins me to face him.

"You aren't going anywhere," he demands, the words a promise.

"Let me leave," I ask in a low voice, pulling away.

Something in my expression widens his eyes. Whatever it is gives me the ability to pull my arm from his hand. Uncaring that I'm in a pair of jeans, a t-shirt, and barefoot, I turn and head for the elevators.

"Vincent," Saint calls out, and the tall, dark-suited man moves into the hallway, blocking my path. No longer in control of the discord of my emotions, I fist my hands at my sides and spin around.

"Let me go!" I cry.

Straightening to his full height and crossing his arms over his chest, he makes a very imposing image. Even in sweatpants and a white t-shirt, the darkness of his deeds surround him like an aura of death and blood.

And, because I'm a terrible, sick girl, my body fucking heats. My own demons writhe along my skin, wanting to bare their most fragile secrets to this creature before me.

"No," he asserts.

I open my mouth to argue, but he's not finished.

"You want me to release you? Tell me who sends the dolls," he bargains, though we both know he won't—not until he's grown bored, or whatever.

"Shouldn't you be home with your wife and family?" It sounds like jealousy, because it partly is, and that makes me even angrier with him. What should I care about his wife, his family? I'm well aware of how these men work, and so are their wives.

His expression doesn't change, but my peripheral vision doesn't miss the way Sketch's head snaps to Saint.

"Careful, doll," he warns.

"I thought I was a dead girl," I retort.

Dropping his arms, he comes for me. Fear zaps up my spine,

tightening my muscles, in preparation to flee. Well, fuck that. Instead, I stand my ground and lift my chin.

"You were a dead girl," he explains from a couple feet away.

Closing the distance, his arm shoots out, grabbing me by the back of my head. Pulling me into his body, my hands come up and press against his heaving chest.

"Now, you're my doll to do with as I please," he finishes.

"I hate you," I growl, trying to turn my head from him, but his other hand comes up, capturing my chin. Unable to move, all I have left to shut him out are my eyes.

"Dante," Jacob pleas from somewhere behind me.

"You don't," he states, ignoring him.

The beat of his heart thuds against my palm, every heavy breath fans over my face, and the caress of his hand beneath my chin sparks my body to life.

His mouth against mine, not caring about our audience, he says, "You belong to me."

Fingers press into the flesh of my jaw, accentuating his claim, before he brushes his thumb along my skin. "And I belong to you."

At his declaration, my eyes snap open, surprised by the honesty I find in the depths of his.

Both of his hands move to palm the sides of my face, his forehead pressing to mine.

"The ground will be littered with the bodies of those who have and would hurt you," he vows. "I will lay each one at your feet and carve your name into their flesh as a reminder to others."

"Why?" I ask on a whisper.

"You belong—"

"To you," I finish with what I assume is the rest.

I'm wrong.

"With me," he corrects, running his thumbs over my cheek bones.

One moment, he threatens to kill me. The next, I belong to him. And now, I have his complete devotion. This connection we share makes no sense and things are moving too fast for me to process. There's so much that could bring it crashing down around us, leaving a very bloody scene.

"Sir," Jacob steps close to Saint, placing a hand on his tense shoulder. "We have a situation."

He holds an iPad out and Saint yanks it from his hand. Sketch moves in quickly, looking over Saint's shoulder.

"What the fuck do they want?" His question is directed at Jacob, not Saint.

Jacob jerks his head toward me. "They're asking about Meissa Winters," he says. "Apparently, there's been a missing person's report filed."

It's like being punched in the stomach. All the air rushes out of me and I frantically search my mind for someone who would miss me enough to file a report.

Saint's hard eyes snap from the tablet to me, then shift to Sketch.

"How'd you miss that?" His question is full of disgust as he slaps the iPad into Sketch's chest.

"Sure, let's pretend for a fucking second that she," he motions to me, "doesn't have one goddamn relative, friend, or close connection, and have me add police reports for a fucking ghost to my list of things to do!"

"You should've caught it," Saint growls.

"We need to address the situation," Jacob interjects, "and this isn't helping."

"I say give her to them," Sketch starts, earning a glare from Saint. "Don't fucking look at me like that. Your goddamn obsession with teen runaway pussy is distracting you from more important—"

Saint's hand around his throat chokes off the end of his sentence.

"I would be careful with what you let your mouth run about," he warns.

The muscles in his forearm flex and his knuckles start to whiten. Sketch drops the iPad to the floor.

This is my fault. If I'd just kept my fucking distance from these people at the club and ignored Tricia, I wouldn't be about to watch someone be choked to death. These two have a fucked up friendship, but it is exactly that. Now, I'm going to be the reason for its demise.

Before I can stop myself, I grab Saint's arm, and scream, "Stop!"

His hand immediately releases Sketch, who stumbles back.

Using the dining table to lean back on, he clasps his throat and gasps for air.

The feel of his stare is like a thousand bricks on top of me, and I quickly step away from him. Glancing to his face, I find exactly what I expect: his eyes on me. Without moving them, he orders, "Bring up our guests."

My eyes widen, and once again, I'm trying to figure out who would send the police for me.

The smirk that contorts Saint's face, along with the raise of one eyebrow, tells me he has an idea, and it sends cold realization up my spine. Panic clogs my throat and tears burn behind my eyes. Taking deep breaths, I try to pull myself together.

"Mei, are you okay?" Jacob asks, stepping forward.

I step back, raising a hand to stop him.

"She's fine," Saint rumbles. "She just figured out who's looking for her."

"Who?" Jacob asks.

"The same person sending her gifts," Saint enlightens the room.

"Fuck," Sketch rasps.

"My God," Jacob whispers.

"Sir," Russ appears from direction of the elevator hallway.

One man and a woman follow, both dressed in dark slacks, a button-down shirt, and a jacket. Their curious eyes focus on me, the woman's narrowing at my black eye.

Well, I wanted to leave. I guess my wish will be granted. Escorted from this prison by the police and delivered right into the hands of my past.

No. That can't happen.

"Marcus," Saint greets. "What do I owe the pleasure of you and Darla's visit?"

From anyone else, it would sound cheesy, but Saint makes it sound almost threatening.

"What happened to her face?"

"Darla," Marcus warns.

"A misunderstanding," Saint freely answers. "One that I will have taken care of soon."

At his admission, I straighten my back and fight the urge to search his face for answers.

"Good to know," she states, crossing her arms over her chest.

"Now, the business of your visit?" Saint presses.

"Mr. Ruggiano, we have reason to believe you have a Meissa Winters in your possession." It's a statement, not a question, and the detective's eyes shift to me.

"As you can see, Miss Winters is perfectly well," Saint says, motioning over my body.

Both their eyes come to me.

"Miss, a report has been filed that you have been missing for some time now," the one called Marcus says. "Do you know why they would think it wasn't of your own choice?"

"I have no idea," I say, making a choice that keeps me from my past, and even I'm surprised by how calm I sound.

"Miss Winters," Darla beings, dropping her arms from her chest. "If there is something wrong, if you need help—"

"What help could I possibly need?" The question is so flippant and snobby, so unlike me, I can only pray my own shock doesn't show.

To prove my point, I turn, making my way to Saint. At his side, I lean into him, wrapping an arm around his bicep.

"You can—"

"Darla," Marcus warns again, "she said she doesn't need help and we can both see she's fine."

She glares at him before spinning and stalking away.

"Thank you, Sain—Mr. Ruggiano," Marcus says, then turns to me. "Good evening, Miss."

Russ and Vincent follow them out of the room toward the elevators.

Adrenalin pumps through me making every muscle twitch and my heart beat rapidly.

"They're gone," Vincent announces upon his return.

Releasing Saint's arm, I stumble back and catch myself on the back of the couch. He turns, facing me.

"You finally have your chance to escape," he taunts, stalking toward me, "and you don't take it?"

Silence fills the room as tears pool at the inner corners of my eyes, lingering like a threat to my sanity.

"Good," Sketch rasps, "fucking thing it was Marcus."

"Why is that a good thing?" I ask, avoiding Saint's observation.

"You're terrified of him," he states, thinking he has it all figured out.

Ignoring him, I focus on what Sketch said, piecing it together.

"Marcus works for you," I say, then accuse, "Did you send them here just to scare answers out of me?"

One thick brow arches over his right eye, amusement dancing in them.

"Maybe," he shrugs.

"You bastard," I shout, pushing away from the couch. "What...who are you?"

"Remember," he says in a low warning, "you chose me over freedom."

Giving a half grin, he takes a step back.

"Vincent, get Frank and the car. We're going to the estate," he announces.

"Are you sure about this?" Jacob asks, inching closer to my side.

Saint's eyes narrow on him before he reaches out, takes my hand, and pulls me to him. Glancing over my shoulder, I don't miss the way Jacob stares at our intertwined hands. His face scrunches like he's trying to work through something in his head.

"You don't need me to go, right?" Sketch asks with a hint of nervousness.

Everyone's hesitation worries me. Maybe I've pushed too far and for too much.

"Thirty minutes," is all Saint says before dragging me back upstairs.

chapter seventeen

Mei

The drive to the estate is long and quiet. A loaded silence not even Sketch seems eager to disrupt. Torn between fear of not knowing where this place is or what will happen when we reach it, I'm also seething about Saint's stunt with the police. Deflecting his touches and avoiding as much contact as possible, I angle my body away from him and lean against the door.

Undeterred, he wraps an arm around my waist, pulling my back to his side.

I hate the way my body heats and skin tingles at his touch. That even when I hate him, he gets this kind of reaction from me.

Closing my eyes, I inhale through my nose, clench my jaw, and growl through my teeth, "Let go."

"As clever as it would make me, I did not send the detectives for you."

Mouth gaping, I repeat his admission in my head. I'm mulling over the words a third time when I blurt, "Why would you let me believe you did?"

"You needed an emotional outlet."

At his deceptively calm response, I twist my body and look up at him.

Seeing the confusion on my face, he explains, "With everything that's happened today, and this new ballsy move of your doll sender, your emotions were all over the place."

"So, you decided anger was the way to go?"

His hand comes up, taking my chin between his thumb and bent fingers.

"You don't cry when you're angry," he explains. "I'll take your anger before seeing you cry."

Turning my face away, I swallow hard. He's making me feel things again. Only this time, it's with his words.

After two and a half hours of watching the scenery change from cityscape to suburb to rural, nothing but dark green forest passes by in a blur. No houses. No passing cars. No sign of human life to be found, and no matter how his words make me feel, apprehension creeps back in, and I find myself staring unseeing out the window.

In the middle of nowhere, who can hear you scream?

As the car slows, I refocus on what's outside the window. A small stone cottage sits on the side of the road. The ivy climbing up its side is well maintained and the face of a young boy peeks over the window sill.

"That's the property manager's house," Saint states as the car takes a left just past the house.

There's a depth and apprehension to his voice, making me worry more about this new location—a destination that creates unease in everyone bound for it.

Settling back into the seat, the trees grow fewer and farther between, until we reach a large house. Dipping my head, I try to get a better view out the front window. The estate is not what I expected, especially in the middle of the all this wilderness.

Circling a courtyard, the car parks in front of four stone steps leading to a large dark wooden door.

The car opens, Frank stepping back to allow Saint to climb out. Before stepping away from the car, he reaches back, offering me his hand, palm up. Swallowing, I slip my hand into his.

He helps me from the car, and I realize how wrong I was. This isn't a house. It's a mansion.

While it's the made of the same light beige stone as the cute family cottage we passed, this place is more like those Italian castle-villa hybrids I've seen in pictures. It's so unexpected, I can only stare up at the imposing dwelling. The longer I do, the more the late day shadows give it an eerie feel.

I jump when his hand comes to my lower back, but allow Saint to guide me through the large entrance. Jacob enters behind us, announcing, "The second-floor guest rooms have been prepared," before opening it.

"The master suite?" Saint asks, standing close at my back.

"Ready," Jacob confirms.

Inside, I glance around a large entrance way. The walls are almost the same color as the exterior, but are a larger exposed stone. Lined with lanterns, they are cast in a warm glow. Tile squares in muted red, brown, and tans decorate the floors.

A press against my back puts me in motion. Walking through a tall stone archway, we enter a large indoor courtyard. It's decorated the same as the entrance, aside from the large plants growing in the center. Glancing up, I find a ceiling made of glass, revealing a darkening sky and the first stars of the night.

"It's retractable," Jacob advises.

Licking my lips, I glance around the vast room. The courtyard looks to be the center of the house, separating different sections and rooms. Each of the four walls have a large archway leading into areas unknown to me. Though, I'm drawn to the one opposite us. There's a clear view of the sky and I can't help but wonder if it's a large window or open to the outside. I also notice the floor drops away to what are probably stairs.

Commotion fills the room around us, pulling my attention from the view. Sketch, Vince, Russ, and a couple other men I've seen, but haven't learned their names, file into the room.

I catch Sketch giving the archway I admired an apprehensive look before quickly looking away. He focuses on the floor, resituating his black backpack over his shoulder.

"I'll be in the office," he mumbles, turning to walk away.

"You have free reign of the house," Saint calls out behind him, more than likely making sure everyone knows I have his permission. Part of me bristles, while the other is relieved and ready to find a way out of here.

"Are you sure you—?" Jacob begins.

Spinning back to face us, he says, "She's free to go where she wants," leaving no room for further argument.

Closing the distance he just created between us, his fingers find my chin and bring my face to him.

"It's thirty-two acres of land," he says, warning in his words. "Forest, crops, a lake, and a lot of land to cover."

He steps closer into my personal space, causing me to raise my head to keep eye contact.

"No one knows these grounds better than me." Definitely a warning. "Especially in the dark."

Sliding his hand from my chin, down the side of my neck, over my shoulder, and down my arm, he takes my hand. Stepping back, he turns, and pulls me behind him.

"Come," he instructs, the same gleam of excitement I saw in him earlier back.

Saint tugs me along, down a hallway to a stone staircase. We climb to the second floor and find another hallway. Reaching the end of the corridor, Saint opens a set of double wooden doors and leads me inside.

"This is the master," he explains, releasing my hand. "This will be our room while we're here," he adds. "The bathroom is through there."

Following where he points, I walk into the bathroom. On my left, in an enclave, is a claw foot tub. Identical sheer panels line the entrance, a privacy curtain. To my right is a double sink vanity and large mirror. At the far end of the bathroom is a glass shower with a bench. Yet, the largest extravagance in this room is another set of glass double doors.

Moving to them, I push them open and find another sunken in room. This one holds a built in hot tub that could seat at least six.

"My mother called it her sanctuary."

Saint's admission surprises me. I turn, meet his eyes, and wait for him to tell me more. He doesn't. At least, not about his mother.

"I have things to handle," he states, turning around to leave.

My curiosity getting the best of me, I follow him out of the bathroom, and blurt, "Why are we here?"

Figuring I opened the dialogue, I might as well keep going.

"And why is everyone so nervous about this place?" I add, trying to understand what the hell is going on.

"You want to know who I am."

It's not a question, but still, I nod. "Yes."

"Everyone else," he straightens to his full height, lifting his chin, "already knows *what* I am."

Without further explanation, he exits the room, leaving me standing in the middle of the bedroom.

Exhaling a breath, I cross the room and open the French doors. Stepping onto the patio, motion lights bring it to life. I'm drawn to a stone wall and plant my palms on it before glancing over. A twelve foot drop down to a covered swimming pool that looks like no one has used it in years.

Following the concrete walkway around the pool, I find a stone staircase leading down from the patio. My flight instincts kick in and my feet itch to run down the stairs. I close my eyes, curling my fingers into the stone.

Freedom. *Grab your backpack, unlatch the lock, and go,* I mentally instruct. *It would be as easy as...*

Opening my eyes, I scan the privacy fence around the pool area, looking for a gate. When I find it, my body tenses, ready to flee, until I glance at the dense forest around the house. Saint's warning echoes in my mind before I shake it off.

You've survived worse than trees, I silently argue with my apprehension. *You survived the dirty, cold, dark streets of Chicago. He only wants to scare you—or he'd prefer to hunt you down and kill you.*

Running my hands through my hair, I take a deep breath and exhale.

At least test the gate. You're only checking the place out, right?

Just as my body starts to move, a figure in black emerges from the shadows just outside the fence. He's hard to see in the dark, but his suit alone tells me he's one of Saint's men. Beeps break the silence before the gate swings open.

Releasing the stone wall, I take quiet backward steps to avoid being seen.

Before the gate falls out of sight, I watch the suited man open a wooden box and punch a code. Three loud beeps fill the air, a small light turns red, and he closes the box. He glances around, probably curious about the motion lights, so I duck into a darkened part of the patio.

Well, there goes that idea.

As I return to the master bedroom and close the doors, I hear, "Perimeter check complete."

Leaning my forehead against the doors, I resign myself to my newest prison. Pushing off the doors, I take a deep breath before leaving the master suite.

Descending the stairs, I'm back in the first-floor hallway. My stomach announces its neglect the moment my feet hit the stone floor and I search for the kitchen.

Upon entrance into the large courtyard, my eyes lift to the glass ceiling. It reminds me of doll cases. Shaking my head, I push the memories away and rush through the archway I watched Sketch disappear into earlier. On my left is a long credenza with picture frames. It's the first time I've found any type of photograph and my curiosity sets my feet in motion.

Starting on the right, I lean down and glance over the frames. They're mainly of a man and woman. Two are candid photos taken somewhere outside this house, another is the same couple's wedding picture, and the rest are posed formal photographs.

Assuming they are Saint's relatives, perhaps his parents, I straighten. Turning around, I find another hallway, like the one on the other side of the house that leads to the bedrooms.

Halfway down the corridor, a muffled scream stops me, sending a chill up my spine. Twisting my neck, I look behind me and find nothing. Pressing my back to the wall, I look back and forth, waiting. Nothing enters the hallway and no more screams follow.

Gathering all my courage, I push forward and enter a massive kitchen.

"Are you hungry?" Jacob's question startles me, and he puts his hands up, palms out. "I didn't mean to frighten you," he reassures.

His words are sincere, but I don't miss the look of pity on his face. I open my mouth to ask what's going on, but my stomach once again protests how long it's been empty.

The pity is washed away by a smile.

"I have roasted chicken," he says, making his way to a pot on top of the stove. "As well as potatoes and carrots," he adds.

In practiced moves, Jacob retrieves a plate, silverware, and a glass. After plating the food, he turns to find me unmoved.

"Please sit, Mei." He motions to the island with a dip of his head, and I tentatively take a seat at the very end.

Placing the plate and cutlery on the counter top, he steps back, and asks, "What would you like to drink?"

"Water's fine," I respond.

With a nod, he sets to it and fills the glass before placing it in front of me.

Picking up the fork, I move the food around. I know it's not rational, but I can't help to wonder if it's drugged or poisoned in some way.

"I can assure you, it's not going to hurt you," he states, reading my thoughts before stabbing a carrot with his own fork and putting it in his mouth. I watch him chew and swallow.

"See." He grins, amused by my distrust.

I frown.

With a sigh, he places his palms to the counter, putting his weight on them.

"He would kill anyone that hurt you," he says. "That includes me."

Pursing my lips, I push away my irrational fear of the food and dig in. The savory flavor of the chicken is like an explosion on my tongue. My eyes find Jacob, who is once again smiling.

"I'm glad you like it."

"It's amazing," I say around a mouthful.

Barely taking time to breathe, I plow my way through the meal. There's nothing that could come between me and my dinner—nothing except the blood curdling scream that fills the room.

Dropping my fork, I push out of the chair and spin toward the direction of the sound.

"What—?"

Another scream. The agony and pain in it makes my stomach knot.

I take a step forward, and it leads to another exit from the room. One I didn't take the time to pay attention to.

"Mei," Jacob says in caution.

Glancing over my shoulder, my eyes meet his worry-filled ones.

"You..." his words trail off.

"I, what?"

He shakes his head. "There's no coming back from what you'll find down there," he warns, but doesn't move to stop me.

I instinctively know, deep inside, how right he is, but I also can't stop myself from following the next cry filling the air.

Through the archway, I find Russ at the bottom of a small stairwell. His back against a wall, he stands guard to an open door.

At my descent, he doesn't look at me. In fact, it seems like he's doing his best to avoid noticing me at all.

Stepping inside the open doorway, cries and howling carrying up from yet another set of stairs.

This place is like a damn labyrinth.

Taking a step down, I wait for Russ to stop me. When he doesn't, I continue down the flight.

It's another stairway, but this one is darker, colder. The cries grow louder, calling to the darkest part of me. Pausing on the last step, I brace my hands against each wall.

This is your last chance to turn around and get the fuck out of here. If you continue, you're going to unleash every single one of your demons.

At the thought, the sharp tingle of my sins prickle along my flesh. Swallowing, I try to ease my suddenly dry throat.

The scream that rents the air when I release the wall and take the final step is almost enough to make me run. Almost.

Saint

Entering the office, I find Sketch at a table in the corner of the room, his laptops open and data flashing across the screens.

"Have you found anything?"

My question brings his eyes to me.

"Regarding which of the many anythings you have me looking

to?" he snaps.

Lifting one brow, my mouth twitches.

"You find this amusing," he shouts, pushing back in the chair.

I shrug.

"Christ, Saint, do you even..." his words fall away with a shake of his head.

I know he has a hard time coming here since the last time, the only time, he was here, wasn't under pleasant circumstances.

Keeping my voice level, I say, "Don't blame me for your mistakes."

Anger flashes in his eyes before he yanks his shirt is over his head. Chest heaving, he points to the scars on chest—scars now camouflaged by tattoos.

"You practically fucking flayed me," he growls.

Dropping my voice low, I remind him, "You stole three million dollars."

"I hid it," he argues. "I didn't fucking steal it! I just moved it to—"

"To fuck with Angelo," I finish for him. "I know what you did. You're lucky I was already suspicious of him then or you wouldn't have left here with your life."

His mouth opens, but closes when I lift a brow in silent challenge. Running his hands through his hair, he calms his rage. Eyes closed and face pinched, he asks, "Are you really going to do this with her here?"

Letting the tension leave my body, I straighten my spine and respond, "Yes."

He visibly swallows, dropping back into the office chair.

"You're going to fucking terrify her, Dante." On my given name, his eyes find mine.

Anger simmers in my gut. His concern for her is out of character and unacceptable. The creature tugs on the bones caging all my demons, wanting to punish him for any feelings he has where my dead girl is concerned. Yet, another part of me, a very fucking small part, finds comfort in the idea that he worries for her.

"You don't know her like I do," I admit.

"I don't care how fucked up her past or present was, is, could have been," he argues, "she's not going to be able to handle *The*

Saint."

I shrug, turning for the door.

"I guess we'll find out."

"You better have a goddamn therapist on fucking call," he shouts at my back. "Or the asylum on speed dial."

Grinning, I make my way to the stairway leading to my sanctuary.

They know nothing about her. They haven't seen the dark glint in her eye, the way she dances within my darkest parts and lays herself on the creature's alter. Yet, as I approach Russ at the doorway, a sliver of doubt finds its way into my mind. This may be the very thing that sends her running. Showing her exactly who I am may be taking her too far.

"Sir?" Russ inquires.

Shaking my head, I say, "She can go wherever she wishes."

His body tenses, and before he asks, I answer, "Anywhere."

Then, I descend into the place my demons can be set free— where my current prey waits for my retribution.

Opening the large door at the end of the long hallway, I leave it ajar. It's my private summons for her to descend into hell and play.

Pulling the bowie knife from the man's body, blood sprays over my chest and chin.

His scream fills the room, an invitation to my creature like a mating call. My heart thumps an excited rhythm, blood pounds between my ears, and euphoria rushes through my veins. Slipping a dagger from my waist, I stab the fucking bastard in the knee. The puncture is practiced and precise, sliding behind his knee cap. This time, his screams die.

His black out creates a silence that allows me to hear her gasp. Turning my head, I find Mei standing in the doorway. One hand on her stomach, the other over her mouth, she stares wide-eyed, taking in the bruises, blood, and mangled flesh.

The asshole's head lolls to the side, starting to regain consciousness.

This is it. She finally understands. She sees the creature at its worst. The very thing grown men cower from and my absolute jubilation in the acts I perform.

A strange sensation ripples across my blood-spattered flesh. Fear. I haven't feared anyone or anything since I was a boy. Not since it was beaten and tortured out of me.

Looking at her, I feel fear. Afraid she'll look at me the way everyone else does. That she'll too recoil at my presence. From the others, it thrills me. To know each of them would fall at my feet from a simple annoyed look feeds into the power.

But not Mei. If she rejects the monster, then the world is damned, and so is she. I won't let her go. I may free her from the demons plaguing her, chasing her, but she will never be free from the real monster—me.

Meeting her eyes, I straighten my spine and lift my chin.

She steps back. The creature, already angry his current plaything has blacked out, fills with a new fury. Her retreat, her rejection, hurts in unexpected ways. Every muscle tenses in preparation for the chase.

"You wanted to see, to know, what I am," I sneer, the anger seeping into my words. "Well," I lift my blood-covered arms out to my sides, "here I am."

Her hand leaves her mouth, reaching for the door frame.

Tightening my grip on the handle of the knife, I fight the urge to charge at her like a mad bull.

Confusion furrows my brow when the room brightens, bathing the blood-drenched walls in soft white light. I blink at the suddenness and Arman groans.

Eyes adjusting, I watch her hand move from the dimming switch to her side. She scans the room, taking it all in. With a slow, tentative step, she walks the perimeter. Touching her fingers over the plastic lined walls, she smears the blood dripping down them.

Dropping my arms to my sides and keeping my gaze on her, I run the sides of the blade along my pants to clean it.

Stopping at the table, standing over the tools laid out, she runs her bloody fingers across the instruments before selecting one of the polished wooden handles.

Still tense and unsure, I study her every move.

Turning on her heels, she spares me a brief glance before focusing on the man bleeding out in the chair between us. The familiar gleam in her eye ignites a fire in my chest. Her darkness shines like a beacon of malice.

Taking a deep breath, I hope—hope for something I shouldn't. I begin tapping the knife against my leg, unable to contain my eagerness.

Determination lining her forehead, Mei steps forward, closing the distance between her and my prey. When she fists the asshole's hair and places the serrated blade to his throat, my anxiousness turns primal. Blood rushes to my cock, hardening it.

The man gurgles, coughs, and opens his eyes. When they fix on her, they widen. She tilts her head to the left and removes the blade. Disappointment doesn't have a chance to douse the fire behind my ribs before she's straddling his lap.

"You remember me, don't you?" she asks, pressing closer to his body.

He stays silent, unwilling to confess.

Pissed he's denying her anything she wants, I stride next to them, and growl, "Answer her."

"Y-Yes," he stutters.

The grin that spreads across her lips makes my dick twitch.

In a swift motion, she cocks back the fist holding the knife and slams her knuckles into his face.

He groans, and she laughs.

"Now your face matches mine," she whispers harshly.

The mention of the mark he left on her cheek stokes my fury.

"I'm sorry," he rasps. "I'm so—"

Her arm arcs upward before slicing down, silencing his unwanted apologies. My cock lengthens and throbs painfully against the confines of my pants.

Instead of removing the knife, she releases the handle, leaving it protruding from his neck. Pushing out of his lap, she stands between his legs. Gripping the dagger in his knee, she pulls it free and cuts the plastic ties restraining him.

Blood covers her shirt, making it cling to her braless chest. Her hard nipples poke through, calling for my touch.

She's more than I'd hoped. Dragging my eyes up her body, I find her watching me.

Instead of the fear and disgust I expected, I find heat and desire. Fuck, I've never wanted anything more than her.

Reaching out with my empty hand, I grab the protruding handle and yank the blade from his neck. Her nostrils flare before she pushes the dead bastard to the floor.

Stepping over his legs, she stands before me. Hands pressed to my chest, they slide up to wrap around my neck and pull my head down. Her mouth attacks mine with a ferocious hunger as she writhes against me.

The knives fall from my hands, clanging against the concrete floor. Taking her ass into my hands, I squeeze. When she shoves against me, I release her and frown.

Fisting my shirt in one hand, she uses the dagger still in her hand to cut the material open and runs her hands down my bare chest. Thin streaks of blood leave a trail over my skin.

She drops the dagger to the floor and slips her fingers into the waist of my pants, tugging me to the chair. Undoing my zipper and the button closure, she drops down, taking my pants with her.

Her tongue swipes the tip of my cock, making it jump, before sucking me into the depths of her warm mouth. Stabbing my fingers into her hair, I grip the back of her head and guide her lips along my shaft. Glancing down, I watch her mouth slide along my length. And in my peripheral, I notice the pool of blood surrounding us.

Her eyes flash open, capturing mine, and rapture sweeps through me.

I fuck her face faster, harder, deeper.

She gags, and I try to ease up, but the grip of her hands on the back of my thighs prevents me. So, I thrust my hips forward, feeling her saliva coat my shaft and run over my balls. The sensation causes them to tighten until the ache becomes painful.

Releasing my dick from her mouth, she slides up my body and shoves me into the chair. In a swift movement, her ruined shirt is torn over her head and pants are pushed down her legs. She comes to stand between my legs, skin stained bloody pink.

I reach out, palm her ass, and tug her to me. She places one hand on my shoulder while the other moves down my chest and around my cock. Moving to straddle me, she positions me at her entrance. The heat of her pussy warms my tip, causing my dick to pulse in anticipation.

Tightening my grip on each globe of her ass, I pull her down.

Her pussy is so wet, I slide deep inside with one thrust. Her head drop back, a curse falling from her lips.

Glancing over Mei's shoulder, I find our reflection in the dirty, cracked wall mirror across the room. Slipping my hand up her back, I watch it leave smeared blood prints along her spine and my arousal soars to a whole new level.

One hand splayed on her right shoulder blade, the other on her ass, I urge her to move and order, "Fuck me, Mei."

Grinding against me, she brings her forehead to mine, and whispers, "Dahlia."

The heat of her breath across my lips and the admission makes every muscle tense. I still her, and the creature rushes forth, ready to possess her body and own her soul. Her eyes snap open and meet mine.

"Dahlia?" I ask, though I already know she just handed me a piece of her puzzle. Possibly the one to unlock all the secrets I crave to own.

A slow, malevolent smile spreads across her mouth, and lift us from the chair, carrying her to the table holding my tools. Knives fall from the surface, clanging against the concrete floor as I plant her on top.

Pulling her to the edge, I grip her left thigh with bruising strength, spread her wide, and enter her in one hard thrust.

"Tell me again," I demand, refusing to move until she gives me what I want.

"Dah-lia," she says, the end of the word made raspy by my sudden grip on her neck.

I fuck her.

I fuck her hard, rough, ruthless. And she takes it, thrives on it, and comes around it.

"Dahlia," I groan as her pussy contracts.

Tightening my hand on her neck, she arches her back and gasps. I lift her thigh higher and thrust into her until my balls throb and my release explodes into her body.

Breathing labored, I release her thigh and press my palm to the table for support. Everything about tonight went beyond any dark, deviant fantasy I could desire.

Sliding my hand to the back of her neck, I pull her face to mine. "Dahlia," I whisper and take her mouth.

Chapter eighteen

Mei

A loud cracking sound wrenches me from a dreamless sleep. A flash of lightening brightens the dark bedroom and a second clap of thunder sounds even closer than the last.

Pressing a hand to my chest, I'm not surprised at the rapid thumping. I close my eyes, trying to calm my erratic heart, but flashes of memories from the night before assault me.

Plastic walls.

Knives.

Blood.

So. Much. Blood.

Me.

Saint.

My name.

Scrambling to the middle of the massive bed, I push to my knees and take a deep breath. I search every shadowed corner, anticipating Saint to emerge from one, but where I expect brimstone walls, fire pits, and death, I only find the soft beige and tan master suite. It's unchanged and I'm alone. More memories rush forward, clearing the remaining fog of sleep from my mind.

Closing my eyes, I inhale through my nose and exhale, trying to will away the awful deeds of the night before. The way my shock didn't melt away into horror and repulsion, as a normal, sane person would. Instead, a hunger, deep and dark, twisted its way through my body until my fingertips tingled and I craved more. How the smooth handle of the knife had been a contrast to the jagged edge of the blade. The moment every insidious urge bloomed beneath my pale skin, bringing forth all the grave mistakes and sins of my past.

Expecting to find bloodstains, I lift my hands in front of my face and open my eyes. They're clean. Lowering them, I glance down my naked body and find nothing that would give away the fact that I'd lost what was left of my soul.

A shiver slides up my spine. Wrapping my arms around myself, I slip out of the bed.

What have I done?

On wobbly legs, I stumble to the bathroom, touch the light panel, and freeze.

Cold realization prickles my skin. The shaking starts in my hand, travels up my arm, and moves over my body.

You know what you did, what you unleashed, a small voice whispers.

Shaking my head, I try to free myself of the fear, shame, and panic welling up within me. Forcing my feet to move, I take care to avoid the dried bloody footprints and streaks. Ones made last night when Saint carried both our blood-covered bodies to the shower. If this is the state of the bathroom floor, then there are more streaks and prints on the stairs, hallway walls, and bedroom door.

The familiar dark urges I've kept buried swirl freely inside. I wait for the horror, repulsion, something other than the complete satisfaction I feel.

He got off easy, the voice reinforces in softly. *Remember what he did when you were just a girl? Do you remember how he hurt you? Do you think you were the only one he hurt all these years? He tried to repeat the attack just weeks ago.* The voice grows louder, refusing to be ignored.

The image of every brutal mark on Arman's body, the blood dripping to the floor, and his bound hands flashes in my mind. The same satisfaction of seeing his hands turning purple settles in my chest like last night.

"No," I choke out, slipping into the glass shower stall.

I want to disagree, argue that no one deserves what we did last night, but deep down, I know all too well that some people do, and that's when the next memory replays.

The serrated blade I'd held, as I turned all my malevolent desires onto one man—the man who starred in my childhood nightmares and marked me as a woman.

Uncaring about the water temperature, I twist knobs until cold water sprays my skin. The shock of it settles some of my impending breakdown. Wrapping my arms around my body once more, I lean back against the tiled wall. As the water warms, tears start to slip over my cheeks.

Sliding down the wall to the floor, I pull my legs to my chest and latch my arms around them. Face buried in my knees, I try to block it all out, to forget, but I've made a horrible mistake. The moment my eyes shut, everything plays out like a twisted snuff film in my head.

He wouldn't approve. All the unnecessary mess. The thoughts burrow deeper into my mind. *Father would never leave so many marks on perfectly good skin.*

Rocking on the floor of the shower, I slap a hand over my mouth and stifle a sob.

Lifting my other hand, I open my eyes and expect to see his hair—the hair I still feel against my palm. Shutting my lids once again, the knife against his neck accompanies the scent of blood and fear I recall pouring out of Arman's body while I made sure he remembered the fear of a young girl and the anger of the woman holding his life in her hands.

Another cry breaks through the hand on my mouth, recalling how I didn't allow him to confess his sins or beg for forgiveness. Because he didn't deserve that. His apologies fell on a bad girl's ears.

The memories play out so vividly, so intense, a metallic scent fills my nose and teases my taste buds. Echoes of painful groans fill my ears, until they're replaced by Saint and my moans of pleasure.

"Oh God!" The sobbed words slip between the fingers pressed to my mouth.

Daddy wouldn't approve of the methods, but he would have been proud of one thing: I remembered his anatomy lessons.

My internal struggle between right and wrong, good and bad,

and should and shouldn't has drawn a line in the blood-stained floor. And it's falling on the wrong side. All of my demons run untethered beneath my flesh, free to act on all my unnatural desires.

Hitting my head against the tile wall, I try to knock sense into myself—repeatedly—trying my hardest not to let the same satisfactions and pleasures from last night creep back in.

"Mei." His deep baritone is followed by hands on my arms. "Christ," he growls, "the water is freezing."

Saint's arms wrap around me and lift me from the floor, interrupting my downward spiral. Carrying me out of the shower, he takes me back to bed, wrapping the sheet around my body and draping the comforter across my shoulders.

"What happened?" His hands grasp the sides of my face.

I close my eyes, just now noticing the chattering of my teeth.

"Jesus, Mei," he scoffs, pushing away from me.

At his retreat, I open my eyes, afraid he's finally repulsed enough to walk away. But he only turns on the fireplace before returning to me.

Kneeling on the floor between my legs, he takes my face in his hands once again before searching my scalp with his fingertips. I wince when he touches the place I hit against the wall.

"What. Happened," he says, his question now a demand.

Shaking my head, I try to free his hold on me, but it doesn't work.

"Let go," I rasp.

His brow furrows.

"There's one thing we need to be absolutely fucking clear about." The harshness of his voice makes me swallow the lump of emotion in my throat. "You belong to me, Dahlia."

At my real name, I stiffen, staring at him.

"You gave that to me," he responds to my reaction. "I didn't take it, and I sure as fuck won't give it back."

"Tell me last night was a bad dream," I beg, reaching up and latching my hands onto his wrists. "That it was only a nightmare."

The left corner of his mouth curls into a devious smirk.

"Last night was the most beautiful thing I've ever seen," he rumbles, daring me to argue.

A sob lodges in my throat and tears blur my vision.

"Is that what this is about?" he asks, incredulous. "Last night?"

I try to turn away again, but it's impossible with his hold on my face. Too bad he can't stop the tears from coming.

"Look at me," he demands.

I squeeze my eyes shut. Releasing my face, he stands.

"Don't waste tears on that worthless asshole," he states, his words a vehement decree.

He's angry at me? My own anger flares to life and I snap my eyes open.

"I'm not crying over *him*," I say through clenched teeth.

Saint lifts one brow, challenging my statement.

Shoving the blankets from my body, I climb to my feet. Standing on the mattress and forcing him to raise his head to meet my eyes, I shout, "I mourn the loss of what little soul I had left."

He blinks at my declaration.

"I've fought so hard to keep..." I trail off, unable to find the right words.

"To keep what?" he presses, placing his hands on my bare hips.

"To not let it out," I try to explain, praying he'll understand.

"Let what out?" he pushes.

My frustration with him not getting it and with myself for not being able to find the right words wins out. "The darkness he put inside me."

Eyes wide and nostrils flaring, his fingers flex into the flesh of my hips.

"Who put in you?" Saint asks, but I ignore the question.

"And now, I can feel it everywhere," I continue, lifting my palms between us. "It's beneath my skin, in my veins, free." Dropping my hands, I meet his heated stare. "There's no escaping it now." My voice cracks.

"It's perfect," he says with little emotion.

"It's terrifying," I counter.

"It's you." He pulls me toward him.

His hands slip over my skin, one pressing to my lower back the other sliding up between my shoulder blades.

"Dahlia, it's you."

"I can't be that," I tell him.

"Why? Who says you can't?"

"I can't," I snap.

"Well, I can't allow a man like Arman to live," he growls, arms tightening.

My eyes widen, and I retort, "So, you just get to kill every asshole?"

"If they fall out of line, then I do what is requested and necessary to protect the family." He pauses, moving one hand to the curve of my ass. "And if they touch you, then yes. I absolutely get to kill them."

I open my mouth to argue, but he's not finished.

"However, after last night, I can see I won't need to."

It's my turn to furrow my brow in confusion.

"You, my deadly doll," he starts, hands sliding to my ribs. "Are capable of gorgeous vengeance," he finishes, pressing his lips to my stomach. "You are a goddess among mortals."

"What's right and wrong is being swallowed up," I whisper, the words weak and lacking vehemence.

"Righteousness is subjective. And last night, it secured your fate to be at my side."

I stiffen, and he lifts his head.

"Mei," he says, returning to my false name, my mask.

I drop my face to meet his gaze.

"You've killed me again," I admit in a low voice.

Everything I'd built and buried has crumbled around me. I can don the Mei mask, but Dahlia has been reborn. He's resurrected her without understanding the crazy, dark, and twisted things that follow her.

Pleased with himself, he grins. "What are you so afraid of?"

"How much I like it," I only half lie, keeping my past to myself.

His touch on my ribs tightens. Eyes still on mine, he drops his chin, just a little. Then his tongue snakes out, tasting the skin above my belly button.

"You." He presses a kiss to the same spot. "Have." His lips move over my skin. "Nothing." Full, soft, hot, and moving lower. "To worry about," he finishes, kissing just above my mound before slipping his tongue between my thighs.

I gasp.

Licking, tasting, he continues his assault and moves his hands over my hips to my thighs. Curving them around the backs of my legs, he pulls my legs out, causing me to fall back on the bed. Before I can catch my breath, he's between my legs.

"Just thinking about last night..." He closes his eyes, licking his bottom lip. Instead of finishing, he buries his face between my thighs.

He's thorough, hard, and as demanding as ever. Ordering me to call his name, not Saint, but Dante, and to admit that I, Dahlia, belong to him alone. And this time, they aren't just demands I expect from him, but things I desperately want myself. Saint owning my name, body, and soul should terrify me, but I can't find the desire to dwell on it.

Exhausted by both my mini breakdown and the deliciously dirty things Saint did to my body, I lie stomach down in the bed. Head turned away from Saint, my eyes focus on a dark stone in the wall. With each blink, my eyelids grow heavier, until I can no longer keep them open.

The warmth of Saint's body presses along my side, his hand sliding across on my lower back, his calloused fingers moving over my bared skin. Palming my right ass cheek, he splays his fingers. Pressing his mouth to my shoulder, he says, "Which birth control, if any, are you on?"

His hand flexes against my flesh before moving lower, curving between my thighs and running his fingers through our mixed releases.

My eyes snap open, mind racing to count down the days of my last period.

"I know it's a requirement at the club," he continues. His fingers move lazily against me as if this isn't a moment to panic. "But," he says, pressing another kiss to my shoulder, "I'm well aware rules aren't always upheld."

"I—" I choke, unable to answer him.

"You what?" His voice grows more serious, perhaps noticing the tension in my body.

His hand disappears from between my legs, gripping my right arm. Rolling to his back, he pulls me against his chest. Sliding a hand into my hair, he fists, bringing my face to his.

"You aren't on anything?" he says, his voice rough and low.

My body, as it always does with him, reacts opposite of the way it should. Clit throbbing, my lower body flares to life, and I can only pray my nipples aren't noticeably hard.

When a muscle ticks in his jaw, I rush to get my words out.

"No—" I blurt.

Before I can finish, his hand tightens in my hair.

"No." It's not a question.

"Yes—" I try again to explain.

"Yes?" Now, it's a question. An annoyed one accompanied by a furrow. "Which is it?"

"You asked if I wasn't on anything," I explained.

"And you said you weren't," he growled.

Wincing when I try to shake my head, I try to clarify, "I said no, meaning I am on something."

His hand flexes once more in my hair before easing.

"I get a shot every few months at the clinic," I rush out before he cuts me off like before. "It's good for another four weeks at least."

Brow still furrowed, his lips thin. The look is all I need to know he doesn't believe me. He thinks I'm lying.

Placing my hand on his chest, I reassure, "I swear, I've been getting the shot since I started at the club and learned about Planned Parenthood."

"How effective is it?" he asks in the same low voice.

"Ninety-nine percent. I typically go five days early, before it runs out, to be sure I'm not late with—"

"You won't need to make further appointments," he cuts me off—again.

Closing my mouth, I wait for him to explain. Maybe he has a personal doctor I'm supposed to use. Something like that, but he says nothing more.

Instead, releasing my body back to the mattress, he climbs from the bed. The quick, jerky movements make his displeasure clear, but for the life of me, I can't figure out why. Naked, he disappears into the bathroom, roughly closing the door behind him.

Confused, unsure, and a little afraid, I pull myself up. Back to the headboard and knees to my chest, I stare at the wooden door he's shut himself away behind. Minutes feel like hours until he emerges. Still naked, he crosses the room. At the fireplace, he places his hands on the mantel and bows his head.

"There's something you need to understand and reconcile

yourself to now," he orders.

Swallowing the lump in my throat, I drop my legs, stretching them out, and sit up straight.

He's going to tell me he doesn't want children, forbid me from ever getting pregnant. Surprisingly, a small twinge of regret pangs in my chest, but it's smothered at the thought of being a mother. I would make a terrible mother. The only time I experienced a true mother was snuffed out by my past in one blood and terror filled night.

How could someone as twisted as me ever deserve or raise a child? I've reconciled myself to all of it before he finally makes his declaration.

"You're mine," he reminds. "You and I both know it." He twists his head to look over his shoulder at me.

Knowing what he wants and before he can ask, I say, "Yes."

At my confirmation, he pushes away from the mantel. Crossing his arms over his chest, he approaches the foot of the bed. Eyes locked to mine, he holds my gaze for long moments before continuing.

"I'm not used to things being out of my reach," he states. "It may take time, but I get what I want. Do you understand?"

I give a small nod, and the lines around his eyes soften, a warmth creeping in.

"But the time it's taking with you is driving me mad," he growls, and I furrow my brow.

"I just said I'm yours," I say, but the words sound like a question.

Dropping his hands, he clenches his fists at his sides.

"But I want all of you," he says through clenched teeth.

I open my mouth, but he's not finished, so I snap it shut.

"Your secrets, your past, your present, and your future will belong to me, Mei."

I stiffen.

"Don't think for one moment I won't possess every last part of you." His words border on threatening.

A part of me bristles, reminded by another man who desired to possess things, women, children...dolls.

"Physically, emotionally, legally, and in blood, I want you." He runs his hands over his face, shouting, "It's driving me to distraction and I can't afford distractions right now."

I jump, dropping my eyes to the mattress. His last statement plants a seed of curiosity.

The bed dips, drawing my eyes to Saint. He crawls up my body, straddling my thighs. Taking my head in both his hands, he confesses in a low voice, "I need to possess you the way you possess me. Because the power you hold over me..." he lets the words fade, but they embolden me.

Placing my hands on his knees, I slide them up and down his thighs. He closes his eyes and smiles.

Stretching my neck, I press my lips to his. Instead of him invading my mouth as I expect, he pulls away.

"You'll no longer need the shot," he states.

My hands freeze on his thighs.

"You'll be pregnant sooner than later. I'll make sure of it, by fucking you often." His mouth conquers mine, demanding and taking. Pulling away and panting, he continues, "and without anything between us."

Shaking my head, I whisper, "I can't be someone's mother."

"You will make a fierce mother." He sounds so sure of it, but I know differently.

Before I can argue, he repeats his words from earlier, "Reconcile yourself to it. I will have all of you. The way you have all of me."

Panicking at the thought of impending motherhood, defiance pushes the next words from my mouth. "I don't have all of you," I snap. "Your wife has a part."

The right side of his mouth curves, amused. It pisses me off and I try to pull away. Saint tightens the hold on my head, forcing my eyes to his.

"I like your jealousy," he taunts.

Grabbing his wrists, I try to pull his hands off me.

"Stop," he orders. "She has a piece of paper," he concedes. "Which will be dissolved in time."

My eyes widen as shame sends a chill up my spine. Marriage, children, partner in crime, and homewrecker are just some of the things he's decided I should accept. I won't deny the small thrill tingling my stomach, but I'm not sure I can be this creature he's decided I'm to be.

"When I said legally, I meant, you will be mine in marriage," he clarifies, bringing his face close to mine and adding, "Among the other ways I'll have you."

Nose to nose, he sweeps his tongue over my mouth before sucking on my bottom lip and nipping. My gasp grants him full access, something he doesn't hesitate to take. My hands still resting on his thighs, he releases my head to place his over mine. His fingers flex before guiding them to his chest and trapping them there.

For a moment, I can see everything in a picture perfect package. Husband, wife, two children, a dog, cat, and a goldfish all wrapped up in a white house with blue trim and a picket fence. For most, this is the dream, the perfect deal, but for me, it feels like a terrible lie. Reality—my reality—invades the dream, and the house melts into a dungeon, a man tied to a chair in the middle of the room, Saint with his knives, and children playing in a pool of blood.

Before he can notice my panic, there's a knock at the door.

Saint breaks the kiss, staring down at me with narrowed eyes. Perhaps he did notice.

"I sent down for food while I was in the bathroom," he states, still studying me.

After a moment, he seems satisfied with whatever he finds. Without moving off me or covering our nakedness, he shouts over his shoulder, "Enter."

"Saint," I hiss, yanking at my trapped hands.

He grins.

A rattling of dishes is followed by Jacob asking, "Anything else?"

The exasperation is evident in his tone. My chest heats, and I stiffen, trying to shrink down behind Saint's large body.

"No," Saint dismisses.

"You're lucky I didn't send one of the men up instead of me," Jacob lectures. "They may not be so quick to avert their eyes."

"They would learn," Saint retorts, his words a promise of punishments and pain.

"Th—" my thanks stopped by the glare darkening Saint's face.

Rolling my eyes, I lean around Saint, and respond, "Thank you."

The moment the door is closed, Saint's fingers lift my chin.

"I'll bring the food over while you tell me exactly what you do with Jacob," he states, releasing my chin.

He's halfway to the food tray when I decide to use his own words to taunt him, "I do believe I like your jealousy."

Saint stops and turns to face me. The light of the fireplace casts shadows across his naked body. Between the tattoos and lack of light, it's difficult to make out the scars marring his skin. Straightening to his full height, he warns, "Careful of the game you play, doll. My jealousy comes with a death sentence."

Pushing to my knees, I place my hands on my hips, and retort, "After last night, are you so sure mine doesn't?"

A large, devious grin spreads across his face. Food forgotten, he stalks back to the bed, tackling me.

Chapter nineteen

Saint

Three days and I still can't get it out of my head. The way she tore away her mask, released her darkest nature, and gave up a piece of her true self to me.

Finding her in the shower the following morning broken and punishing herself awakened a part of me I thought long dead. My chest felt as if someone carved out my heart and lungs, the ache growing and twisting my insides. Her mental break doing enough of a number on me to force out demands I knew she wasn't, isn't, ready for yet. Selfishly worrying she would be lost to a broken mind, or renew her efforts to get away from me, drove me to foolishly expose my plans where she's concerned.

Desperation isn't something I often experience, but when I do it's unpleasant for everyone involved. Having one tiny little woman possess every thought and desire, who stirs a million buried emotions, brings out the primeval male in me.

Well aware of the way I've craved her from the beginning. Now, after watching her come to life and embracing the deepest parts she hides from herself, I want her tied to me by lust, desire, marriage, children, and terrible deeds. But who the fuck tells someone they are going to get them pregnant just to make sure they're tied to you forever? An obsessed man afraid the person he wants most will disappear in a puff of smoke or puddle of blood.

Three days ago, she almost broke mentally. While she still struggles internally, trying to come to terms with this awakening, her sleep has become much less agitated. She's rising from the black pit of regret and shame, wearing them like her own personal armor.

"If you were anyone else..." Jacob says, taking a seat across from my desk.

Leaning back into my leather office chair, I steeple my hands touching the tip of my fingers to my lips.

"I wouldn't have believed it, but..." he starts again, staring, unfocused, at a spot on the desk.

The right corner of my mouth curls.

"You seem to have a hard time finishing sentences," I state.

His eyes snap to mine.

"Russ went down there."

At Jacob's words, all amusement drains from my body. Dropping my hands, I grip the arms of the chair. Every muscle tenses, preparing to stand.

He lifts a hand, palm out. "Stop," his tone makes me pause. "He heard her yell and only went down to make sure you weren't in any danger." A small smile spreads on his mouth. "That boy is more loyal than you deserve," he teases.

Settling back into the chair, I lift one brow.

"When you emerged from the basement..." he hesitates again.

This time I know it's because of the morbid picture Mei and I presented. Our bodies covered in blood and her wrapped around me, we'd emerged like something nightmares and horror stories are made of. The Saint and his Deadly Little Doll.

"Yes?" I press.

Our eyes meet and he confesses, "I thought she... that you may have killed her."

I stiffen at his honesty.

"But then she moved, wrapping tighter around you, holding on like you were the center of her universe." There's awe in his voice that I don't particularly care for. "And once you passed us, she glanced over your shoulder."

Furrowing my brow, I'm impatient for him to get to the point.

"Dante," he licks his lips, "Her eyes were so menacing." He shakes his head. "And that fucking smile..." he swallows hard, and finishes, "I've only seen that once before," he pauses, making sure I'm paying attention. "The day I watched you kill your mother. You wore the same look."

Leaning my elbows to the desk, I glance away from the intensity in his eyes. We haven't spoken of that day since he first came to work for me.

"I don't know if what you unleashed is a good or bad thing. I just hope you can handle it." I don't miss the scolding tone.

"Your concerns are noted," I state, staring off into the shadows of my office.

The moment I enter the living room, finding Mei burrowed into the sofa, her eyes move from the TV to me.

"You won't be going back to the penthouse, so get comfortable here," I order.

"And my chosen prison guards will be?"

Her bold question makes me smile. Moving to the small liquor shelf, I take a tumbler glass in one hand and a bottle of Vodka in the other. I pour half a glass and respond, "They're for your protection."

Turning around, I find Mei watching me from a knelt position on the sofa. Her elbows resting on the top of the back cushions. She pulls her lips to one side and lifts one brow over a disbelieving eye.

"Is that what you tell yourself to feel better about keeping prisoners?"

I step up to the back of the couch, slide my free hand into her hair and fist. Tugging her head back just a bit, I bring the tumbler glass to her mouth. When I press the edge to her lip, she opens and accepts the clear liquor.

"Don't swallow."

Her face scrunches in confusion at my demand.

Taking the glass away, I crush my mouth to hers and drink from her mouth. When I pull back, she sways forward wanting more. I lick my bottom lip and grin around the glass as I finish the last of the Vodka.

Releasing her head, I return the glass to the shelf, turn around, and tell her, "You are free to leave whenever you want."

Her eyes narrow and she voices her skepticism, "What game are you playing now?"

"It's not a game," I admit.

"I'm free?" She asks, adding, "To leave and not come back?"

She pushes off the couch, standing with the large oversized piece of furniture between us. Apprehension flares to life in my veins making me feel overheated and tense.

The silence stretching out between us becoming too much for me to bear, I ask, "Where would you like to go, Mei?" Before she has time to even think, let alone answer, I add, "Back to your apartment where the first doll arrived?" She visibly tenses. "Back to the club where the second doll was delivered?" This time is a noticeable swallow. "Or do you still have plans to hop on a bus and run?"

Fisting her hand at her sides, she lifts her chin defiantly. Fuck, if she isn't a gorgeous contradiction. Small, but deadly. Scared, but fierce. Free, but mine.

"My ticket *is* exchangeable," she states. "I could —"

"How far do you think you'll get?" My question is harsher than intended, but her just thinking about leaving is enough to provoke my creature.

"From Chicago or from you?" She presses, again reading me too well. I'm not sure when this particular shift in our interactions occurred. Nor am I sure why it doesn't bother me more.

"You already know the answer to that," I say much calmer than I feel.

"Then I'm not exactly free, am I?" She challenges.

Moving around the couch, I stand before her once again.

"Do you want to be free of me?"

Her eyes soften at my question, telling me just how much I've given away.

"It's you who may want to be free of me," she says, looking away.

"You mean free of Dahlia."

She snaps her eyes back to me at the mention of her real name. A mix of fear and concern swirling in them.

Reaching up, I cup her face. "Tell me who he is and it will all go away," I promise.

Pulling away from my touch, she shakes her head.

"Doesn't it bother you how..." she pauses, turning a hard glare on me, "Just how easily I... You have no idea what you're unleashing." Turning away from me, she moves to the French doors, staring outside.

"Then tell me," my words more demanding now.

Her body shakes and, on a humorless laugh, she says, "I wish I knew."

"Sir?" Jacob appears in the open entry.

Without taking my eyes off her, I answer, "Yes?"

"You have a call," he states.

Moving my eyes to him, I furrow my brow.

"Tell them I'll—"

"You'll want to take this," he insists. "It's..." his eyes shift to Mei and then back to me.

I nod, giving him the okay to speak.

"Angelo."

"Wow, that news traveled quickly," Sketch says, leaning against the frame of the door. "I bet you are on the naughty list now," he teases.

Shooting him a glare only brings a smile to his face.

I glance back to Mei and tell her, "We aren't done with this conversation."

Her body tenses, but she says nothing.

Ending my verbal reprimand with Angelo, I squeeze the phone until I hear it crack. Having basically threatened me for *disobedience*, he'd ended the call issuing orders. I'm supposed to apologize to Arman's uncle – publicly – and to bring the *woman who has me pussy whipped* to Felix's upcoming birthday party. Whatever he has planned, I need to figure out and do it quick.

Shouting, I release my pent up rage and frustration. My office door jerks open, Jacob filling the doorway with Sketch on his heels.

Focusing on nothing, I order, "Get Felix."

"On it," Jacob says, ducking out of the room.

"Bad call?" Sketch asks, sarcasm thick.

Snapping my head in his direction, the look I give is enough to wipe the smirk off his face.

"Don't you have research to finish?" I remind him of the information I recently handed over.

Not wanting to share her with anyone, not even something as simple as her name, it had taken until this morning for me to give Sketch Mei's real first name. His victorious grin made me believe it wouldn't take much longer. Soon I would know her past and strip her down to each secret she harbors.

"The searches are running," he says, quickly adding, "It's still not much to go on, but I'm sure we'll get hits soon."

"For your sake, I hope so," I growl, pushing out of my chair and stalking to the neatly lined liquor bottles.

"I'm working with what I've got," he argues.

"You're running out of time," I tell him, giving him my back.

"Time for what?" He presses.

"Next weekend is Felix's birthday celebration," I inform. "Family is expected."

Sketch snorts.

"I'm positive Aunt Rosario would rather drink poison than have me show up," he says around a laugh. "It's almost tempting, just to see how red her face can get. Plus, there is the sick joy I get calling Angelo Uncle Angie."

Turning around, I lock my eyes on him and tell him, "You'll be attending."

"What?" His brow furrows.

"Angelo is up to something."

Taking a seat once again, I motion for him to sit. When he does, I give him a recap of my call and end the conversation with, "So, I'm going to need you there."

"And you're bringing Felix on board." He nods his head toward the door where Jacob left moments ago to track down Felix.

I nod.

"What the fuck is the plan here, Saint?" He runs his hand through his overgrown hair. "You're already pushing Angelo to the edge and bringing me will definitely be another insult. This game is going to get bloodier and I'm still not sure what the ending will be, but I don't want mine to be at the hands of those fucking cunts."

Sketch, the bastard son of Maurizio Bianchi and nephew of Angelo's wife, has plenty of reasons to hate our aunt and uncle. His revenge had been elaborate, sick, and compelling enough for my services to be requested—to erase the black mark on Rosario's family.

"Sir," Jacob enters with quick strides, "Felix." He hands me another burner cell.

Taking the device, I bring it to my ear.

"Things are escalating," I say in place of greeting.

"Well, what the fuck did you expect when you slice and diced Arman?! Christ, Dante, what were you thinking?" He shouts.

"That the asshole touched something that belongs to me," I say, making it clear I regret nothing. "And he was dealt with accordingly."

"Fuck," he exclaims. "You of all people hooking up with a whore."

"Careful, Felix," I warn.

"Did you learn nothing from my situation with Vicky?"

"This is nothing like your penchant for gold digging women who will let you degrade them for your own satisfaction." I keep my tone even, without any emotion.

"Fuck you," he growls. "Don't act like I'm the only one with perverse preferences."

Sighing in frustration, I rub the bridge of my nose. Getting into a pissing match with Felix isn't exactly my goal. And getting into what he *thinks* are his preferences, because they really aren't. Sure, he gets off on the sexual games he likes to play, but if it was truly his *thing* he wouldn't be so goddamn miserable with every woman he beds.

"Have you thought about our conversation?" I reroute the conversation.

"Feelers were put out," he confides.

"Really?" His response surprises me. I expected him to think it over, mull on the details, and perhaps do some of his own investigating.

"Don't sound so fucking shocked," he snaps. "I know damn well that your information is thorough. Your little cyber-pet knows his shit."

"I'd like to know where you stand on the obstacle." I don't have to say Angelo for him to know exactly what I'm referring to.

"This isn't going to happen overnight, Dante," he states.

"I realize this."

"Do you?" He presses. "Even if my inquiries draw him out," he refers to Evgeni, "It's a very real possibility that he'll think I'm Angelo's spy or even consider me a lost cause since I belong to this syndicate."

"It's all a significant risk," I admit. "But I can't stand by after all he's done and still doing. We're supposed to be family, in blood and honor."

"And his selfishness and greed have even corrupted the most corrupt of us all," Felix adds, letting me know he understands. "We're all at risk until the obstacle is dealt with."

"Agreed," I say, giving a nod.

My eyes move between Sketch and Jacob before I say, "However," I pause. "I can tell he's planning something for your birthday celebration. I'm not sure, yet, what it is."

I focus on Sketch who nods understanding the silent order I've just given him. Glancing back to Jacob, I watch him straighten to his full height and cross his thick arms over his chest. He may not always approve of the things I do, but the stance he's taken on the matter is clear.

"But I plan to know as much as possible before the party," I finish.

"I'll let you know if anything comes my way," Felix says and then adds, "You know he has loyal followers and this could cause a massive war that splits the family, right?"

"Yes," I admit.

"Alright then," Felix sounds resigned, like he just made his final choice. "I'll see you this weekend and remember I like gifts that give oral."

I toss the phone to the desk.

"He contacted Evgeni?" Sketch asks, eyes wide.

Shaking my head, I explain, "No, made inquiries to draw him out."

"I can't believe Evgeni's never been suspicious. I mean, Felix doesn't exactly resemble the rest of you guys. He has to hold some resemblance to his wife or other family members."

"I never paid much attention until learning the truth and I'm not well versed in the looks of Evgeni's wife or family. Besides, Angelo's a bastard, not stupid. Felix was never really involved with Evgeni. He kept it that way as much as possible. Looking back, I can actually see how well he orchestrated and maneuvered Felix."

His tone disbelieving, he asks, "So, they've never met, at all?"

I shrug, "Maybe once, briefly. I'm called in with most of the international negotiations and I maybe remember once Felix was involved, but Evgeni was barely around. Felix was mostly involved with our southern associates," I explain.

"The Cartel," Sketch says, unmasking my vague reference.

"Yes," I confirm, releasing a sigh of annoyance, "Until a misunderstanding left his brother a captive."

He nods, remembering the month-long ordeal of getting Cosimo, Felix's brother, back and the missing drug shipment straightened out. Sketch had been a major player in getting Cosimo returned.

A beep pulls Sketch's attention away from the conversation. He takes out his cell phone and taps the screen. When his body stills, I study him.

"We have a hit," he practically purrs.

Pushing out of the chair, he focuses back on the screen of his cell phone.

"It's a hit on a Dahlia Dandry," he says, a broad grin on his face.

A smile of my own starts to form until his eyes snap back to mine. All triumph gone, replaced with shock and disbelief.

Heart racing, I rise from my chair. "What is it?"

"She..." he pauses, rapidly scrolling through his phone.

"She what?" I demand, my patience evaporating into a cloud of annoyance.

Dropping his arms to his sides, his rounded eyes come back to me.

"Dahlia Dandry is the daughter of Gilbert Dandry," he says, like I should know who that is. In a jerk of movement, he hurries to the corner table of computers in the office. Dropping into a rolling chair, he starts tapping away on his laptop.

Furrowing my brow, I focus on the name. It's vaguely familiar. Pressure builds at the base of my skull and a memory lingers at the edges of my mind.

"Who is Gilbert Dandry?" I tense at Jacob's question.

So caught up in this new discovery, I forgot he was in the room.

Moving to Sketch's side, I look down at his laptop, trying to focus on the image he's pulled up. He glances up from the screen, catching the confusion on my face.

Sketch leans back in the chair, shakes his head, and motions to the screen.

"She's the daughter of Gilbert Dandry, otherwise known as The Dollhouse Killer."

chapter twenty

Mei

Having not seen or heard from Saint, Sketch, or Jacob, I help myself to the contents of the refrigerator. On a tall stool at the far end of the large kitchen island, I sit on one leg while the other dangles along the side.

Taking a slice of ham and cheese, I roll it up, dip it into a glob of mustard, and bring it to my mouth. I'm mid bite when Jacob enters. He stops short just inside the threshold. There's no greeting or smile on his face. He just stares. I can't completely read the look on his face, but the softening of his eyes is clearly pity.

"Hope you don't mind," I mumble around a mouthful and hold up the half-eaten roll.

I've come to expect the blunt and very verbal Jacob. So, the silence following my comment grows uncomfortable, making the hairs on my arms stand up. Unsure of what's happening, I can only assume I've done something wrong.

With a visible shake of his body, he gives a small that feels off.

"As the lady of the house, you can have whatever you like," he finally speaks, moving from his frozen spot near the doorway.

"I'm not the lady of the house," I correct, watching him open the fridge, take out two bottles of water, and set them on the granite top between us.

"Of course you are," his voice back to the one I've grown familiar with. "Who else would be?"

I don't hesitate in responding, "His wife."

With a look that clearly conveys, *stupid girl*, he uncaps one bottle of water and drinks.

Placing the bottle back on the counter top, he reveals, "She's never stepped foot in this house."

That information shouldn't send a thrill through me, but I'm a warped person. So, even though I don't show it, I still feel it. Reaching out, I take the other bottle, uncap, and drink.

Jacob continues, "This isn't a place he brings people."

Sketch strolls in and, having overheard, is quick to add, "At least not ones he plans on leaving here breathing or with all their parts still intact."

I choke on the water, dribbling some down my chin.

Jacob glares at Sketch and holds a paper napkin out to me. Snatching it out of his hand, I press it to my mouth and wipe over my chin.

Sketch grabs an apple out of a bowl, leaning his hip against the far end of the island. Rubbing the fruit on his t-shirt, he ignores Jacob and focuses on me.

"But given how comfortable you are in the dungeon, I'd say you two twisted fucks are a match made in hell," he taunts, giving a toothy grin before biting into the apple.

"Oh how I wish you wouldn't have been an exception to norm," Jacob grumbles.

Sketch slaps a palm over the center of his chest. "You wound me, Jake," he feigns hurt and then goes on, "Besides, Mei should feel quite at home, given all the experience with—"

Jacob cuts him off and addresses me, "How about you and I do some sparring on the back patio?" He nods to the French doors behind me. "I'll grab some gear and meet you out there."

There's definitely something going on and I'm obviously not supposed to know. So, I nod, saying, "Let me go find something to change into."

Glancing back to Sketch, I find his face uncharacteristically serious. His eyes are directed at me, but he's not seeing me. Instead, he's lost in his own mind.

"I'll get this," Jacob says, taking my plate away and pulling my attention from Sketch.

"Thanks," I mumble, slipping off the stool and padding out of the room.

Hushed arguing follows my exit, but I can't make out what the two are disagreeing about.

The black cut off sweats brush the top of my knees and my cropped gray t-shirt reveal about two inches of skin. The chilly air caresses all my exposed flesh as I step out onto the back patio.

Jacob looks up at my arrival. Sitting on a low stone wall, he secures black gloves onto his hands. They aren't standard boxing gloves, instead they look like the kind MMA fighters use.

Lifting his hands, he explains, "We don't have two sets of boxing gloves here. I figure these will work for a sparring workout until I can get others delivered."

He pushes up to his feet and motions to a red pair.

"They are the smallest I could find, so hopefully they'll work." His eyes trail down my body to my bare feet and back up, meeting my eyes. "This isn't exactly half clothed kind of weather."

At the mention of the temperature, a second cold breeze sweeps up my back making me shiver.

"You should dress warmer," he says in a fatherly tone. It's the same tone I hear from him every time we work out together.

Striding to the wall, I pick up the red gloves and slip them on. Securing them, I say, "Once we start moving, I'll be fine."

"It's your disadvantage," he teases, stretching and warming up.

"And I'll still beat you," I taunt back, giving him a smile.

He returns one and says, "Your smile is quite charming."

"The better to distract *you* with," I retort, hiding my embarrassment behind a joke.

The genuine kindness he shows me coupled with a sincere compliment are things I'm not exactly used to. In my line of work, I usually get lewd comments or false praise and their sole hope is that I'll give them more. Jacob's compliments don't have strings and I don't know how to process that.

"Ready?" He asks, taking a fighting stance.

Opening and closing my hands, I test the fit of the gloves and nod.

"Yep." I take my own stance.

"Ladies first," he offers, wanting me to throw the first jab.

"I respect my elders, so you first," I retort.

He laughs and our dance begins.

Forty minutes and two matches later, the cold is unnoticeable. Sweat drips down my spine and between my breasts. Having gone so many days without a workout, my body is already feeling it. But now, I'd found my stride.

Jacob jabs right, I dodge left. He sweeps a leg, I jump and send a padded jab into his side. But before I can move around his body an arm wraps around my chest. Curling the limb, he pulls my back to his chest and sends a soft hit to my right kidney.

"Damn it," I shout, pissed he caught me.

"Not quick enough," he teases on a laugh.

His laugh dies as quickly as his arm disappears. Glancing over my shoulder, I furrow my brow.

"Explain." Saint's deep demand sends a different kind of shiver through my body.

"The lady—" Jacob starts to explain.

"I'm used to working out a few times a week," I cut him off and turn.

Saint's eyes sweep the length of my body, stopping on my feet.

"You should have shoes on," he grumbles, bringing his eyes to mine.

"I'm fine," I assure.

"Is this what you went to that gym for?" He asks, stepping onto the patio.

I nod.

"Just for the exercise?" He presses, stalking toward me. He stops less than a foot away and lifts a brow.

"No," I shake my head. "I trained with two instructors to learn how to fight."

The corners of his mouth lift just a little at my confession.

"Gloves," he demands, tugging his sweater over his head.

Keeping his eyes on mine, he tosses it off to the side and lifts an expectant hand out to Jacob. Silence falls around us, until the tear of Velcro rips through it like a shout. Jacob places the black gloves in Saint's hand before backing away and out of my peripheral.

"Let's see what you've got, doll," Saint taunts, slipping the gloves over his hands.

A mixture of surprise and fear jolts through my body and I step back. His hands come up and he positions his feet in a manner that makes it clear he knows what he's doing.

Swallowing, I resume my starting stance in front of him.

"Widen your legs," he instructs.

I narrow my eyes, letting him know I don't trust his advice.

"Your balance is compromised," he continues. "One hit and you'll stumble, possibly fall."

"You're twice my size," I snort. "My leg positioning doesn't make a difference. Besides, you'd have to hit me first," I tease.

The giant grin on his face is almost enough to distract me from his first attack.

Almost.

He jabs, I duck. I jab, he dodges. The dance goes on for a solid ten minutes before I come to a conclusion. I'll lose any fair fight with him, so it's time to use other tactics.

He punches out again, but this time I duck under his arm and move around his body. One jab to his side, as I did with Jacob, and he grunts. But this time, I move faster. Now behind him, I jump on his back before he can turn around.

Wrapping my legs around his waist, I bring my arm around his neck. He gets one gloved hand between my arm and his throat, but I lock my hands together and tighten.

In my peripheral, I see Jacob jump to his feet. He hesitates, unsure if an intervention is needed.

It's not.

Saint works his other hand beneath my arm and breaks my hold. The surprise of his release forces me to grab at his shoulders. And before I can drop back to the patio, my back hits the side of the house. It's not enough to seriously hurt me, but the stone is unforgiving, causing me to grunt at the pain and drop my legs from his waist.

In a real fight, I'm sure he'd step away, letting the opponent crumble to the ground so he could finish them off. But with me, he stills, using his body to hold me up.

"Can you stand?" He asks over his shoulder.

Nodding, I pant, "yes."

Slowly, he turns, being sure to keep his body close. Pressing his hands into the stones on either side, he cages me in.

"You're a fierce little thing," he praises, bringing one hand to my face and brushing my stray hairs away. "But I'll always win, Mei," he grins. "Even if I have to fight dirty, cheat, or kill," he continues and I feel like we're no longer talking about sparring. "Whatever it takes," he finishes, pressing his body against mine.

A throat clears behind him. Jacob.

"Go away," he orders.

"Unless you want the crowd you've drawn to watch, I suggest you take this inside."

At Jacob's suggestion, Saint pushes away and turns. The moment his body is out of my way, I see four men in suits seated on the stone wall.

"How is my perimeter?" Saint asks, crossing his sweaty arms over his chest.

The men shoot up and disappear around the corner of the house.

"You can't blame them," Jacob says, a hint of amusement in his voice.

"Can't I?" Saint asks, removing his gloves and holding them out.

"Like you said," Jacob pauses, looking over to me. Saint does the same. "She's a fierce little thing," he finishes, taking the gloves.

"That she is," he agrees, extending an arm to me.

When I hesitate, his brow lifts. Placing my hand in his, he yanks me toward him and removes my gloves.

"We'll be going out to dinner at seven," Saint announces.

"The car will be ready," Jacob responds.

"Until then, we're unavailable."

Keeping one hand secured in his, he guides me along the back patio, down one flight of stairs, passed the pool, and then up the stairs that lead to his room. Once inside, he releases me to close the French doors.

"I like that you can defend yourself," he states, locking the doors.

When he turns to face me, there's a ferocity in his eyes. A riot of butterflies assault my stomach and a lump of nervousness forms at the base of my throat.

"I'll admit, I was curious after you knocked me off the bed back in the penthouse," he continues, starting a slow prowl in my direction.

For each step he advances, I take a step back.

"Don't run from me," he commands.

Swallowing my nerves, I admit, "You scare me."

He stills. His brow furrows and muscle at his jaw ticks.

"I'm the last person you should fear," he growls, closing the distance.

I retreat until my back hits a wall and press myself against it. Saint reaches me, dropping to his knees. It's not what I expected and the unpredictability makes me more nervous.

Large hands grip my hips, holding me in place. His head tilts back.

"The first moment I saw you," his words draw my eyes to his. "I was drawn in."

Tugging on my hips, he brings me closer so that his chin rests against my lower abdomen.

"The first time our eyes met, you ensnared me," he confesses. "And the moment, you pulled away your mask, you became my obsession."

His hands move from my hips, sliding around me until I'm caged within his arms.

"They say giving someone your name gives them power over you."

I stiffen at the words, pressing my hands on his shoulders. I try to twist away and out of his hold. I handed my name, my power, over to him like a fucking foolish girl.

"But..." The word stills my struggle. "With you it's the opposite," he admits. "I've spent my life making sure no one owns me," he declares, squeezing me tighter. "Until you. You've seen the ugliness, danced with my demons, and you didn't run."

Closing my eyes, I drop my head back against the wall. No, I hadn't run. I accepted him, was twistedly turned on by him. And maybe it's because we're alike. More so than he knows.

He releases my lower body long enough to stand and capture my throat in his large hand. My body instantly flushes, wanting to arch into him. And when his thumb slides along my jaw, I bite back a moan.

Lowering his face to the side of my head, he whispers, "Why is it that the creature excites you, but the rest of me scares you? Why do you think that is, Dahlia?"

"I don't know," I answer on a shaky whisper.

"I think you do," he responds. The hand at my throat tenses and his tongue touches my earlobe.

"I don't," I cry, not wanting to admit all the things I work so hard to deny to myself.

"You do," he counters, lifting his head to capture my eyes with his. "It's easier to fear the man, hate him, because you've dealt with mere men for a long time, haven't you?"

Shaking my head, I try to deny his truths.

"But the darker side, the demons, it's too close to home, isn't it?" He presses.

I continue to shake my head in denial.

Easing his hold on my throat, he takes a step back. He drags his hand down my chest, stopping to palm my breast through my shirt.

"When you picked up the knife..." He rubs the pad of his thumb over my nipple. My body responds immediately, the tip hardening. "I was terrified."

Bringing his other hand up, he fists the collar of my tank top, and, with both hands, rips it. The material tears, but not completely. He has to fist the last inch and finish the job. Then his hands are on my stomach, moving up to grip the small piece of cotton holding my bra cups together.

"I wouldn't let myself believe or even hope. In fact, part of me was sure you'd come after me."

There's a small hint of amusement in his voice. He tugs the bra, tearing the material and causing my body to jerk.

"But then..." He closes his eyes and licks his lips. "You did more than..." his words fall away. Eyes flashing open, the same ferocity burns in them. His jaw tense, he grounds out, "You were made for me."

Dipping his fingertips into the waist of my cut off sweats, he shoves them down my body until they pool around my feet.

"My vow, to you, the other night wasn't just words," he states, pulling his t-shirt over his head. "I will possess you, own you, in every possible way I can," he promises, undoing his pants and shoving them to the floor with his underwear.

His cock springs forward, needy and hard. My clit pulses and I clench seeking relief.

Pressing his naked body to mine, he lays his hands on my hips. Lowering his head, he kisses the side of my jaw before burying his face in my neck. Then he slides his body down mine, making sure my hard nipples rub against his chest. His calloused fingers slip over my hips, down and around to palm the back of my thighs before he lifts me high against the wall.

"Hold on," he orders, positioning the head of his cock at my entrance.

I grip his shoulders as he lowers me onto him.

"Yes," I cry out, feeling every inch of him enter me.

He doesn't wait, jerking his hips back and thrusting up into me, rough and repeatedly.

Coherent words aren't possible. Everything he admitted, promised, and the way his thrusts punish me for daring to think differently.

When I come, he pushes me even further, digging his fingers into my ass, and making damn sure I don't fucking forget. He owns me, and I own him. His obsession is overwhelming and scary, but knowing I also possess him only makes me come again.

His thrusts become erratic, frantic, and my lower back slams against the wall until he curses against my neck.

Body going slack, he presses into me, his chest rising and falling with heavy panting.

Running my hands from his shoulders into his hair, I turn my head and press my lips just below his ear. He stills, holding his breath. So, I kiss him again.

Lifting his head from my neck, he drops my legs and grabs the sides of my face.

"Nothing will take you from me," he declares. "There is nothing that I will allow to keep me from the one person meant for me. Do you understand?" His fingers flex against my head.

Knowing that even if I was sane enough to not want anything to do with him, he still wouldn't let me go. That should be all I need to reject him. To continue to put up my fight and work harder to get away. But I'm clearly not sane. In fact, pleasure rolls through my body with every pledge of possessiveness. My own linger at the tip of my tongue, wanting nothing more than to own every deep dark piece of his soul.

"Yes," I whisper.

Returning a brief nod, he releases my head and takes a step back.

Body still at a slight arch, I flatten my palms to the wall on either side me for support.

His eyes drift down my body. Stopping at my thighs, he licks his bottom lip. He gives a slow blink, opening his eyes to focus on mine.

"As much as I hate to wash away the cum dripping down your thighs..." he hesitates, glancing down once more.

I press my legs together and feel exactly what he's talking about. Noticing the movement, a grin of satisfaction spreads across his face.

Reaching out and taking my hand from the wall, he guides me through the bathroom, passed the shower, and into the spa room. Stepping into the steamy water, he guides me to follow him.

Seating himself in a corner, he turns my body and positions me in front of him. My back to his chest, his groin against my ass, he sweeps my hair to one side.

"Relax," he says in the same way he does most things. A command.

It's a command that my body is too eager to follow. The large hot tub immediately soothes any aches from my workout and from Saint fucking me. But as my body goes lax, my mind does not.

In a short period of time, I've completely submitted to my captor. Logic sends up every red flag, alerting me to the insanity of it all. He hunted me down, took me, and kept me locked away in his penthouse. Then he brought me here, unleashing my terrible urges and twisted desires. And the entire time, I've allowed myself to sink into the promise of his dark manipulative devotion.

I wait for the fear to take hold. The panic that usually works its way into my veins and muscles, pushing me to run, secure my mask, and protect myself. But it doesn't come. In its place is something far more dangerous and terrifying. My own obsession. With the very man who's uncovering my secrets, killed me over and over again, and left his mark so deep on my soul.

Realization stirs the evil parts of me. Stretching through my chest, limbs, and causing a throb between my thighs, I turn and straddle my captor, my killer, my demon.

"We have dinner plans." No matter his warning, his hands still come to my ass, squeezing as I roll my hips against him.

Stabbing my fingers into his damp hair, I grip and tug his face to mine. His eyes widen with a mix of surprise and approval flashing in them. Crushing our mouths together, a deep sound vibrates his chest.

Closing my eyes, I hum my satisfaction, but images immediately begin to play behind my closed eyelids. His knives, the feel of his hand at my throat, the way my body burns from just a look, how each touch leaves a mark, and the way he looked at me three nights ago, covered in the blood of the second person I killed. A person he delivered to me with a zip tie bow at their wrists.

Without penetration, I drop my head back and grind down hard against his length.

"That's it," he urges, "Use me. Take what's yours."

My captor. My killer. My demon. Mine.

I cry out as my orgasm crashes over my body, mixing with awareness and knowledge.

Not only that Saint is mine, but that there is absolutely no question of how much it pleases me.

chapter twenty-one

Mei

The next morning, I wake up sore and bruised, but a hot shower helps ease any discomfort.

Walking the hallways and descending the stairs, everything feels different. Any hesitation or suspicion I'd once held disappeared overnight. I move with an ease through the house I hadn't felt until now.

While these feelings are new and very dominant, there is still a small niggling of caution in the back of my mind. Warnings trying to go off in my head, it's too fast, too far, too much. Don't trust anyone.

Pushing the mental struggle away for later, I enter the kitchen and find Jacob setting a place at the island. The smell of bacon, butter, and toast fill the room.

"Good morning," he says around a smile, but, like yesterday, it feels guarded. He motions to the place setting, indicating for me to sit.

"How do you like your eggs?"

"I can make—"

Sketch stumbles in and says on a yawn, "Don't give her anything sharp."

He rubs his bare stomach, drawing my attention to his half naked body. Wearing only a pair of loose shorts, the waistband hanging low on his hips, he puts all his tattoos and toned abdomen on display. But it's the raised skin that takes my focus. Three long scars decorate the center of his chest. All of them camouflaged behind a large black skull tattoo with extended bat wings stretching over his pectorals.

"Quit checking me out," he taunts.

I avert my eyes, but want to ask if Saint gave him the scars.

"I'm not trying to get tossed into the dungeon of death because you can't resist me," he continues.

"It's not my fault you're walking around half dressed," I blurt. "If I look where you are actually covered then I'm left staring at where your vagina is located."

Jacob coughs, covering a laugh.

"Awww..." Sketch coos, a sneer curling his lip. "Look who's biting back again. Don't think just because you're probably the most fucked up person in this house that—"

The slam of a metal bowl to granite makes me jump and draws my eyes to Jacob.

Focused on Sketch, Jacob gives him an undeniable shut the fuck up look.

"Whatever," Sketch grumbles, pulling open the fridge and leaning inside. Once he finds what he's looking for, he leaves in silence.

"So, about those eggs?"

"Scrambled," I reply, all too aware that their hiding something. I don't know what it is, yet, and I'm not sure I want to. But the warnings have returned, screaming louder in my head than before.

Jacob doesn't make my eggs how I requested. No, he turned the scrambled eggs I'm used to into a culinary masterpiece.

"I have no idea what you put in those eggs and I don't even care. Not even if it's heroin. They were amazing. Thank you," I praise his cooking.

"You are very welcome," he gives a mock bow.

While helping to clear my dishes and the pans, Jacob surprises me.

"Everything is waiting on the back patio if you are interested, of course."

Smiling up at him, I say, "I would love that. It's amazing how quickly you fall out of practice." Stretching my arms and rolling my shoulders, I walk to the set of French doors.

"Yes, it is," he responds.

Reaching the doors first, he pushes them open. I stop short just outside them.

In only a pair of low slung sweat shorts, Saint stands at the center of the stone patio. He crosses one arm over his chest, curling his other arm under it to stretch the muscles in his extended arm. Then he repeats the warm up on the opposite arm.

"Good morning," he greets dropping both arms and shaking them out at his sides.

The sky is clear today, allowing the sun to highlight each rise and dip of his chest muscles. The black ink on his shoulders and pectorals look wet in the warm rays, and each abdominal muscle rippling with each move he makes.

Clearing my throat and giving myself a small mental shake, I finally respond, "Morning."

Locating the same gloves I used yesterday, I move to them. Warmth fills my back as I slip the red leather over my right hand.

Brushing my braid over my shoulder, Saint plants his lips to the back of my neck. Instead of pulling away, he says against my skin, "You'll spar with me, not Jacob."

Annoyance tingles over my skin. Remaining silent, I slide on the other glove and secure it.

"Mei?" He presses, wanting confirmation.

"And when you aren't around?" I ask, fidgeting with the closure on the other glove even though it's already secured.

Large warm hands grip where my shoulder and biceps meet.

"There's a workout room," he offers. "I'll have a punching bag installed."

"I don't just punch," I retort, my annoyance leaking out. "That's why a sparring partner works best."

His hands tighten and his mouth lifts from my neck.

"I think skipping a day or two won't be detrimental," he growls against the back of my head.

"And those times when you're gone longer?" I push, not knowing exactly why I'm forcing an argument before I go one on one with him in a match.

"An unnecessary worry," he grounds out. "If it's more than a day or two, you'll be brought to me."

I'll be brought to him. The words echo in my head. The thought of being put away like a toy until he's ready to play makes my blood pressure rise. Turning to face him, Saint takes a step back.

"Different partners offer different..." I hesitate and then finish, "experiences."

His jaw flexes and his gloved hands return to my biceps, pulling me closer.

"In this partnership, there is only you and me."

I snort, knowing damn well he could still turn to his wife whenever he pleases. While all I'm asking for is a work out partner.

"No," I challenge, pushing my face into his. "There's only you for me, it's not the same for you." I shrug off his hold on my arms and finish, "But I'm only referring to sparring workouts. And when you aren't around, I'll do them with whoever is willing."

Crossing his arms over his bare chest, he lifts a brow and curls the right side of his mouth up.

"And don't go threatening people," I add in a shout.

His grin falls, the eyebrow lowering to meet the other in a scowl.

"Only Jacob," he concedes.

"Fine," I agree, then add, "But don't force him to leave when you do or I choose whoever is willing."

Brow still low in displeasure, a muscle in his jaw ticks. He doesn't respond, instead dropping his arms, he takes three steps back to the center of the patio and goes into a fight stance.

Moving in front of him, I lift my fists and spread my feet apart. Our dance begins.

"A personal shopper will be arriving this afternoon," he says as if we aren't throwing jabs at each other.

"For what?" I ask, grunting when his fist catches my shoulder.

"Conversation is distracting," Jacob scolds from the sideline.

"For whatever you need," Saint says, ignoring the reprimand.

"Raise your arm, Mei," Jacob instructs.

I listen.

"You mean clothes."

"I mean whatever you need," he repeats.

"So, tampons, girl razors, and wax are options?"

My question distracts him and I land a punch in his side.

"Good," Jacob praises. "But watch your aim."

"Wax?" Saint asks, deflecting my right leg when I kick.

"Yep," I retort, jabbing out and missing him.

His brow lifts, wanting clarification.

"To wax my legs," I answer, quickly adding, "And other places."

"I see." His tone gives away his amusement.

"I guess I'm not allowed to shop for myself." It's not a question.

"Not right now," is all he says.

Sending a jab at his head, he catches my wrist and yanks me forward. Instead of crashing into his chest, he sidesteps. Using his other arm, he bands it around my neck, pulling my back to his front.

"Damn it," I grunt, grabbing at his forearm.

He doesn't cut off my airway. The pressure is just enough to secure me.

"You'll also need to choose a dress for an upcoming dinner," Saint says in my ear. "It's Felix's birthday and you will be at my side, along with another engagement before the party."

I stiffen, remembering the last party he took me. Noticing the change in me, he releases my neck and spins me around. Recapturing me in his arms, pulls me against his chest, digs his fingers into my hair, and tilts my head back.

His fierce hazel eyes lock on mine.

"You will be at my side and Sketch will be there as well," he tries to reassure.

Pursing my lips at Sketch's name, I deadpan, "Yeah that makes me feel better."

The fingers in my hair tighten.

"No one will touch you again," Saint promises. "I've made it known what you are to me."

"Your mistress," I whisper. The words are more painful to say than I expect, so I wasn't prepared to hide the cringe on my face.

"My everything," he corrects, slamming his mouth to mine.

As promised, a personal shopper arrives after lunch and keeps me busy for over two hours looking through fashion books, taking measurements, and pictures. Saint makes one appearance informing the shopper that he will handle jewelry. He also, before making his exit, makes one requirement.

"No panty hose," he states, "Garters only."

"Would you also like to choose my underwear?" I blurt.

"Preferably none," he retorts, exiting the room.

The playful responses are a new development, so I'm left wide eyed and flush with embarrassment. The shopper simply smiles knowingly and soldiers on. At the end of our visit, the shopper accepts a list of personal items I created. She doesn't bat an eye or ask questions. Instead, she shoves it into a small portfolio and promises to return tomorrow.

More exhausted than I thought possible from looking through magazines and books, I lounge back into the leather couch with the remote in hand.

It takes me a couple tries, but I finally get the channel guide to come up. Scrolling through the cable channels, I accidentally hit the wrong button and bring up a show called Dexter. I'm instantly entranced by the duality of the character and his process, getting lost in the shows dynamic.

"Uh oh, you've got competition," Sketch's voice breaks through a particularly intense scene.

Twisting my head, I find Sketch and Saint standing just inside the room. I'm not sure how long I've been watching, but I am certain that my annoyance at being interrupted is evident on my face.

Stepping down and entering the room, Sketch sits two cushions away. Settling in, he continues, "Someone has a thing for twisted fucks."

Looking back to the TV, I lift one hand out toward him and flip my middle finger at him.

A burst of laughter comes from him, but I move my attention to Saint when he says, "We'll be going back into the city tomorrow night."

My muscles tense and I take a breath.

"You'll be visiting your old hooking grounds," Sketch taunts.

"I," Saint's voice raises, silencing him, "Have a meeting with a few of the men at the club." When he says 'the club', his eyes land on me.

My throat suddenly feels hot and dry, so I just give a nod.

Seeing my panic, Saint reassures, "You will be safe."

Clenching my jaw, I bite back a snort and the urge to remind him how unsafe I was last time.

My nightmare replays the night Felix shot Vicky. Only this time, she's dancing at the party where Arman attacked me and it's not Felix who's pulling the trigger—it's me.

After a night of terrible dreams waking me up early, I'm filled with nervous tension and unease. Dressing in a pair of blue yoga capris, sports bra, and gray tank top, I decide the best way to get it out of my system is to work it out.

Reaching the first floor, I find it quiet. It's not that there has been a lot of noise since we've been here, but this silence feels loaded. Like someone or something would jump out at any moment.

Steeling my resolve, I cross through the large courtyard to the other side of the house and into the kitchen. This morning there is no Jacob or smells of breakfast. While my nervous stomach is thankful for the lack of bacon and eggs, I was hoping Jacob would be here to show me where to find the workout room.

Returning to the courtyard, my eyes travel to a hallway I haven't walked. My stomach flips, a nervous action, but I chalk it up to my dreams and the anxiousness toward tonight's plans. Brushing off my panicky feelings, I make my way toward it.

Reaching the far end, my eyes travel of their own accord to the stairs leading to the basement.

I wonder if he's still down there, rotting away like the garbage he is.

Giving myself a mental shake, I turn and enter the hallway.

The first door is open, revealing a restroom. The second door is closed. Flexing my fingers a couple times, I reach out and twist the handle. It opens without effort to a linen closet and cleaning supplies. Closing the door, I rest my forehead to the wood and release a heavy exhale.

"He said you can go where you want," I remind myself on a

whisper.

The words are supposed to reassure me I'm doing something or going somewhere off limits, but when I reach double wooden doors, it all flies out the window.

Gripping both golden door handles, I hesitate before pushing them down, finding them unlocked and easily opened.

It wouldn't be unlocked if the room is off limits.

Even though it's not the workout room, a calm settles over me. The book filled shelves line two walls. A large dark brown wooden desk sits against a wall with a large painting and fireplace behind it. The other wall has two windows with a liquor shelf between them. In the far corner is a makeshift desk with computers and electronic devices littering the top.

Sketch.

Turning to leave, my eyes catch the familiar red yarn peeking out of a box on the corner of the large desk.

Why would he bring that here?

Unable to resist the lure of my past, I take tentative steps and flip the lid. A warm feeling of home warms my belly.

There she lays, black button eyes staring back from a dingy worn cloth face. Part of her smile has rubbed off and there's a black smudge near her chin. Lifting a hand, I let it hover just above the frayed yarn on her head. Her familiar face and all the memories she carries come back.

"But the hair makes me hot," I whine.

"You don't match without the hair, doll," my father says, fixing the red wig back on my head.

"No," I shout, forcing myself back to reality and snatching my hand back.

With quick, jerky movements, I grab the lid and close the rag doll away. My ears fill with the rush of my blood and pounding of my heart. Pressing both palms to the surface of the desk, I close my eyes and drop my chin. Breathing in through my nose and out my mouth, I try to restore some semblance of calm.

Nervousness still tingling along my body, I lift my head on my next inhale. Exhaling, I open my eyes, and that's when I see it.

Moving around the desk, I grab a black and white picture peeking out from beneath a manila folder. My reaction is instantaneous and the printed out article crinkles from the shake of my hand.

Home. I stare at the house of my childhood and read the caption.

Local House of Horrors. Authorities still trying to determine the body count.

It's not the first time I've seen this photo. I came across it multiple times during my online searches at the public library. I really shouldn't be surprised to find it in Saint's office. He's not the type to rest until he gets all the answers he wants.

Setting the article back on the desk, I pick up the folder and review the contents. Dropping it back on the desk, I take a step back. New articles fan out, but it's the photo of my father staring up, taunting me from the desk, I can't look away from.

Local craftsmen of celebrated dollhouses and signature dolls believed to be involved in a more sinister craft.

Gilbert Dandry suspected to be The Dollhouse Killer.

Covering my mouth, I swallow a sob and blink back the tears.

With my free hand, I spread out the other documents and clippings. Headline after headline appear. The one discovering an unknown catatonic woman locked away in a pristine room. The next highlighting the discovery of her identity as Lisa Michaels, previously believed to be a runaway. Another revealing the name of the woman who escaped The Dollhouse Killer. The last I glance at announces the unearthing of mass graves, mutilated bodies, and well-preserved victims.

Wrapping both arms around my middle, I try to hold it together. His familiar presence and the sound of multiple sets of feet make me tense. The weight of their eyes is enough to snap the fragile string holding my sanity together.

"Mei—" Saint begins.

"What have you done?" I ask, staring down at the black and white paper trail.

Sketch snorts, "Us? I'd say you've grown up around some pretty fucked up shit Doll Face."

Closing my eyes, I lower my chin and take one breath. On my exhale, I snap my eyes open. Glaring at Sketch from under my furrowed brow, I smirk.

"You have no idea," I taunt.

"You believe it's your father," Saint pulls my attention to him.

"He won't ever stop," I whisper.

"He's dead," Saint states, approaching me.

As he rounds the desk, I skirt around to the side, needing distance from him—from all of it. Lifting my chin, I study his face, wondering if he's stating a confirmed fact or a promise.

"There's no way he's still alive." Saint grabs another folder from under the pile and tosses it in my direction.

Staring at it, I can't bring myself to read any more.

"He was seriously ill," Saint continues, and I raise one brow at him.

"You think." It's not a question. "He kidnapped women, and men, so he could have live dolls. So, his *favorite little doll* could play with them."

"Jesus," Sketch scoffs.

"He doesn't exist," I snap at his exclamation, shoving the papers back at Saint.

"You have no idea what you've done," I say on a humorless laugh.

"It's not your father," Saint growls, straightening to his full height. "Who else could it be?"

"There is no one else," I cry. "He's the only one. It was just him and me until the day one of our dolls tricked me." I clamp a hand over my mouth.

"One of *your* dolls?" Sketch asks, disbelief in his voice.

I remove my hand from my mouth. There's no need to hide anything now. He's unleashed every demon possessed skeleton in my closet. Leaning forward, I press my palms to the desk and drop my head.

"Your information is wrong, Saint. The *only* person on this planet obsessed with getting his little doll back is my father."

"It's impossible—"

"No," I shout, making his eyes widen. "Nothing is impossible."

I push away from the desk and cross my arms over my chest.

"He captured and collected more women and men than those," I point to the papers, "files can tell you. They only document the ones they confirmed."

Dropping my arms to my sides, I straighten and fight back the tears.

"You were tricked by someone he kidnapped, one of *your* dolls?" Sketch asks, still analyzing my admission and making a point to note he didn't miss the way I said *our*.

"Yes, your file will mention Sara Franklin as rescuing me from the house during her escape." I can't keep the smirk off my face. "Fact is, Sketch," I say his name like an insult, "I let her free." His mouth opens, but before he can say a word, I finish, "Because I wanted to play with my new doll."

His mouth snaps shut.

"She could talk. The others couldn't."

I watch his eyes round.

"That's right." I move my eyes back to Saint. He's watching, observing, evaluating. "I grew up with the dolls you've been asking me about, but those stuffed dolls," I nod toward the box holding the ragdoll, "were only inspiration for the dolls my father made me believe were normal to have."

Saint moves, rounding the desk. I begin my retreat, terrified of what will happen once he gets his hands on me.

"You should've seen the terror and disgust in the eyes of my first psychologist. She was very pretty, but the look of horror on her face when I asked if my daddy got her for me," I continue. "Or the other psychiatrists and doctors who couldn't hide their feelings when I didn't know how to interact with other children. And then there were the dolls," I say on another humorless laugh.

Moving to put more space between us, his eyes track every evasive step I make.

"I'd never seen a Barbie Doll, so of course I wanted to make one," I drop my voice, "just like my father showed me."

Saint stops three feet away from me. His face still blank, revealing nothing.

"Fucking hell," Sketch rasps.

"The nurse at the hospital needed twenty-eight stitches to close up the wound on her neck." I shrug. "And I needed to be bathed three times to get the blood out of my hair and off my skin."

"Come here," Saint growls.

"You want all the dirty, terrible details of my past, you got them," I lash out. "The first time my father came for me, regardless of the blood coating the floor, I was still ready to go with him. I *wanted* to go back to my dolls. How sick is that?"

"Dahlia," he says, his voice a warning.

"It wasn't until he plunged a knife into my foster brother right in front of me that I finally had a normal reaction. I finally feared him. You see, it was too bloody, unclean, imprecise. That's the only reason I knew it was different, and terror finally switched on. I ran."

My eyes lose focus and I'm right back to that night.

"We ran," I whisper.

"Kayla," Saint offers.

I nod, my mind flashing forward to the second time my father came for me.

"The next time I was ready to fight back, but..." The face of the police officer flashes in my mind and a sob escapes my mouth. "I thought he was my father," I cry.

Strong arms come around me, pinning mine to my sides and pressing my face into his chest. His familiar scent invades my senses, bringing with it a sense of comfort and safety.

"He didn't die." Saint's words halt my sobs.

Pulling my head back, I look up at him, and whisper, "That's impossible."

"You injured him, but he pulled through," Saint says so factual, I start to worry about how calm he's being. "If you read the files, you'll find the cop survived. The only thing the police were ever looking for was a missing girl, and your father was terminally ill. He can't be the one sending the dolls to you. In fact, I'm not so sure he was the one who came for you the second time."

Shaking my head, I swallow the lump of unshed tears.

"There's no one else," I say. "It was just..."

"Just?"

"I found out later Lisa Michaels, my mother, was in the house, but I never saw her," I admit. "It wasn't until much later when I read a news article online that I found out she was in the house and put into a long-term care facility."

"Why didn't you go with your mother's family?" Sketch's question sounds farther away than he really is.

Snorting, I move my eyes to him. "Why would they want an abomination—a reminder of what happened to their daughter?"

"Did they tell you that?" I don't miss the disgust or hint of anger in Saint's question.

"Not directly," I hiccup. "And the exact words were *'we can't bring that abomination around our family. You saw what she did to that poor nurse, heard the things she said. It's too dangerous for our other children, grandchildren, and she would be a constant reminder of what our daughter suffered.'*"

"You memorized it word for word," Saint says low, even.

"I was young, not stupid," I snap. "Besides, they were right. I was dangerous."

"You were a fucking kid," Sketch argues.

"Mei, if you didn't know your own mother was in the house, you can't be sure your father didn't have an accomplice, apprentice, or someone else in the house," Saint brings the conversation back on track.

"I...I don't know," I whisper, dropping my forehead to his chest.

Fisting his gray, long sleeved shirt, I swallow hard. The cacophony of emotions start taking their toll and exhaustion washes over me. My body sags, Saint taking my weight.

"I've done things," I whisper against his chest.

"We've all done things," he counters, still too calm.

"How long?"

Knowing exactly what I'm asking, he admits, "Three days."

"My name." It's not a question.

A sudden wave of betrayal and anger surges through my limbs. Shoving at his chest, his arms fall away.

"I gave that to you," I shout. Backing away, I point to Sketch. "And you gave it to him."

For the first time in this room, emotion flares to life on Saint's face. His brow furrows and lips thin.

"You gave him my name. I suppose he should have me too!"

Rage gleaming in his eyes, he charges. I try to retreat, but he bends at the waist and puts a shoulder in my stomach.

"Put me down," I shout, fisting the back of his shirt.

Ass in the air, he carries me to the desk and drops me on top.

Shoving his body between my legs, I'm forced to open them. When he moves into my body, I lean back, taking my weight on my palms behind me. His hands plant on either side of me, his heaving chest a few inches from mine.

"Dante Santino Ruggiano," he grounds out.

"What?" I ask, confused.

"My name," he clarifies.

Furrowing my brow, I'm not sure what to do with that.

"Your past is documented in black and white, but mine floats in the shadows," he continues. "We aren't that different, Dahlia."

My mouth pops open, ready to object, but he has more to say.

"I killed my mother when I was fifteen years old," he confesses.

I snap my mouth shut.

"And my uncle, Felix's father," he says, before adding, "Then I hunted my father like an animal to slaughter him."

Biting my lip, I fight the wave of relief and pleasure at his words. We're both dark and damaged.

"Your father twisted you, tried to create his ultimate trophy." He lifts his right hand to my face.

"His doll," I whisper.

He nods. "Yes. Well, my uncle, Angelo, twisted me into his ultimate killer. A creature he's now lost control of."

Mimicking his act, I lift one shaking hand and place it to the side of his face. He closes his eyes, leaning into my touch.

"He thought you were for him, but you were always meant to be mine."

Remembering Sketch is still in the room, I tense at his declaration. Saint's eyes open with a lingering need for accession fogging them.

"I don't care about your sins," he says, "I have my own." His fingers flex against my scalp. "And quite honestly, I need your soul to be as dark and corrupted," he confesses. "It's the only way mine won't destroy you. I can't destroy you."

Tears fill my eyes, one blink setting them free.

"You're so fucking perfect, and I'm terrified of you," he admits, bringing his left hand to the other side of my face. "It's like my demons conjured you just to torment me and I'm scared they'll take you away."

"You resurrected all my demons and ghosts," I sniff. "He'll come for me."

"I hope so," he growls. "Because there isn't a god or devil who will save him from The Saint."

chapter twenty-two

Mei

Standing naked in the master bathroom of Saint's Chicago penthouse, I stare into the large vanity mirror. From mid-thigh to the top of my wet head, I scan my reflection.

Light bruising on my thighs, evidence from the way Saint fucked me three nights ago. When we'd entered the rear of the car, a wave of relief washed over me. And the farther we drove away from the club, the more relaxed I'd felt. Then, Saint brought it all back in one question.

"Was it how rough he was being or just the act of watching?"

My mouth floods with saliva, butterflies riot in my belly, and I cross my legs to ease the throb at just the mention of Felix and the blonde.

"Perhaps it was all of it," Saint verbalizes the thought.

His hand clamps on my knee, pulling my legs apart. Gripping the hem of my dress, I try to keep it from riding up.

In a fluid motion, he slides from the seat next to me. Knees to the floor of the car, he moves between my legs, grabs my hands, and pulls them away from the skirt. The material slides over my bare thighs to the crease of my lap. With a wrist in each of his large hands, he secures my arms to the seat on both sides.

    His eyes search my face, seeking an answer I'm hesitant to give.

    Part of me wants to confess my history with watching men roughly fuck women, pleasuring myself later at the memories, and how much the way he takes everything from me makes my body zing to life. The other part wants to keep my mouth shut and not give him any more of myself.

    The grin that spreads across his face and the familiar dark gleam in his eyes makes me squirm.

    Saint presses his body closer and takes my chin in his hand.

    "Have I mentioned how much I adore your little chin lifts and the challenge in your eyes," he divulges, and then his tongue swipes over my bottom lip. Gripping my chin tighter, he raises his head and demands, "Tell me what had your ass squirming back there."

    Pressing my lips together, I refuse to answer.

    "I have ways."

    His words a low growl, he releases my body, only to shove both hands between my legs. The material of my dress rolls to my waist and I grab his wrists. Curling his fingers beneath my thighs, he tugs hard. My hands fly out, the left finding purchase on the door and the right slapping against the leather seat. When he jerks my ass to the edge of the seat, I dig my heels into the carpet and try to push back up.

    Saint doesn't allow it.

    "Tell me." He thrusts hard between my legs. "Is it the roughness?"

    His eyes search mine, but still, I give him nothing.

    "Very well," he states.

    Releasing my thighs, he reaches between them and fists the crotch of my panties. Yanking them to the side, he uses the fingers of his free hand to slide through my wetness. A wide, cocky smile spreads across his face.

    The asshole.

    "And there's my defiant girl," he praises, slipping a finger inside me.

    Tensing my thigh muscles, my hips jerk forward, wanting more. Then the car moves over a bump, reminding me we aren't alone.

    I grab his wrist and glance around his body.

"Eyes on me," he orders.

I comply, but ground out, "Are you going to kill him after he watches?"

"Maybe," he grins.

My eyes widen, and I tense.

He chuckles before proceeding to fuck me most of the ride home.

Given that Frank was the one to drive us to the penthouse yesterday afternoon, I'm sure he didn't suffer the same fate as Arman.

Moving my gaze from my thighs over my stomach, breasts, and shoulders until I meet my own eyes, I swallow the lump of a million emotions.

Placing my hand on my stomach, I slowly glide it up my body, stopping to touch the purple hickey mark on my left breast. I close my eyes and recall the way I'd demanded he suck harder as I rode him last night.

Opening my lids and dropping my hand, I sweep another look over myself. As much as I wanted to hate everything, to hate him, I don't. Hell, the evidence of how much I'm thriving is staring back at me in the mirror. Eating regular full and mostly balanced meals, along with not adhering to my previous workout routine, has added a roundness to my hips, stomach, and breasts. My hair and skin are less dull and sullen. And while I've fought against the darkest part of myself, unleashing it on Arman over a week ago and just a few nights ago with Felix is the worst kind of addiction. I feel free. Not to mention how invigorating it is to embrace my dirty and often depraved desires knowing Saint won't be repulsed by them. He welcomes, even craves, them.

There's no warning knock before the bathroom door opens. Saint enters, prowling toward me. His eyes rake over my bare body, pausing on the marks he left on my skin. I turn to face him, giving him the full view of his handiwork. The way his mouth twitches at each mark makes my clit tingle.

"You have," he begins, placing his hands on my hips, "two hours." His hands slip around and grip my ass, pulling my hips against him. "Can you be ready?"

I give a nod.

Moving one hand back around to my front, his finger slips past my lips to circle my clit. I fist the cotton covering his biceps and gasp.

His face drops to my neck. "I'm tempted to fuck you," he says, licking my skin and dipping his finger lower.

"I have to get ready." My hands now at the waist of his pants, I unbutton and lower his zipper.

"Part of getting ready," he growls, walking me backward to the vanity, "will be for the evidence of my fucking you to be between your legs all night."

Then he shoves a finger inside me. The invasion and words cause my pussy to spasm.

Lifting me onto the vanity, I spread my legs wide and lean back onto my palms. Glancing down my body, I watch his finger move in and out. Pressing my hips upward, I meet the thrust of his hand. The tingle in my clit turns into a burn. I drop my head back, ready for the fire to consume my body.

"No," I whine when his hand disappears, only to soon moan, "Yes," when his cock enters me.

His fingers slide over my nipple, rubbing my own wetness into my skin before he leans down and takes the tip into his mouth.

A hand slaps to my lower back and the other between my shoulder blades as he wraps me in the cocoon of his arms. Propping my weight onto my palms, I push my hips out, giving him free access to piston faster and harder into me.

"Yes," I exclaim.

Releasing my nipple, his hands slide down under my ass. Squeezing, my ass cheeks spread and his thrusts grow punishing. He's doing exactly what he said he would do, making sure I feel him between my legs for the rest of the night. The friction and his intent cause my climax to claw its way along my inner thighs and over my belly.

"Tell me what you want, Mei," he demands, accentuating it with thrusts.

Lifting my head, I meet his eyes and exclaim, "I want to feel you between my thighs and in my pussy for the rest of the night."

Lifting my lower body off the vanity and holding my weight, he drives into me. My body jostles back and forth. His hip bones dig into my thighs. There's a hint of pain accompanying the pleasure, causing a second orgasm to suddenly rush through me. Roaring out his own release, he thrusts one last time before stilling inside me.

An hour later, hair and make-up done, and legs still sore, I exit the bathroom wrapped in a towel. Preparing to get dressed, I enter the walk-in closet and pause.

Saint stands at his rack of suits with only a towel around his waist. Hair still damp, I watch a water droplet slide down his neck and slip over the large tattoo on his back. The partially extended wings made up of knives are like a warning you get too late. Because once you can see his tattoo, you're dead, close to it, or you're me—tied to him through sins, blood, and flesh.

A shiver runs up my spine, and regardless of how sore I am, the desire is there to strip away the towel and drop to my knees. Suppressing the urges, I turn to what is now my side of the closet and scan the row of clothing. I've gone from a woman with only enough clothes to get her through a week and that will fit into a backpack to one with expensive designer dresses, shirts, pants, and lingerie in both the walk-in closet here at the penthouse and a full wardrobe back at the estate. It feels overwhelming and surreal.

Taking a deep breath, I exhale slowly, and grab a gold dress from the selection.

The stylist must have a thing for dresses with a conservative neckline and a low back, because this one, like the black mini dress, dips down in the back. One difference, this long-sleeved gold number is covered in sparkles from neck to hem.

Hanging the dress on a wall hook, I pull open the top drawer of the built-in dresser. My fingers linger over a bra before remembering the open back. Moving on to panties, I choose a pair and step into them.

"Put on the heels," Saint orders.

Glancing over my shoulder, I find him buttoning up his black dress shirt. His eyes move from me to the floor, then back. Looking down, I see a pair of strappy gold heels. These aren't the type you can just slip into. No, these involve wrapping them up your leg.

"Put them on." His repeat command sends a shiver along my spine and heat gathers between my legs. I should want to fight, rebel against his orders, but instead, lust rolls through my body.

Bending at the waist, I place my foot into one shoe, wrap the long strings around my calf, and secure them just below my knee. Leaning back against the closet wall, I put on the other heel, then stand motionless, letting him look. The weight of his eyes feels like a million flames licking across my skin. I want nothing more than for them to find their way between my thighs and burn me.

Resting his loose tie around his neck, he steps close. His hand comes up, collaring my neck and flexing. Dragging the hand down to the valley between my breasts, he flattens his palm.

His tongue slips out, wetting his bottom lip.

In a sudden movement, he brings both hands to each side of my neck and uses his thumbs to tilt my face up. His eyes move between mine, like he's looking for something. When I furrow my brow, he blinks, releases me, and walks away.

I quickly slip into the dress and exit the walk-in closet.

Saint stands at a tall dresser with his back to me. He's finished dressing, his dark suit only accentuating the ominous figure he creates.

"If I could leave you behind tonight, I would." His words cause a sharp pain behind my ribs. "I don't know what's going to happen this evening," he adds, turning to face me. "Things are in a precarious place."

It's only a small waver in his voice and a quick flash in his eye, but I don't miss the apprehension and fear.

"You'll be by my or Sketch's side the entire night." His voice quickly becomes an command. "Do you understand?"

Fear lodges in my throat, but before I can answer, he continues, "I need you to understand, Mei. Tonight, you don't question or hesitate."

Swallowing hard and straightening my spine, I nod.

We stay in a silent stare down for a few minutes before he finally seems convinced. Then he closes the distance between us. Reaching into his pocket, he orders, "Turn around."

I immediately turn without question or delay, hoping it helps prove I'll do as he requested.

A gold necklace dangles in front of my face before Saint brings it to my neck. Reaching up, I move my hair to the side and he secures the clasp at the back of my neck.

"Don't take it off," is all he says.

Dropping my hair, I glance down to the pendant resting against my chest. A gold circle stamped with the look of a compass.

Forty minutes later, Frank delivers Saint, Sketch, and myself to an understated brick building. Vincent and Russ maneuver around our vehicle and find a place to park ahead of us.

Stepping out of the car, Saint leads me beneath the green awning. Costa's Italian Restaurant is spelled out in white script on the front window. Through the glass, every table looks full. And when we enter the establishment, all eyes feel like they're on us.

Instead of waiting for the hostess, Saint places his hand to the small of my back, urging me to continue. He guides me through the restaurant to a back hallway. At the end of the corridor, past a kitchen door and bathrooms, are double wooden doors. Two men standing on either side nod and push them open, revealing a private dining room.

Where it felt as if all the people out front were staring, it's very clear that the ones in this room definitely are. There's a brief lull in conversation as they study us.

Saint slips an arm around my waist. Hand gripping my hip, he pulls me close to his side and leads us into the room. Tilting my head back, I look up at him. His eyes sweep the room.

"Dante," a deep Italian accented voice calls.

Saint's fingers tighten on my hip.

"Come." The voice draws my attention, and Saint leads us toward it.

At a table against the back wall, four women dripping in an array of jewels, designer dresses, and flawless makeup are seated beside three men in suits with an air of arrogance. The one in the center is obviously in charge, but it's the large man standing behind him I can't look away from.

Wrinkles and graying hair expose how much time has passed since I last laid eyes on him—since the day a man called Max bought my innocence and delivered me further into darkness. His familiar dark eyes meet mine. With a slight tilt of his head, he furrows his brow.

I stiffen.

Noticing my reaction and pulling me tighter into his side, Saint's mouth comes to my ear, "You okay?"

No! I silently scream in my head. Every instinct to run kicking in, I make note of the two emergency exits located along the back wall with my peripheral vision.

Allowing myself to move my eyes to the man who called us over, I clench my jaw.

"Dante," the man I currently stare at says like it's a question.

"Angelo," Saint finally greets, and it almost breaks me.

Thankfully, Saint tucks me into a chair at the table before I collapse.

My eyes move back and forth between Angelo and Max before I drop them to an empty wine glass. Unseeing the way the light reflects off the rim, that night so many years ago flashes through my mind. Max buying and delivering me to the man who would tear away my innocence. Looking from under my lashes, I take in Angelo. A man who, after praising his son for killing a piece of me, would wait until the room was cleared out before shoving his cock down my throat.

Saint takes the seat next to me. His hand comes to my thigh and squeezes.

Knowing he can sense my discomfort and panic, I take a deep breath, place my hand over his, and on my exhale, I put my mask in place. I won't let my emotions or past effect Saint, though I'm sure he'll demand answers later—answers he'll soon find he doesn't want.

"Where's Felix?" Saint's question pulls me from my own thoughts.

"Coming." Angelo waves the question off. "He's making a special entrance as the guest of honor," he concludes before moving his eyes to me.

"So, this is your new..." he hesitates a moment before finishing, "acquisition?"

"This is Mei," Saint introduces. "Mei," he addresses me, "this is my Uncle Angelo and..." He motions to the blonde woman at his side, but before he can finish, Sketch appears.

"Aunt Rosie," he coos. "It's so good to see you."

Her lips press into a disapproving line.

Pulling out the empty chair on my left, Sketch steps close to the table.

"That's for Felix," she snaps, nostrils flaring.

"Should I pull up a chair from another table?" His question is laced in so much sarcasm, I try not to laugh.

"I don't know why you're here at all." Her words are filled with so much disgust, they surprise me. Her eyes move from him to Saint. "You should've left your mutt at home."

"Aunt Rosario, you know Maurizio is family," Saint counters.

She scoffs, lifting her chin. "He's the son of the help, not family," she retorts.

Tension rolls off Sketch in waves, causing a protective and possessive side of me to emerge. I've said worse things to him, but as far as I'm concerned, only I get to be a heinous bitch to him. Not this overly made up and plastic faced cunt.

"I understand," Saint acquiesces, making me bristle. "But he's one of *my* men, so he's *family*." I relax and Sketch calms at his stressing of those two words.

Rosario's face contorts, looking like she's sucked on a lemon.

"Now, now, dearest," Angelo finally chimes in, patting her arm. "Maurizio can take the empty seat there." He motions to the table next to us. "This one *is* reserved for the birthday boy," Angelo explains.

I'm not sure what it is about his words, but everything feels loaded with double meaning. It's frustrating and frightening.

"Thanks, Uncle Angie," Sketch quips, moving to the other table.

A scowl forms on Angelo's face, but disappears at the approach of a man. He walks to Angelo's side, leans down, and speaks close to his ear. His eyes light up, and a large smile spreads on his face.

Pushing out of his chair, Angelo claps his hands together, and announces, "Our special guests have arrived."

Guests? I glance to Saint. His eyes narrowed on Angelo.

One of the emergency exit doors bangs open and two men in dark gray suits drag a man into the room.

"Here he is now," Angelo cheers.

The room fills with apprehension and uncertainty.

Felix is tossed out into an empty space in the center of the room. One of the dark gray suits uses his foot to shove the man onto his back.

I gasp.

"What is this?" Saint asks, pushing up from his chair.

Felix lies on the restaurant floor in the same clothes he wore at the strip club three nights ago. Except now, the expensive suit is dirty, torn, and stained. Blood covers his face, seeping from a wound above one of his swollen and bruised eyes. One of his legs lays in an awkward position and a deep bruise rings his neck.

"Do you think I'm stupid?" Angelo shouts.

Everyone's attention moves from Felix to him.

Angelo rounds the table, yelling down at Felix's motionless body, "You're a traitor just like your fucking father!"

Drawing a gun, he points it at Felix's head.

"Angelo," Saint shouts.

Gun still pointed on Felix, he slowly turns his head to Saint.

"Don't think for one second you are getting off either," Angelo sneers, pulling the trigger.

The room erupts into female screams.

Saint takes a step forward, drawing me behind his body, and Angelo bursts into laughter.

Glancing around Saint's body, I search Felix for a bullet wound until red starts to spread over his right shoulder.

"Get down," Saint growls over his shoulder. When I don't listen, instead watching for any signs of life from Felix, he twists. Using his big hand, he grasps my shoulder and shoves me to the floor. "Under the table," he orders, turning back to Angelo.

Angelo turns, holding the gun on Saint.

"No," I cry.

When I try to get up from the floor, Saint steps back, blocking me under the table.

"I gave you everything," Angelo exclaims. "And you repay me the same way your mother did."

"By not loving you," Saint quips.

Angelo's face contorts into rage and he brings the gun across Saint's face.

"Traitor," he screams, shoving the barrel to Saint's chest.

Leaning in close, he licks his lips, and growls, "I have a special gift for traitors."

The moment the words leave Angelo's mouth, the emergency door bangs open again. There's a moment of clanging and glass breaking.

"Bring her to me." Angelo's words are filled with annoyance.

The rage pouring off Saint make me both curious and afraid to know who was just brought in the room.

"What did you do to her?" Saint growls.

Peering out from under the table, a dark-haired woman is tugged to stand behind Angelo.

The abuse she's suffered is all over her face. The black eye, bloody lip, and swollen cheek all physical evidence, but it's the disheveled clothes and faraway, haunted look in her eyes that rings too close to home. Her violation runs deeper than skin and bone.

"Giuliana swore she wasn't a part of your schemes," Angelo begins, waving the gun at her, before turning it back on Saint, "But...I had to be thorough." The sick smile on his face makes my stomach knot. "You understand?"

"You sick fuck," Saint spits at him.

"If it makes you feel better," Angelo continues, ignoring Saint, "I believe her and will be taking her into my home once you are..." he pauses, "unable to provide for her."

"What?" Rosario hisses, knowing damn well what the asshole is suggesting.

Rolling his eyes, Angelo swings his arm to the left and pulls the trigger.

Screams fill the room and I bury my head in the floor, but I still hear Rosario's body hit the ground.

"Well, looks like I'll have plenty of room for you now, my dear." His words draw my attention back to Giuliana.

Angelo holds the gun on Saint, but reaches out with his other hand to brush her disheveled hair from her face. The moment his fingers touch her cheek, I see it.

A fire lights in her chocolate eyes.

"Never again," she cries out, her left arm arching through the air, light catching on the metal before she lands a steak knife in the front of Angelo's throat.

It's then I remember the clang of dishes and sound of broken glass. She must have grabbed it from a table in passing.

Angelo gags, dropping the gun and gripping the handle sticking out. Giuliana shoves the knife deeper. A shot rings out, catching Giuliana in the temple. She crumbles to the floor next to Felix.

"Don't," Max warns as Angelo yanks the knife from his throat.

Blood bubbles out of his mouth and over his chin to mingle with the blood pouring from his neck. The front of his shirt saturates with red. I can't look away. My dark urges rise, wanting to add our own slashes to his body. I want my own vengeance, cutting off his cock and shoving it in his own mouth, or in the hole in his neck.

Crawling out from under the table, I stand next to Saint and take in the carnage.

Max kneels next to Angelo, hand over his throat. I want to gut him too.

Taking a step forward, Saint puts his arm out, stopping me.

Wrinkling my brow, I glance up to find him scanning the room.

Following his gaze, I take in the full scene. A jolt of surprise runs through me.

Half of the wait staff holds a gun to someone's head.

"Did you do this?" I ask on a whisper.

"No," he responds as all the emergency exits and main room entrance open.

Two figures clothed in black, long sleeve shirts, black pants, and Kevlar vests enter from each of the emergency exits behind us, while four more arrive through the main entrance. It only takes a couple minutes to realize they are all women, all dressed in black, with face shields revealing only their eyes.

"Kanojo wa tōchaku suru," one of them announces.

The four at the main door part, allowing a woman to enter the room. She too is dressed head to toe in black, but her face shield is different. At her approach, the design comes into focus and makes sense.

It's the face of a Geisha.

chapter twenty-three

Saint

The minute the waitresses pulled guns, I knew she was near.

The Geisha approaches. Dark hair pulled into a tight bun and dressed in black, aside from her face shield, she's not exactly an imposing figure. A good head shorter than me and thin, it's easy to see how the men she's killed would underestimate her.

Instead of stepping around the bodies littering the floor, she uses her long legs to step over them. Glancing down as she passes, she stops next to Giuliana. Squatting down, she places her gloved hand on her chest.

Lifting the hand, she makes a circular motion before placing the same hand on Felix.

Two woman wearing waitress uniforms come forward, picking Giuliana off the floor.

"Stop," I demand.

The Geisha's head snaps to me, but other women don't acknowledge I've spoken.

"Her family will—"

"Will want their daughter to live," she speaks for the first time, standing back to her full height.

Muffled by the face shield, I still make out the Japanese accent.

My mind drifts to my sister, wondering if The Geisha knows where she is.

"She's alive?" Mei asks, the hope in her question clear.

The Geisha's eyes move from me to Mei.

Wanting to keep Mei off her radar, I move, blocking The Geisha's view.

"What do you want?" I ask, crossing my arms over my chest.

Her head tilts.

"It was his time," she states.

Furrowing my brow, I glance to Felix.

"Not him," she hisses. "Him!" She points to Angelo.

"You cunt," Max shouts from his kneeling position, pulling a gun.

Before he can lock onto his target, her leg shoots out. The heel of the boot knocks the weapon from his hand, sending it skittering across the floor. A second woman in black pushes up to his back, a sword to his throat.

"Yameru," The Geisha exclaims. "Kare wa sugu ni shinudarou." Her eyes move to me, and she finishes, "Ichido kore wa kare ga naniwoshita ka o shiru."

"Hai." The woman drops her sword.

"Who's sending you for our men?" I ask, not expecting a response.

"Sending me?" I don't miss the humorless laugh behind the words. "Theresa Ann Costa sends me," she growls.

Every muscle tenses at the mention of my mother. Clenching my jaw, I ground out, "Then she sends you for me."

Her eyes grow round, flaring with anger.

Moving into my personal space, she leans in close.

"I am here for all of you," she says, her words a threat.

Lifting my arms out at my sides, I lift one brow.

"Here I am," I bait her, wanting her emotions to get the better of her. "Shall I tell you exactly how I killed her?"

Anger fills the space between us, thick and hostile. Reaching behind herself, she pulls a gun from a holster.

At the same time, Max goes for his gun, and the woman behind him swings her sword, landing a blow to the side of his neck.

Collapsing to the floor, he slaps a hand over the gaping wound, the blood pouring through his fingers.

The Geisha doesn't waver or get distracted.

I wait for the press of the barrel and burn of the bullet tearing into my flesh.

"No!" Mei shouts, slipping around my body, placing herself between us.

"Mei," I growl, gripping her biceps.

My knife brushes along my chest as she slides it out of my jacket. Spinning, Mei wields the blade, catching The Geisha's forearm with the sharp edge.

The Geisha steps back, gripping her arm. Eyes fixed on Mei, she gets a personal introduction to my deadly little doll.

Even unable to see it, I can picture the determined and fierce look on Mei's face. What I don't miss is the flash of approval in The Geisha's eyes as she slowly moves, giving a wide berth and coming to stand on our left. Regardless of any respect she may have felt, The Geisha brings her gun back up. This time, it's pointed at Mei.

"It is a shame to have to kill you," she tells Mei. "But...I have a debt to repay."

"I don't give a fuck about your debt," Mei spits at her.

Sliding my arm around her waist, I'm prepared to throw Mei out of the way and take the bullet.

"See," Sketch says, appearing at The Geisha's back, his own gun pressed against her neck. "If anyone gets to kill Doll, it's going to be me."

Instead of dropping her weapon or surrendering, The Geisha leans back into Sketch. His eyes flare in surprise, but he holds his position. Her hips swirl back, pressing her ass against his groin. Then, she leans her neck against the gun.

"The fuck?" Sketch grounds out.

I can see the cocky smile shining in her eyes right before she yells, "Minagoroshi ni suru!"

I don't know a lot of Japanese, but I know *kill them*. Gunfire and mayhem ensue.

Tossing Mei to the floor, a bullet tears through my suit, grazing my shoulder. Grabbing the back of her dress, I drag her across the floor behind a table. Sketch appears at my side, handing me a gun.

"That bitch is crazy!" he shouts, flipping the table onto its side.

"She got away?" I exclaim, leaning around the wood and shooting.

"Don't fucking start," he shouts back.

A woman's cry pulls my attention away from the battle to the scene behind us.

"Christ," Sketch exclaims, taking in the sight.

Mei stands over a dead waitress, chest heaving, blood splattering her dress and dripping from my knife, a menacing curl to her lip. Eyes meeting mine from under her lashes, the deviant glimmer I've come to know and worship shines. My dick, uncaring of the chaos around us, twitches. And the creature claws at my gut, torn between spilling more blood and fucking Mei in the red pool at her feet.

A bullet piercing the table near my head gets my urges under control.

"Get her out of here," I order Sketch before turning to Mei. "Go with him!"

Keeping her promise to listen, she nods, taking the hand he offers. The moment their fingers twist together, I want to break his arm, but the need for her to be safe overrides the impulse.

My attention split between the ongoing battle and getting Mei out, I step from behind the table and cover their escape through an emergency exit. The moment they clear the doorway, I focus on the task at hand.

Popping off rounds, I scan the room until I find my target.

Figures in black move around the room with a speed and agility that would be impressive if they weren't attacking us. One appears out of the gun smoke, sword drawn and lifted. Before she can swing down, I raise my gun and shoot. The bullet enters the base of her throat, stilling her. Dropping the sword, her hands come to her neck. Wide eyes on me, her mouth opens like she's about to speak, but only blood gushes out over her chin.

When she drops to the floor, I lift my eyes and lock them with The Geisha.

Standing about twelve feet in front of me, next to the main dining room entrance, she raises her arm. Holding a gun out in my direction, she shoots. Orange and red flares fly from the wide barrel, lighting the room. They arc in separate directions, landing on opposite sides of me. As more smoke fills the room, I watch her disappear through the main door. A loud whistling sound fills the room, and I cover my ears while watching her women quickly fall back and vanish.

Coughing, I bend low to avoid the flare smoke and work my way through toppled furniture and bodies. When I reach the main doors to the private dining area, the sprinklers burst to life. Smoke starts to clear, the fire dies, and the room is reduced to the sounds of aftermath. In place of gunfire and shouting, there's water, cries of pain, sobbing women, furniture scraping the floor, and glass crunching.

I feel Vincent at my side before he asks, "Where did they go?"

Unable to take my eyes from the empty corridor beyond the open door, I growl, "Got away."

"That was her," one of Angelo's lieutenants says, adding, "She needs to be dealt with!"

No shit, asshole.

"Saint," Russ shouts.

Dragging my eyes away from The Geisha's non-existent trail, I find him on his knees. Fingers pressed to the side of Felix's neck, Russ says, "He's still alive."

"Vince!" My call brings him back to my side, awaiting my orders. "Call the cleaners, then gather men to clear away the dead bodies."

Giving a quick nod, he moves into action.

Lifting my gaze, I survey the destruction. Bodies, blood, and glass litter the floor. My eyes catch on one of our men cradling a woman's lifeless body. His large hand palms the side of her dark brown head, pressing her into his chest. He buries his face in the top of her hair.

I'm unexpectedly struck with a need to make sure Mei is safe, that Sketch got her back to the penthouse. My hand moves on a subconscious mission to retrieve my cell from my pocket, but the man's cry stops me.

"No," the sob rips from his throat.

Feeling the weight of their eyes, I look up and find the remains of our crew staring. With Angelo and his second, Max, dead, the line of succession falls to the underbosses. With half of them lost in the battle, the men in this room await someone to take the reins. And apparently, that someone is me. It's a move I'm hesitant to make, because the moment I start giving direction and take charge is when I seize the role as head of the family.

"Baby, stay with me." The man's cries snap me into action.

Moving in a practiced motion of a man who's taken part in too many gun fights and territory battles, I scan the room.

"Where's Doc?" I call out. "Is he still—?"

"Right here," he answers from the back of the room.

Walking in the direction of his voice, I find him pressing balled up napkins into a bullet wound in one of our lieutenant's chest.

"Who else can we call?" I ask.

He nods to the cell phone on the floor. "I already made a call."

"How far out?"

He shrugs. "Maybe ten."

Giving a quick nod, I turn to Russ.

"Get Jacob here and tell him he's going to need extra hands."

He pulls his cell from his jacket and touches the screen.

Slipping off my coat, I roll up my sleeves and return to Doc.

"What do you need us to do?"

Doc starts giving orders, and I ensure they're carried out.

With the injured handled, I sit at the bar, a glass of vodka in my blood-stained hand while the cleaners separate and remove dead bodies. Unfortunately, the dark brown-haired woman being one of them.

Jacob slides into the barstool next to me and says, "You know what you've done."

He already knows the answer.

"It's a heavy burden to carry," he continues. "While we are all aware Angelo was a sick motherfucker to begin with, the weight of his responsibilities couldn't be denied."

"I'm aware," I grumble, draining the last of the liquor from the glass.

"Most of the underbosses were here tonight so he could obviously do a show of strength with Felix. Half of them are dead now."

"Want to tell me something I don't already know?" I slam the glass onto the bar.

"You're going to be fine," he says.

The words send a jolt of surprise up my spine. Twisting on the stool, I stare at his profile.

"I know you didn't ask," Jacob continues. "And that you would never." His eyes come to mine. "But just in case, I thought you should know."

An uncomfortable warmth tries to form in my chest, but my darkness snuffs it out before I can identify the cause.

"Besides," he adds, "The Saint knows no fear, right?" He grins.

Shaking my head, I pull my cell phone from the inside pocket of my jacket. Bringing up Mei's name, I touch the screen. It goes straight to voicemail and I try Sketch.

"All I ask," Jacob says, nodding to my phone, "is that you don't give that little bastard any more power than he has."

The right side of my mouth begins to curl, until Sketch doesn't answer either. Another unfamiliar feeling prickles across my skin.

Jacob's smile drops, noticing the shift in my mood, and he asks, "What's wrong?"

Retrying the call, I slip from the barstool. Voicemail. Again. The feeling grows, and I finally recognize it.

"You're wrong," I say. "I feel fear."

Spinning away from him, I look around the room.

"Vincent," I shout, causing him to jump to his feet. "I need the car. Now!"

With a single nod, he rushes from the room.

Stalking to the door, I exit with Russ and Jacob close on my heels. Keeping the phone to my ear, I relentlessly dial Sketch and Mei.

For the briefest moment, jealousy rises from the pit of my stomach, thinking they're together.

Frank stands by the car, waiting with the door open. Before I slip inside, I turn to the men at my back.

"We'll take the main road to the penthouse and I need you two to take alternate routes. Find Sketch and Mei," I order.

Their eyes widen, finally realizing the issue.

Once inside the car, Frank hurries to the driver's side, climbs in, and peels away from the curb.

Mei

Sketch uses the butt of his gun to crack the windshield of a dark blue car parked behind the restaurant, then knocks the glass out and unlocks the door. Shoving me into the driver's seat, he pushes in right behind me.

"Scooch, doll Face," he orders.

I hop to the passenger side as he sinks down into the seat. Cracking part of the lower dash, he yanks wires down and starts tearing, biting, and twisting them. The engine roars to life, he sits up, and slams the door shut. We shoot out of the back alley and around the building, almost sideswiping two parked cars.

"Seat belt," Sketch instructs, turning onto another street, and my body sways at the speed he's going.

"What about you?" I ask, securing the belt into place over my lap.

"Awww, you worried about me?" He glances at me, wearing a big smile.

"You—" I begin to set him straight, but my words are cut short.

The crunch of metal fills my ears and the car lurches to the right. A large truck with dark tinted windows is pressed to the front driver side fender and they aren't stopping.

"The fuck," Sketch exclaims, white knuckling the steering wheel and slamming on the brakes.

Our car spins in the middle of the road and Sketch jerks the steering wheel to the right, stomping the gas pedal. My body is jolted to the left as he speeds away from the truck.

"What the fuck?" he shouts, bringing his seatbelt across his chest. "A little help here," he yells, shaking the metal piece near his leg.

Grabbing it, I fumble with the latch, trying to lock it into place. Once successful, I turn in my seat and ask, "Who is it?"

The minute the question leaves my mouth, the truck hits us

from behind, sending my body toward the windshield before slamming back into the seat.

"Hold on," Sketch orders, taking a left at the next cross street.

The turn is too sharp.

"Fuck!" Sketch shouts just as I yell his name.

The squeal of the tires fills my ears. When the car tilts, it feels as if everything goes into slow motion. A feeling of weightlessness takes over my body, only to be impeded by the safety strap across my lap and chest.

Metal crunching and scraping, a shower of sparks, and the smell of burning rubber fill my senses. My window finally surrenders under the pressure of the car sliding on its side. Crossing my arms over my face, I clench my eyes shut and shield myself from the shards of glass.

There's another hard crash and we bounce off something. My hands fly to the ceiling, bracing as we flip completely over. Now upside down, the seatbelt digs into my lap, a sharp pain shooting across my thighs. Sliding over the blacktop, the roof begins to heat from the friction. Opening my eyes, I watch through the cracking front windshield as the concrete barrier grows closer, bigger.

Knowing our fate, I scream.

"Hold on," Sketch shouts over all the noise.

We collide with the immovable object, causing the necklace Saint gave me to fly in my mouth. A sharp pain shoots down my arm, my head snaps back against the headrest, and the taste of copper hits my taste buds. Spitting the necklace from between my lips, I cry out. The impact was enough to make my head instantly ache and blur my vision. At the snap of his seatbelt, I watch as Sketch falls from his seat. Legs trapped beneath the steering column, his body drapes over the wheel.

He's not moving.

In an attempt to clear my vision, I give my head a shake. It's a mistake. The small throb at the back of my head splits, pulsating between each temple. Being upside down, all the blood rushes to my head, causing the pulse to intensify and gather behind my eyes. Crying out from the pain, I squeeze my eyes shut and bring both hands to hold each side of my head.

Releasing one side, I search blindly for the latch of my belt.

Hoping getting right side up will alleviate the pressure in my skull, I prod at the release for what feels like hours.

Distracted by the escalating pain, I don't brace before finally freeing myself. My body drops from the seat, head first, and everything goes black.

Saint

My hands tighten around my cell, reading the text one more time.

Instead of a phone call, Russ sent their location and a short message.

You need to get here.

As Frank maneuvers through back streets, I can't take my eyes from the screen. Those five words have done something I never thought possible. My ever present creature is silent. In place of the rage and bloodthirst is a stabbing between my ribs, almost enough to take the air from my lungs. It's like nothing I've ever known.

"We're here, sir," Frank announces, slowing the car.

Before it's in park, I'm out of the passenger door.

"Saint..." Vincent begins, stepping in front of me.

Shoving him out of the way, my eyes widen at the overturned car.

"Where the fuck is she?" I roar, charging the vehicle.

Russ's head pops up from the other side.

"She's not here," he states, his brow creased in concern.

"What do you mean she's not here?" I ground out, rounding the car.

My eyes drop to Sketch's prone body before snapping back up to Russ.

"He's alive." Russ is quick to assure. "Just unconscious. We need a doc—"

"You need," I move into his personal space, "to tell me where Mei is."

"She was gone when we got here," Vincent says from close behind me.

"Find her," I clip out.

"Saint," Vincent starts again.

At his hesitation, I turn and lift one brow.

"Someone caused their accident," he finally divulges, motioning to the smashed rear fender.

"How do you know?" I ask.

"There's black paint marks and scraping on the front driver side and bumper," he explains.

I open my mouth to argue that it could've happened during the crash, but Russ's next comment stops me.

"And that same someone used a crowbar to open the passenger door."

My eyes move to the car door. Sure enough, there are two obvious places where the door was pried open.

"I couldn't get the driver's door to budge," Russ continues. "We had to pull him out through the passenger's side."

Glancing back down to Sketch, I watch his chest rise and fall.

Another car arrives with Jacob climbing from the driver's seat. His eyes scan the area, searching for the person I was sure I'd find dead at the scene.

The pain from earlier dissipates. The creature no longer silent, he burrows under my flesh, letting my demons run loose through my veins.

"She's not here," I snap, angry someone took her from me. I'm also not pleased by the fact that Jacob cares so much.

"Where—?"

"Get Sketch in the car," I order, cutting Jacob off.

Vincent and Russ jump into action. Lifting him off the ground, his head lolls back. They carry Sketch's motionless body to Jacob. He opens the rear door and they put Sketch's lanky ass inside.

"Clean the car and meet us at the penthouse," I instruct, rounding Jacob's car and climbing into the passenger seat.

The moment I slam the door shut, sirens blare in a distance and passersby start gathering.

Jacob slides back into his seat, starts the car, and pulls away from the wreckage.

"What happened?" he asks, turning right onto the next street.

I know what he's really asking, and it's taking everything in me not to gut the fucker.

"Someone took her," I divulge.

"Who would do that?" he presses, keeping his eyes on the road.

"I don't know, but I will find out," I declare, my words an oath. "And they will suffer at the hands of every demon I have."

Smart enough to keep his mouth shut, Jacob focuses on getting us home without drawing attention from passing law officers and emergency vehicles.

"Once I reclaim what belongs to me, we will be discussing your interests in Mei."

"You're fucked," Sketch rasps, coughing around the words.

Twisting in the passenger seat, I glance down at him.

"My chest," he barely gets the words out.

"Don't try to speak," Jacob instructs. "You could have a collapsed lung."

"Tell me you can track her," I say, though it sounds more like a plea.

Sketch's eyes snap to mine and widen.

"She's gone?" He grimaces.

"Stop talking," Jacob warns.

At my silence, he nods.

Turning back around, my hand comes to my chest and finds nothing. Then I remember Mei removed my knife during our confrontation with The Geisha.

Fisting the lapel of my suit jacket, I close my eyes and take a deep breath.

"We'll find her," Jacob reassures.

"I'll find her," I correct, my jaw clenching. "You will stay the fuck away from her."

"Jesus, you really think—"

"Another time," I cut him off.

Pulling out my cell, I begin to make necessary calls.

"He needs a hospital, not to be playing on an iPad," the doctor groans.

"I have," Sketch inhales, "to work," he finishes, planting his palm to his chest.

The doctor's eyes move to me.

"His lung was partially collapsed," he reminds me. "It's going to collapse again if he doesn't rest and let his body heal."

I want to agree with him, but Mei's also been gone for roughly forty-five minutes and I need the information he can provide.

"Here," Sketch grunts, holding the tablet out.

Grabbing it from him, I look at the screen. He settles back into the guest room bed.

"She's," he breathes out, cringing, "almost an hour," he pauses, "outside the city."

"They're headed south on Interstate fifty-five," I finish, glancing to his face.

He gives a nod.

"The range." He takes a breath. "They're taking," another breath, "her out of range."

"Fuck," I grumble, tucking the tablet under my arm. Before exiting the room, I turn around and say, "Keep him in bed. Tie him down if you have to."

Sketch's long arm comes up to flip his middle finger in my direction.

When I reach the first floor, Russ, Vincent, and four other men look at me expectantly.

"We need to move," I instruct.

"We have a problem." Jacob's statement draws my attention.

He holds up the security feed on his own tablet.

Two uniformed officers are in the lobby of my building.

"They're waiting to come up and speak with you about an incident." Jacob lifts his brows.

"I swept that car and lit it up," Russ states.

"It's the restaurant," I groan, running a hand over my face. "Show them up," I instruct.

Removing the tablet from under my arm, I glance down at the dot moving along I-55 South. It blinks once, twice, enrapturing me in its hypnotic wink before disappearing. The glass groans in protest to my grip.

"Mr. Ruggiano, Officers—" Jacob begins to introduce.

"No," I rasp, shaking the tablet, like it will magically make the dot appear.

"What do you—?"

"NO!" I shout, flinging the useless piece of technology across the room.

Dropping my head, I gnash my teeth together and breathe slowly through my nose.

There's a crack of glass and a crash of metal on the floor.

"She's gone," I say through clenched teeth.

"Who's gone, Mr. Ruggiano?" one of the officers asks.

Blind rage courses through my veins. The creature unleashed, I draw both my guns, holding them on the officers in my penthouse. The rush of blood pounds between my ears and pressure builds behind my eyes.

"Dante," Jacob yells, putting a hand up.

"Sir," Vincent exclaims, placing a firm hand on my shoulder.

The officers pull their own weapons.

"Sir, put down the guns," one orders.

She's gone! every one of my demons scream from within me.

"I said put the guns down," he demands again.

Snorting, my lip curls back. Lowering my weapons, I watch them relax.

"Place your hands on your head and step—" My bullet in his chest cuts him off.

A shot fills the air and a searing pain lances my left shoulder. Unblinking, I slightly pivot my torso and pull the trigger again. This bullet pierces his neck. His gun clangs to the hardwood, causing it to fire and catching him in the leg. The second shot knocks the dying man to the floor.

"Damn it, Dante," Jacob screams. "Do you have any idea what you just—"

When I move the gun to him, he shuts his mouth.

In a voice that feels foreign and out of body, I order, "Call the cleaner and sort it out."

Lowering the weapon, I don't spare a glance at the lifeless officers.

"You're going to have every cop in Chicago targeting you for this," Jacob hisses.

"Then I'll kill them all," I state, my voice still detached and cold.

"What if they had families?" Jacob snaps, trying for guilt. I ignore him and turn to leave.

"Killing them doesn't bring her back," he tosses out, his words stilling me.

Spinning around, I level a glare at him. To his credit, he doesn't waver or back down.

"I know this feeling is new for you, but it doesn't give you free reign to murder whoever you want," he reprimands.

Lifting my brows, I stride into his personal space. Chest to chest, I bring my face close to his. The flash of worry in his eyes is the only sign of weakness I need. The creature feeds off the fear.

"As head of the family," I stress, "I have reign to do as I please."

"Then you're no better than Angelo," he sneers. "Like father, like son!"

Balling my hands into fists, every muscle tenses.

"Go ahead, Saint," he spits out my nickname like it tastes bad. "Murder me too."

The realization of his words hits home. Unclenching my hands, I take a step back and look over at the dead officers.

Unwilling to admit how right he is, I say, "Make sure their families are compensated."

Turning away from the evidence of my breakdown, I drop my guns on the floor and exit the living space.

At the liquor cabinet, I grab a full bottle of vodka, uncap it, and chug.

An onslaught of pain, sorrow, and regret make me feel off kilter. Gripping the edge of the small bar, I drop to my knees and press my forehead against the dark wooden cabinet. The trembling starts in my hands before climbing up my arms and across my chest. When the first tear falls from my chin, it shocks all my emotions into submission.

Reaching out, I touch the droplet, smearing it over the hard wood floor before lifting the finger in front of my face.

"We'll find her," Jacob assures my back.

Still captivated by the salty remnant of emotion, I say, "Call me what you want, Jacob, but..." I rub my finger and thumb together, "I will destroy every single person who played a part in taking her from me. And if they hurt her..." Balling my hand into a fist, I close my eyes.

"I won't kill them. Not at first."

chapter twenty-four

Mei

Reaching, stretching, I try to get to the surface, but something weighs heavy on my chest. Kicking my legs, I try to scream. Instead of noise coming out, I inhale deep. The pressure on my body lessens and moments of bright flash before me. Pushing my body harder, I release my breath on a gasp and open my eyes.

Blinking at a sudden invasion of continuous light, I attempt to bring my arms up to shield my face. They're so heavy and breathing takes too much effort.

Is this dying?

"She's waking." A female voice pings through my skull.

I groan and try to roll to my side.

Am I tied down? Trapped?

A surge of adrenalin spikes my panic. Tremors move along my limbs as I gasp for breath I can't catch.

"Calm down," she whispers. "You're fine."

"What are you doing?" a man booms, causing my head to thump.

"Calm down, Andy," she snaps. "I'm increasing the IV to flush out the drug."

My body shakes and ice moves through my veins.

"You gave her too much," he accuses. "I told you the second shot wasn't needed."

"She was coming to in the van. I had to do something!"

Each angry word beats between my temples.

"Eeee...nou-nou-nough." My plea falls from chattering lips.

"Shhh, Dahlia, you're safe," he softly coos.

"Get the heating blanket," the woman orders, but much quieter.

Focusing on inhaling and exhaling, I try to open my eyes once more. The light pierces my pupils like needles to skin and I immediately return to the darkness behind my lids.

Something settles over my body and begins to warm. My limbs slowly go from jerking to twitching and a wave of exhaustion sweeps over me. Soon, I'm lost to sleep once again.

Stretching my arms over my head, I try to work out the stiffness in my muscles. When I open my eyes, I inhale sharp, shove up in the bed, and scramble back against the headboard.

"No," I whisper, taking in the softly lit room. "It can't be." I shake my head.

The light pink walls, pink paisley valances, and thick gauzy sheers are suffocating. Glancing down at the bed, my bottom lip starts to tremble. My feet feel imprisoned in the soft white comforter with pink bows.

He called me Dahlia.

Closing my eyes, I try to block it all out, but I'm a twisted kind of person. The longing builds until I can't help but seek out the things I already know I'll find.

Opening my eyes, a humorless laugh leaves my mouth.

The ornate white shelves with green ivy trim.

"Im-possible," I stutter. The police collected everything in my father's house. Every part of the home was evidence, so how did it all get here?

So many glass and button eyes bore into me, their lifeless stare something I wish didn't feel so comforting and familiar. The urge to cradle each one and revel in the many secrets they carry is so powerful and inviting. Tightening my grip on the headboard, I look away from the shelves.

My eyes fall to the white tea party table and floor-to-ceiling mirror. The glass calls to me like an old friend. *The shadow.* It makes no sense, now knowing it was just the imagination of a twisted child's mind. Still, I seek out the dark figure who kept me company during my solitude. My only link to social interaction, beside my father and his dolls.

His dolls? They were just as much yours, a voice whispers at the back of my mind.

Opening my mouth to protest, I find it clogged with fear, panic, and, as horrible as it makes me, relief. *I'm home.*

Everything is exactly as I remember. The décor, the furniture, the location of the small bathroom, and the closet. It's closed, but I don't need to see inside. Even knowing, I swallow down the lump at the base in my throat and climb off the bed.

Reaching the closet door, I slip my fingers over the knob and twist. Yanking the door open, I jump back.

"No," I cry, backing away.

Ruffles, bows, stripes, and polka dots, every little girl's fantasy dress hang like dead men from a noose. Above them, the decapitated heads of Styrofoam display wigs of yarn and real hair. All of them different from the next, an assortment of styles to please a doll maker.

Shaking my head, I rush to the bedroom door. Trying the knob, I find it locked. Raising my fists, I pound against the polished white wood.

Dread twisting my stomach, I head for the first of two windows and throw open the gauzy sheers. Tears burn the back of my eyes and the tip of my nose tingles when I find it boarded up. Conscious the other will be just the same, I can't not check, so I hurry and pull back the drapes.

Stumbling away, I reach the ceiling high mirror and take in my appearance.

"Oh God," I gasp.

Dressed in a light blue baby doll dress, accented with white knee socks, apron, and wrist length lace gloves, my makeup has been removed and a blue bow adorns my head.

Lifting one hand, I place it on the glass. I'm exactly what my father always wanted. But that's not the sickest part. No, it's how consoled I am in my costume.

The tears break free, streaming over my flushed cheeks.

He's dead. He's supposed to be dead.

A sob bursts from my mouth and I drop to my knees. Wrapping my arms around myself, I try to hold myself together.

"No," I shout, wiping the wetness from my face.

The scratch of the lace infuriates me.

"NO!" I rip the gloves from my hands.

Tugging on the apron, two arms come around me.

"It's okay," he hushes.

The shock of his touch, his voice, stills me.

"You're home now," he coos, running a hand over my hair.

"No," I shout, crawling away.

The thick pink carpet burns my bare knees.

"This isn't my home," I protest.

Reaching the wall, I climb to my feet and find a light switch. Flipping it, I turn to face this unknown man and jerk back.

"I told you she wasn't worth all this trouble," Caroline moves close to John's side, leaning her head on his shoulder. "She's been turned against her family," she continues. "A traitor!"

"Enough," he shouts, his voice deep and authoritative. It's also *too* familiar. Too much like *his.*

Shrugging her off him and taking a step toward me, he halts when I jerk back against the wall.

"Why are you doing this?" I ask my former neighbors.

"Why?" she asks, her question sounding more like a taunt.

"We're your family," John reasons, placing a hand to his chest. "You should be with us."

Shaking my head, I argue, "I'm not your family. I don't know what my father told you, but —"

"Our father is of no matter now," he roars, closing the distance until there's only a foot between us.

Caroline moves close to his back and sneers over John's shoulder. "We took care of him long ago," she informs.

The words dance around my head, but only one thing sticks out.

"Our father?" I ask in a whisper.

John smiles.

"You don't have to worry about him," he assures, lifting a hand to cup my face.

The soft look in his eyes sends a chill up my spine. My skin prickles with awareness.

"You're insane," I accuse.

Sidestepping, I put distance between us.

"I don't have a brother and sister."

The moment the words fly from my lips, I remember what Saint said before.

"If you didn't know your own mother was in the house, you can't be sure your father didn't have an accomplice, apprentice, or someone else in the house."

"You would believe you were his only child," Caroline scoffs, stepping around John. "Sorry to disappoint you, *little sister*."

"I never..." I search my mind for any clue or hint of them in my past.

Eyes landing on my discarded glove, realization smacks me in the face.

My room was always clean, but I never straightened it.

My clothes were always neat, but I didn't launder them.

Meals and snacks were always ready on time, but I never saw my father cook.

"Oh, look, she's starting to believe us," she mocks, drawing my eyes back to her.

Tilting her head, she sticks out her bottom lip.

"You," I nod, "you took care of me."

Her cheeks flush and nostrils flare.

"I was a servant," she shouts.

"I didn't know," my voice cracks.

"Of course not," she seethes, stepping closer. "We wouldn't *dare* speak or touch you," she exaggerates. "We weren't allowed."

Blinking the tears from my eyes, nausea makes my mouth water. Swallowing, I shake my head.

"I don't," I hiccup, and try again, "I don't understand."

"Father forbade it," John states.

There's a change in his stance, anger vibrating just beyond his eyes.

"But why would—"

"Because YOU were his *precious little doll*," she shouts, taking a step forward.

John grabs her arm, holding her back.

"Molly," he says in warning.

My eyes widen, and she smirks, crossing her arms over her chest. "You thought our real names were Caroline and John?" With a snort, she glances over her shoulder. "She's dumber than I thought, Andy."

Molly and Andy, my sister and brother. Not Caroline and John, the new neighbors in my apartment building.

"Just like *Mei* is your real name," she taunts, rolling her eyes.

"Enough." His order silences her.

"Let me go," I plea.

"Let you go?" His face contorts with anger.

I take a step back, my thighs meeting the footboard of my childhood bed.

"Let you go," he repeats on a shout. "You belong with your family."

Clenching my teeth, I fight the protest at the tip of my tongue.

"I've spent years looking for you," he informs.

Closing the distance between us, he cups my face in both of his calloused hands.

"I was so close all those years ago." His eyes search my face, lingering on my mouth. "But you ran from me."

My body jerks at his admission, wanting to run now.

"It was you?" I ask what I already know.

The night my life forever changed from foster kid to runaway on the streets. It wasn't my father who came for me, but my brother.

His face dips close.

"You belong with me." His words warm my lips.

The sudden memory of what I'd heard from my neighbor's apartment assaults me. Her moans and his grunts.

"Your mother almost ruined everything. Our father thought he could take away what he promised," he continues, "but I took care of them both."

"What?" Molly asks in a shout.

"No," I rasp.

Pressing my hands to his chest, I shove him away before his mouth comes to mine.

Jumping over the footboard, I scramble across the bed until I put plenty of space between us.

"Andy," Molly demands his attention, but his eyes stay on me, longing and fury battling in them.

"When that whore got pregnant," Andy ignores our sister, "he promised me you!" He points a long finger at me.

I shake my head in silent rejection.

"Yes," he counters, moving around the bed.

Climbing off the mattress, I skirt around, keeping the bed between us.

"He was so obsessed with your mother," he scoffs.

"Enough to kill our mother when she discovered what he was doing," Molly adds, distracting me long enough for him to reach over the bed and grab for me.

The brush of his fingers can't find purchase when I jerk my arm away and take half a step back.

"The bastard strangled her in front of us and made us bury her." Her words filled with disgust, she continues, "All so he could console his precious Sara."

"All I did was try to stop her," Andy says.

Confused by the different recollection of events, I'm not sure what to believe.

"She had you bundled in blankets, trying to take you from me." A muscle ticks in his jaw. "It's not my fault she lost her balance," he shouts.

Shifting my eyes to the bedroom door, I notice it's cracked open. Glancing around, I try to find a way to get by Molly and out of the prison of my past. Andy's next words sidetrack me from my plotting.

"When her head hit the railing, I was sure she was dead." He can't keep the small smile off his face. "I cradled you in my arms, holding you to my chest." His arms move, acting out his words. "I took you back to your room, kissed you on the head, and placed you safely in your bed."

His eyes close, and I take the opportunity to inch farther away from him and the bed.

"That's where he found me." His eyes snap open, anger drawing his brows down. "That's when he took you away from me and punished us for your mother's betrayal."

No longer able to hold my tongue, I snap, "She just wanted to be free."

"What did I tell you?" Molly shouts, rushing to his side. "She's a betrayer, just like her mother."

With her out of the way, I rush to the door and throw it open.

I don't have time to figure out which way to go, so I turn left and run down the hallway.

"Dahlia!" Andy shouts.

Halfway down flight of stairs, I trip. The edge of each step finds the perfect place of impact, creating the worst pain in my hip, thigh, and ribs.

"No!" he shouts again.

His voice is enough to keep my adrenalin pumping.

Jumping to my feet, I round the second-floor landing. At the top of the next staircase, I can see the front door. The minute I can see freedom, it's snatched away by my hair.

"You know what to do with her," Molly's voice carries down the stairs.

Hand fisted in my hair, he spins me around and backs me against the railing, his free hand coming to my throat and tightening.

Where Saint instills lust and desire with his grip, my brother's fills me with fear.

Grasping at his wrist, I try to pull his tightening hand from my neck.

"Everything I've done has been for you," he says through clenched teeth. "I killed our father to free you of him, came to save you from that imposter family, made sure you had everything you loved waiting for you, and saved you from the criminal! And this is how you repay my devotion?"

Releasing my hair, he pushes me over the railing by my neck.

Molly appears at his side, a satisfied grin on her face.

"If you survive the fall, I won't take care of you the way father forced me to care of your mother." She can't keep the revulsion from her voice.

Meeting my brother's eyes, I choke out, "Please."

The sharp lines of his face smoothing, some of the anger eases in his eyes.

Molly, seeing his resolve die, shoves both hands into my

stomach.

"No!" Andy shouts.

The weight of my body shifts, my ass and thighs sliding over the railing. Gripping his wrist tighter with my left hand, I flail my right arm, trying to find purchase on the railing. Curling my knees around it, I twist my feet into the spindles.

Andy's hand tightens on my neck, cutting off my airway and blurring my vision. Then his free hand shoots out, fisting the front of my apron. Tugging me forward, he brings me back from the brink of falling. Releasing my neck and apron, he puts his arms around my body, pulling me close.

Coughing around the pain in my throat, I gulp at the air.

"Are you okay?" His eyes search my face.

Looking away from his intense gaze, I continue coughing and trying to swallow.

"What are you doing?" Andy's question makes me tense.

"She betrayed you," Molly hisses. "Betrayed us. If you can't do what needs to be done, then I will."

Taking my weight in one of his arms, the other arcs out and catches the side of her face. It's Molly's turn to hold on to the railing.

Shuffling us closer to her, he moves me to the side, but doesn't let go. Then his face is in hers.

"If you touch her again, I'll sell you to the highest bidder," he threatens.

Highest bidder?

"I'm pregnant," she whimpers.

Oh my God.

His body tenses for a brief second before both arms come around me again.

"I'm sure I have a buyer for that too," he states.

Bidders? Buyers? What the fuck is he into?

Then he's dragging me back toward the stairs.

Shaking my head, I dig my feet into the floor.

"No," I rasp.

His arms disappear, only to grip me by both biceps.

"I don't want to hurt you, Dahlia. Come on," he orders, tugging me toward the stairs.

"No!"

Kicking out, I catch his kneecap with my foot.

He groans, but doesn't release me.

"Stop it!" He shakes my body.

My head snaps back so hard, spots float in my vision.

Pressure on my stomach makes me aware once more. Tossing me over his shoulder, he straps my thighs down with his arm and carries me, screaming and hitting, back to the bedroom.

Once inside, he drops me down on the bed.

I bounce once, then scramble back and away from him.

Chest rising and falling, his hard eyes follow my every move.

"You just need time to settle in," he tells me.

I shake my head. "I'll never settle in," I inform him, watching his jaw tighten. "And I'll never stop fighting you."

Straightening to his full height, he rolls his head, pops and cracks coming from his neck.

"Perhaps you'll change your mind after some time in your bedroom. You'd be amazing what a couple days in isolation can bring a person to accept."

Eyes widening, I watch him turn and move to the bedroom door.

"Stop," I croak at his back. "Let me go!"

Without another word or looking back, he shuts me inside my nightmare.

Pushing off the bed, I fling myself at the door. Pounding my fists against the wood, I try to scream, but the trauma to my throat makes it painful and pointless.

Leaning back against the door, I slide to the floor, curl into a ball, and cry.

Please find me, Saint. Please.

The silence, pink walls, dolls, and more silence are bearable. At least, for the days I think have passed.

I'd been so sure they couldn't isolate me—not completely and without starving me. But I'd been wrong, so wrong. Through angry tears, I stripped away the bow on my head, tore off the knee socks, and ripped the blue dress to shreds. I'd left them all in a pile in the center of the room for them to find.

At some point during that first night, a box of non-perishable food items was put in the room and the shredded dress removed. And the tiny bathroom, nothing like the one I had as a child, provided the barest of essentials. A sink, toilet, and two pink towels were all the little white room contained, but it was a source of water.

Lying on the floor, my head on my outstretched arm and wearing only a white slip, I stare at the light coming from beneath the door. I'd unsuccessfully tried to stay awake last night to catch someone coming in, but eventually passed out. But it never fails. When I wake up, a new box will be just inside the door with the old one removed.

Each time I fall asleep, exhausted from effort of trying to keep my eyes open, I wake unknowing how long I've been out, if it's day or night, or even what time it is. Everything blurs together into one long, never-ending day.

Rolling onto my back, I throw an arm over my face.

"You said I belong to you, so where are you?" I ask, wanting nothing more than Saint to bust down the door.

He's forgotten all about you, an ever-growing voice whispers inside my head.

Covering my face with both hands, I shake my head and let the tears fall.

You're home, so BE home.

"NO!" I scream, slapping my hands to the carpet on either side of my prone body.

Poor little doll. You were lost, but now are found.

"I'm not a doll," I tell the empty room. "I'm..." The words fall away when I see movement in my peripheral. Turning my head, I squint, trying to make out what's on the other side of the small opening beneath the door.

Two feet stand just outside.

Taking a deep breath, I hold it and swear the door moves just a fraction. Then the feet are gone.

"Come back," I cry on an exhale.

Rolling to my stomach, I rise onto my knees, staring down at the pink carpet. The color makes me sick, this room makes me sick, and my family disgusts me. Pushing onto my feet, I glance over my shoulder at the bed. It's the only thing in disarray, because I'd been in it when they snuck into the room.

Spinning around, I focus my anger on the little table. The teacups and saucers sit in perfect order with the teapot at the center.

With my mind on destruction, I charge the table. Reaching out for the porcelain teapot, a movement in the mirror catches my attention. Stilling, I glance behind me and find nothing. Turning back to the mirror, I watch the dark figure move.

I'm hallucinating. The days of isolation have me imagining things, just like I did as a child.

"You aren't real," I tell the mirror, like that will make the shadow disappear—a shadow that is much larger than it had been when I was young.

A light flicks on from behind the mirror, bringing Andy into view.

"It was you," I choke out, realizing I'd spent my childhood playing with the shadow of my psychopathic brother.

He grins and nods the confirmation.

A wave of nausea washes over me, bile rising to the base of my throat. Hurrying from the mirror to the bathroom, I drop to my knees before the toilet.

Emptying what little I have in my stomach, I flush the toilet and move to the sink to wash out my mouth and splash cold water on my face.

He's fucking with you. He's been fucking with you since you were a kid. Now...now he thinks you're just a doll for him to play with.

Disgusted with myself, I'd avoided the mirror until now, not wanting to see my defeat. Bracing myself on the sides of the sink, I lift my head. Expecting to find Andy looking back, I find the face looking back isn't him, though it's still unwanted.

In place of the woman I'd become with Saint, I stare into the eyes of the scared girl of my past. My anger and disgust turn into rage. Squeezing the porcelain beneath my palms, I refuse to look away from my reflection.

Look what you've become. What you've allowed them to make you. You are not Dahlia the victim. You are Mei the survivor.

"So, fucking survive," I order. "Survive," I shout, hitting the mirror.

The glass cracks, splitting my face in two, and my plotting begins.

After washing my face, hands, and hair in the sink, I braid my dark hair and twist it onto my head. Before climbing into the bed, I enter the closet and change into a yellow ruffle nightgown.

Giving the mirror my back, so he can't see the tears streaming down my face, I mentally assure myself I can do this. Over and over, I repeat it to myself, until I finally fall into a deep sleep.

You are a master of masks.

You are a master of masks.

chapter twenty-five

Mei

When I wake up, I take a deep breath and begin to play my part.

Dressing in a blue and white striped knee-length dress, white ruffled petticoat, pale blue knee socks, and white gloves, I unbraid my hair and wrap the waves in a blue ribbon. I even go as far as to slip the black patent Mary Jane shoes on my feet.

Hesitating for the briefest moment, I take a deep breath and look myself over in the mirror. Pulling my hypothetical mask in place, I grin wide. Twisting back and forth, I make the skirt twirl.

With a small skip in my step, I walk to the wall of dolls.

Closing my eyes, I take another fortifying breath before reaching out and pulling two from the wall.

Katie, in her kitty paw dress and ears. Ruby, with her pioneer dress and freckled face. And finally, Margo, a throwback design to the kewpie doll. The moment they're in my arms, memories swirl in my mind. Not the day these two were gifted to me, but the day my father introduced me to my *real dolls*.

Setting both of them into their respective chairs at the tea party, I put on my little act. It's not a difficult part to play. In fact, everything comes rushing back like it was just yesterday.

For the days that follow, I keep my routine in place—dressing the part, having the tea parties, even sleeping with the god awful dolls and stuffed animals. The only problem, it's not horrible. It's familiar and comforting.

When the door finally opens, I don't move a muscle. Fearing it's my imagination, I keep my eyes on the table.

"Dahlia?"

At his call, I allow myself to look up at him. Mask in place, I smile.

Picking up the teapot, I ask, "Do you want to join us?"

His eyes scrutinize me, scanning my face and the table.

"If I let you out of your room, will you behave yourself?"

The thrill coursing through my veins is clearly visible by the way his eyes narrow.

Quick to recover, I jump to my feet and clasp my hands in front of me.

"Really?" I ask, playing on my real excitement. "I'd like that very much."

The lines around his eyes smooth out and he offers his hand.

"Come," he orders, and I obey.

The moment my hand slides against his palm, I fight the roil in my stomach.

Exiting the room, I exhale and revel in the view out the window. The sun is still high in the sky and there's a light dusting of snow on the ground.

He says nothing as he leads me down the stairs and through the house, which is fine by me. It gives me every opportunity to see the layout of this place.

While my room is almost an identical rebuild, the rest of the house is not. It definitely has the old Victorian feel, but it's missing the ornate woodwork and dark wood flooring. This home is much lighter, more exposed brick and tile.

Passing through a kitchen, I'm *finally* able to see a clock. I don't even care if it's the right time, just that I have time back—I'm not having it stripped away in unknown increments.

The rattling of a chain and a creak brings my attention back on figuring out our destination. A cold breeze sweeps through the open door, around my bare knees and up the skirt of my dress.

"You'll need this." He releases my hand to throw a large black coat over my shoulders before putting on his own.

Slipping my arms inside, my fingers are barely visible.

"We'll get you a prettier one," he promises, cupping my face in his hand.

Swallowing down the bile in my throat, I force a smile.

We fall back into silence and he leads me to a large metal building. The fading red paint hints that it may have once been a barn. Glancing around the vast space and no visible sign of neighbors or life, I realize two things. One, this could have once been a farm, and two, there's nowhere for me to run.

At the large barn door, he grips an oversized metal handle.

"You can't be serious?" Molly shouts, trudging toward us.

"Not now," he snaps, making her steps falter.

The wounded look on her face is quickly replaced with pure hatred when she finds me watching.

Realizing the threat she sees in me, I move in closer to Andy's side. His eyes slide down to me, brow furrowing.

"I'm cold," I explain, pressing closer.

He drapes an arm along my shoulders, pulling me into his side.

Glancing over the hand he rests on me, I find Molly staring daggers.

I know it's a dangerous game to play, but with nowhere to run, I need to figure out another way out of this twisted hell.

At my smile, her eyes widen.

The sight of her jealous rage is cut off when Andy guides me into the barn.

Looking ahead, the smile melts from my face and my mouth goes dry. To stop the scream bubbling up, I clench my teeth together. But it can't stop the screaming in my head.

No, no, no, no!

The heat of his body presses against my back and his mouth comes to my ear. It takes everything not to elbow him in the face and run.

"I know how much you loved them," he hushes, wrapping his arms around my waist.

Squeezing my eyes closed, I fight to keep calm. Still feigning cold, I wrap my arms around myself.

Straightening, he asks over my head, "You don't like them?"

Shaking my head, I want to scream, *No, you sick fuck! I don't like them!* Instead, I say, "No, I'm just...surprised."

When he moves from behind me, I'm forced to open my eyes again and take in the contents of the barn.

Five glass cases line the far wall, four of them containing another piece of my past.

"Come," he demands, gripping the coat at my chest.

As he drags me forward, I see exactly what kind of dolls are inside.

The first, a replica of my kewpie doll. The second, a replica of Katie, matched all the way down to the kitten ears on her head. The third and fourth, also matching dolls in my room.

At the empty case, he turns a bright smile in my direction.

"I have this one waiting for you," he reveals.

Sliding my eyes from his face to the empty case, my vision blurs and dizziness assaults me.

"Dahlia," he calls out, catching me by the shoulders.

"I'm okay," I say, forcing another smile. "Just too much excitement," I lie, feigning a look of adoration.

"You should rest."

Taking my hand, he pulls us back toward the barn door.

"What's that?" I motion to the large packing crate.

"That is business growth," Andy explains, tugging me over to the massive wooden box.

Glancing inside, I find another doll, but this one isn't like mine. She's *altered*. Arms outstretched and secured, she has what looks like butterfly wings sewn into her skin. The colorful pattern drapes from her underarms down to her side. Then, there are her legs. Her skin looks like it was melted together and wrapped in string, giving it a wormlike appearance.

Gasping, I step back and shake my head.

Molly snorts from somewhere behind me, but I can't look away from the abomination.

"She doesn't like your work, Andy," she taunts.

"I know it's not what you're used to," he's quick to explain.

Moving into my line of vision, he continues, "It's a special order. There are specs that—"

"Order?" I choke out.

Pride brightens his face and he nods.

"No more custom dollhouses or doll furniture," he clarifies. "That's in the past for our family. People pay good money for the custom dolls we can provide."

"Daddy wouldn't approve," the words slip from my lips like a devoted daughter, shocking me and enraging Andy.

"He no longer has a say," he shouts, stomping toward me. Face in mine, he yells, "I'm making the decisions now!"

Saint

Seven days, I've had to divide my attention between the needy fucking underbosses in our syndicate, law enforcement questioning my involvement in the crash as well as the two missing officers they'll never find, and dealing with Giuliana's pissed off parents, all while trying to get Mei back.

Giuliana miraculously showed up in a hospital the day after The Geisha's attack. The hospital stated she'd been treated and stable when brought in by two men from a homeless shelter. Neither one had any information, other than having been paid a large sum and provided a car to transport her.

Needless to say, her parents had her transported from the hospital here to one in New York near them. Her father, after admitting his knowledge of our fake sham of a marriage, threatened to kill me if I showed up to see her.

"Keep your people away from us," he'd shouted before hanging up.

Some would call it guilt, but as much of an asshole it makes me, it's more like indebted. So, while I understand his anger, I also know Giuliana will need extensive medical assistance and have made arrangements with the hospital for all her expenses and updates from the doctors.

This is now one less distraction to deal with.

And if it weren't for my inner circle making it clear early on I wouldn't be the only one dedicating time to the search, I would've laid waste to half of our organization.

Jacob contacted his police department connections and found the truck from the accident had been abandoned in a parking garage, but it was a closed garage without working security cameras.

However, defying the doctor's orders, Sketch left bedrest to analyze the area we last got a signal of Mei's location and to review ATV camera feeds from near the parking garage and along I-55 south. He located two possible vehicles they could've switched over to. One, a white SUV, which turned out to be a cheating spouse, and the other, a dark van. We found it traveled I-55, but the footage didn't provide a clear view of the plates. It also disappeared forty-five minutes passed Odell.

Vincent and Russ have been down there for almost three days, trying to find anything that would lead us to her.

"Felix is awake," Jacob states, pulling me away from photos Sketch got of The Geisha coming out of the restaurant.

"That's good news," I respond.

I'm genuinely happy my cousin is alive and awake, but Mei needs to be found and The Geisha needs to be dealt with before the underbosses and captains get anxious and start doing something stupid in revenge.

"Do you want the car?"

"For what?"

I stare at the armor truck that carried The Geisha and her crew away from the scene.

Where the fuck did she get an armored truck without someone knowing?

There should've been red flags caught by at least five of our associates when she secured it, but not one informed us. Which brings my suspicion of a rat in our ranks back to my number one thought.

"Dante," Jacob shouts.

Lifting my head, I raise a brow.

"You didn't hear anything I said, did you?" he asks, disappointment clear on his face.

Running a hand over my face, I groan.

"Fuck, I've got enough to deal with here." I motion to my desk.

"You aren't going to deal with it all this afternoon," he

reprimands. "So, go see your cousin."

It's not a request.

"And what do you suppose I tell him?" I toss the photos on my desk, shoving back into my chair. "I don't have a single fucking answer to give him."

"Answer to what?"

Spinning in my chair, I glance out to the city skyline. "To every fucking question I'd ask if I were in his position." I can't keep the defeat from my voice and I hate it. I absolutely fucking despise it.

My normality, any control I thought I had, disappeared with Mei. Once my citadel, the penthouse is now a haunting reminder of her. And even considering returning to the estate makes the creature flare to life, but not in anxious anticipation as before. No, now the place I used to indulge my darkest urges, where many suffered at the edge of my blade, has become a taunting reminder. Because my deadly beautiful doll isn't there.

Mei's done the impossible. She ensnares the man I am and possesses the creature inside.

Spinning back to the desk, I slam my fist onto the hard wood. "Fuck!"

"We'll find her," Jacob reassures, knowing exactly what weighs upon me the most.

Looking up from beneath my lashes, my nostrils flare, and I inform, "And he will regret every touch, word, and act that occurred where she's concerned."

Pushing up from the chair, it slides back and slams into the glass wall.

"She belongs to me," I declare.

The creature rises up, tearing down the mask of normality I wear.

I don't miss the step back Jacob takes when I slide my knife free of my jacket.

Flipping it through my fingers, I ignore each nick of the newly sharpened edge.

Without another word, I walk around the desk and out of the room.

Jacob doesn't follow. He knows better than to engage the monster exiting the room.

Fisting the handle of the knife, I extend my arm and run the edge along the wall. All the way to the elevator. Once outside the building, I come face to profile with Frank. Clearly warned of my mood and destination, he keeps his eyes downcast.

When we reach the abandoned warehouse, two of our soldiers approach the car. The moment I exit, they dissolve back into the building's shadow.

I don't acknowledge any of the men as I stride to a large brown metal door. It opens when I'm three feet away and closes upon my entrance.

The creature thrives on the smell of blood and decay of the room.

The shuffle of bodies and scrape of chains draws my eyes.

I grin when I see how far they've moved away from the corpse I left in here with them.

Their wide eyes follow my every move as I come to stand over them.

"Still playing the *I don't know anything* card?" I ask.

Squatting down, I rip the duct tape from their mouths.

"I paid for them," the one on my left blurts the moment his lips are free. "They were supposed to be fucking escorts."

"An escort?" I scoff, not believing anything he says. "You're a captain," I remind him. Then, moving my eyes to the other man, I say, "And you're a fucking underboss." Lifting my knife, I bring it to his eye. He closes them, and I press the tip to the lid. "A made fucking man, but you had to resort to prostitutes for a *family* gathering."

These two fuckers each brought a woman with them who ended up being part of The Geisha's soldiers. The fact that they lived, when these women were killing whoever closest to them, puts up a lot of red flags.

"It's done all the time," the man on my knife argues.

"Yes," I hiss, keeping my eyes on the other guy. "But they don't survive when the blood thirsty vipers are at their side. They get their necks slit or a bullet in the head, just like the others."

Shifting my weight forward, I send the knife through his soft flesh. It slips with ease, like his eye is made of butter, until the hilt snags on his cheekbone.

He shouts for the briefest of moments, the shock taking over quickly and making him pass out.

"Fuck!" Leftie shouts, scurrying back, only to shout again when he bumps into what's left of one of the women they brought to the dinner. "Christ!"

Yanking my knife out of the eye socket, his body slumps over.

Movement from my next victim, draws my gaze. He's pressed his body back against the concrete wall.

"Please," he begs. "I don't know anything. I didn't know," he cries. Reaching my blood-stained knife and hand in his direction, he clenches his eyes shut and cringes away. Wiping the flat sides of the blade on each of his cheeks, I clean it.

"I'll visit again soon," I warn. "Hopefully, you'll have something of more use to me."

At the metal door, I pound three times, pause, then tap twice. It slides open and I exit.

The creature's need for pain and thirst for blood has been appeased. But to make sure none of these motherfuckers forget who I am, I leave the evidence of it on my hands and clothes.

"We can't sit by any longer," Michael, a captain campaigning for underboss status, interjects into the discussion, and murmurs of agreement follow.

"And what do you propose we do, Michael?" Lorenzo, an underboss from the west side of Chicago asks.

"We rally." He slaps the large table I sit at the head of. "We have resources, so let's put them into play. Find this cunt and show her who's she's dealing with!"

Fed up with everyone's demands, suggestions, and bickering, I turned my chair almost an hour ago. Out of the thirty men in this room, only a handful aren't leftovers from The Geisha's attack. And only half of them are worth anything.

Lorenzo being one of those with any sense and understanding, I'm quick to enter the conversation on his behalf.

"Do you have resources I'm not aware of?" I stare down at my half empty tumbler, running my fingers along the rim.

"I..." Michael hesitates.

I'm not sure whether he's surprised I joined the conversation or scared to admit secrets he's been keeping.

Twisting my neck and lifting my eyes to his face, I press, "You?"

"We all have connections to explore," he quickly explains. "Someone has to know something about—"

Sweeping my glass from the table, it shatters against the wall. Pushing out of my seat, palms flat to the shiny wood, I take two deep breaths, exhale sharply, and lift my head. One after the next, I meet everyone's eyes, stopping on Michael.

"Do you think Angelo sat on his ass, not bothering to find the person responsible for killing off his men?"

At his prolonged silence, I lift my brow in a silent answer-the-fucking-question way.

"Angelo's mental state was clearly compromised," he argues.

I'll give the guy credit. He's got balls.

"Everyone's either witnessed or heard about his behavior before he was killed." He sits back in his chair, a smug look on his face. "By *your* wife."

Straightening to my full height, I cross my arms over my chest and give a nod.

"You're right, on both counts," I agree. "We'll never really know where his head was at and that's because *my wife* stuck a knife in the throat of the man who attacked and abused her for information and his own pleasure."

The cocky grin falls from his face.

"Angelo brought his death upon himself," I announce to the table. "If any of you want to challenge me, please do it now."

The room falls silent.

Dropping my arms, I round the table behind their seated bodies.

"Come on," I encourage. "Let's get this over with now, because I can fucking guarantee I won't fight you for it."

Thirty sets of eyes come to me, following me as I come full circle.

"Michael," I call him out.

He sits straighter, looking uncomfortable.

"Do you think you can sit as head of this organization?"

Squaring his shoulders, he nods. "Yeah, I could do it."

"By all means," I take a step back and motion to the chair I sat in moments before, "it's there for you to take."

"I didn't say I wanted it," Michael counters.

The right side of my mouth twitches, but I quell the urge and scan the men once more.

"Lorenzo?" I ask, knowing his tenure is one of the greatest in this room.

"Perhaps if I were younger," he teases. "My time for that has passed."

"Anyone?" I exclaim. "Because I need you to understand and be sure you're ready to take on the fucking mess we're currently in."

"None of us are questioning your ability," an underboss from the northside breaks the silence.

"Though, you are distracted by other matters at the moment," another captain wannabe boss adds, obviously referring to the search for Mei.

Keeping my eyes on the table, I ask the room, "If your daughter or wife were taken, what would you do?"

Lifting my head, I catch a couple of them shifting uncomfortably.

"Exactly. Now, I want you to understand something else." Taking another deep breath, I divulge, "Angelo had been working all our connections to get his hands on The Geisha."

"Yes, but—"

Cutting Michael off, I continue, "I've been working with my own contacts for information and have gotten bits and pieces."

"And you aren't sharing that information?" Lorenzo interrupts.

Meeting his eyes, I answer, "No." Moving my gaze back around the room, I add, "She had access to armored trucks, floor plans, vital information—like Felix being targeted and beaten by Angelo's men." Scanning the room, I see realization dawning. "How do you think she got all those things without one alarm or red flag being thrown up?"

"Fuck," Michael breathes, running a hand through his curly hair.

"Yeah," I concur. "Fuck is right."

Each of them glance around the room, like the rat is going to jump up and announce their betrayal.

"Until—"

At the sudden pounding on the door, everyone is out of their seats, guns raised.

"Saint!" Sketch yells between beating on the wood.

Nodding to a man nearby, he grabs the handle. Two others cover him and he pulls the door open.

Unfazed by the weapons drawn on him, Sketch raises his own gun.

"Oooh, look, mine's bigger than yours." He grins before pushing a gun away. "Get that shit out of my face," he orders.

"Who the fuck are you to disrupt—" one of the lieutenants begins.

Ignoring the man, Sketch shoves past him, his eyes fixed on me.

"We need to talk. Now," he says, his chest rising and falling heavily.

"You're going to relapse," Jacob reprimands from the corner he's been sitting.

Sketch lifts his arm out and flips his middle finger at Jacob. Eyes still on mine, he repeats, "We. Need. To. Talk."

Mei. He's found her.

"Out," I announce.

"You can't be serious," a deep voice says in disbelief.

Lifting the gun still in my hand, I aim at the ceiling and fire two shots before turning to face them again.

"Do I look like I'm fucking joking?"

Between the roar behind my words and the gunfire, they evacuate with lightning speed.

When the door closes, leaving only Jacob, Sketch, and me in the room, I give all my attention to the man who barged in on a sit down of the top made men in the organization.

"She contacted you," he states.

"How?"

Sketch reaches into a bag slung over his shoulder, pulling out a brown, yellow, and red pattern box.

Furrowing my brow, I take it from him and look it over.

"It's a Japanese Trick Box," Sketch explains.

Not Mei. The Geisha.

I don't see him, but I feel Jacob move to my side.

"Here," Sketch takes the box back.

"What if the trick had been death?" Jacob asks the same thing I'm thinking. "She could've rigged that thing with anthrax for Christ's sake."

Ignoring Jacob, he slides a hidden panel, pops open a corner of another side, and moves a couple other panels until he lifts the top and sets it on the table.

Looking down into the box, I find a dried poppy flower and a gold chain.

Sketch reaches inside, pinches the chain, and lifts it into the air.

"Oh hell," Jacob breathes, taking a step away from me.

"I'll murder the bitch with my bare hands," I shout, snatching Mei's necklace out of his hand.

"Wait," Sketch exclaims, retrieving a piece of wrinkled paper. "It was folded like a fan," he explains, flattening the gold paper on the table.

Konnichiwa, Dante.

It's time for you to face your greatest sin.

You're cordially invited to talk in the last place Teresa Costa-Ruggiano spoke her final words.

8 PM

PS...I have something you want, but I have conditions.

Glancing at my wrist, I curse.

"It's seven-thirty," Jacob verbalizes what my watch already told me.

"We'll never make it across town in time," I rumble, balling the paper in my fist.

"That's why I interrupted," Sketch explains.

Nodding, I order, "Collect everything. I have to try to get there."

"Frank, get the car—" Jacob calls before I ask, the door closing behind me and cutting off the rest of his conversation.

It's 8:10 when I enter the abandoned building by the shipping docks. I'm immediately reminded of the last time I stepped foot in this decrepit place. My mother's face flashes in my mind, her words echoing between my ears.

"I forgive you."

"I didn't think you were coming."

The lean, deadly woman steps out of the shadows, hair still tightly wound on top her head and dressed entirely in black, aside from the shield across her face.

"Your message didn't make it to me until forty minutes ago," I explain, focusing my attention on her as well as tracking anything in my peripheral.

"I see," she says, the gleam in her eye leading me to believe she was well aware of my meeting.

"Where is she?" I demand, tired of this drawn out game.

"Who?" she asks. "And be sure you know which *who* you really want to find."

"Don't give me riddles," I warn.

She shrugs. "I'm just offering you some sound advice."

Moving to the center of the room, she gives me her back. This act makes me scan the warehouse for her soldiers.

"I'm not going to kill you," she says, her back still to me. "Not today anyway," she adds, then spins around, and asks, "Is this where you did it?" Her head drops to the stained floor.

My silence causing her to grow agitated, she shouts, "Is it!"

"No," I answer honestly.

Lifting my arm, I point to a spot three feet to her left. The place my mother's knees touched, where she stayed strong until the very end.

Her eyes follow my motion, then she walks to where I pointed. Arms at her sides, she drops her head back, and whispers something I can't make out.

Head snapping back up in my direction, she asks, "Do you remember the exact spot you murder all your victims?"

Clenching my teeth, I want nothing more than to gut her or shoot her for asking so many questions.

"I won't die alone," she says, surprising me for a second.

Her ability to read people—me—is impressive, but annoying as fuck.

"So, your little army is here." It's not a question. It's more a taunt.

With a slight tilt to her head, she crosses her arms over her chest and admits, "No."

"What makes you so sure you can—"

"I have no doubt you will fatally wound me," she cuts me off. "But you should know, I will succeed in doing the same to you."

"No," I finally answer her question.

Her brow furrows.

"I don't remember every spot," I clarify.

The confusion melts away.

"I have something you want, but I also have a condition," she finally cuts to the chase. "Agree to my condition, then I will help you."

"Why would you help me?" I ask, suspicious.

"I'll just say you have something I need, so this one time, we're going to help each other," she asserts.

"Why would I help you? You just killed half of my organization," I remind.

Lifting one shoulder, she counters, "I did you a favor. Besides, I'm not the one who killed your father."

I stiffen.

"Your wife did that," she finishes, confirming she somehow knows Angelo was my biological father. "Rightfully so, too, if you ask me," she adds.

"What do you want?"

"Answers," she responds immediately. "No more, no less."

"I'm afraid you'll have to clarify."

"I need answers you can provide," she explains.

"For?"

"Ah, ah, ah," she waggles a finger at me, "that's not part of this deal."

"What makes you think I have these answers you seek?"

Her laugh is muffled by the face shield, but still audible.

"Answer all my questions and I'll give you her," she states.

"You know where she is?"

"Which she?" The Geisha presses, lifting one brow.

Then, it clicks. *She knows where Mei and my sister are.*

"Choices, choices," she taunts. "Choose wisely, killer dearest."

"You know about my sister."

"Is that the she you wish to know about?"

Tightening my jaw, I fist my hands at my sides so I don't physically lash out. My palm burning to unsheathe my blade.

"Who will it be?" she provokes. "The long-lost girl you've never known, or the recently stolen pet?"

The answer surges through me, the finality of it feeling like the only correct response.

I've never known my sister, and who says this woman is the only one who can give me answers on her whereabouts.

"Where's Mei?" I ask.

I don't miss the flicker of surprise in her hazel eyes.

"I have five questions," she states. "Answer them to my satisfaction, and you'll have what you seek."

"Fine," I say through clenched teeth.

"First question," she announces, raising her fist in the air, one finger extended—her middle finger. "Did you know? Before you even arrived in this building, did you know you would kill her?"

A sharp pain zips across my chest, remembering that day so many years ago.

"No," I answer honestly.

Her eyes search my face before giving a quick nod.

"Second question," she flips a second finger up. "Did he watch her die?" she asks, her lip curling.

"Yes," I admit. "He watched very closely."

The muscle in her left check ticks. Dropping her countdown

fingers, she stands tall.

"Is there anyone else left who was there?"

Slowly, but surely, the connections start to form. Each death at the hands of The Geisha have been those in attendance to my mother and uncle's deaths.

"Just Felix, and myself, of course."

"Of course," she echoes.

"But Felix played no real part," I assure her.

"No part?" she snorts. "He was there," she sneers.

Mouth suddenly dry, I force swallow a couple times before divulging, "We were both brought to watch, learn, and then act. Angelo liked twisted games. The same applied to the day we were brought into the family fold. He wanted me to take care of my mother and for Felix to take care of his father."

"And you," she strides forward, "wanted all the glory." Her arms flail out, arching through the air. "So, you shot them both," she states, her words laced in disgust.

She doesn't need to understand my reasons, so I remain silent.

"Answer me," she demands. "Why did you obey him without question or second thought to your mother?"

Taking one large step forward, putting less than two feet between us, I lean in close.

"My shot was quick and clean," I clip out. "Angelo would've done much worse if I hadn't acted. The same goes for Felix's father. So, when he hesitated, I took things into my own hands."

My chest rises and falls slowly, the creature stirring, wanting nothing more than to end this bitch right now.

"You protected Felix," she says, surprising lacing her words.

"I saved two people from a fate worse than a quick death," I correct, not willing to admit more.

Dropping her voice to a whisper, she says, "Last question. What did she say to you?"

"What makes you think she was allowed to say anything?" I retort, not wanting to share my last moment with her.

"Tell me," she presses.

"She told me I wasn't like them." I pause for a long moment, then finish, "Then she told me she forgave me."

The Geisha's eyes widen and she takes quick steps backwards.

Shaking her head, she protests, "No."

"Yes," I counter, then add, "My mother always saw the good in people, even if there wasn't any in them. Like me."

Hands on her hips, she lifts her chin, like she's going to further argue the matter.

Before she can say a word, knowing she's helping my sister, I say, "So, tell my sister I understand her wanting us dead and I forgive her."

"Your forgiveness isn't necessary. I'm sure she could care less," The Geisha retorts.

Turning on her heels, she starts walking away.

"We had a deal." At my reminder, she pauses.

Without looking back, she says, "I may not be of this country, but even I know a town as small as Towanda is the perfect rural place to hide in plain sight."

"Quit with the riddles and tell me where in Towanda," I shout, taking one step in her direction.

Glancing over her shoulder, she quirks an eyebrow.

"I didn't say I had an address."

My eyes are drawn to a black rope descending from the ceiling.

"Thought you came alone," I call her out.

Shrugging, she twists her arm and leg in the rope line.

"I lied."

With those final words, she ascends through an open ceiling panel and disappears.

Exiting the building, I hear the distinct sound of a helicopter and watch a black one rise from the roof before disappearing into the dark sky.

Pulling my cell from my coat, I lift it to my ear.

"Did you get that?"

"Got it," Sketch responds. "Already sent Vincent and Russ instructions to head farther south to Towanda."

"Good." I slip into the back of my waiting car. "Did you confirm the necklace is Mei's?"

"Yeah, the tracking chip is inside, along with your fingerprints," he confirms.

"Make sure Vince and Russ cover as much ground as possible before I get down there."

"Shouldn't you wait until we've got something?" he asks, quickly adding, "I don't trust the bitch at all. For all we know, she's setting you up."

"She had the necklace, Maurizio. I don't doubt she's up to something, but she had Mei's necklace. I have to go."

"Jacob says to swing by the penthouse. He'll have your necessities ready to go."

"Fine," I agree, knowing Jacob is the only other person who can access my knife collection.

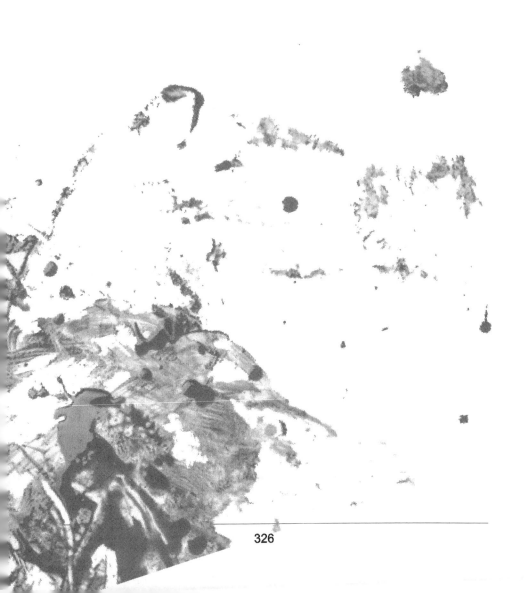

epilogue

Mei

Every day, it gets easier and easier. To the point where I'm no longer worried about Andy discovering my deception. No, I'm more concerned about the person I'm twisting into with every passing day.

After Andy's blow up in the barn, I was locked back in my room with the dresses and the dolls. Each time I glanced at one of them, I only saw the women in the barn. The images tear through my mind, resurrecting memories of a time I've tried to forget. Worst of all is the sick desire I have to revisit the barn, because it's not to free them.

Since being locked back in my room, I've created a new routine. One designed to put me back in *my brother's* good graces. Showing interest in all the dolls, talking to and playing with them—all of it is meant for *him*. What I didn't plan on were the side effects it would have on my own mental stability.

This morning, I step into a pink pleated dress with a white peter pan collar and puffed cap sleeves. As I began rolling the white socks to my knees, long buried desires tease at my thoughts. Separating my locks into pigtails and securing pink bows to each one brings forward dark urges.

Glancing at myself in the mirror, my reflection knowingly

mocks me with reminders of who and what I really am.

A monster wrapped in a cute package.

Finished dressing, I move to the doll shelves and stare at them until my eyes grow dry and I'm forced to blink.

Gripping the bottom shelf with both hands, I jerk it downward. It barely comes away from the wall, but it's enough to send the dolls tumbling. I repeat the process with the next shelf, then the next, until the floor is littered with disheveled dolls.

Looking down, I find Polly Dolly staring up from the heap, her pink pleated dress with the peter pan collar taunting me the same way the mirror had.

Sitting cross-legged in the middle of the bed, I hold Polly Dolly's head in one hand, her body in the other, and keep unfocused eyes downcast.

"What—?" Molly starts. "You're going to clean that up," she grounds out.

Head still down, I lift my eyes and look at her from under my lashes. Allowing my eyes to focus, I raise one side of my mouth in a mocking grin.

Straightening, she fidgets uncomfortably for a moment, then squares her shoulders and stomps to the side of my bed.

"I'm not picking them up," she snaps.

"I didn't ask you to," I retort.

"You little..." Her hands clench and release. "You've always been spoiled," she states, like it will mean anything to me. "Come on. Pick them up," she orders, throwing an arm out toward the pile of dolls.

When I don't move to obey, she grips my bicep in her hand and yanks me from the bed.

"Pick them up," she shouts, dragging me to the lifeless stuffed bodies.

"No!" I yank my arm from her grasp.

Spinning around, her face flushes red and angry lines crease her face.

"You will do what I say," she bites out.

This time, I laugh out loud, incensing her more.

With both hands, she shoves me, and confesses, "I've always hated you." She shoves again. "The way father doted on his precious

Dahlia—his doll. The way Andy would spend hours watching you through that fucking mirror, trying to play with you when I was right there!" She shoves again, and my back hits the wall next to the door. "No one ever paid attention to me. Not once did father praise *me* or give *me* gifts." Getting in my face, she takes my chin in her cold hand. "Even when you were gone, finally gone," she sighs, "all they *ever* did was talk about you, plot to find you."

Thrusting my face away, she takes a step back and looks me over.

"You disgust me. This little part you play, that you've always played for them," she snorts. "I saw you," she says, low and menacing.

Tilting my head, I furrow my brow.

"Who do you think let you out of your room?" she asks, making realization pour over me. "Who do you think made sure you could get into those off-limits places? Huh?"

Crossing her arms over her chest, she sneers.

"Yes, precious Dahlia, I saw the things you would do in Father's work room when you thought no one could see."

Memories of going through his detailed notes, books, all the pictures, and the dolls he wasn't finished with flit through my mind. The unfinished were never to be bothered and were locked away in Father's workroom, but I'd liked them. The way their eyes would move or tear up when I would poke at their limbs. How the sound of their voices, muffled by sealed lips, made my fingers tingle with excitement.

"I wanted you to get caught!" Her shout pulls me from dark, shameful memories. "For once, I wanted him to see you weren't his perfect little doll. But, no, you had to ruin that too by releasing that woman and bringing the cops."

Her eyes grow watery, just a blink away from escaping.

Focused on her impending tears, I wait for empathy, shame, or something other than what I feel right now. But nothing arrives to replace the disgust raising the hairs on my body.

Dropping her voice low, she says, "But if you're gone..."

Her thought dies off, but not before I understand them.

In a flash of movement, she brings a familiar large silver needle to my neck.

Wrapping my hands around her wrist, I try to stop her.

"I'll make you the doll you always pretended to be," she

threatens, pressing the point into my skin.

"There's only one problem," I rush out, and she stills.

Rolling my eyes, I explain, "That's not how it's done."

Bringing my knee up between her legs, she groans and stumbles back.

Ripping the needle from her hand, I look it over and purse my lips.

"Daddy would be so disappointed," I chastise. "It's not even the correct gauge."

Balling my empty right hand, I land a punch into the left side of her face. She falls onto the floor.

With swift steps, I come to stand over her. Gripping her brown locks, I yank her head to the side.

"But I can make it work," I reassure before jabbing the needle into her neck.

It misses the target area.

"Stop!" she cries, clawing at my arm.

Extracting the instrument, a laugh escapes my mouth.

"I'm out of practice," I admit before sticking her again.

"No, stop," she shouts, but her words fall on deaf ears.

Carotid Artery penetrated, just like Daddy's books taught me, blood spurts from the open end of the needle.

The carpet saturates and Molly's movements slow. Her head lolls back and I watch the life drain from her eyes. The needle slides out of her neck as she crumbles to the floor.

Chest heaving, adrenaline coursing through my veins, I stand over her body and close my eyes. Taking two deep breaths, I drop the needle and back away from my work. Stepping awkwardly on a doll head, I lose my footing and fall into the pile of stuffed babies.

"You were jealous of the attention." I give a humorless laugh, and roll out of the dolls. "You wanted this," I shout at her lifeless body, motioning to the room. "You can have it," I hiss.

Stomping forward, I grab beneath her arms and drag her to the bed, a red trail following.

Leaving her on the bed, I rush to the closet and rip down everything I'll need. Stripping her from her 1950's inspired blue dress takes more effort and strength than I anticipated, but in the end, I dress her in yellow polka dots and white ruffles. The final touch being a blonde wig and yellow floral hair clip.

Trying to pull her from the bed, it feels like she's gotten heavier, so I untuck the blanket beneath her and use it to haul her across the floor.

At the bedroom door, I try the knob. It opens. I make my way out of the room, through the hallway, and down the first flight of stairs, my older sister dragging behind me.

At the second-floor landing, I stop and listen.

Nothing, so I bring us down to the first floor.

Passing through the entryway and living room, I enter the dining room and stop. Staring at the large table, the dark urges swirl beneath my skin.

"You wanted to be precious and coveted," I announce, like she's still alive. Then, my words turn colder, harder. "Let me show you what that's like, Dolly Molly."

I tug her body along the hard floor, pull, lift, and shove Molly into place. Straightening, I stand over her and blow a stray curl out of my face. I brush my glove-covered hands over the front of my dress and see the stains. Lifting my hands, I stare at the gloves.

Red.

Blood.

The darkest parts of the stain start at the tips of my fingers, fading to a wet orangish pink near my palms. Glancing down my body, most of the stains look more dirty than bloody. All except where the blood had spurted out the end of needle and sprayed across the pleated pink.

"Ruin the dress, ruin the doll," I whisper.

Clenching my eyes and covering them with the stained gloves, I try to keep the memory from surfacing, but it forces itself into the forefront of my mind.

"What have you done?" he shouts, gripping my arm and shaking me. "What have I told you!"

Flinching, I sob, "Please, Daddy, don't."

"Look what you did!" Using his free hand, he fists the material near the dark purple paint mark I'd only made worse by trying to wash it out in my bathroom sink.

He drags me over to the hooks lining the wall and rips the dark blue smock down.

Shoving it in my face, he demands, "What's this, Dahlia?"

"Th-Th-The..." I stutter nervously.

"The smock!" he screams, throwing it on the floor. Stomping on it, he continues, "Useless since you didn't use it!"

"I'm sorry," I cry.

"You know the punishment for ruining your dresses," he sneers.

Shaking my head, my bottom lip quivering, I blink the new tears from my eyes.

Leaning down, bringing his face close to mine, he bites out, "Yes."

No crying or pleading ever works, but I still do it the entire way to the showcase room.

Inside, he throws me to the center of the room. I land on my side, but quickly sit up to my butt. Eyes wide, I watch him pull the rope next to one glass panel and flip a silver switch.

The dark blue curtain pulls back and light flickers, revealing Princess. The bright light causes her to body to jerk in awareness. Lifting her crown-wearing head, she slowly opens her lovely blue eyes. It also catches on the silvery blue color of her dress, casting multicolor spots on the wall. The same dress I'm wearing, that I've ruined with paint.

They always move so slow. I wish they could play with me better.

Princess's fingers twitch, her eyes following my father's movements.

"Please, Daddy," I beg once more, pushing up on my knees.

Dropping his head, he shakes it.

"When will you listen and be a good girl." It's not a question.

Removing a key from his back pocket, he opens the glass case, shoves the door wide, and climbs inside. Princess's eyes widen and her body twitches a little more.

"What won't you do again, Dahlia?" he asks, moving behind Princess.

At my hesitation, he repeats, "What. Won't. You. Do!"

"Ruin my dress," I half whisper, half sob.

Reaching behind his body, he yanks a large piece of plastic out and starts wrapping her head. Princess jerks harder, finally able to lift *her arms to her face, her gloved hands slipping over the slick material.*

He wraps it tighter, the exertion showing in the red creeping up his neck, before circling it around her once more. This time, her neck. Next will be her shoulders.

Princess tries to move her legs, but the ankle bracelets won't let her.

The dolls don't like when Daddy puts them away.

"What have you done?"

The voice is so like Daddy's. I twist around, needle still in my hand.

Andy's wide eyes focus on the doll behind me.

"Dahl—"

"She wanted to be me," I cut him off, glancing at the doll in the chair. "Now, she's exactly what I am." I move my eyes back to my shocked brother. "Inside," I add.

He moves his gaze from Dolly Molly to the large embalming needle in my hand. Then his eyes move up my body to my face.

Sadness, apprehension, then fear flicker on his face. His fear sends a thrill through me. Licking my lips, I take a step toward him. He backs away. Thrill morphs to power. A surge of it rushing over me.

"I thought you wanted me back?"

At my question, he straightens to his full height, crossing his arms over his chest. With the lift of his chin, I can't help but focus on the necessary spot to use the needle in my hand next.

"Molly was—" he starts.

"Dolly Molly," I correct.

He drops his eyes to the manic grin sliding over my lips and swallows hard.

"She's your sister," he states, meeting my eyes once again.

"Now, she's my doll," I counter.

Closing the distance between us, I place my gloved hand on his folded arms.

"And we already have the perfect place for her," I allude to the empty case in the barn.

My eyes drop once more to his neck and I tighten my fist around the base of the needle. The urges rise up, tensing my muscles, preparing for my next strike.

Before I can act on my impulses, something flares in his eyes, and I think it's excitement.

Andy drops his arms, saying, "Stay here."

Then, he's gone, out of the room in a flash of movement.

Turning to the large wooden table, I place the needle down and lean my palms against the top. My chest rapidly rising and falling, I try to fight the needs and longings pushing me to commit terrible acts, but there isn't enough time.

At the heavy footfalls on the staircase, I push away from the table and steel my resolve.

Andy rushes back into the room with one of my dolls in his hand. Before I can ask, he moves to my side. Grabbing my arm, he pulls me along behind him.

"I have something for you," he explains.

At a door in the far corner of the kitchen, he undoes a sliding chain, two bolt locks, and the lock on the knob. Excitement increases the force used to open the door. It slams into the wall, making me jump. Then, we're descending a narrow flight of stairs into darkness.

Run, Dahlia! Don't go down there! a voice screams in my head. *You'll never resurface from the dark.* The words echo between my ears, making me stop on the last step.

Andy releases my arm, and within seconds, bright white light chases the shadows of the basement away. But it's not a basement, I realize, scanning the large open space. It's a work room.

Medical tables, trays, and machines clutter the space. Along with two metal tables. One's empty, the other holds a body shaped white sheet. A scream rises into my throat, but I swallow it down.

"I was going to surprise you." His voice draws my eyes back to him. "Now, we can be the team we were meant to be," he explains.

His hands come to my waist, lifting from the step and holding me close to his chest.

Pressing my hands against his shoulders, I can't help the nausea churning and my instinct to push him away. Assuming I want to be put down, to explore, he sets my feet to the cement floor.

I take three steps back, leaving my eyes on him.

"Let me show you," he says, brushing against me as he passes by.

No! I want to scream and run back up the stairs.

"Here," he announces.

Being truly twisted and knowing nothing he could show me is good, I still turn my head in his direction. Standing beside one of the metal tables, he throws back the white sheet.

"She's just for you." The words drip with devotion.

Then, he lifts the doll he retrieved.

It's the redheaded farm girl doll. Ruby.

Dropping my eyes from the toy to the redheaded woman on the table, a sharp pain slices through my chest. Recognition crawls across my memories and I rush to his side.

No, no, no.

Candy lies prone, motionless, her fair freckled skin fully exposed down to the small strip of red hair between her legs. Closing my eyes, moments of the past play behind my lids.

Candy's bright white and wide smile. Candy trying to console me after Tricia's advice to hook up with a rich man. Candy with a text book on her lap in between performances, her glasses on the end of her nose and highlighter in hand.

NO!

"She'll be perfect," he coos, running a hand over her disheveled hair.

"Don't touch her," I shout, slapping his hand away.

"What's the matter?"

The look on his face tells me he really has no idea.

Dropping my chin, I take a deep breath and exhale heavily. Once again, the desires will not be denied. Looking at him from beneath my lashes, I curl my lip and shove both hands into his chest.

He stumbles back against the empty table and the rattle of the metal echoes around the room.

Catching sight of the tray full of instruments, I slap my hand down and fist around the first one I can. Swinging my arm around, I run the sharp edge of the scalpel over his chest.

"Stop," he cries out, surprised.

Eyes locked to his throat, I prepare for my second strike. So focused on where the perfect artery lies pulsing beneath his skin, I don't see his movement. I don't realize what he's doing, until the barrel of the gun is pressed to my forehead.

"Stop," he shouts. I drop my arms to the side and lean into the gun.

"Please do it," I ground out. "Put me out of my fucking misery," I shout, tears streaming over my cheeks.

"Why?" he chokes out, devastation creasing the skin around his eyes.

"Why," I mimic, following it with a snort. "Because I'm Not. Your. Doll!"

His jaw flexes and a muscle twitches in his left cheek.

"You were meant for me," he argues. "He promised you to me!"

With a defiant lift of my chin, I raise one brow.

"You forget," I say. "He took your doll away in punishment," I taunt.

"It wasn't my fault," he screams.

The metal digs into my skin, and the pain is a welcome distraction from my crumbling sanity.

"That's not what Daddy said," I continue to jibe.

"Don't call him that," he screams, turning sideways and straightening the arm holding the gun. "I hate the way you call him that," he confesses. "You did from the very start," he continues. "And I could see the perverse light in his eyes every time you did."

"Do you want to be Daddy?" I ask, switching into sweet little girl mode.

The hypocritical psychopath in front of me gets the same perverse gleam in his eyes. Bringing my empty hand up, I slip my fingers over his hand.

Tilting my head, I ask, "Is that what you want, Daddy?"

Curling my hand around his, I pull the gun deeper into my flesh.

Dropping my voice so low, I practically growl, "Because I won't."

Anger flares in his eyes and I glance away, focusing on his neck. With a wide arc, I bring the needle up, my target that patch of vulnerable flesh.

He bats my arm away, knocking me off balance.

"I did everything for you," he shouts, waving the gun in my face.

"I never asked for any of it," I yell back. "Not from him. Not from you! I didn't even know you." He flinches at the words. Raising one brow, I continue to taunt. "You. Didn't. Exist. To. Me."

Pain flashes in his eyes before rage contorts his features. Nostrils flaring and lip curled, he lines the gun up between my eyes.

"I wouldn't do that if I were you," a muffled woman's voice says.

Light catches on a blade resting against Andy's throat.

The gun wavers.

No longer focused on me, I take two steps back and one to the left. Surprise and panic battle for dominant emotion the moment her face shield comes into view.

As before, her shiny dark hair is twisted in a sleek bun atop her head. She wears solid black, from her neck down to her fingers and toes.

Her eyes shift to me, but she continues to speak to Andy. "Thank you. I know someone who wouldn't be very happy if you had done that, and I fear he's more violent than you."

"He's a criminal," Andy bites out, knowing exactly who she refers to.

The Geisha nods, moving her eyes to him. "Oh, I agree."

"If he tries to take her, I'll kill him," Andy threatens.

With a sigh, she rolls her eyes back to me. "You're like a magnet for possessive sociopaths. Aren't you sick of it?"

The question sends a jolt of agreement through my body. My hand tightens around the needle still in my grip.

"You could end it all," she says, her words a low seduction. "Change your own fate."

"I—"

"No father, brother, sister..." She pauses. "Or Saint," she spits out his name like a curse, "to force their will on you."

Sliding my eyes down her face, across her bent arm, I stop at the steel blade. The anticipation builds, wanting nothing more than for it to puncture his skin. Hypnotized by the possibility, I release the embalming needle and close the distance between us.

Stripping the gun from his hand, I turn it on him.

"That's it," she encourages. At the same time, her blade retracts from his throat. "You call the shots now," she says in a rush.

"On the table," I order, nodding my head behind him.

"Dahlia, we're fam—"

"Now!" I scream.

Snapping his mouth closed, he hops onto it. Legs dangling over the side, he crosses his arms over his chest in a silent challenge.

"Here." Her voice next to my ear makes me jump, but the syringe she dangles in my face distracts me from her closeness.

Snatching it from her hand, I take two steps toward my brother. My past. My captor. The nightmare that won't let me be.

"Dahlia," he coos. "You and I—"

Jerking my hand back, I stab the syringe into this thigh and press the plunger.

"Are NOT going to be together," I finish for him.

Hurt and anger twist his face. Making a grab for my hand, his fingers brush my knuckles. I yank it back, and instead of my hand, he pulls the needle from his leg.

"What huhvvvv..." his words slur and body sways.

Using the gun, I nudge him onto his side, then lift his legs onto the table and shove him to his back.

Rounding the table, I glance around the trays and machines. My eyes find Candy and my step falters. I bump into a small instrument table. The metal tools clang as I use one hand to steady it.

Still focused on Candy, rage boils anew, my darkest urges running along my spine and beneath my skin. The rush feels like a high, making me dizzy.

Dropping my head, I inhale and lock my gaze on the injection tubes, long needles, and forceps.

Fingering each of them, I close my eyes.

Don't do this, the voice in the back of my mind instructs. *You'll never come back from this.*

"I suppose," The Geisha interrupts my internal struggle, "you could just go on playing happy little family with brother dearest." The way her voice carries from different parts of the room, I know she's moving. "Or you could go back to your murdering criminal to be kept like a good little pet," she taunts. "Then again, what will he think when he sees what you did to your own sister."

Snapping my head in her direction, I glare.

Raising both hands, palms out, she says, "Now, now, don't point your needles at me. I'm quite impressed with your work."

"It's *not* my *work*," I correct, snatching the twelve-inch-long, wide gauge, stainless steel needle from the tray.

"Why deny what you are?" she counters. "Huh?"

"You have no idea what I am," I inform, turning from the tray to my prone brother.

"Are you so sure about that?"

"Yes," I answer, but look at Andy's face.

His eyes are open with an occasional slow blink.

"Dah—" he tries to speak.

"You're not a victim," The Geisha continues.

"Why are you still here?" I snap.

"You're *not* a doll either," she says, her voice giving away her amusement. "Though, the dresses do suit you."

"What do you want!" I scream, raising the gun and leveling it at her.

Her cheeks rise, giving away her grin.

"I want—no, I'm not like those who wish to own you, possess you, and tell you what you are. I would just like," she stresses the word, "to see you in black."

Snorting, I drop the gun and set it on the table next to Andy's head.

"This is pretty drastic for a recruitment." I can't keep the disbelief or sarcasm out of my words.

"You..." Andy's lazy word draws my attention. "Mine," he breathes out.

His face blurs, then morphs into my father, and my past replays in my head. Dolls, dresses, punishments, solitude, perfection, touches, caresses, lessons...

"You've only ever known possession," she continues her campaign. "I'm offering you freedom, true independence, and family."

Closing my eyes only makes my memories more vivid.

Picking up a scalpel, I bring it to Andy's neck and slice through the skin. I drop the blade on his chest and probe the opening with my fingers.

I use my thumb and first finger to part his flesh. With my other hand, I bring the needle to the opening. Letting it hover there, I lift my eyes to The Geisha. I don't miss the flash of fear in hers and quirk an eyebrow.

"Second thinking your offer?" I ask.

Lifting her chin, she narrows her eyes on me.

The Geisha doesn't like being read the way she does to others.

The longer she stares, the more familiar her eyes become. Something in the harsh, cold glare makes goose pimples rise along my arms.

"Of course not," she snaps, her brows lifting in challenge.

She's a fool. The urges have gone too far. The memories are too real. Dahlia has taken over.

"How about now?" I ask, shoving the needle into Andy's exposed artery.

There's a quick spurt of blood from the open side of the needle before a slower stream begins.

His mouth opens on a gargle before the next words fall from his lips.

"Wel...come...home...Doll..."

My lungs seize. I can't breathe. Releasing the needle, I shake my head and back away. Tears stream over my cheeks as a sob wrenches free. Clawing at my chest and pulling at the collar of my dress, I fight for air.

The Geisha steps forward, her mouth moving, but all I hear is the sound of my heart. A deafening thump between my ears.

Opening my mouth for more air, a scream finally breaks through the thumping in my head. Then, I realize the scream is mine.

"Mei." His voice silences everything. "What did you do to her?" he accuses.

"Of course you found her," The Geisha says, ignoring his question.

"No thanks to you," he barks.

Reaching out, I grip the edges of the metal table. My fingers slip on the blood running over the edge.

"Mei?" his voice softens. "It's okay," he assures.

Looking up and meeting his eyes, I find something I never thought I'd see. Pity. And in this moment, I know it's something I never wanted to see there.

"It's okay?" I ask sullenly.

"It will be." His words are like a command for the universe to fix everything broken inside me, but it's too late for that.

Grabbing the gun from the table, I aim it at his chest.

"Mei," he warns. "Put the gun down."

"Another man, another order." The Geisha's words float into my ears like a seduction for the darkest parts of me.

"I'll deal with you soon enough," Saint promises.

"She saved me," I tell him.

The hard, determined look on his face doesn't change.

"For her own gain, I'm sure," he counters. "You can't trust her, Mei."

In my peripheral, I see Russ and Vincent descend the basement stairs. Guns pulled, they have them trained on me.

This time, The Geisha's voice comes from farther behind me. "When they can't control their pet..." she practically sings, "punishments happen," she ends in a rougher voice.

"Shut the fuck up," Saint yells before redirecting to me. "She's a liar and monster. It's just a game for her, Mei."

"My name is not Mei!" I shout.

Saint's head jerks back, almost as if I slapped him.

"Don't you see," I cry, gripping the gun tighter. "There were never monsters under my bed." A solo tear slips over my blood-stained face. "No, they stood in bright daylight. They sat at the dinner table, tucked you into bed, called you daughter." Curling the right side of my mouth, I snort. "They dress you up, call you their doll, and make you think that shit is normal," I shout, holding the gun steadily on his chest.

"He gave me dolls, Saint," I confess. "I played with them. I believed they were toys, *my* toys, *I* taunted them and made them cry for not playing the way I wanted."

Realization spreads across his face, widening his eyes.

"Finally, you're catching on," I exclaim. "I remember all my doll's names, their clothes, the way each had a different scent, and that my favorites could blink," I sigh. "I even remember how some of them were made. And where I should feel disgust and horror, I feel fondness and peace in my childhood memories."

Allowing my eyes to fall out of focus for just a moment, I finish on a whisper, "I was created, just like one of these damn dolls," I scream, using my free hand to motion to Candy's body. "And my creator unleashed his monsters years ago." I glance to the man dying on the table in front of me.

"The one created to do his bidding, persuaded by the promise of his very own specially designed doll," I inform, using the barrel of the gun to point at my chest. "He honestly believed I was made for him alone," I snort. "But he didn't count on the doll maker wanting to keep the special doll locked away in a special room all for him, just like his first precious doll."

"Your mother," Saint says, not asking, but confirming.

I nod.

"Sound familiar, Saint," I taunt. "Locking me away, his possession, his doll."

Slowly, I bring the gun to my temple.

"Dahlia, don't," Saint orders, using my true name. The name encompassing all the horrible deeds I've done.

"I can feel it deep inside, clawing against my ribs and squeezing the air from my lungs, refusing to be locked away."

Everything inside me twists and convulses, the need to succumb to the evil becoming too much.

"Release it, Dahlia," he demands, parting his feet and straightening to his full height. He doesn't advance, instead broadening his chest and stretching his arms out at his sides.

Dropping my arm and the gun from my head, I lock eyes with him and my mouth parts in surprise. He's making himself my target.

"I've done horrible things," he confesses, "and that includes the things I've done to you."

Furrowing my brow in confusion, more tears begin streaming over my cheeks.

"My obsession with you and all the lies brought this misery back into your life," he says, taking the blame for something as inevitable as my descent into hell.

"This is your chance," The Geisha urges. "Your freedom from all of it, all of them."

"Shut up!" I shout over my shoulder, silencing her. "You're no better than them."

While distracted by her, Saint steps toward me. I lift the gun, aiming for his chest.

"Stop," I demand, shaking my head. "Don't," I warn, knowing if he gets too close I'll succumb to him like always.

He pauses.

"Your father was the monster in our past. He," he nods to Andy, "was the monster of your present. But, *I'm* the monster in your bed, Dahlia," Saint explains.

The truth of the words hits me like a battering ram to the chest.

"In the end, the monster always gets what it wants," I whisper.

"Exactly," he growls, lunging for the gun in my hand.

Before he can, I pull the trigger. The bullet finds its target, stopping him a foot away from reaching me. Red blossoms at the center of his dress shirt. Glancing down, his hand instinctually moves to the wound. Bringing his eyes back up to mine, he reaches out with the bloody hand and cups my face.

No. No. No!

"I forgive you, dead girl," he says around the blood forming at the corners of his mouth.

My head throbs, like it's being split in two, and a shrill scream fills the room. My scream.

A broken heart must be what death sounds like.

He collapses to the floor and the room erupts. Gunshots echo off the cement walls and a sharp burn starts in my left arm before I drop behind the table for coverage. When I do, I catch The Geisha's black form slipping through a door I hadn't noticed.

Crawling under the table with Candy on it, I follow her. Once through the door, I yank it shut and lock it. Spinning, I find her climbing through a small basement window. Two sets of hands grip her arms, hauling her out.

Rushing to them, I grab her leg, preventing her escape.

She kicks and twists, her foot making contact with my jaw. The force of the hit causes me to release her and I stumble to the wall for support. The moment the pounding starts on the door, I push toward her again.

The Geisha is gone, but a small black backpack hangs from the corner.

"Mei!" This time, it's Sketch.

Then there's a loud thump against the door. Shoving an old desk across the floor, I hope to slow them down. Knowing if they get in here, I'm dead, because *I killed Saint.*

My chest aches and tears fill my eyes.

The door starts to buckle at the next hit.

Wiping at my eyes, I push a chair beneath the window, grab the backpack, and climb out. The metal frame hurts my fingers and scrapes my shin, but I successfully pull myself to freedom. Cold air whips around me, making me shiver.

The sound of a helicopter lures me around the corner of the house. It hovers a couple feet from the ground and The Geisha grabs the bottom, pulling herself up.

Gripping the side of the aircraft, she turns and spots me. I lift her bag in the air, and she stills before giving a slight bow of her head. Then, they're gone.

Commotion comes from the front of the house and I run to the barn. Inside, I rush to the large open crate and glance down into it once more. Entire body shaking, I climb in, burrow into the packaging straw, and tug the butterfly doll over me.

It takes hours before I'm sure they're gone. And when I'm sure, I sob. Loudly and freely.

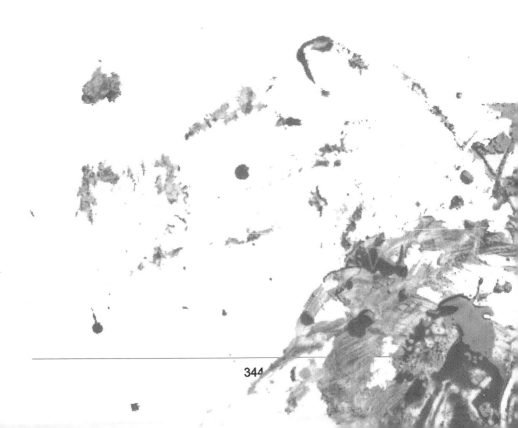

Saint

"Which one of you shot her?" I rasp around the pain in my chest.

"You need to rest," Jacob scolds from the chair next to my hospital bed.

"I need to find her," I correct.

"She shot you," Vincent snaps.

Turning my glare on him, I clench my jaw.

"It wasn't him," Sketch says, and my eyes flash to him.

"I only tried to slow her, disable her," he continues.

"I'll kill you," I say around a cough, and add, "After you find her."

"Fine. Just do as Jacob says," he concedes.

Tossing the white sheet off my body, I push up.

"For Christ's sake, Dante," Jacob exclaims. "You had surgery two days ago to remove a bullet from your chest—you know, the one that almost pierced your heart."

"I'm," I groan, sitting up and throwing my legs over the edge of the bed, "well aware."

"Get your ass in that bed or I'll kill you myself," Jacob threatens, pulling his jacket back to reveal he's strapped.

An eerie silence falls over the room.

"The likelihood of you finding her anytime soon isn't great, Dante," he explains. "Didn't you listen to anything they told you about the helicopter?"

"Sir," Russ interjects, "I don't know where else she would've gone or how she'd get away without having been on that chopper."

Falling back into the bed, I rub a hand over my face.

I refuse to believe Mei willingly followed that crazy bitch. Then again, she seemed to be playing Mei really well when I arrived.

Not surprised she knew exactly where to find Mei, I hadn't expected her to be in that basement with her. Now, I can only wonder at the reason she was there. What does she have to gain?

"She wouldn't have gone with The Geisha." When I say it out loud, I believe I'm right.

"You don't know that," Sketch argues. "None of us expected to find that house...like that," he sneers in disgust. "We have no idea how fucked up that girl reall—"

A chime cuts him off, his eyes widening. Reaching inside his jacket, he pulls out a cell phone and focuses on the screen.

"What is it?" I press, annoyed.

"Nothing," he clips, slipping it back into the jacket.

It chimes again, and I lift a brow.

"It doesn't have anything to do with Mei," he assures.

"Then what does it have to do with, Maurizio?"

His forehead creases and mouth thins.

"I've got a knife and a basement," I warn.

"Someone's researching me," he says.

Dropping my scowl, I stare, waiting for an explanation.

"I have algorithms set up on myself, just like you and everyone else," he explains. "It gives me a heads up before something heads our way. I ramped them up, made them more complicated after those cops showed unexpectedly."

I nod, urging him to continue.

"Right now, all I know, is my name has suddenly become popular," he concludes.

"No matter what it is," I start, rubbing my chest, "it won't touch you."

Wincing at a sharp pain shooting from behind my rib to right shoulder, I clench my eyes shut and teeth tight.

"That's it." Jacob steps forward, pressing two buttons on my IV machine.

The drugs move quickly, turning the room fuzzy and taking

away the pain.

"Find me The Geisha," I mumble.

Then, the world falls away.

Two weeks, they forced me to stay in the hospital. Upon my release, every member of our syndicate sent gifts of well wishes or delivered them in person. The penthouse has become a revolving door of people. None of them the one I need.

I'm back where I started. Searching, waiting, tortured by every minute that goes by.

Unable to sleep, I stand at the bar in the penthouse. The Vodka Tonic in my tumbler glass goes untouched, deciding to drink directly from the liquor bottle instead. Watching the tonic bubbles float to the top, my mind plays the scene on repeat.

We'd found her sister at the dining room table when we first arrived and followed the trail of blood streaks to a bedroom straight out of a horror movie. All the dolls, pink, bows, lace, and blood. So much blood.

At first, when I found her standing between two dead bodies laid out on metal tables, I wasn't sure what was going on. The uncertainty, unknowing, only escalated the helplessness I'd felt watching her breakdown in front of me.

Her eyes told me so much, but without all the information, like the man on the table being her brother and the other body a girl from the strip club, I hadn't quite gotten her inner struggle. The battle she was waging between what she believes is good and bad. I played the whole scene wrong and paid the price once more—losing her, again.

Lifting the clear bottle to my lips, I tilt my head back and drink.

The hairs on my arms raise and the back of my neck prickles with awareness. Slamming the bottle down on the bar, the weight of eyes on my back almost as heavy as the one in my chest. The air in the room changes, charging with something different than Jacob or Sketch being in the room.

"Are you going to continue hiding or *try* to finally kill me?" I ask.

"Who's hiding?" she counters in her familiar muffled voice. "Though, it is disappointing to find you breathing."

Twisting around, I swear for a moment I see Mei standing on the stairs. Blinking, the tall lithe women comes into focus. The Geisha stands on the same step Mei once stood frozen.

"I want her back," I inform, not wanting to play her games or hear riddles.

"You want something," she says, moving back to a more natural pose. "And what you want has something I want."

Translations:

(Japanese) **Kanojo** wa tōchaku suru: She Arrives
(Japanese) **Yameru:** Stop!

(Japanese) **Kare wa sugu ni shinudarou."** Her eyes move to me, and she
finishes, "Ichido kore wa kare ga naniwoshita ka o shiru: He'll die soon
enough. Once this one finds out what he's done.

(Japanese) **Minagoroshi ni suru:** Kill them all!

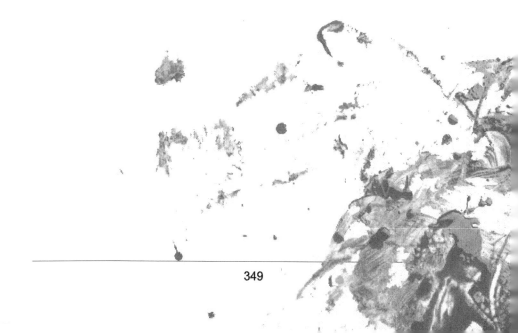

ABOUT THE AUTHOR

Sadie Grubor
Sadie Grubor is a Haribo Gummy Candy Whore & a foul-mouthed writer of smexy times and characters who typically have immature and inappropriate humor. Yes, this is a reflection of her. She can only hope you respect her in the morning, but doesn't expect it.

At some point, she may offend you. Yes, she realizes this and owns it. Trying to change this outcome has proved futile in the past. It's best to just let her trashy mouth weed out the classy folk. Everyone is better off that way.

Sadie's darker side: V Fiorello
Where bad guys deserve love.

www.facebook.com/groups/GruborGroupies
www.facebook.com/authorsadiegrubor
www.facebook.com/sadiegrubor
www.twitter.com/sadiegrubor
www.sadiegrubor.tumblr.com
www.instagram.com/sadiegrubor
www.goodreads.com/author/show/6470181.Sadie_Grubor
www.sadiegrubor.com
BLOG: www.booknerdrevelation.com

ABOUT THE EDITOR

Monica Black – Freelance Editor
This is where you can find her, but she's really, really, really, really, really, busy, so she can't…. OKAY, perhaps I'm being a bit selfish. I'll still be pouty about it, just saying!

www.facebook.com/wordnerdediting
www.wordnerdediting.com

THE

GEISHA
A DOLL FACE NOVEL
BOOK 2

"Through discipline and talent, a geisha will emerge."

A woman in a Yakuza crime lord's world, her business was to sell a dream---of attraction, seduction, and devotion to the wealthiest and most powerful men in Japan. But behind the painted face and silk robes lay the blackest of hearts, the darkest deceiver, and stealthiest of assassins.

Born into a world of fear and lies, The Geisha has created a life of revenge. She has been molded into the perfect killer, the embodiment of her life and circumstance. The Geisha has one weakness she will stop at nothing to reclaim, even recruiting help from a man she wishes death. A man

Once upon a time, being a geisha was one of the few ways a woman of "common birth" could achieve wealth, status and fame. Now, The Geisha is one of the few Yakuza members no man, or woman, wants to at any cost.

HER name strikes fear in those brave enough to speak it.
HER presence causes panic for those unlucky enough to be in it.
But not HIM.
HE isn't afraid of her.
HE won't leave her alone.
HE has a death wish SHE is more than happy to grant.
(After he's served his purpose.)
Coming 2018...

OTHERBOOKS
BY SADIE GRUBOR - V FIORELLO

The Doll Face Series (writing as V Fiorello – dark erotic)
Doll Face
Book 2 – TBA – Tentative Release February/March 2018

Falling Stars Series (contemporary)
Falling Stars
Stellar Evolution (a Falling Stars novella)
Hidden in the Stars (a Falling Stars novel) book 2
Stellar Collision (a Falling Stars novella)
Snare (a Falling Stars novel) book 3
Refrain & Reprise (a Falling Stars novella – standalone)
**Coming soon….. Book 4 in the series **

Modern Arrangements Trilogy (contemporary)
Save the Date
Here Comes the Bride
Happily Ever Addendum
Terms and Conditions

Stand Alones: (contemporary)
Live-In-Position
All Grown Up
VEGAS follows you home

47508970R00198

Made in the USA
Middletown, DE
31 August 2017